Valley of Promises

22436

Valley of
Promises

45357

Bonnie Leon

BROADMAN
& HOLMAN
PUBLISHERS

Nashville, Tennessee

0-8054-2153-X

Published by Broadman & Holman Publishers
Nashville, Tennessee

Dewey Decimal Classification: 813
Subject Heading: HISTORICAL FICTION—ALASKA /
FICTION—LAND SETTLEMENT AND PIONEER LIFE
Library of Congress Card Catalog Number: 2001025492

Library of Congress Cataloging-in-Publication Data
Leon, Bonnie.
  Valley of promises / Bonnie Leon.
    p.   cm. — (The Matanuska series ; bk. 1)
  ISBN 0-8054-2153-X (pbk.)
    1. Alaska—Fiction. 2. Land settlement—Fiction. 3. Frontier
and pioneer life—Fiction. I. Title.
  PS3562.E533 V35   2001
  813'.54—dc21

                                             2001025492
                                                  CIP

1 2 3 4 5 6 7 8 9 10 05 04 03 02 01

Dedication

In Memory of Lucille Bohn
Who invited me into her home and told me her story.

Acknowledgments

Each time I begin a project I am delighted
to watch as partnerships grow.
I owe thanks to many.

Thank you to my cousins, Billy, Kenny, and Sue Hightower, and friend Lucille Bohn who helped bring their homeland to life for me. Their willingness to share their experiences and knowledge helped me see the spectacular and sometimes formidable place called Alaska.

There are also my writing cohorts. They walked through the pages with me, often putting in extra hours so I could meet my deadline. Ann, Billy, B. C., Ellen, Julia, and Shirley, I can't thank you enough. You ladies are great.

And to Vicki Crumpton, my editor, who willingly and skillfully jumped in to make this a better book, thanks for your dedication. I don't tell you often enough how much I appreciate your hard work and your commitment to excellence.

Chapter One

LAUREL HASPER LEANED HER TALL, SLENDER FRAME AGAINST THE weathered porch railing and studied her father. *He's always seemed invincible,* she thought, trying to swallow the hurt. Now he looked beaten, the droop of his shoulders and his heavy step revealing his grief. The last five years had taken a toll. First the depression, then the drought had drained Will Hasper's spirit and stolen his dreams.

Dirt swirled into the air, dusting last summer's dead cornfields. Merciless sun splintered the haze into thousands of dusky red particles, creating a flaming sunset.

The beauty didn't soothe Laurel. The red cloud represented the end of their farm and so many others. The Midwest ranches were dead, carried away one piece of ground at a time. The air tasted like dust as it had for months. Laurel longed for the day when the air would again hold sweet moisture.

Sweeping off his hat, Will used the back of his hand to wipe grime and sweat from his face. His weary, gray-blue eyes closed a moment. He dropped to one knee, tenderly ran his hand over the dry ground, scooped up a handful of soil and watched it sift through his fingers. The wind caught the particles and swept them away.

Fighting tears, Laurel turned away and looked heavenward. "Why, God? Why?" Bitterness touched her voice. She gazed out at their once fertile farm. Again, there would be no crops, only wind and dust. A dry, frigid winter had sucked the remaining life from the land.

Will stood, planted his hat on his head, and marched back to the house. With little more than a glance at Laurel, he leaped onto the porch and brushed past her. "Laurel, get your brothers." Pulling open the door, he stepped into the house. "Jean, we need to talk."

Laurel found her brothers playing in a desiccated apple orchard. Justin and Brian were hanging from a limb while Luke twisted the branch of a dead tree.

"What are you doing?" Laurel demanded.

Justin and Brian quickly dropped to the ground. Luke let loose of the limb, and the dead branch hung limp.

Hands on hips, Laurel continued, "Isn't it bad enough the weather has all but destroyed our orchard? Do you have to finish the job?"

Sixteen-year-old Luke stripped off a piece of bark, then turned a defiant look on his sister. "What difference does it make? Everything's dead anyway."

"Yeah. Everything's dead," eleven-year-old Justin agreed, reaching up and slinging an arm over his brother's shoulders.

"It's wrong, that's all." Laurel hesitated. "The rains might return."

Luke gazed up at a cloudless sky, then gave his sister an insolent look. "You think so, huh?" His dark looks turned stormy as he broke a brittle branch from the doomed tree and shoved it close to her face. "Do you see any life here?"

"You never know. God can do anything."

"If he was going to do something, he would have." Luke shook his head in disgust. "You know, for a nineteen-year-old, you're not too smart." He cast the stick to the ground.

Laurel thought of a dozen brutal responses but held her tongue. She knew Luke's words came from fear and anger. He loved the farm. How could she fault him for that? "Daddy wants us up at the house."

The youngest of the boys, six-year-old Brian, ducked beneath the crippled branch, and standing beside his sister, faced his brothers. "It could happen, you know. It could rain."

Laurel ruffled his thick blond hair. "That's right. Anything can happen." She headed toward the house with Brian beside her, then stopped and looked back to find Luke and Justin staring after her. "You better git moving if you don't want to feel the strap across your backsides."

While the children filed into the house, Will stood at the front window and stared out at a fence line choked with tumbleweeds. He didn't seem to notice his family had assembled and were sitting around the wooden dining table waiting for him to speak.

Jean Hasper cleared her throat. Will turned and walked to the table, smiled gently at his wife, then reached out and touched baby Susie's cheek. She giggled and snuggled closer to her mother. He then studied each face at the table, shoved his hands into his jean pockets, and paced the wooden floor. His boots echoed on the aged planking. Finally he stopped, cleared his throat, and looked hard at his family.

"We've had some tough times these past years. Real tough," Will began. "The land has dried up, the farm is all but gone, and it doesn't look like the weather is going to change, anyway not soon enough for us." He glanced out the window. "Everyone's suffering. Some of our neighbors have already had to leave. More are going." Will swallowed hard. "I didn't want to be one of them, but . . ." He studied the floor, then looked up at his family. "I've been thinking, and I've decided we have to do something, and we can't wait." His eyes met Jean's. "The government is offering a new start to families like us, folks about to lose their farms and people on subsistence."

Laurel's stomach plummeted. Her father couldn't be suggesting they leave the farm!

"What kinda new start?" asked Brian.

"Well, they're choosing families who're willing to move." He hurried on. "I know it'll be hard to leave, but the way I see it, we got no choice." He hesitated. "I think this is God's answer for us. In fact, I'm sure of it."

Laurel had seen the ads, but she couldn't believe her father would consider leaving. Hoping she was wrong and needing to hear the words, she asked, "Where? Where are the farms?"

Will didn't speak.

Jean answered softly. "A place called the Matanuska Valley. In Alaska."

Silence enveloped the room.

"Alaska!" Justin whooped, shattering the silence. "Wow! Alaska!" He jumped out of his chair and started prancing around the room. "We're going to Alaska! We're going to Alaska!" He turned and looked at his father. "Will we see Eskimos and igloos?"

Will chuckled. "Probably not. The Matanuska Valley is farm country. There's good land and lots of timber for homes and barns."

"Daddy, how do you know they'll choose us? They don't take just anybody," Laurel said.

"From what I heard, they want hardy folks and having children is a plus. They don't want people who are too young or too old, and the ones chosen should know something about farming." He shrugged. "Sounds like us."

Laurel folded her arms over her chest. "And what if they don't pick us?"

"They will. I'm going down to the courthouse first thing tomorrow and fill out the papers."

Laurel chewed a fingernail. Alaska was at the end of the world! She had plans. When the depression ended, she was going to attend the University of Wisconsin. Tears burned the back of her eyes, but she gritted her teeth and held them back. She wasn't going to cry.

"I know it'll be hard to leave friends, but we'll make new ones," Will said.

Laurel stared out the window without seeing. Anger replaced sorrow. Without looking at her father, she said, "I won't go."

For a long moment no one spoke. Finally, Will asked, "What will you do?"

Tipping her chin up slightly, Laurel looked at her father. "I don't know, but I'm not going to Alaska."

"You need a plan," Will said. "What do you think you'll do when we move away? There's nothing for you here."

Laurel didn't know what she was going to do. What could she do? She shrugged.

Will opened his mouth, then clamped it shut. A few moments later he slowly and deliberately asked, "What is it you want?"

"I planned to go to the university in Madison. I want to get my teaching degree."

"How will you pay for it? You can't make it without family to help. There's no work." Will swiped his hand through his hair. "Laurel, it's hard to accept something other than our dreams, but fantasies won't put bread on the table. I made less than two hundred dollars last year." His voice had a sharp edge to it.

Jean rested her hand on Laurel's arm. "Everyone has a right to dream," she said gently. She turned to her daughter who looked so much like her, thick auburn hair and hazel eyes that radiated strength and stubbornness. "I know this is hard, honey, but we have no choice. We've waited, prayed, and hoped we could stay, but God has another plan for us."

"There has to be another way. Something . . ." Laurel searched for a solution, but helplessness and a sense of being trapped trampled over her. She pushed out of the chair and hurried to the door. Hitting the screen with the palms of her hands, she walked out, letting the door slam behind her. Striding across the porch, she leaned on the railing and stared down at a scorched flowerbed. "The rains will come," she nearly shouted. "They will!" She heard the squeak of the door and her father's steps on the porch. "It can't last. It'll rain." Unable to hold back tears any longer, she began to sob.

Will stood beside her and rested a callused hand on her back. His voice gentle, he said, "Even if it rained tomorrow, it's too late. It will take more than one good season to bring back the farm."

Laurel leaned against her father. Immediately his arm went around her shoulders and he hugged her. "I wish we didn't have to do this, sugar. I really do."

Laurel didn't answer. She couldn't trust herself to speak.

The screen door complained again. Brian hurried to his sister and hugged her about the legs. He pressed his cheek against her floral cotton dress. "It won't be so bad, Laurel. It'll be fun."

"Yeah," Justin added. He stood beside Laurel and looked up at her, his blue eyes alight with anticipation. He smiled broadly. "Just think, we'll be pioneers in a new frontier!"

Laurel wiped her tears and tried to smile. She cupped Justin's chin in her hand. "New frontier, huh? That sounds like something you got out of one of your books." She patted his cheek. Crossing to the old rocker that had graced their front porch for forty years, Laurel ran her hand over the armrest, then stood behind it, rocking it gently. Her grandfather had told her many stories while he rocked and she sat at his feet. She looked at her father. "How can we leave our home? I don't know any other place."

Will stepped in front of the rocker, caught hold of the arms, and stopped it. His eyes sad, he said gently, "You're old enough to understand that sometimes decisions just have to be made; people do what they must." He glanced at Jean who stood in the doorway. "Laurel, you're grown now and can go your own way if you choose . . . and . . ." His eyes glistened.

Remorse and family loyalty grabbed hold of Laurel's rebellion. "No . . . I didn't mean . . ." She rested her hand on her father's. "I'm sorry. You're right. Moving is the only answer. I just didn't want to believe it." Her eyes traveled over her family. "I'll go."

Chapter Two

WILL DRAINED THE LAST OF HIS COFFEE, THEN GLANCED AROUND THE ROOM cluttered with boxes and luggage. "You outdid yourself," he said. "It couldn't be easy cooking in the middle of all this mess."

"I figured our last meal here ought to be a good one." Jean smiled, but it didn't touch her eyes.

Will looked at the front door. "Where'd Luke disappear to?"

Brian leaned his elbows on the table, resting his face in his hands. "He said he was going for a walk. He didn't look too good."

Spearing the last of his eggs, Justin quietly added, "I think he's saying good-bye. You know . . ."

Will stared at the last of his coffee in the bottom of his cup. "I wish this weren't so hard on everyone." He stood and deposited his plate and cup in the sink, and offered Jean an apologetic smile. "Thanks for the breakfast. Thanks for everything." He bent and kissed her.

She caressed his cheek. "We'll be fine."

Catching Jean's hand, he looked at Laurel and the boys. "We got to remember how God has blessed us. We have a lot to be thankful for."

Her stomach churning, Laurel stared at her eggs. *Thankful? We're leaving our home. How can we be thankful?*

Will walked to the door, took his hat off its hook, and planted it on his head. "I better get to it. There's a lot to be done."

Laurel nibbled on her biscuit and studied her parents. In spite of the hardships, their faith had remained steady. Just as her father was about to step out the door, she asked, "Daddy, are you *really* thankful? I mean—you're about to leave behind your life, everything you've known."

Will removed his hat. His short-cropped hair was scrambled, some of it standing on end. He returned to the table and, resting his hands on the well-worn wood, he looked directly at his oldest child. "My life isn't this farm." He looked at Jean, the boys, then back at Laurel. "My life is you, my family. There's nothing on this earth more important to me." His eyes roamed the cluttered room, then lingered at the window. "I love this place. It's the only home I've known, but another home is waiting for us." He straightened. "Maybe it won't feel comfortable at first, but . . . Well, look at it this way. When you buy a new pair of boots, they feel stiff and uncomfortable for a while, then gradually mold to your foot as you wear them, and before you know it, they're a perfect fit."

An engine backfired, and the clatter of a vehicle bouncing over the rutted driveway carried from outside. "That'll be Joe," Will said.

Jean walked to the sink. "It was kind of him to help."

"He's a good friend." Will strode to the door and opened it. "Looks like David's with him. That'll make the work go faster. We should be able to get our things loaded and be on the road before the day heats up." He put on his hat, adjusted it, then looked at Justin and Brian. "Time to finish your packing."

Jean secured her cotton apron snugly around her waist. "Boys, could you take your bags out onto the porch? After that you can carry the box of toys out. That'll be a big help."

Justin and Brian raced to the bedroom. Brian poked his head out the door and in a small voice asked, "What about Luke? What about his stuff?"

"He'll take care of it. Don't worry." Jean walked to the sink, turned on the faucet, and sprinkled detergent into rising water. "I'll wash, you dry." Susie's wail resonated from the back of the house. "Oh, dear. I'd hoped she'd wait a bit longer."

Justin jogged into the kitchen. "I'll take care of her. I know how." He grabbed the baby's bottle of milk out of the ice box and plunked it into a pot on the back of the stove.

"Thank you," Jean said. "You're a good boy. She'll need changing."

"I'm eleven. I can do it," Justin said confidently before hurrying to his parents' bedroom where his baby sister hollered for attention.

Laurel cleared the table while Jean scrubbed and rinsed the dishes, then set them on a towel to dry. The house was oddly quiet. Usually her mother sang along to the radio or hummed church hymns while she worked. Today, the radio had been packed, and Jean was silent. Laurel dried and gently wrapped each dish and cup in paper, then pressed them securely into a box partially filled with wood shavings. She glanced at the old phonograph resting against the wall beneath the front room window. "Mama, we're taking the phonograph aren't we?"

"I don't think there's going to be room. We have a fifteen-hundred-pound limit." She looked at the family treasure. "It's awfully big. Maybe."

Justin returned to the kitchen carrying eight-month-old Susie. He was small for his age, so the baby looked big in his arms. He snatched the bottle out of the hot water, sat on an overstuffed chair, and snuggled the baby as she eagerly devoured her breakfast.

David pulled open the front door and peeked inside. He nodded at Mrs. Hasper and smiled at Laurel. "Can I get some help moving furniture out onto the porch?"

"I'm done here," Laurel said to her long-time friend.

David stepped inside, propping the door with a wooden chair. "Where do you want to start?"

Laurel looked around the room. "How about the sofa? Might as well get the heaviest piece out first. We won't have room for the piano."

While Will and Joe loaded the farm equipment, Laurel and David hauled furniture and boxes onto the porch. The boys carried out their personal things.

Tired and drained, Laurel sat on a chair, stretched out her legs, and studied the crowded porch, then the two pickups. Her heart sank. They'd have to leave so much behind.

With Susie propped on one hip, Jean stepped through the door and eyed their belongings. A sad smile touched her lips. "In the beginning your father and I had so little. It's hard to believe we've collected so much over the last twenty years."

Will walked up the steps. "We've got the tools loaded. Good thing the government's supplying some of what we'll need. Otherwise we would only have room to pack bare necessities." He smiled at his wife. "What do you want me to take first?"

Jean scanned the furnishings. "Well, all the boxes, and we have to take the washing machine. I'm not living without one."

"I suppose you ladies could go down to the river to wash your clothes," Will grinned.

"We won't be doing any wash at the river," Jean said firmly. "Just because we're living in Alaska doesn't mean we have to be uncivilized." Her eyes moved over their belongings. "I don't want to leave the sofa. And we'll need the dining table and chairs." She sighed. "Do you think you can find room for the beds and dressers?"

"I'll do my best."

Jean walked back inside.

Laurel followed. "Mama, you're not thinking of leaving the china cabinet? It was Grandma's. You've always loved it."

Her eyes sad, Jean said, "I don't think there's going to be room."

"What about the china? That was Grandma's too. Great Grandma gave it to her . . ."

"I know, for her wedding. Grandma always treasured her china. I wish we could take it with us. But . . ." Jean swept back a wisp of auburn hair. "I promised the dishes to Grace. She's always admired them." She wrapped an arm around Laurel's shoulders. "They'll have a good home."

"Can't we ship them?"

"It would take money we don't have." Jean sighed.

"And the rocker?" Laurel asked, afraid to hear the answer. "We can't leave it."

"We'll try."

Laurel's insides ached, and she fought tears. "Mama, we don't have to leave. It's not too late. You and Daddy are always talking about how God will take care of us. Why can't you trust him with this?"

Jean turned her daughter around to face her, firmly placing her hands on Laurel's shoulders. "God can take care of us, but sometimes we're forced into action by circumstances. Going to Alaska may be exactly what God wants." She squeezed Laurel's shoulders gently. "We can't stay. We've talked about this. There's good farmland and lots of fishing and hunting in the Matanuska. It will be a good place for a new start."

"And what about bears and wolves, and snow higher than the rooftop?" Laurel asked, sounding defiant. She hadn't meant to.

"The man your father talked to said the stories about bears and wolves are exaggerated, and we're used to snow. If we give it a chance, we'll be happy there."

"I'll see if Daddy needs help," Laurel said with resignation and walked out the door.

A wheelbarrow, grinder, hog troughs, chicken feeders, cider press, pitchforks, axes, shovels, pails, plow, horse collars, harnesses, and tack were piled up past the wood slats of Joe's beaten pickup. No room remained for sleds, wagon wheels, or Will's wood lathe. Laurel knew what a sacrifice it was for her father to leave his lathe. He loved working with wood.

Their two Belgians stood in the paddock. Although a bit thinner than when they were in their prime, Jake and Cooper were still magnificent. Laurel strolled to the fence, and Jake stretched his muzzle out to her. She stroked his chestnut neck. "I'll miss you," she said, pressing her forehead against his broad face. She straightened, ran her hand down his nose, then gave Cooper a pat and walked to her father's pickup.

It was nearly full, and several items were still on the porch. Laurel's dresser stood off to one side. She let her eyes roam over the old wood. A dent marred the top drawer. Laurel smiled. She'd been thirteen when David had decided he was in love with Jessica Hopkins. Laurel had been so angry she'd grabbed a music box he'd given her for her thirteenth birthday and thrown it across her room. It had smashed against the chest of drawers and broken into pieces. The scar remained.

David stepped onto the porch. "Hi." He shoved his hands in the pockets of his overalls. "So, you ready?"

"If being packed means I'm ready, then I guess I am."

David tapped the toe of his boot against an uneven plank on the porch. "I can't believe you're moving." He looked at Laurel. "You're old enough to stay."

"I thought I could stay—go to school maybe. But Daddy and Mama said I was being foolish. In these hard times it's not easy to make it on your own."

"You wouldn't have to live on your own. You could stay with us."

"I don't think that's exactly proper." Laurel's eyes slid to the loaded truck. "Besides, my family will need me. It's going to take all of us to make it." A soft smile touched her lips. "I was thinking of coming back, though, after they're settled. I want to go to college so I can teach."

"I'll be here." David rammed his toe into the planking. "My life's not exactly exciting, but I'm a good farmer. My dad and I are gonna make something out of our land. The drought won't last forever."

"Hey, David. We need your help," Joe called. "Get on the other end of this sofa, would ya?"

His voice barely more than a whisper, David continued in a hurry, "Do you think when you come back, we could . . . well, do you think we could talk about getting married?"

Laurel knew David had been in love with her since his boyhood, except for the temporary diversion of Jessica Hopkins. She studied him. He was tall with calm blue eyes and an easy smile. She loved him, but he felt more like a brother than a mate. When she married, she wanted it to be with a man she loved passionately, someone she couldn't live without. She met his eyes. "You know I love you, but not like that. We'll always be friends." She planted a gentle kiss on his cheek. "I'll write. Will you?"

"Yeah. I'll write."

"David, come on," Joe called, his voice laced with irritation. He grabbed hold of the couch.

"I'm comin'," David said and hurried to help his father.

Laurel wandered to the barn and stopped in front of a wooden bucket with a sprig of a tree growing in it. The previous spring she'd taken it from one of her grandfather's apple trees, hoping to save a remnant of their farm's early beginnings.

"I hope there's room for you," she said, kneeling beside the pot. She pressed her hands against the cool, damp soil. Although the ranch had dried up, this little tree had flourished; its green leaves were supple and glossy.

She ran into the barn, found a piece of burlap and some string, and returned to the seedling. Carefully loosening the roots and keeping a good dirt ball, she removed it from the bucket, set it in the burlap, then pulled the material up around the roots and tied it. Hopefully it would live to be replanted. She picked it up, cradling it against her chest.

Luke stepped around the corner of the barn and nearly plowed into her. Brother and sister stared at each other. "For crying out loud, Laurel. Watch where you're going." Luke's eyes wandered to the tiny tree. "You taking that thing?"

"It's not a thing. And, yes. It's part of this ranch and belongs with us. It'll be our first apple tree on the new farm." Laurel studied her brother. Since their father's announcement, Luke's dark good looks had turned brooding, and he'd been quieter than usual. "Are you all right, Luke? You've been acting strangely."

"Yeah, I'm fine." He glanced at the house. "No. I'm not." He looked at Laurel. "My friends are here."

"You'll make new friends."

"Yeah, but not . . ." He shook his head. "I don't know. I don't think I'm going to like it much."

It was Lucinda he was going to miss. He and the pretty blonde had been going around together for several months. "Did you see Lucinda this morning?" Laurel asked.

"We took a walk," he said morosely, staring at the ground.

"I'm sorry, Luke. It's hard for all of us."

"Yeah, but you don't have someone special you're leaving."

"I do . . ." Laurel began, then stopped. Luke was hurting, and she didn't need to make it worse. "You'll meet someone else."

"There's no one else for me."

"You're only sixteen. There will be lots of pretty girls in your future." He said nothing but instead worked his jaw.

"Mama's looking for you. She needs you to get the last of your things packed."

"They're packed." Keeping his eyes on the ground, Luke shoved his hands in his pockets and trudged toward the house.

Holding the sapling against her, Laurel left the cool shade of the barn and walked to the truck. She was glad to see that the rocker and chest of drawers rested on top of the sofa. She looked back at the porch. Grandma's phonograph and the china cabinet still stood by the front door. *Well, we aren't leaving this,* Laurel thought with determination and approached her father. "I have the seedling. Where do you want it?"

Will eyed the plant. "Laurel, I just don't see how we can take it."

"It's part of this farm. It came from one of Grandpa's original trees. It will be like having part of him with us."

Shaking his head, Will walked to the truck, restacked several boxes, and moved the radio and clock, leaving a tiny space in the front corner of the pickup bed. "All right. We'll put it here, but you'll have to keep it with you on the ship. I don't even know if we're allowed to take plants."

"They won't care about one little tree," Laurel said, handing him the seedling.

Will set the plant in the corner of the truck, then pulled a rope tight over the back of the pickup and cinched it.

Brian ran up. "Is it time to go?"

"Yep. There's just enough room for you children in back." Will lifted the blond-headed six-year-old and set him on a heap of blankets and pillows. "That ought to be comfortable."

Luke and Justin climbed in beside Brian. Jean handed the baby to Laurel and joined Will. They stood, their arms intertwined, and looked at the house. Laurel pressed her face against her baby sister's soft curls and let her eyes wander over the farmhouse. The roof needed repair, the porch sagged on one end, and the outside walls needed a new coat of paint, but Laurel didn't see any of that. All she saw was home, the only home she'd ever known.

"Your grandpa always liked an adventure," Will said. "If he were here today, he'd be excited."

"Grandpa loved the farm," Laurel said.

Wind gusted, raising dust around the house. When the dust settled, the house looked lonely, the windows bare, abandoned possessions stacked on the porch. "I wish we didn't have to leave so much."

Jean gently brushed a stray curl off Laurel's cheek and tucked the wavy strand into the young woman's long hair. "Things aren't important. What matters is we're together." She took the baby, cradling her against her shoulder as she walked to the pickup.

Laurel followed. Jean climbed in, and Laurel slid onto the seat beside her.

Will sat behind the wheel, pushed in the clutch, and turned the key. The engine fired. "Alaska, here we come," he said, but there was no joy in his voice.

Chapter Three

A ROCK JABBED LAUREL'S SHOULDER. SHE ROLLED OVER, FLUFFED HER NEARLY flat feather pillow, then settled back on a thin wool blanket. She couldn't get any relief from the unyielding ground and its pebbles. Laurel stared at a black sky speckled with shimmering stars. Her eyes settled on a hazy patch called the Milky Way, then moved on to the Big Dipper and the Little Dipper.

Many nights she and her grandfather had lain side by side in cool grasses and studied the heavens. He'd pointed out stars, filling her in on scientific details and legends. Laurel smiled softly. She'd always loved spending time with Grandpa Hasper. When he'd died, her world had buckled. He'd been her dearest friend and confidant.

Laurel turned onto her side, bundling deeper into her quilt. *Tomorrow we'll be on the train.* She closed her eyes and tried to quiet her mind but couldn't rein in wandering thoughts. The train would carry them to Seattle, and from there they would board a ship that would take them to Seward, where another train would carry them on to Palmer in the Matanuska Valley. There they would try to build a new life, a life she wanted no part of. *As soon as I'm not needed, I'll return and go to school,* she told herself.

The next thing Laurel heard was the sound of clanging cookware. She pulled her blanket up over her head, trying to shut out the noise and dawn's light. She'd been having a lovely dream. Her bare feet had been skipping through lush, cool grasses and clusters of flowers.

Someone stripped back her quilt. Laurel opened her eyes. Brian's grinning face was only inches from hers. "Brian! What are you doing?"

"Laurel's awake," the six-year-old called. He grinned, freckles crinkling over his nose. "It's time to get up."

"You scared me."

"I was watching you sleep. Did you know your eyes move when you're sleeping?"

Laurel smiled. "Yes, I know. And so do yours." She grabbed him and tickled his sides.

Giggling, Brian wriggled free. "Hurry up. Breakfast is ready. After we eat we're going to the train! I've never ridden on a train!" He tugged on her hand. "Come on, Laurel. Get up."

"All right. All right." Laurel forced herself to sit. "I can't sleep anyway."

Laurel stood, smoothed her skirt and blouse, and ran her hands through her thick wavy hair. Stiff and sore, she pressed her hands against the small of her back and stretched from side to side, then backwards. "It's going to take a little time to work out these kinks," she said, reaching for her toes.

"I don't have any kinks," Brian said, raising his arms straight up over his head, then proudly bending forward until his fingertips touched the toes of his shoes.

"You're young." Laurel retrieved a brush out of her bag and, with quick, short passes, pulled it through her hair. Using a ribbon, she gathered it into a loose ponytail and secured it. "Mama, I'm going to wash up at the lake."

"You better get a move on," Will said. "Breakfast is nearly ready, and we've got to hustle if we're going to make the train."

"I'll hurry," Laurel assured him, grabbing a towel and heading for the beach.

Yesterday she'd been so enthralled with Lake Michigan's beauty that she hadn't noticed the toll the drought had taken. The water level was so low that the natural water line could be seen on the dried and fractured bank. Dead bushes clung to parched earth high on the embankment. *No place has been spared,* Laurel thought sadly.

Joe led the way to the railway station. Laurel had rarely visited any city, and the bray of horns, grinding gears of buses, and exhaust fumes were enough to send her straight back to the farm.

Laurel looked through the back window at the boys and smiled. Brian and Justin gazed eagerly at towering buildings crowding the streets, colorful marquees shading doorways, and people hurrying along the sidewalks.

Most of the people were nicely dressed and seemed in a hurry.

Maybe she *could* make it in the city on her own. "Do you think folks here have jobs?"

"It's like anywhere else. Some do and some don't," Will said. "Unemployment is high everywhere. I'd say a good share of these folks are out looking for work." Joe slowed, and so did Will.

"Do you think they have enough to eat?" Laurel pressed.

"With government soup lines I don't suppose anyone has to go hungry, but I expect some are."

Laurel's eyes fell upon a young woman sitting in a doorway. She looked weary and wretched. Two blond-headed children sat on her lap. Their oversized clothing was threadbare and dirty.

Joe turned into the railway station, and Will followed. "This is it." He drove through a parking area where other pickups loaded with furniture and farm equipment were already parked. "Seems a lot of folks are moving," he said, parking in an empty space.

People waited. Some stood alone; others visited. Confusion painted some of the faces, worry etched others, and some were alight with anticipation. A group of older boys played Kick the Can while other youngsters hung close to parents.

"Where do we go?" Jean asked.

"Well, I s'pose we should check in at the ticket office." Will stepped out of the truck, stopped to speak to Joe a moment, then taking long, unhurried steps, walked to the terminal and disappeared inside.

Laurel fought to relax tight muscles. "I think I'll take a look around," she told her mother, opening the door and stepping out. "Do you mind?"

"No, but don't wander too far."

"I won't."

Brian and Justin jumped out of the back. "Where you goin'?" Justin asked.

"For a walk."

"Can we go?"

Laurel wanted to be alone, but when she looked at Justin's expectant eyes and Brian's playful smile, she couldn't resist. "Mama, is it all right if the boys come with me?"

Jean smiled and nodded.

"OK, hold my hand," Laurel said. "I'm not taking a chance of losing either of you." Each boy clasped one of his sister's hands and nearly dragged her toward the terminal. Luke jumped out of the truck and walked in the opposite direction.

"Do you think that's our train?" Brian asked, pointing at one waiting alongside the depot. A line of parked trucks was being unloaded, their possessions disappearing into boxcars.

"Probably."

Justin studied the passenger cars. "I don't think so," he said. "There aren't any people on it."

"That's just cause it's not time yet," Brian argued.

"Maybe," Justin shrugged.

Without warning, the train's whistle shrieked. Laurel jumped. The boys tightened their hold on her hands. "Maybe we should go back to the truck," Laurel said.

Justin nodded, his eyes wide and a little frightened.

"I want to see the rest of the train," Brian said.

Laurel glanced at the parking lot. The truck was still parked. "All right, but just a little while longer."

They walked the length of the train. Doors on some of the boxcars were open. Brian broke free of Laurel's grasp and ran to one car. He jumped and jumped, trying to see inside. "Lift me up." When Laurel didn't respond immediately, he said, "Please."

Curious herself, Laurel hefted Brian and peeked inside. Assorted furniture, boxes, and household items were stacked against the walls. "There sure is a lot of stuff," the little boy said. "Where are they going to put ours?"

"There are other boxcars. I'm sure there's plenty of room." Laurel set the boy on the ground.

She looked back at their pickup. Her father was backing it out of its place. "We better get back."

Laurel started walking but stopped short when she looked into a camera pointed directly at her. For a moment she didn't know what to do. She'd never liked having her picture taken. She smiled briefly and continued on. The man behind the camera stepped in front of her, walking backward while continuing to snap photographs. At first Laurel tried to ignore him, but finally, too disconcerted, she stopped. Arms folded over her chest, she frowned at the stranger. Lowering his camera, he flashed a charming smile. Laurel ignored his friendly overtures but couldn't help noticing deep blue eyes set in a likable, handsome face. Looking almost boyish, he brushed a brown curl off his forehead. "Are you always so rude?" she asked.

"Always," he said.

"What are you doing?"

"Taking your picture."

"I can see that. Why?"

"I'm a reporter. It's my job. And you have a face readers will love."

Laurel felt her cheeks heat up.

"You're blushing."

"I am not." Deciding she didn't like the man, Laurel started walking again.

He joined her.

"It's impolite to follow people and take pictures of them without their permission."

"I wasn't following you. I was walking ahead of you. I guess you could say I was leading." He chuckled.

Laurel's irritation swelled. She hurried her steps and, without looking at him, said, "I would appreciate it if you would not take my photograph again."

"Can't promise. Sometimes my camera has a mind of its own. And you wouldn't want to get me fired, would you? If my boss found out I didn't get photographs of the prettiest girl on the train, he'd have my hide."

Laurel tried not to smile. She kept walking. "What kind of reporter are you?"

"I work for the *Chicago Tribune*. I'm writing about the colonists. You're a colonist, aren't you?"

"Yes. Are you going with us?"

"Yep. It's big news. The administration's grand experiment." He gave her a sideways grin. "Can't you see the headlines? Government lends a helping hand."

"I've already seen it—everywhere, in every newspaper," Laurel said derisively.

"We're just reporting the news." The man walked beside Laurel, clearly comfortable with himself and with her.

Laurel wished he would leave her alone.

"So, where you from?" he asked, taking out a writing tablet and pencil from his front pocket.

Laurel eyed the tablet. "You're going to write down what I say?"

"It's news."

"I'm sure I don't have anything to say that anyone would want to read." Laurel wasn't about to have her family's misfortune plastered across the front page of any newspaper. She walked faster. Brian and Justin were forced to trot to keep up.

"Just tell me how you joined up with the colonists."

"Please, leave me alone."

"Are you really a newspaper reporter?" Justin asked.

"Justin," Laurel snapped and yanked on his hand. She glanced back. The reporter stood, arms folded over his chest, a curious smile on his face.

Her father leaned against the rear bumper of their truck. He was visiting with Joe and David. Luke stood off a little, watching the loading. "Daddy, how much longer will it be?" Laurel asked.

"Not long." He pulled out a pocket watch and looked at it. "It's eleven now, and the train is supposed to leave by noon. They'll have to move quickly."

Luke stood beside his father, hands shoved into his pants pockets. "Do you really think we can make a go of it in Alaska?"

"Sure do." Will gently gripped Luke's shoulder. "During the summer months the days are long. The sun barely sets before it rises again. From what I hear, the vegetables grow fast and big because of the long days. And the soil's good. All we have to do is work hard. And I know we can do that."

"Yeah, but it's so different from home," Luke said.

"It is. There are mountains, big ones. And they say there are rivers full of fish, the likes we've never seen. Plus lots of wild game."

"Will we be doing a lot of hunting?"

"You betcha. I've seen pictures of moose and caribou. One moose would nearly see us through a winter. And I heard there are mountain sheep too."

"I wouldn't mind setting my sights on a moose," David said.

Luke nodded. "It sure would be something to bring one down, or a bear."

Laurel smiled. It was good to see Luke catching on to the idea of living in Alaska. Now if only she could.

"We're ready for you," a man called from the doorway of a boxcar and motioned for Will and Joe to pull forward.

"That's us," Will said and climbed into his truck. Joe hopped into his, and the two steered the vehicles alongside the train.

"Let's get this stuff loaded," the man said. Will, Joe, David, and Luke went to work unloading while two men climbed inside the boxcar and grabbed the belongings. A man with a cigar clenched between his teeth and a dirty blue hat tagged each item, then recorded it on a form attached to a clipboard.

The trucks were emptied and parked in front of the station. Will climbed out, gently closed the door of the 1927 pickup, and turned to Joe, handing him the keys. "It's yours. Do what you can with it."

"If I sell it, I'll send you the money."

"Thanks. I appreciate that. You're a good friend, Joe." Will gripped his neighbor's hand and shook it.

Joe glanced at the train, then back at Will. "I wish you weren't goin'. You'll be missed. I wish you luck, friend. Me and Grace will be prayin' for you."

"We thank you for that. And if you ever have need of an adventure, come north. We'll put you up till you find a place to settle."

The train's whistle pierced the air and a porter called, "Board!" A band played "My Country 'Tis of Thee," and people converged on the train.

"They're certainly making a lot of this," Jean said, taking Will's arm.

He gathered up the baby and kissed her cheek. Then he wrapped his free arm around his wife. "We're the new pioneers." He nodded to Joe and David. "I hope we'll see you again one day."

"Me too," Joe said and climbed into his truck. "David, you ready?"

David glanced at Laurel, then back at his father. "Can I have a minute?" Joe nodded. David stepped onto the platform. "Can we talk?"

"Sure," Laurel said. She'd been hoping for a way to say a proper good-bye. She followed David to the end of the platform. Facing one another, neither spoke. Laurel took a slow, even breath and reached for David's hands. It was time to say good-bye. But what did a person say to a comrade she was probably never going to see again?

She looked up at David. "You've always been a good friend. I can't remember a time when you weren't there for me." Tears brimmed. "I'm going to miss you."

"Laurel, please stay. We can have a life together."

Laurel searched his eyes. "I'll never forget you or our friendship." She stood on tiptoes and kissed his cheek, then turned and hurried to her family.

Chapter Four

LAUREL PLUMPED HER PILLOW, REPOSITIONED IT AGAINST THE WINDOW, THEN rested her cheek against the padding. The cotton casing felt cool, a welcome contrast to the stuffy, overly warm passenger compartment. She gazed at the desolate countryside. Hour upon hour it had rolled past her window—dried-up pastures, deserted farmhouses, and dry creek beds. The bony fingers of drought had touched so much of the country.

The rhythmic cadence of the train's wheels rolling across steel rails enticed her to sleep. She closed her eyes, then struggled to open them. Too many hours had already been lost to slumber.

Brian dropped into the seat beside her. "You're looking chipper."

Laurel glanced at her brother, wishing he'd left her to her dreaming. She wasn't in the mood for his energy. "I was just thinking."

"About what?"

Laurel sighed. Obviously he wasn't going to let her alone. She straightened and looked into his flushed face. "I was kind of dreaming. Have you been playing tag again?"

"Yep. Were you asleep when you were dreaming? I have lots of dreams."

"No, not exactly. Does Mama know you're running through the cars?"

"She said it was all right." Brian pulled his legs up under him and balanced on his knees, making him taller and giving him a better view out the window. "What were you dreaming about?"

"Why do you ask so many questions?"

Brian didn't respond but waited for Laurel's reply.

"I was thinking how I'd like to lie in the cool grass beneath a big shade tree," she finally said.

"Oh, is that all? If I was going to have a dream, it would be about catching tadpoles and frogs at the creek." His mouth drooped in a frown. "But there isn't no creek anymore. I liked catching tadpoles."

Feeling her brother's unhappiness, Laurel circled an arm around the little boy's shoulders. "I know. I remember how we used to hide in the weeds and watch the baby ducks."

"Yeah," Brian said, snuggling close. He stared out the window. "Mr. Prosser told me we get to cross some real big mountains."

"Who's Mr. Prosser?"

"Oh, just a man. He's real tall. I met him when Justin and I were playing tag. He's got a wife. Her name's Mrs. Prosser. She's kind of old but real nice."

A sleeping Susie resting on her shoulder, Jean Hasper sat across from her son and daughter. "I like them too," she said softly. "They'll be good neighbors." Gently, she laid Susie on the seat beside her.

"They have a big boy like Luke," Brian added. "His name's Jason."

Laurel studied her mother. She looked tired and thin. "Mama, are you feeling all right? You look worn-out."

Jean rested her hand on her abdomen. "I guess I am. It takes a lot out of a person to chase after your brothers and see to this family."

Laurel felt bad for not noticing. She'd been so engrossed in her own needs that she'd forgotten to think of anyone else's. "I should have been more help. I'm sorry." Laurel offered her mother an apologetic smile, then asked, "Where's Daddy?"

"He's in the dining car chatting with Mr. Prosser. You know how it is. Men love to talk about farming and hunting. They have big dreams about our new farms." She sighed. "I hope they come true."

Laurel returned to gazing out the window. They passed another tumbled-down fence and deserted house with prairie dust piled to the windows. "It's worse than I thought."

"I know," Jean said softly. "So many people suffering."

Brian slid off his seat. "Can I go play?"

"All right, but I don't want you disturbing the other passengers. Maybe you can find something to do that's quiet?"

"OK. Bye." Brian dashed down the aisle.

Jean watched him until he disappeared into the next car. "I wonder if he'll ever settle down." She bent and pulled a picnic basket out from beneath her seat. "Are you hungry? We still have sandwiches, fruit, and some sugar cookies." She held out a cheese sandwich. "You haven't eaten much since we left."

"I haven't been hungry," Laurel said, accepting the food. Taking a bite, she said, "Daddy was right. We did have to leave. The land is never going to come back."

Jean's eyes turned to the dead prairie. "It will—one day." She patted her daughter's hand. "I know it's hard to see now, but time has a way of healing things—even land."

Laurel knew her mother was referring to more than just dried-up prairies, but she didn't feel like talking about her feelings, so she took another bite of the stale sandwich and said nothing.

"Laurel, you've been awfully quiet since we left home. Are you all right? Is there something you'd like to talk about?"

Laurel could feel tears build but blinked them back. "It's just hard—leaving home and going to a place we've never seen. And the drought seems to have no end. I'm beginning to be afraid Seattle and Alaska will be like this—dead."

"I can't believe the government would move us to another place that's dried up. Can you?"

Laurel shook her head.

"I was told Washington's always green and gets lots of rain. Alaska's even further north. I'm sure we have nothing to worry about."

Laurel leaned her head against the window. "I wish we could have stayed in Wisconsin. I already miss home . . . and David."

"Me too." Jean smoothed a blond curl on Susie's head. "God will take care of us."

"I know," Laurel said, but didn't feel peace. She'd heard her parents and others say that very thing many times, but she didn't have the trust they did.

"I'm looking forward to seeing the valley. I think it's going to be a surprise blessing—beautiful and perfect."

Susie whimpered and opened her eyes. She placed a thumb in her mouth and laid her cheek against her mother's cotton dress. Out of habit, Jean rocked gently back and forth. "Life is full of unexpected blessings." She stood and winced, pressing a hand to the small of her back.

"Mama, I can take her for a while."

"No. That's all right. She seems happier if we move from place to place. I think I'll walk down to the dining car and see what your father's up to." She braced herself against the seat to keep her balance. "Why don't you come with us? You can have some tea to wash down that sandwich."

"Maybe later." Laurel didn't feel like being sociable.

"I'll see you after a while," Jean said, heading toward the back of the car. Laurel took in the disorderly compartment. Clothes were strung on makeshift clotheslines, giving off a familiar odor of wet flannel and cotton. Some children cried, others played, and adults slept or visited quietly. Three little boys she didn't know were caught up in a game of hide-and-seek. One turned and faced the wall, hands over his eyes, and counted while two others ran, then ducked behind a seat. *How wonderful to be a child,* she thought. *No worries except what game to play next.*

Resting her head against her pillow, she tried to find a comfortable position. The hours of sitting were taking a toll. Her body ached, and Laurel wondered how she would tolerate three more days of traveling.

Gradually, the sun slid down the sky and touched the top of distant hills. Its light dimmed, and shadows stretched between rolling mounds. Laurel tried to sleep, but her mind wouldn't quiet so she gave up and thumbed through a magazine.

Jean returned with Susie hanging over one arm. The little girl chattered while swinging her legs and arms. "You're a busy little thing," Jean said and dropped onto the seat. Resting a hand on her stomach, she said, "Oh, dear. I'm full. The government has certainly provided good food. You should go back and get something. Tonight it's chicken soup and biscuits."

"Maybe later."

Luke sauntered down the aisle and sprawled out in the seat across from Laurel. "You want to play a game of cards?" He took out a deck from his front pocket. "I learned a new game—Hearts. I'll show you."

"All right," Laurel said, setting her magazine aside.

Luke pulled out a game board from beneath the seat, laid it across his knees, and proceeded to shuffle the cards.

While Susie did her best to scramble away from her mother, Jean removed the baby's clothing, changed her diaper, then dressed her in flannel pajamas. "Luke, could you find your brothers before you begin? I'd like to get them settled down for the night. It's getting late."

Luke looked as if he would argue, but instead he gathered up the cards and returned the wooden board to the floor. "All right. I'll be right back. Don't forget we have a game," he told Laurel pointedly.

"I won't." She stood and moved into the aisle. After stretching from side to side, she reached her arms over her head. "I'm stiff. I think I'll walk a little, maybe have some dinner. I won't be gone long. When Luke gets back, tell him I haven't forgotten our game."

The harmonic sounds of a mouth organ began, and Laurel craned her neck around to see who was playing. It was Mr. Volasko, a man who smiled often, making his overlarge mustache move up and down like an anxious caterpillar. His eyes always seemed to be dancing.

The car quieted and people listened. Laurel leaned against the end of her seat and watched as the old man made his way down the aisle, taking time to notice and smile at each child. Some grinned at the gregarious man while others pulled back in fear.

The reporter Laurel had met at the train depot also moved about the car, engrossed in taking photographs. His camera clicked again and again, snapping pictures of Mr. Volasko, then those watching and clapping.

Caught up by the gaiety, Laurel clapped and joined in a song she'd learned the previous evening, "When It's Springtime in Alaska." The final words of the song echoed through Laurel's mind—*and we have come to stay.*

Early the following morning the train stopped to take on water and supplies at a small station alongside a creek. Will and the boys headed upstream to do some fishing while Laurel helped her mother with the wash. Susie lay on a quilt in the grass, happy to play with her feet.

A breeze blew across damp grass, raising goose bumps on Laurel's arms. It felt good to be free of the stuffy train. She closed her eyes and tilted her face toward the sun.

"Laurel, daydreaming isn't going to get the wash done," Jean said with a smile.

"I'm sorry. I'm just so happy to be outdoors." She grabbed a bar of soap and a pair of her father's blue jeans and kneeled beside her mother. Laurel gave her mother a sideways smile. "I thought you told Daddy we weren't going to wash our clothes in a river."

Dipping a diaper, Jean said, "At the time I couldn't imagine it." She sat back on her heels and pushed a loose strand of hair off her face. "I guess we'll be doing lots of things we didn't plan on."

Laurel scrubbed, rinsed, and hung the blue jeans on a makeshift clothesline. Next she washed a pair of Justin's pants. After that she sat on the bank and gazed downstream. Trees hugged the bank and green grass blanketed the ground beneath them. She longed to sit in the shade and dip her feet in the creek. With a sigh, she returned to washing clothes. When only one dress and a blouse remained, she asked, "Mama, do you mind if I take a walk?"

"Where?"

"Down the creek a ways."

"That's fine, but don't go far. I don't know how long we'll be here."

"I'll listen for the whistle." Feeling like a child just released from school, Laurel wanted to skip. But knowing it was undignified for a woman to do such a thing, she forced herself to walk. When the train was out of sight, she sat in the shade of a willow rooted in the bank, then laid back and stared up at the tree. Its branches reached nearly to the ground, and Laurel felt protected, almost as if she were home. Laurel sat up and removed her shoes and stockings. Dipping her feet into the cold water made her shiver.

A click disturbed her quiet mood. She looked into the face of the annoying, young reporter. "You again? Have you no manners?"

"Why? What did I do?"

"You should ask people if they want their photograph taken. It's rude to poke that camera into someone's face and snap a picture."

"I'm just doing my job." He placed a foot on a log, rested his arm on his thigh, and smiled down at Laurel. "It's just a photograph."

Embarrassed that he'd found her barefooted and daydreaming, she quickly pulled on her stockings while trying to keep her skirt pulled down over her ankles. She pushed her feet into shoes, laced them, and stood. "Please take pictures of someone else." Laurel walked away muttering, "All I wanted was a few minutes alone."

The man followed. "I had to take the photograph. You looked so content and peaceful." He pointed the camera at her.

The word *content* caught Laurel by surprise. She'd wanted contentment but thought it had eluded her. The man snapped another picture.

"Stop that!"

"All right." He let the camera hang on a strap around his neck.

"Why are you following me?"

"It's my job. And . . . you're the prettiest thing in this God-forsaken place."

No man had ever spoken to Laurel this way, not even David. Stumped for a response, she stared at the stream.

He said, "I'd like to live along a river some day."

"We used to. Before things dried up, I'd fall asleep listening to the creek alongside our house." She bent and plucked a piece of grass, sneaking a glance at the man. Tall and lean, he stood comfortably, staring at the stream. A shock of hair had fallen onto his forehead. He brushed it back unconsciously, but it immediately fell back to his brow. "It would feel wonderful to wash off some of this traveling dirt," Laurel said.

"Why don't you?" he asked, looking at her with a grin and leaning against a tree.

Laurel could feel her face heat up.

"There are some bushes along the creek over there." He pointed downstream. "No one would see you."

That was it. Laurel turned and headed back toward the train.

The reporter gently captured her arm. "Walk with me? I promise not to take any more pictures."

Laurel jerked her arm out of his grasp.

"I could use some company."

Laurel didn't know how to respond. He was rude and arrogant, but at this moment his eyes and voice were gentle. *He's most certainly a philanderer. I'd be a fool to give him the time of day.*

"We can walk along the creek a ways. Just for a few minutes?"

While trying to find a gracious way to refuse, she brushed dirt and grass from her skirt.

"When I was a boy, I used to go fishing whenever I could. Sometimes I'd just walk along the river behind the . . . the river near where I lived."

"Where are you from?"

"Chicago."

Before Laurel knew it, they were walking. "Shouldn't we go back? They'll be leaving soon."

"They'll blow the whistle."

For several moments silence hung between them. Finally Laurel said, "I don't know your name."

"I know yours," the man said in his usual arrogant tone. "Laurel Hasper." He smiled.

"And yours?"

"Adam Dunnavant." He held out a hand.

Laurel stopped, looked at his hand a moment, then shook it. It was callused. *Unusual for a reporter,* she thought and continued walking. "So, what do you do besides snap pictures and take notes?"

"Not a lot."

"Your hands are rough, not what I would expect of a reporter," she said, knowing she was being forward.

Adam glanced at his hands. He didn't answer right away. "I help out at a school near my apartment."

"What kind of school?"

"An orphanage."

Laurel was surprised Adam would volunteer his time for anything. "Did you grow up in Chicago?"

"Mostly. I was born in Nebraska."

"Oh, so you and your parents moved to Chicago from Nebraska?"

Adam was quiet for a long moment. "Not exactly. My parents died when I was a baby."

"Oh. I'm sorry."

"Don't be. I don't remember them." He picked up a stone and skipped it across a quiet pool.

"Did you live with relatives?" Laurel didn't understand why she was so curious about Adam or why she felt free to probe. Maybe it had something to do with the way *he* charged into people's lives.

"No."

Her curiosity piqued, Laurel tentatively asked, "Who raised you?"

Adam looked at her with a half smile. "Are you always so nosy?"

"Aren't you?"

Adam tossed another stone. "I grew up in an orphanage." Ripples spread outward, reaching toward shore.

Laurel had never known anyone who'd been raised in an orphanage. Images of starving, beaten children filled her mind. "You lived there your entire life?"

"Don't sound so horrified. It wasn't that bad. I was adopted once, but . . ." He kept walking and grabbed hold of a branch, breaking it off a bush as he moved past. "My adoptive parents divorced shortly after I went to live with them. I guess things were bad before I got there, and they thought having a child would help. It didn't. Anyway, I was sent back." Adam's jaw twitched, but he kept his easy pace.

"It must have been awful for you."

He stopped and, wearing an amused look, said, "It wasn't a tragedy. It was my life. I'm OK." He tossed the branch and watched it sail out over the stream, drop into an eddy, then bob through rapids. "I'm happy, and I have a good job—one that will take me places."

"How long have you been a reporter?"

"I started at the newspaper about four years ago."

"I've never known a reporter before. What do you do exactly?"

"I find news and write about it."

"Did you always want to work for a newspaper?"

"No. Actually, I stumbled into the job. When I was a kid, I used to sell papers on the street. I was good at it. Sometimes I'd hang out by the office, and I got to know some of the reporters. They started asking me for favors. You know, get them coffee, donuts, stuff like that. One of them, Joe, let me tag along on some of his stories."

"How old were you then?"

"Oh, about seventeen, eighteen. Eventually I wrote a story and asked Joe to take a look at it." Adam gave Laurel a sideways grin. "Old Joe—he was tough. He told me it was awful." He shoved his hands into his pockets. "I don't know why I'm telling you all this."

"Go on. I'm interested."

"Well, I kept writing and Joe kept evaluating. He'd point out what I was doing wrong and what I was doing right. And I got better. By the time I left the orphanage, the *Tribune* had hired me on as a copyboy. With the money I earned, I bought myself a camera and began taking pictures to go along with the pieces I wrote. One day I got a chance at a good story."

"About what?" Laurel asked, forgetting she hadn't wanted to talk to Adam.

"I came across a family sitting in the street, their possessions scattered all around. They couldn't pay the rent, and the landlord booted them out. It happens a lot. I took some pictures and wrote about how they landed there." He shrugged. "The boss liked it. After that they started sending me out on more stories, and eventually I became a full-fledged reporter."

Laurel kept walking and began to wonder why she'd been so angry with Adam. He didn't seem so bad. Maybe he *was* just doing his job.

The train whistle blew. "We've got to go," Laurel said and headed back.

Adam followed. When they reached the train, everyone had already boarded. Adam handed Laurel up the stairway.

A bird-thin woman with mousy brown hair, a red nose, and round wire-framed glasses circling blue eyes stood just inside the door. The smell of camphor oil emanated from her. "Oh, Adam, there you are," she said in a high-pitched voice. "I was wondering where you'd gone off to. I was beginning to worry."

"You don't need to worry about me." He glanced at Laurel. "Laurel, I'd like you to meet Miram Dexter."

Miram grabbed Laurel's hand. "Nice to meet you."

"Hello," Laurel said, squeezing past the frail woman.

"I was hoping we could sit together," Miram told Adam. "I have so much to tell you." She took his arm and steered him toward the back of the car. Adam tipped his hat and gave Laurel a helpless smile as he allowed Miram to lead him to a seat.

Laurel sat across from them and took out a novel. A tall man with curling black hair stood in the aisle beside her. "Do you mind if I join you? I'll go if you like."

Laurel set her book in her lap. "No. Please, sit."

The young man sat beside Laurel. "I'm Robert Lundeen. I'm from outside Jefferson."

"Laurel Hasper. My family had a farm near Madison."

"I know." He blushed and said, "I asked." He started to rise. "I should let you get back to your reading."

"No. Please stay." She glanced at Adam, "I could use some company."

Chapter Five

ROLLING HILLS BLANKETED WITH SPRING GRASSES MOVED PAST THE window. Laurel wondered where the dense green forests she'd been told about were. Wasn't Washington known for its lush vegetation? There were no trees here—not a single cedar, fir, or pine. Was it possible the drought had reached this far? *Don't be silly,* she told herself. *There would be dead trees.*

But, she wondered, *if Washington isn't what we were told it would be, then what about Alaska? Did they lie about it too?* She closed her eyes and tried to quiet her apprehension.

"Mind if I join you?" Adam asked. Before she could answer, he sat across from her.

"Do I have a choice?" She stared out the window. The train had descended into a deep gorge and moved across a large, slow-moving river.

"That's the Columbia," Adam said. "I've heard there's good fishing along some stretches. Maybe one day I'll get to fish it."

The train chugged up the other side of the gorge and continued across open meadows. "I thought Washington was supposed to be forested," Laurel said.

"Western Washington. Once we get closer to the Cascade Range, you'll see a few trees."

Laurel studied the snow-capped mountains. They were still a long way off, but she could see they were rugged and steep. In the shadows the white deepened to lavender.

"Seattle and the Pacific Ocean wait for us on the other side." Adam dropped his right leg over his left and folded his arms over his chest. He stared at the distant peaks. Today is the day. We'll soon be free of this train." Adam leaned on his legs. "You look a little under the weather."

"I'm fine. In fact, I'm excited about getting to Seattle. We'll be closer to reaching Alaska. I'm very happy," she added, knowing she was saying too much and hoping he didn't pick up on her apprehensions.

"Have you ever been to Seattle?"

"No," Laurel answered, wishing he were less inquisitive.

"It's a great city, one of my favorites when it's not raining. Do you have a favorite?"

Laurel gritted her teeth, embarrassed at her lack of worldly experience. "Actually, I've never been out of Wisconsin. My family's stayed close to home. We never had much reason to travel."

Then she asked, "What's Seattle like?"

"I'd say it's a big little city. Not as big as Chicago, but a good-sized town. It sits right on Puget Sound, a real pretty bay. The restaurants are good, and Woodland Park is a nice place if you like that kind of thing. Plus, the nightclubs are always hopping."

Laurel had no experience with clubs or city life. She said simply, "Oh," then let her eyes roam over the countryside. A farmhouse and barn sat on a rise in the distance. A tall silo filled the sky just west of the house. Miles of barbed-wire fences cut across open land, and an occasional cluster of cattle huddled against the wind. They looked healthier than the livestock she'd seen in the upper Midwest.

"I suppose you hope to have a ranch one day," Adam said.

"No. That's my father's dream." She folded her hands in her lap. "I intend to go to school."

Adam raised one eyebrow. "What is it you want to do?"

"I'd like to teach history to the upper grades."

"A history buff, huh?" He grinned. "Knowing history can come in handy, but I doubt there's much call for it in Alaska."

Laurel bristled at his know-it-all tone. "I don't plan to stay in Alaska." The words were out before she could stop them. Inwardly she rebuked her loose mouth. Already there had been talk that the colonists were soft and wouldn't make it. And now she'd told this reporter she wasn't going to stay.

"You haven't even gotten there and you're planning to leave?"

"Not my family, just me. I want to go to school, and there's no place in Alaska to get my degree." She sat a little straighter. "My father and mother are very committed to making a new start and staying in Alaska."

Adam nodded.

Laurel knew that Adam would jot down her words in his notebook the moment he had the opportunity. She wanted to throttle him but instead forced an exterior calm and stared at the passing grasslands.

Prairie gave way to foothills, and farms with rows of fruit trees loaded with pink and white blossoms dotted the landscape. The train began its ascent into the mountains where rock crannies were interspersed with pine and fir. Discarded needles tinged the earth a red hue.

A man started singing, "We'll be comin' round the mountain when we come. We'll be comin' round the mountain when we come . . ." Others took up the chorus, and Laurel couldn't resist. She joined in, then Adam. They smiled at each other, both caught up in the anticipation and fun.

After a while the singing died down, and passengers returned to reading books, playing cards, visiting, and gazing at passing scenery. Laurel tried to concentrate on the view, and although Adam had stopped his questions, she wished he would sit somewhere else.

For a long while the train followed a clear stream that bounced over rocks and washed into pools before heading down the mountain the way they'd come. Giant spruce and pine clung to steep embankments, but as the train climbed, the evergreens became sparse. Engines labored, and the train slowed as it wound its way along a steep slope.

Gradually the trees disappeared altogether, leaving graveled ridges, low-growing bushes, and clusters of wildflowers amid green meadows. Snow lay in ravines and padded the base of trees. Mountaintops were hidden in deep piles of white, while granite ridges pushed up, free of snow. Wind lifted white powder off a distant peak.

"It's so beautiful," Laurel whispered.

"It is. I've got to get pictures." Adam said, moving toward the end of the car.

Laurel didn't know what to make of the man. One moment he was thoughtless and insensitive, and the next he was passionate about a view.

The train crested the pass and began its descent. Snow lessened, trees reappeared, and the underbrush thickened. A dense forest of giant cedars and firs shaded thickets of berry bushes, thistles, and vine maple. Tiny white and purple flowers pushed through a thick carpet of dead leaves and ferns.

Adam dropped into his seat and hefted his camera. "I got some great pictures."

"I didn't know you took photographs of scenery."

"It's not part of my job, but sometimes I can't help myself."

Jean and Will sat across from Adam and Laurel. Will nodded at Adam. "So, I expect after you get to Seattle you'll wrap up your work and head home?"

"I'm tagging along all the way to Alaska, and I'll stay awhile to get more of the story."

"Oh. Well, it'll be good to have you," Will said. He patted Laurel's leg. "We're about halfway there. After Seattle, we'll be in Seward."

Jean gazed up and down the aisle. "I hope Luke's watching after Susie."

"He's fine. Stop worrying and enjoy the free time," Will said.

"There's not much of that to be had." Jean sighed. "I need to get our things folded and packed if we're nearly to Seattle." She stood.

"I'll help," Laurel said.

"No. There's not much." Jean unclipped the clothing she'd strung above the seats behind them. "Adam, could you reach under that seat and pull out the suitcase?"

Adam did as he was asked, resting the bag between himself and a pile of clothes. Jean opened the suitcase and placed the clothes inside. "I was beginning to think these would never dry." She glanced at the quilt draped over the back of Laurel's seat. "Would you like me to pack that?"

"No. I'm a little cold. I think I'll keep it." She pulled the coverlet down and draped it over her legs.

Breathless, Justin joined the family. "Are we almost to Seattle?"

"Almost. Do you have your things packed?"

"Yep. But I don't know about Brian. He's been goofing off all morning." He gazed out the window. "Do you think we're going to like it in Alaska?"

"Of course we are." Jean rested a hand on his shoulder. "I guess I'd better round up Brian—and Luke and Susie too."

Adam stood and squeezed past Jean and Justin. "I've got work to do.

I'll be seeing more of you, I'm sure." He tipped his hat to the family and walked away.

Will leaned toward Laurel. "Has he been bothering you?"

"No, not really. He's just trying to be friendly."

"I wish you wouldn't spend so much time with him. He's city people, not like us."

"You don't have to worry. He's not interested in me, and I'm certainly not interested in him."

"Good." Will stood and draped an arm over Jean's shoulders. "I'm sure he's a fine person, but it's going to take a real special man to impress my little girl." He winked at Laurel. "I've met a few on this trip."

The train slowed as it entered Seattle. Concrete buildings pressed in from both sides, their countless windows staring down on the newcomers. Laurel caught sight of a man peering at them from one of the buildings and wondered if he had any idea that the train was loaded with Alaskan pioneers. *Alaskan pioneers,* Laurel said to herself. She liked the sound. *I'm an Alaskan pioneer.*

"Look," called Brian, clambering over his sister to get to the window. "There's a bridge." The Haspers gazed at the overpass, and Brian bounced up and down. "Seattle! Seattle! We're in Seattle!"

"Shush," Jean said. He stopped bouncing, smiled at his mother, then turned his attention outside again.

Laurel looked toward the south and caught sight of an immense mountain enveloped in white. "What's that?"

"Mount Rainier," said Luke. "Some people were talking about it yesterday. It's big but nothing compared to Mount McKinley in Alaska. McKinley's the tallest mountain in North America."

"You mean it's bigger than that one?" Justin asked.

"Yep. Plus, from what I understand, Mount McKinley isn't far from where we'll be living." Luke leaned against the seat. "I plan on climbing it one day. Jason told me we could do it together."

"Who's Jason?" Laurel asked.

"You know, Jason Prosser, my new friend. His family's going to the Matanuska too."

Laurel nodded, then lifted Susie onto her lap and held the little girl up to the window. "So, Susie, what do you think of Seattle?"

The little girl grinned and nodded her head, blond curls tumbling onto her forehead. She planted her hands on the window and pressed her nose to the glass.

"King Street Station," called a porter.

The train slowed. A tall tower with a clock rose from a three-story building with rows of windows trimmed in white. Laurel heard the clank of couplings, and gradually they came to a stop. Brian and Justin tumbled out of their seat and into the aisle.

"Boys," Will said sternly, grabbing hold of the back of Brian's jacket. "We'll go together. This is a big city. I don't want you wandering off."

Brian pouted but only for an instant. This was too exciting a moment to waste on a mood. He stood beside his father. "Can I carry something?"

"Sure." Will handed him a small suitcase.

Laurel stood, anxious to get a look at the city. They had only two days in Seattle, and she intended to make the most of them.

"This is it," Will said with a smile. The line of people in the aisle moved, and the family shuffled forward.

Laurel followed her mother down the steps and onto the walkway alongside the train. She breathed in mingled odors of exhaust, tobacco, fried food, and damp earth. The air felt cool and humid. Puddles left from an earlier rain forced her to pay attention to where she placed her feet.

Influential-looking men stood on a platform. The colonists crowded around. One man wearing a pinstripe suit stood in front of a microphone. He tapped the speaker, sending it into a squealing rant. Grimacing, he leaned away from the microphone, scanned the crowd, then smiled. "Welcome, colonists. Welcome." The buzz of conversation died.

A city official reached out to a baby cradled in a woman's arms, lifted him up to the crowd, then planted a kiss on the child's cheek. Flashbulbs popped. Wearing a plastic smile, he patted the child's bottom and handed him back to his mother.

The man at the podium looked slightly ill at ease but smiled at the baby-kissing official and the colonists. "You have come to the greatest city on earth. Welcome. We wish only good things for your future. Now it is my pleasure to introduce—"

Another squeal from the microphone drowned out his words. Still wearing an artificial smile, the man who'd kissed the baby walked up the wooden steps leading to the stage and stood in front of the microphone. The first man stepped aside and sat in a chair at the back of the platform. The official at the loudspeaker cleared his throat and, in a soft voice, said, "We hope your stay in this fine city will be a happy one. We've arranged special outings for you while you're here, and we wish you luck as you journey north to your new homes." Spreading his arms, he added, "Welcome."

Another man replaced the second. He droned on about Seattle and what a privilege it was to be a part of the government's grand experiment. "It's all a bunch of political hogwash," Adam stated sourly.

Laurel turned, surprised to find him at her shoulder. "How do you know? Maybe they mean what they say. They're helping us, aren't they?"

"Yeah, but this is nothing more than a chance to look good."

The city representatives finished their speeches and spent more time pinching babies' cheeks and smiling for the cameras. Several women worked their way through the crowd, handing out badges. One with short curly hair approached Laurel. She handed her a button that read, Matanuska Pioneer. "What is this?" Laurel asked.

"If you wear the pin you get free transportation on any street car, admission to a motion picture theater, plus entrance to some of the pubs and nightclubs here in town. There will be sightseeing trips too, and a picnic at Woodland Park." She smiled sweetly. "We want you to enjoy your visit."

"Thank you." Laurel pinned the button to her coat. She hadn't expected such special treatment.

After the speeches were over, information about upcoming events was given, then Boy Scouts helped carry the colonists' baggage to the nearby Frye Hotel. Laurel stepped through the door into the foyer and onto soft carpeting. The lobby was impeccably clean with cushioned chairs, a sofa, and floral carpeting. The travelers quieted as they took in the plush surroundings. Will joined a line forming at the front desk. Jean sat with Susie in her lap. Laurel kept watch over her two youngest brothers, but even they were silently gaping at the accommodations. Laurel thought her mother looked tired and hoped their stay in Seattle would rejuvenate her.

"We're on the third floor," Will said, dangling a key.

"Oh, boy!" Brian yelled.

A short man, nearly as wide as he was tall and wearing a dark blue uniform, picked up two suitcases. Will grabbed another and asked, "Luke, could you carry that one?" Luke hefted the suitcase. Brian still had a tight hold on the bag he'd been given.

"This way, please," the bellhop said and headed toward a double door.

He pushed a button on the wall, waited, and doors opened. He stepped inside, and the Haspers followed.

Justin gazed at the walls and ceiling. "Is this an elevator?"

"Of course it's an elevator," Luke said testily.

"Luke," Will said, a warning in his voice.

Laurel felt a thrill as the doors closed and the lift carried them upward. Her stomach turned over just a bit at first, then she couldn't even tell they were moving. When they stopped her stomach dropped again. Pressing her hand against her abdomen, she joined her family as they followed the bellboy into a narrow corridor. It had the same flowered carpeting as the lobby and muffled their steps as they walked to their room.

The bellboy stopped in front of room 322, pulled out a key from his pocket, and turned it in the lock. Pushing open the door, he stepped inside. "I hope you have a pleasant stay," he said in a practiced tone, then walked out and closed the door.

The hallway carpet continued into the large room. A double bed sat on one wall with a four-drawer dresser on the opposite wall. A small table with two cushioned chairs sat beneath the only window. A door led into a smaller adjoining room with a double bed, chest of drawers, and two cots.

"This is neat," Brian cried, throwing himself across the bed. Arms flung above his head, he lay flat on his stomach. "I like it here. Can we stay?"

"Don't be a drip. Of course we can't stay," Luke said. "This is a hotel. You don't live in hotels."

"Enough of that. Your father already warned you," Jean said. She returned to the larger room. "Oh, look—flowers." She walked to the table and bent to smell a bouquet of daffodils and tulips. "They're beautiful. I never expected this."

"Hey, look!" Justin called, digging into a box beside the bed.

Brian joined his brother. "Toys!" He lifted out a truck and ball, then looked at his mother. "Are these for us?"

Will walked to the box and looked inside. He picked up a plastic doll with blond curls. "I guess so. Why else would they be here?"

"I think we should check first," Jean said. "I can't imagine the hotel giving the children toys."

Justin shoved his hand into a baseball mitt. "Can we play with them until we find out?"

"No. Put everything back."

A knock sounded at the door, and Will opened it. The bellboy stood with a shabby brown sweater held at arm's length. "Does this belong to one of your children, sir?"

"Jean? Is this ours?"

"That's Justin's. Thank you," she said, taking the sweater.

"No problem, ma'am." He turned to leave.

"Oh, before you go. Could you tell us why there's a box of toys in our room?"

"Those were donated for the children, ma'am. Every family got one."

"Oh, boy!" Justin said, snatching up the mitt and pushing his hand inside the stiff leather. Brian emptied a box of Tinker Toys onto the floor. "I think I'm going to like Alaska."

"Have a nice day," the bellboy said with a smile as he closed the door.

"I can't believe they've done all this," Jean said, her eyes shimmering with unshed tears.

"Maybe they're being nice because they know what's ahead," Luke teased. He looked out the window at the street below. "This is a swell place. Do you think we'll get to see the city?"

"Some of it," Will said, picking up a *Seattle Times* left on the table. He scanned the front page. "There's a story here about us. It says the government has high hopes for the colony and that men have been sent ahead to get the living quarters ready."

Exhausted, Laurel fell into a chair. "What do you think it will be like?"

Will shrugged. "We won't know until we get there."

Chapter Six

LAUREL SAT AT THE HOTEL WINDOW, ONE ELBOW RESTING ON THE SILL, HER face in her hand. Rain splattered the glass. "I hate this rain. I wanted to explore the city."

Brian climbed onto the chair beside her, and resting on his knees, pressed his face against the pane and blew fog onto the glass. "Do you think it'll stop? I want to go to the park."

Will joined his son and tousled his blond hair. "Listen to yourselves. For months we prayed for and hoped for rain, and now all you can do is complain about it."

"I just wanted to go to the picnic," Brian said.

Justin glanced up from a Sherlock Holmes mystery. "Rain's OK. This is a good book."

Jean set her embroidery in her lap. "There must be something else we can do."

Luke walked om the adjoining room. "It's really coming down." He dropped a yo-yo from his hand and watched it spin toward the floor, then with a flip of his wrist, he pulled it back up into his hand. "How many times have we been here?"

"None," Justin said, looking up from his book.

"And how many times are we going to come back?"

"Probably never," Brian said.

"Well, let's go down to the waterfront anyway, rain or no rain. I'll bet our ship is docked. We could get a look at it."

Justin shut his book. "You really think we could see the boat?"

Luke released the yo-yo again. "I'd bet ya.'"

"I was kind of hoping we could visit some of the local stores," Jean said. "We'll see the ship tomorrow."

"Why don't you, Laurel, and the baby go shopping while me and the boys take a walk down to the wharf?" Will asked.

"Please, Mommy. Please," Brian begged.

"Could we?" Justin asked.

"That sounds good to me," Laurel told her mother.

"What will it be like on the boat? Will it be safe?" Justin asked. "I mean, could we sink?"

"We certainly won't sink," Jean said. "The government wouldn't send us out on the ocean in an unsafe ship."

"I hope you're right." Luke flung his yo-yo toward the floor.

A rap sounded at the door. Brian charged across the room and swung open the door, then stared up at Robert Lundeen. "Who are you?"

"Brian, remember your manners," Jean said.

Laurel stood. "Hello, Robert." She looked at her family. "You remember Robert Lundeen, don't you?"

"Oh, yeah. You were on the train," Brian said.

Before Robert could answer, Will strode across the room, shook the young man's hand, and said, "Hello. Good to see you. Come in."

Holding his hat in his hands, Robert stepped inside. "Mrs. Hasper," he said with a nod and a smile.

"Nice to see you again, Robert," Jean said kindly.

Will closed the door. "How have you been getting on?"

"Good. My mother's a bit done in; she's happy to be here. My sisters are in a lather to see the sights."

"Yeah, we were just tossing around some ideas," Will said.

Gripping the brim of his hat, Robert looked at Laurel. "I was wondering, since the picnic was canceled . . . I thought maybe you'd like to see a movie? Our badges will get us in free." He tapped the button pinned to his jacket.

Laurel was taken by surprise. She hadn't expected an invitation. She looked at her parents. "Would it be all right with you?"

Will glanced at Jean. "I thought you and your mother were going shopping."

"We can go another time," Jean said.

Still uncertain she even wanted to go, Laurel asked, "Are you sure?"

"Yes. Actually, I'm kind of tired. I think I'd just as soon take a nap."

Surprised at her mother's sudden change of heart and wondering if it had anything to do with this handsome farmer, Laurel hesitated. She looked at Robert. "Do you know where the theater is?"

"The desk clerk said it's only a couple blocks from here. And the first show starts at one-thirty." He shuffled his hat from one hand to the other. "Do you like Fred Astaire and Ginger Rogers?"

"Yes. They're great."

Robert smiled. "Their new movie, *Top Hat,* is playing. Plus another one called *Mutiny on the Bounty.*"

"I heard *Top Hat* is supposed to be good." The idea of a Fred Astaire and Ginger Rogers movie was enough to sway Laurel. She looked at the tall man. He was handsome; his dark brown eyes were gentle, and he'd seemed a gentleman. "Mama, are you sure?"

"Yes. You two go along."

"All right then. I'll get my coat." When she returned to the main room, Robert was already standing at the door.

He opened it. "We won't be late," he promised Will.

"See that you're not."

Robert followed Laurel into the hallway, escorted her to the lift, and pushed the elevator button. They waited silently, careful not to make eye contact. When the elevator arrived, they stepped inside and stared at the doors as they closed. Neither said a word.

Clutching her purse against her stomach, Laurel cast Robert a cautious smile. She didn't know why she felt awkward. When they'd visited on the train, she'd sensed an easy rapport between them. Of course they hadn't been on a date. *This isn't exactly a date,* she told herself.

The ride to the lobby felt interminably long, and Laurel was grateful when the doors opened. Robert smiled and allowed Laurel to step out first.

"I'll get directions," he said and walked to the desk. His stride was stiff and formal, and he looked self-conscious. The clerk was away from the desk, so Robert waited. Finally he touched a bell sitting on the counter, and its sharp chime resonated throughout the lobby.

A man wearing a stylish, dark blue suit and sporting a small mustache appeared. "May I help you?"

Laurel gazed out the window. Rain splattered into shallow puddles on the sidewalk, cascaded into gutters, and rushed to grated drains where it swirled away and disappeared somewhere beneath the city.

The elevator opened with a ding, and Adam Dunnavant stepped out. He smiled and tipped his hat to Laurel. Glancing around the room, he asked, "May I ask why you're standing in the lobby?"

"I'm waiting for Robert." She nodded toward her date. "We're going to the movies."

"Oh?" He cocked an eyebrow. "What are you going to see?"

"*Top Hat* and *Mutiny on the Bounty.* Have you heard of them?"

"No, can't say I have." Adam leaned against the wall, took a cigarette case out of his pocket, tapped out a cigarette, and lit it. He inhaled deeply, then slowly exhaled. He glanced at the cigarette. "Nasty habit. I keep planning to quit, but . . ."

Laurel nodded, wondering why anyone would want to smoke.

Gazing out at the dreary boulevard, he said, "It's a good day for a movie."

Without thinking, Laurel asked, "Would you like to go?" The moment the words were out, she wished she could take them back. What was she thinking?

"You sure Robert won't mind?" He flicked ashes into a standing ashtray.

"Of course not," she said, hoping she was right and that it would seem less like a date with Adam along. "Three will be more fun than two."

Adam took another drag on his cigarette. "All right. You talked me into it. And maybe I can get some information for my story."

"Please, no story."

"All right. It'd be hard to take notes in a dark theater anyway."

Robert returned, and shaking Adam's hand soundly, said, "Nice to see you again. How's your story coming along?"

"Good."

Laurel touched Robert's arm. "I asked Adam to join us. I hope you don't mind."

After a slight pause Robert said, "Course not. But we better get moving. The matinee begins in twenty minutes, and it's two blocks from here."

Seated in the dark theater and sandwiched between the two men, Laurel knew she'd made a mistake by inviting Adam. Although the two had bantered in a friendly way as they walked to the theater, friction sizzled. Now no one spoke as they waited for the film to begin. When the lights finally flashed onto the screen, Laurel relaxed.

After watching a newsreel about rising tensions in Europe, which showed footage of a nervous-looking man called Adolf Hitler, they saw a cartoon. Finally, the title *Mutiny on the Bounty* filled the screen and dramatic music resonated through the theater. Laurel felt her anxiety slip away.

By the time the reel ended and intermission was announced, Laurel had nearly forgotten about the tension between Robert and Adam. Robert leaned close and asked, "Can I get you something from the snack bar?"

Laurel was thirsty, but she knew money was scarce, so she said, "No, I'm fine."

"I'm going to stretch my legs," Adam said and stood. "I'll be back in a few minutes." He ambled up the aisle.

"So, what did you think of the movie?" Robert asked.

"I didn't really like it much. It was disturbing, but I have to admit Charles Laughton made a perfect Captain Bligh."

"Yeah, I agree." Robert leaned back in his seat, stretching his arms over his head. "I wonder what it would be like to start a new life on an island away from everything you've ever known?"

"I think we're about to find out."

Robert chuckled. "I guess you're right. Living in the Alaskan wilderness is kind of like that."

The theater lights blinked as Adam returned to his seat. "Looks like I made it just in time." The room went dark. Lights settled on the screen, and a glossy floor appeared with two pairs of dancing feet, a man's and a woman's. The scene dissolved into a shot of a black top hat.

The movie ended with Fred Astaire and Ginger Rogers happily dancing off into their future. Laurel wished that one day she'd find that kind of love.

She considered her parents. They'd always said they loved each other, but Laurel had rarely seen passion between them. They were almost always kind to each other and embraced often, but they shared very few kisses, in public anyway. She remembered how her mother's eyes turned warm when she looked at Will and her father's often shined with admiration for Jean. *They are devoted. That's what I want.*

"So, what do you say to a soda?" Adam asked, taking Laurel by the elbow and escorting her up the aisle.

Robert followed. "Do you know a place?" he asked, his voice tight and prickly as he took long strides to catch up.

"Well, I was out and about early this morning, and there's a soda shop not far from here." Adam looked over his shoulder at Robert. "What do you say?"

"I guess it's up to Laurel." Robert sounded surly.

Both men looked at her. The tension had returned, and Laurel wished she were somewhere else.

"Well," Adam pressed.

Mentally she calculated how much money she had. "I guess, if that's what you want."

"Great," Adam said, picking up the pace.

With Robert on one side and Adam on the other, Laurel was escorted into the brightly lit theater lobby, then out double doors into cool evening air. The rain had stopped.

"It's this way," Adam said as he turned right, careful to keep his hand on Laurel's elbow.

Laurel would have preferred he not touch her. His hand felt possessive. He seemed awfully bold for a man she'd met only six days ago. Still, there was something captivating about Adam.

Another group of people moved past, forcing Robert to stop, step aside, and wait. Adam kept walking. He talked about the city and what he'd seen that morning when he'd been out. Laurel slowed her pace, hoping to give Robert time to catch up.

"Here we are," Adam said, stopping in front of a small soda shop. He opened the door and stepped aside. "After you."

Laurel walked inside. A long bar stretched across one wall. A man behind the counter glanced up and nodded, then returned to washing tall drinking glasses.

"Do you want to sit at the bar or at a table?" Adam asked, looking at a cluster of tables on the opposite end of the room.

"The bar," Laurel said, crossing to a stool and sitting. Adam sat on one side and Robert on the other. She turned to one, then to the other. "It's a good thing this chair swivels," she quipped.

"I'm buying," Robert told Laurel. "Anything you want."

Laurel considered telling him she could pay but knew it would hurt his pride, so she said, "Thank you." Drumming her fingertips on the counter, she searched for something inexpensive. "Hmm. There are so many choices. I guess I'll have a root beer."

Robert placed exact change in front of him. "A root beer, please, and a Coca-Cola."

Adam set a dollar bill on the counter. "Let me cover it. It's on the company."

"No. I'll take care of ours," Robert said evenly.

Adam shrugged. He studied the menu. "I'm in the mood for something special. I think I'll have a banana split."

After the drinks and dessert were served, the three mismatched companions fell silent. Finally Adam took out his pad and pencil. "I haven't gotten your story yet, Robert. How did you end up with the colonists?"

Laurel stared at his pencil, then asked, "Can't you think about anything else?"

Adam carefully picked a nut off the top of his banana split and ate it. "I could, but there are some things I still don't understand."

Laurel's anger grew. "All you wanted was a story!"

"Why are you so mad? It's my job."

"This was supposed to be time with friends—nothing more."

"All right, all right." He tucked his pencil and pad back into his pocket. "But I am interested in knowing how Robert ended up here . . . as a friend," he added.

"I don't mind telling you." Robert took a drink of his soda. "Like so many of the folks in Wisconsin, our farm was dying because of the drought. When my dad heard about the project, he decided we ought to join the colonists—we needed a new start." He took another sip. "A week before we were set to leave, he died." Robert gazed at his drink.

"Oh, Robert. I didn't know," Laurel said, reaching out and placing a hand over his.

Robert glanced at her hand, then at Laurel. His eyes were moist. "The doctor said it was his heart."

"But you and your family made the trip anyway. Why?" Adam asked.

"Moving to Alaska was my father's dream since he was a boy. He'd probably read every book ever written about Alaska. After he died, we decided it's what he would have wanted us to do. The government agent said I was old enough to be listed as head of the household. So here we are."

"Do you know what you have ahead of you?" Adam asked. "This isn't going to be a picnic. It's gonna be tough."

"I'm ready." Robert had a stubborn set to his jaw.

"Have you managed a farm on your own?" Adam pressed.

"No. But . . ."

"If I were you, I'd go back home," Adam said.

"There's no turning back, not for us."

Adam took a bite of banana, then leaned his arms on the counter and looked directly into Robert's eyes. "Look, I wasn't going to say anything. I want to believe this 'experiment' can be done, but I have to tell you, this whole thing is madness. Life isn't the same in Alaska as it is anywhere else. You colonists think you're on some kind of lark, but I'm telling you . . . it's not what you think. Things are going to get serious—real serious, real soon."

Robert leaned toward Adam. "I'm not on a lark. I know how it's going to be, and I'm ready."

Laurel searched for something she could say to change the subject. She glanced out the window. "The rain has started up again," she said. Neither man paid attention.

"This whole colony thing isn't going to work," Adam said. "Even the experts say it's doomed." He glanced at his melting ice cream. "I've been with you folks for a week now, and I like you. There are a lot of good people in this project. I hate to see anyone get hurt, or worse, end up stranded in the wilderness. Furthermore, something you probably haven't heard is that the homesteaders who already live there are real unhappy you're coming."

"What are you talking about?" Laurel asked. "Why would anyone be upset because of us? And why do you think this is going to fail?"

"The homesteaders settled there on their own with no help, and they don't appreciate interlopers on government apron strings." He shook his head in disgust. "And you know as well as I do that government projects don't work."

"What about the CCC and WPA?" Laurel argued.

"Those are exceptions."

"This will be too. All the government is doing is moving families there, then helping us get on our feet. We'll each have forty acres to work. We know farming. We can do it."

"A lot of the families have never farmed." Adam paused.

Robert stood. "Even if some folks going aren't farmers, they're hard-working and determined, and they'll make it. What one person doesn't know, someone else will; we'll work together."

"That's right," Laurel said, but she wasn't so sure. *What if they didn't make it? Then what?*

Chapter Seven

THE BUS BUMPED TO A STOP, AND EXHAUST ROLLED IN THROUGH OPEN windows. The noxious fumes didn't help Laurel's already tumbling stomach. The door whooshed open and she stood, cradling her apple seedling against her chest. She stepped into the aisle behind Justin who was struggling to dislodge his suitcase from between two seats.

Finally, yanking it free, he peered out the window, then looked up at his sister. "That's it! That's our boat!"

Laurel gazed at a white ship docked alongside the pier. Above the waterline were two rows of small round windows and *U.S. Navy Transport, St. Mihiel* written on the port side. Masts and rigging crowded an upper deck. Resting in the center of the ship was a pilot-house; its long row of square windows looked out over the bow. A squat smokestack sat behind and above the wheelhouse and, like a sentry, watched over the ship.

"I'm glad the ship's white," Miram Dexter said from behind Laurel. "White represents purity. That's got to be a good sign."

"I was told she's overloaded," a man wearing a tattered jacket and wool cap said. "So we'll have to sail the open sea route."

Miram glanced up at black clouds. "Oh, dear! What if there's a storm?" She pressed a white handkerchief to her pale face. "I'll be sick for sure."

Laurel could feel her stomach muscles tighten. They'd been told the ship would take the quiet waters of the Inside Passage. She turned to the man with the wool cap. "Are you sure about being overloaded?"

He stuck out a whiskered chin. "That's what I was told."

"Hey, get a move on!" someone shouted.

"I'm sorry," Laurel murmured and closed the gap between herself and Justin. When it was Laurel's turn to walk down the steps, she peered to see around the seedling, carefully placing her feet on one step then the next. She left the bus, and a cold mist touched her face.

"Let me carry that," her father said.

Laurel pulled the sapling closer. "No, that's all right. I've got it."

"OK." Will hefted a large suitcase with one hand, took Jean's arm with the other, and led his family to the dock.

Brian studied the *St. Mihiel*. "It's a real pretty boat."

"It is," Jean said. She turned so the baby could see the ship. "See, Susie, that's going to be our home for the next five days. It'll be fun."

Laurel wished she could believe her mother's words, but if they had to travel on the open sea, she doubted it would be enjoyable, especially if the weather was bad.

Mr. Prosser bumped against her. He tipped his hat, exposing graying hair. "Sorry." The wrinkles in his face deepened with his smile.

"It's all right." Laurel pushed closer to her father and shifted her grip. Her arms ached from holding the plant. She searched for a less crowded spot but couldn't find one.

"Is it true the boat is overloaded?" Miram asked in a whiny voice. "I think it's awful we're being forced to sail in the open sea."

Laurel offered what she hoped was a compassionate smile and said, "I'm sure the captain knows what he's doing."

Miram waved a gloved hand at a seaman standing on a pile of crates. "Sir? Sir." The man looked at her. "Is it true we're overloaded?"

"This ship can carry a lot more than what you have here," he said.

"But is it true we're not taking the Inside Passage? That's what we were told." Her voice reached a higher pitch with each word. Sniffling, she pushed her glasses back into place by crinkling her cheek. The motion stretched her mouth into a grimace and squeezed her eye into an unattractive wink. She dabbed at her nose with her handkerchief.

"I can't say which way you'll be heading, ma'am, but the *St. Mihiel* is a sturdy ship and will take good care of you either way."

"Are we taking the Inside Passage, or aren't we?" a heavyset man standing beside Miram asked.

The sailor nudged back his cap. "That was the plan . . ."

"So, has the plan changed?" the man pressed, a note of sarcasm in his voice.

The crowd quieted, waiting for the sailor's answer.

"I'm not the one makin' the decisions."

The crowd pressed in closer, crushing Laurel against her father. She pushed at the people closest to her, needing to get free of the squeeze. A hand rested on her shoulder, and Laurel turned and looked into Adam Dunnavant's eyes.

Wearing his boyish smile, he said calmly, "That looks heavy. Can I carry it for you?"

Shaking off the sense of being suffocated, Laurel tried to focus on his face. "No, I can carry it." She didn't want any help from Adam Dunnavant.

"Are you all right? You look a little pale."

Although Laurel nodded yes, she wasn't at all sure she was.

"There's nothing to worry about. It's just a little crowded." He gently squeezed her shoulder.

Laurel's stomach did a somersault. "I'm fine. I wasn't worried," she lied.

"Good."

Laurel glanced at the boat. "I wish we could board. I'd like to get started."

"Everything's going to work out fine," Adam said.

"That's not what you were saying last night." Laurel shifted her tree and wished she could find a place to set it down.

"Sometimes I can be too cynical. You shouldn't listen to me all the time." He smiled.

Laurel couldn't help but return the gesture. His intense blue eyes stared into hers, and he leaned close. Blushing, Laurel tried to step back, but there was nowhere for her to go. The crowd moved, and Adam was pushed against her. They were too close. Laurel couldn't look at him, so she searched the crowd. "I . . . I wonder where Robert is?"

"Can't help you there," he said, his mouth forming a hard line. "Haven't seen him."

Two men wearing white uniforms approached the top of the gangplank. One remained on deck, standing at the entrance, while the other ambled down the catwalk and opened the gate at the bottom. "All right, one person at a time, please," he said, stepping aside while people boarded.

Passengers made their way up the footbridge, and Laurel felt an odd mix of relief at being freed from the mob and anxiety. With the seedling still in her arms, she walked up the gangplank.

Adam stepped in front of her. Walking backwards, camera pressed against his eye, he snapped a picture. "That'll be a good one." Before Laurel could say anything, he turned and hurried up the catwalk.

Once on board Laurel walked to the railing and deposited the seedling on the wooden deck. Standing beside her mother, she shook her aching arms, leaned on the balustrade, and looked down on the docks. Families were still boarding. The more adventurous children raced ahead of their parents; the timid clung tightly to their hands. Hundreds of well-wishers stood on the pier, waving and yelling their good-byes.

Against her will, Laurel searched out Adam. She found him almost immediately. He was taking a photograph of a family. The oldest daughter was openly flirting with him. Laurel felt an uncomfortable resentment.

"We better get your things down to your quarters," Will said, turning and steering Jean toward a porter. "Can you tell us where the women are staying?"

The man pointed at a nearby stairway. "Follow those down until you reach a landing with a sign and an arrow pointing toward the sleeping quarters. The arrows will show you the way."

"We're not staying together?" Jean asked.

"No." Will smiled down at his wife. "They have things laid out the best they can. You ladies and the boys have a room, but . . ." he hesitated, "there aren't enough beds for the men, so they're putting us up on deck."

"On deck! I can't believe it!"

"It's not that bad." He chuckled. "It'll be an adventure."

"Are you sure you didn't misunderstand? You shouldn't have to sleep up here with the livestock."

Will chuckled. "We won't be sleeping with the cows and goats."

"You must have misunderstood," Laurel said.

"No, I got it right." He swung an arm over Luke's shoulders. "We'll be fine."

"I feel awful about this," Jean said.

Will led the way down the staircase to a landing, then along a narrow, musty corridor. He'd been given a slip of paper with their room assignment on it, and when he located the correct cabin, he stopped. "This is it." He turned the knob and opened the door.

The family crowded into the small compartment congested with bunks. Two round windows provided a modest amount of natural light. The quarters were airless and overly warm.

Jean walked to a set of bunks not far from the door, and pressed her hands down on the mattress. "Not bad." She glanced at Laurel. "There's room at the end of the bed for your seedling."

Doing her best to disguise her disappointment, Laurel smiled and stepped all the way inside. She set the tree on the floor at the foot of the bunk.

"Luke and I'll store our bags down here with you." Will shoved the two suitcases under the bed, then pulled Jean and Susie into his arms. "We're almost there."

Jean rested her cheek against his wool shirt. "Yes, but I wish you didn't have to sleep on deck. I hate being separated."

"Me too. But it's only for a few days, and it's not like we haven't slept outdoors before."

"But it's going to be cold; we're heading north."

Will kissed Jean's forehead. "We'll be fine."

Luke leaned against the doorframe. "I'd rather sleep on deck anyway."

"Can I?" Brian asked.

"No." Jean pulled the little boy close to her. "You and Justin will stay with Laurel and the baby and me."

Brian and Justin climbed onto a bottom bunk. Justin lay back, leaving his legs hanging over the side. He stared at the mattress above. "This is neat. It's like a fort."

"I want to sleep on top," Brian said.

Will looked at Luke. "Well, son, we'd better go up and see about our sleeping arrangements. We'll be back after we're settled." He gave Jean a quick kiss.

"Can we come?" Brian asked.

"Sure." Will handed Susie to Jean. "See you ladies later."

Jean turned to Laurel. "Do you want the top or the bottom?"

"With Susie to look after, you should have the bottom."

Jean sat Susie on the mattress, then pushed her suitcase beneath the boys' bed. She sat beside the little girl. "Susie and I will be snug as a bug in a rug." She tweaked the little girl's nose, and Susie giggled.

Laurel set her bag at the end of the bed and climbed onto the upper bunk. She lay down, resting her head on a small, nearly flat pillow and stared at the ceiling.

"I heard there's supposed to be a grand farewell," Jean said. "After I get the baby changed, I'd like to go up."

Cradling the baby, Jean walked into the narrow corridor. Laurel followed, closing the door. They stood for a moment, looking up and down the hallway. "We came in that way, didn't we?" Jean asked.

"I think so." The corridor felt close and tight and smelled of diesel oil and stale sweat. The lights put out a dim glow.

A heavyset woman wearing a pillbox hat and too-tight suit approached them. Miram followed. The woman smiled courteously, stopped in front of the door, and studied the room number.

Miram smiled at Laurel. "Hello again. I'm so glad to see you," she said in her nasal voice. "Are you in this room?"

"Yes."

"Oh, that's wonderful! So are we." She looked at the woman. "Mama, this is my friend Laurel. I met her on the train."

The woman gave Laurel a curt smile and extended a gloved hand. "It's nice to meet you. I'm Margarite Dexter." She gave her daughter a sideways glance. "I apologize for my daughter. She sometimes forgets her manners."

"It's good to meet you, Mrs. Dexter," Laurel said, feeling sorry for Miram, who'd quickly wilted under her mother's disapproval. "This is my mother, Jean Hasper, and my baby sister, Susie."

"Hello." Jean shook Margarite's hand.

Mrs. Dexter peered through the doorway. "So this is our room. Not much, is it?" She walked inside. Miram gave Laurel a helpless smile and followed.

"Poor Miram," Laurel whispered.

"They should be interesting roommates," Jean said, wearing a half smile.

"Hi," Brian called from the bottom of the stairway. "Daddy and Luke got their beds. They're outside!"

Will, Luke, and Justin stepped into the corridor. "We're all set," Will said. "This will make a good story to tell our grandchildren."

"We'll have a story all right," Luke said sourly.

Jean took Will's arm. "It's only a few days. We'll be in Alaska before we know it. Let's go up and say good-bye to Seattle."

On deck, a cool, sharp breeze blew through the rigging, and the air smelled clean. The cloud cover had broken, and the sun peeked through, illuminating Mt. Rainier, which stood like a noble guardian beyond the city. The wharf breathed activity. A few travelers were still boarding, longshoremen loaded the last of the supplies, and the crowd waved flags, whistled, and called greetings. Gray and white gulls screeched as they flew over the water and dove for tidbits in the bay.

Colonists crowded the railing. Mothers cuddled babies while boys and girls ran up and down the decks. Fathers smoked cigars and worked at looking relaxed. Laurel gazed up at a huge smokestack, preparing herself for the blast that would signal their departure.

"Hi there," Robert said, joining her. "So, this is it." He smiled broadly and, hanging onto the rail, leaned out over the water.

"Yep, this is it," Laurel repeated, wishing she could muster some enthusiasm. Knowing it would do no good to dwell on the past, she asked, "Where's your family?"

"Mom and the girls are getting settled in their cabin. They'll be up before we sail."

Laurel studied the crowd of well-wishers on the pier and longed to be one of them. A blast from the ship's pipes echoed across Puget Sound. Laurel jumped. A band played "On Wisconsin," and people shouted farewells. The catwalk was drawn into the ship, and large knotted ropes securing them to the dock were let loose and cast aboard. People yelled and blew party horns; confetti floated from the decks to the pier and into the waters of the bay. Everyone waved. Even Laurel got caught up in the farewell and waved at the crowd below.

The *St. Mihiel* moved away from the dock, and a narrow wedge of water appeared between ship and pier. *This is it,* Laurel thought and looked for her family. She needed them. A kind-looking, plump woman and two young teenaged girls joined Robert.

"Laurel, have you met my mother?"

Laurel shook her head no, wishing the introductions could wait.

"This is my mother, Patricia Lundeen." The woman nodded and smiled. She had kind eyes. Robert laid a hand on what looked like the older of the two girls. She had dark hair and blue eyes. "This is Joanna." She smiled shyly. Nodding at the other girl, he said, "And this is Veronica." She looked like she might be a tomboy-type and offered Laurel a friendly smile. "Family, this is Laurel Hasper."

"It's nice to meet you. I hope we'll get to know each other in the months ahead."

"I'm sure we will," Patricia Lundeen said.

"I'll talk to you later," Laurel told Robert and hurried to join her family.

Brian and Justin leaned against the railing, waving and cheering. Luke remained more detached, but Laurel thought she detected excitement beneath his composed exterior. Will had one arm wrapped about Jean.

"Come on, sugar, join us." Will held an arm out for her.

Laurel gladly slipped into her father's casual embrace. Enjoying the sensation of wind and sun on her face, she could feel the subtle movement of waves beneath the ship.

Gradually the sliver of water between ship and pier grew into a pond, then a lake. As they moved into Puget Sound, the band's playing dimmed and the pier grew smaller. The *St. Mihiel* turned northward, and the city of Seattle blended into the Washington coastline.

Again, Adam's camera sought out Laurel. "Can't you find someone else to take pictures of?" she asked, not really angry.

"You looked so enchanted; how could I resist?" Adam grinned.

Laurel stepped away from her father. "Daddy, I'm going up on the bow. I want to see where we're going."

Will gave her a kiss. "All right." He bent close to her ear. "If you need me to take this young man in hand, I will."

Laurel smiled. "I'm fine." Ignoring Adam, she turned and headed for the bow. Adam caught up to her and matched her strides. She looked at him. "Where do you think you're going?"

"With you."

"I'm not sure just where that is. I might go to my room."

"You wouldn't close yourself off from the view."

Laurel looked back to where Seattle had been. Lush islands like green emeralds dotted the sound. Between stretches of beach, heavy cedar and fir clung to their shorelines. Boats bobbed in the small sea. Laurel stopped and leaned on the balustrade. "It's beautiful here. I wonder if it's anything like Alaska?"

"Not where we're going."

"You've been there?"

"Once, with a man from our office. He took three of us on a fishing trip. I'd have to say I've never seen any place as beautiful. If I believed in God, I'd say he did his best work there." He scanned a nearby shoreline.

"You don't believe in God?"

"I did once, but—not anymore." He stared out over the waves. "This is pretty, but it's not Alaska. You have to experience it to know the difference."

And I will, Laurel thought. *Soon.* She turned her gaze toward an open expanse of water. Her new life wouldn't wait any longer. It lay ahead and rushed to meet her, whether she wanted it to or not.

Chapter Eight

Hours after they left the safe waters of Puget Sound, heavy black clouds rolled in from the north and enveloped the *St. Mihiel*. The ocean turned dark, wind whistled around the heavy-bodied smokestack, and water surged against the ship.

Soon passengers and crew were ill. Some hung over railings, while others lay on their bunks below or makeshift beds on deck. All prayed for deliverance. Will, Laurel, Brian, and Justin seemed unaffected. Luke and Jean had gone pale and were unusually quiet. Susie slept in her mother's arms.

"Luke, you're not looking so good," Will said.

"I'm not feeling so good."

"You, Laurel?"

"I'm fine, and hope I stay that way," she added, glancing at a passenger bolting for the rail.

Will placed an arm over Jean's shoulders and pulled her close. "You look as bad as Luke. You all right?"

Holding Susie in one arm, Jean rested a hand on her stomach. "I'm sick. I need to lie down." The ship lurched over a swell. "Oh, dear." She clapped a hand over her mouth, handed Susie to Will, and lunged for the rail where she emptied her stomach. Resting her face on the top of the balustrade, she said weakly, "I'm really sick. I don't know how I'll take care of Susie or the boys."

Will tenderly brushed her hair back from her face. "Don't worry about anything. We'll look after the kids. You need to get to bed." Handing the baby to Laurel he said, "I'll see to your mother, but I'll need you to take care of Susie and keep an eye on your brothers." He gently lifted Jean and cradled her against his chest.

Laurel held the baby at her shoulder. "Don't worry, Mama. I'll take care of the children."

Her mother managed a small smile.

"Is Mama all right?" Brian asked, watching his father carry his mother to the stairway.

"She's sick, but she'll be all right," Laurel explained just as Luke made a dash for the rail. "Oh, no! Not you too?"

"I've got to lie down," Luke said, staggering to the lounge chair he'd set up as a bed.

"Can I get you something?" Laurel asked, knowing her sixteen-year-old brother would refuse any help. He'd always been annoyingly self-reliant.

"No. I just want to sleep." He closed his eyes and pulled a blanket up under his chin.

Justin and Brian wandered down the deck. Laurel stood at the railing and stared out at the ocean. The swells looked taller and closer together. Whitecaps skipped across the top of waves. She hoped the weather wouldn't get worse. Susie's cheeks gleamed bright red, and her eyes teared. Laurel cuddled her close, hoping to warm the little girl. She kissed the top of her knit hat.

"Hi there," Robert said, joining Laurel. "Looks like you're faring well."

"I'm good."

He held out a hand to Susie, and the little girl grabbed his index finger. "So, you've got baby duty I see."

"Yes. My mother's sick."

"Mine too, and my sisters." He shook his head. "I don't know what to do for them. Thank the Lord for Mrs. Prosser. She shooed me out and took over their care. She's a good woman."

Laurel nodded. "Daddy carried Mama down to our room. He's taking care of her for now. I guess we'll take turns."

Robert leaned on the rail and gazed at the waterline. His eyes wandered out over the ocean as a new set of swells lifted the ship, forcing Robert and Laurel to grab hold of the railing. "It's hard to believe that only a few hours ago we were docked in a calm, sunny harbor."

"Do you think the bad weather will last?" Laurel asked.

"Hope not. But I overheard a couple crewmen say it's a big storm and might hang on the entire trip."

"Oh, no. I wish we'd taken the Inside Passage. Do you know how long it takes to get used to the movement?"

"Depends on the person, but I read somewhere that seasickness usually passes after a couple of days."

"That's under normal conditions," a man's voice said.

Laurel turned and found Adam approaching. She didn't want to talk to him. She nodded curtly and turned her eyes back to the ocean.

Robert's pleasant expression faded.

Adam stepped between Robert and Laurel and rested his arms on the rail. "Not everyone recovers from seasickness, and it's especially tough to shake when the seas are rough." He looked at Laurel, then Robert. "Looks like you two are doing all right."

"I'm fine," Robert said curtly.

Laurel didn't respond. She was angry over the way Adam had shoved his way between her and Robert and into their conversation.

Adam scanned the deck. Several lounge chairs were occupied by the sick. A few individuals still clung to the rail. "Looks like the healthy are in the minority here. I'd guess that at least two-thirds of the passengers and crew are sick." He shook his head. "I even saw a sick dog. Poor thing was lying in the corridor, whining and drooling. He didn't even raise his head to look at me when I passed."

Another wave lifted the ship, and Laurel's stomach turned over. "Please don't talk about it anymore, or I'm going to be sick."

Robert moved around Adam and fixed himself beside Laurel. Pressing his back against the rail, he rested his elbows on the edge. "Laurel, what are your plans once you're settled in Alaska?"

Laurel didn't answer at first, then hesitantly she said, "I'm not settling. Living in Alaska is my parents' plan. I'm not going to stay. Once they're set up, I'll return to Wisconsin and go to college."

"Oh. I didn't know," Robert said, unable to hide his disappointment. "Why college?"

"I've always loved history. I worked with the children at our church, and I'm good with the kids. I thought I'd teach and maybe do historical research."

"You'd be good."

"Please don't say anything to my parents or anyone else. They don't know my plans."

"I won't say a thing," Adam said, stepping backwards and training his camera on Robert. Taking a photograph, he said, "You look awfully glum for a farmer on an adventure." The ship made another steep climb up a wave, and Adam quickly turned his camera toward the bow and clicked off a picture as spray washed onto the deck. Smiling, he said, "That should be a good one." He looked at Laurel, then Robert. "Could you move away from Laurel? Laurel, turn the baby around so I can see her face."

"Sure," Robert said sullenly and stepped aside.

Rather than argue, Laurel did as she was asked. Adam looked through the lens. "You could be that baby's mother. You look very maternal with her in your arms."

"Just take the picture," Laurel said caustically.

Adam took a couple pictures. "Beautiful." He let the camera hang from a strap around his neck.

Robert stepped closer to Laurel. "I'll bet you'll make a good mother."

Adam took out his pencil and writing tablet. "Laurel, what happens if you can't go to school?"

"I don't know. Why?"

"People are interested in the challenges you people are facing." A wind gust snatched at his hat. He caught it before it blew off and resettled it more firmly on his head. "I figure you'll marry and raise a family like your mother—maybe work a farm?"

"You figure? Mr. Dunnavant, you don't know me. You have no idea what I plan to do." Adam kept writing. "And stop taking notes. None of this is anyone else's business."

"Hey, it's my job," he said but let his arms fall to his sides.

Laurel shifted Susie to her other arm. "I want more out of life than being a farmer's wife and raising a passel of kids."

Robert grimaced.

"I believe you'll get it, Laurel. I believe you will." Adam turned to Robert. "And how about you? What if things don't turn out the way you plan?"

Robert's mouth was drawn into a grim line. "What? What did you say?"

"What are your plans if the farm doesn't work out?"

"It will work. My family and I will make it work. We've no other choice."

"Things happen. Things you never count on. You can't *know* you'll succeed."

Robert squared his shoulders. "Like I told you before, I'm a good farmer. We'll pray and work hard, and the farm *will* succeed." His gentle demeanor fell away. "Farming's never easy. It's hard work every day. It takes grit. And I'm plenty determined. So are the others. But you wouldn't know that because you've never farmed. You've no idea what we can or cannot do."

"You may be right, but I've already heard some colonists say they've made a mistake and they're planning to head home."

Robert didn't try to hide his anger. "I don't believe you. I can't think of one of us who is ready to turn back. We know how to work and how to stick with something. Life's never been handed to us. No farmer I know would give up so easily."

"You may want to believe that, but there *are* some who are already set on giving up. I'm no liar."

Robert worked his jaw, then asked, "Do you really believe that?"

Laurel stepped between the two and turned on Adam. "Mr. Dunnavant, you're not a Midwest farmer. And you've no idea what it's like to be one." So angry she could hardly think, she sputtered, "How can you even suggest that Robert or any of the rest of us are so spineless that we would give up at the slightest struggle? I've had enough of you and your bad manners and arrogance." She looked at Robert. "I'll see you later? At dinner?"

Robert smiled. "Dinner."

Laurel turned, and with a tight hold on Susie, walked away.

"So, if you're not ready to give up, how come you're already planning on leaving?" Adam threw after her.

Laurel stopped and glared at him. "You know it has nothing to do with that." She turned and quickly walked toward the stairwell. "I've never met anyone like him," she muttered. "He's the most egotistical, rude man I've ever known." Pulling open the door, she stepped onto the landing. "Enough is enough," she said, slamming the door.

The lighting in the stairway was dim, forcing her to slow her pace and carefully place her feet. By the time she reached her room, her temper had cooled, but her heart still pounded in exasperation. Now, more than ever, she looked forward to docking in Alaska and being rid of him.

She opened the door, and the odor of sweat and vomit hit her. Reluctant to enter, she stood in the doorway with her hand on the knob and studied the room. Several bunks had lumps beneath blankets from which moans emanated. A little girl lay on her side, thumb in her mouth, her face wet with tears.

Will sat in a chair beside Jean's bed. Laurel closed the door. "Is Mama all right?"

"She'll live, but she's awfully sick," Will said wearily.

Laurel sat on the edge of the bed, and Susie squealed her delight at seeing their mother. Laurel had to hold her tight to keep her from crawling on Jean. "Mama, I didn't know you were so sick. Is there anything I can do?"

Without opening her eyes, Jean barely shook her head no.

Will dipped a washcloth into a basin of water and sponged her ashen face. "Looks like it's going to be a long trip."

Laurel took her mother's hand. "Mama, I'm so sorry."

This time Jean managed a weak smile and whispered, "It won't last forever."

"That's right. We'll be in Seward in no time," Will said cheerfully.

"What can I do to help?"

"I need to check on Luke. He looked like he was sick."

"He is."

"Could you stay with your mother while I see to him?"

"Of course."

"While I'm gone, I'll see if I can find something for you to eat."

"No. Don't. I couldn't keep anything down."

"How about something to drink? I heard they have apple juice."

"All right." The ship nosed into a wave, and Jean's face turned gray. Sweat broke out on her upper lip. "I need the basin." Immediately Laurel handed it to her, and Jean wretched. Laurel sponged her face.

His steps heavy, Will left.

Susie whined, then started to cry. "I think she's hungry," Laurel said almost apologetically, knowing that feeding the baby would be difficult for her mother.

"I'll have to nurse her," Jean said weakly. "Here, give her to me." She unbuttoned her blouse and put Susie to her breast.

For several minutes nothing was said. Susie nursed and fell asleep. "Please take her," Jean whispered.

Laurel placed the baby between two pillows at the end of the bed and covered her with a blanket. Susie looked angelic, her face free of worries. Laurel wished her life could be so simple.

Jean stared at the bunk above her. "I hate being sick—not being able to care for my family."

"You always take care of us. Now it's our turn."

Jean nodded, pulled the blanket up under her chin, and closed her eyes. Laurel settled back in the wooden chair and replayed the scene she'd had with Adam. Immediately her anger and frustration returned.

"Is everything all right?" Jean asked. "You look troubled."

"I thought you were asleep. I'm fine."

"I don't believe you." Jean fluffed her pillow and carefully resettled her head.

"It's just that Adam Dunnavant. He makes me so angry."

Jean gave her a questioning look. "What's he done?"

"He as much as said the farmers won't make it in Alaska, and he was so rude to Robert."

"Robert?"

"Robert Lundeen. You met him on the train. Remember, he's the one whose father died just before they left."

"Oh, yes—a nice young man," Jean said weakly. She pushed herself up on one elbow. "Could you give me some water?"

Laurel filled a glass from the pitcher beside the wash basin and held it to her mother's lips. Jean sipped a little, then pushed it away. "I dare not drink anymore." She lay down and was quiet for a few moments. "Oh, this seasickness is a terrible thing. I'll be glad when we get to Seward."

"Adam said the seas are supposed to stay rough all the way there. He thinks he knows everything."

"I hope he's wrong about the bad weather." Jean looked at her daughter. "Why do you care what he thinks?"

"It's just that he's always certain he's right. It's infuriating."

Jean raised an eyebrow. "All you have to do is stay away from him."

"That's just it. I try, but every time I turn around, he's there."

"Walk away."

"I try."

"You sure you don't care about him?"

"Adam? Of course not. I could never be interested in someone like him. When I'm ready to settle down, I want someone steady and decent. Adam's pushy and nothing more than a flirt." She stared at the wall. "I've decided not to talk to him again."

Chapter Nine

"I FOUND ANOTHER PAIR OF SOCKS AND SOME GLOVES," LAUREL SAID, SITTING on the edge of Luke's deck chair where he lay huddled beneath three layers of blankets. "I'll help you put them on." The ship rolled over a large swell, and Laurel nearly toppled off her seat.

Luke peered up at her through miserable eyes and mumbled, "Thanks."

"I'm sorry you're so sick. You aren't feeling any better at all?"

"I don't know, maybe a little."

"I wish there were something I could do. There must be something." She scanned the deck, searching for a steward, but she couldn't find one. Laurel unlaced Luke's shoes and removed them, then pulled on the extra pair of socks and replaced his shoes. She started to push his hand into a glove.

Luke jerked his hand away. "I can do it." He pushed his fingers into the warm wool, then laid back and closed his eyes.

"Hi, kids," Will said, strolling up to Luke and Laurel. Brian was perched on his shoulders, and Justin ambled along the rail, clacking a stick against the braces. "You feeling any better?" he asked.

"Maybe."

"We'll be in Seward soon." Will rested his hand on his son's shoulder. "How much longer?"

"A couple of days."

Luke pulled a blanket over his face. "That's too long." Throwing back the cover, he looked at his father. "I'm never leaving Alaska if it means I have to take a ship."

Will chuckled.

A steward joined them. "Feeling any better, Mr. Hasper?"

"I wish everyone would stop asking me that."

"I have an apple and crackers and some tea for you." Luke shook his head no. The steward looked at Will. "Should I leave them on the table?"

"Why bother? Nothing I eat stays put," Luke muttered.

"Leave it," Will said. "I'll get him to eat something." A large swell lifted the ship, then dropped it into a trough. Will braced himself against a wall.

When the ship settled, the steward set the food and drink on the table. He stared at the boy pityingly. "In all my days of service, I've never seen so many sick." The ship rolled over another wave, and Luke moaned. "Take heart, lad. Only a couple more days."

Laurel knelt beside her brother and rested a hand on his arm. "You need to eat something."

"I can't."

"Just a little." She held up a cracker, but Luke turned his head. "All right then, try a little of the tea." She set down the cracker, dropped a cube of sugar into the tea and stirred, then held the cup out to him.

Luke rolled onto his side, pushed himself up on one elbow, and took the cup. He sipped. "How's Mama?"

"Better, but she's weak and still a bit dizzy. She's worried about you."

Using his pocketknife, Will sliced off a section of apple and held it out. "Try eating a piece of this."

Luke reluctantly took the fruit and nibbled on it.

Adam joined the Haspers, and after tipping his hat to Will and Laurel, looked at Luke. "Sorry to see you're still sick. I was seasick once. It was no picnic, that's for certain."

"Oh, dear Lord!" a woman shrieked. "Somebody help!" Miram Dexter ran onto the deck. "We're sinking! The ship is sinking! We're going to die!" She scanned the deck. "Where are the life jackets? What about lifeboats? Do we have any?" She paced up and down. "Where are they?"

"They're on the upper deck," Laurel said, her heart leaping. "What's wrong? What's happened?"

Seeing Will, Miram sprinted across the deck and grabbed him. "Do something!"

"What's happened?" Will asked, his voice steady.

"There's water pouring into one of the cabins! We're going to sink!"

Will took hold of the hysterical woman's arms. "Miram, calm down. Getting in a panic isn't going to help. What do you mean there's water pouring into a cabin? Which cabin?"

People crowded around. "What's happened?" a woman asked. "Is something wrong?"

Miram closed her eyes and gulped in air. "All right, I'm calm," she assured Will, but her voice said otherwise. It quavered, and its pitch rose with each syllable.

Will gently released her. "All right now, tell me what's happened."

"Nothing happened exactly." Her voice sounded shrill. "I was visiting with Mrs. Prosser and doing some needlework when water started seeping through the wall. At first it was only a little, but then more started coming in, and now it's a lot, and it's flooding the floor!" She held her face in her hands. "Someone has to do something!" Her eyes swept up and down the deck, then scanned the sea. "Dear God, what are we going to do?" She ran to the railing and peered out over choppy waves.

"Laurel, you take care of her," Will said. "I'll see what's going on. And look after the boys." He stopped in front of Miram. "Where is Mrs. Prosser?"

"She went to tell the captain."

Laurel gathered her brothers close. "Daddy, check on Mama. OK?"

He nodded, then taking long strides, hurried to the stairs and disappeared. Adam, Robert, and two others followed.

Luke sat up, his skin sickly pallid. In a voice that sounded more like a boy's than a man's, he asked, "Laurel, what's happening?"

"I don't know, but I'm sure everything will be fine." Laurel wished she could believe her own words. Miram seemed high strung, but Laurel couldn't imagine her making up such a story. She scanned the ocean, searching for land, but there was none.

"What should we do?" Luke asked, grabbing the edge of the chair and struggling to stand. For a moment he looked like he might fall, but he finally managed to gain his balance.

Justin hugged Laurel's legs. "Are we going to sink?"

"I'm sure if something were really wrong an alarm would have sounded." Luke nodded and leaned against the wall. Laurel walked toward Miram who clung to the railing. Taking a slow, deep breath, she joined the young woman and rested a hand on her arm. She could feel Miram's trembling. "Where's your mother?"

Miram's eyes widened. "I don't know." She searched the deck. "Do you think she's all right?"

"I'm sure she is." Pasting on a smile Laurel continued, "And I doubt the boat is sinking. There must be another explanation."

Clutching Laurel's hands, Miram shook her head. "I don't think there is another explanation." Suddenly, she dropped to her knees and squeezed her eyes shut. "Dear Father in heaven, save us. Please don't let this boat sink." Tears coursed down her face, and her glasses fogged. Unexpectedly, she opened her eyes wide. "What if there aren't enough lifeboats?"

"Whining isn't going to help," Laurel said sharply. Miram shut her mouth. Her eyes brimmed with tears, and her chin quivered. Laurel regretted her harsh words. "Miram, I'm sorry. I'm sure there are enough lifeboats. I remember reading that after the Titanic sank, a new law was passed that says all ships must have enough lifeboats for passengers." She gently lifted Miram off her knees. "It doesn't matter anyway. I'm certain the boat's not sinking."

"What other reason can there be for water flooding Mrs. Prosser's cabin?"

"We'll know soon. My father will be back any moment, and he'll tell us."

People were crowding onto the deck, gathering children, and rushing to find life jackets.

Hands trembling, Miram smoothed her hair and resettled her glasses on her nose. "I . . . I'm sure you're right." She glanced at the stairway. "I just wish he'd hurry."

Hoping Miram wouldn't notice her own shaking, Laurel placed an arm around the bird-thin young woman. "We're going to be fine. Everything will be fine."

Miram nodded, then turned frightened eyes to Laurel. "But what if we *are* sinking? What'll we do?"

Trying to keep her tone light, Laurel said, "Well, I guess we get into the lifeboats. Land can't be too far away." She gazed at the rough waters, wondering how many passengers knew how to swim and what would happen to the children. She searched for her brothers. They both sat huddled beside Luke on the deck chair.

Suddenly, the thrum of engines stopped, and Laurel's stomach turned over.

"What's happening?" Miram asked.

The ship's forward progress slowed, then stopped, and they wallowed in the swells. A wave hit broadside and lifted the ship, causing it to list to one side. *We are sinking!* Laurel's mind screamed.

Miram's eyes opened wide and her face turned ashen.

Will stepped onto the deck. Adam and Robert were right behind him. People closed in around the three and began firing questions. Will smiled reassuringly. "We're not sinking. The captain has everything under control. They'll have the problem fixed in no time."

"What problem?" Miram asked, pushing through the crowd. "What's wrong?"

"There's a crack in the hull just below the waterline, and water's seeping into . . ."

"A crack in the hull! Oh, dear Lord! Is the ship breaking up?" a woman shrieked, gathering two little girls close to her.

Purposely keeping his voice low and steady, Will said, "No, the ship's not breaking up. The damage can be repaired. This used to be a navy transport, and there's a diving bell on board. They're going to drop it into the water and fix the tear."

"They can do that?" Miram asked.

"Yep—according to the captain." Will looked over the crowd. "The engines have to be shut down while they do the work."

"More time lost," a rumpled-looking, heavyset man complained. "First they overloaded us so we couldn't take the Inside Passage. Now this." He flicked a cigarette butt over the side. "At this rate, we'll miss the drawing for our land."

"We can't miss the drawing," a young man with long blond hair said. He stood beside the first man who'd complained.

Will knew frustration was high among the colonists. Some were angry, some disenchanted, and others were frightened. There had been growing apprehension about whether the government could be trusted or not, and it wouldn't take much to get people stirred up. He lifted his eyes to the heavyset man. "It's only a few hours holdup. We'll make it in time for the drawing."

Bullying his way through the crowd, the man stood in front of Will. "How can you be sure?"

Will met his defiant eyes and held out a hand. "I'm sorry, but we haven't met. My name's Will Hasper."

The man stared at Will's hand through droopy lids, scrubbed his scraggly beard, then reluctantly shook hands. "Felix Pettersson."

"Glad to meet you, Felix. We still have four days until the drawing. Captain said we should be on our way in ten to twelve hours. That will put us into Seward in plenty of time to make the train to Palmer."

"Why should we believe the captain? Why should we believe anybody? The government's bungled this whole thing from the beginning." Felix lit another cigarette, sucked smoke into his lungs, then blew it in Will's face. "We've been lied to." He turned and looked at the people gathered around. "We can't trust the government officials or the captain."

The younger man with the blond hair walked up to Will and peered at him. "He's right, isn't he? Things ain't been the way they were promised. We had no place to sleep on the train. There are no rooms for the men on this boat. Plus, the ship was jammed, and we've had to put up with rough seas. I ain't had a decent night's sleep since I left home." He brushed the hair out of his eyes. "And now this? A tear in the hull? If we make it, what are we goin' to face when we git to Alaska? Maybe they lied to us about that too? Maybe there ain't no land." He glanced around at the others. Some nodded. He turned back to Will. "I think we been lied to from the beginning."

Will's irritation grew. Already the people had forgotten all that had been done for them—gratitude had been replaced by self-interest. Silently he prayed for patience and composure. Meeting the young man's challenging eyes, he asked, "What's your name? I don't think you told me."

"Ed Ketchum. Up from Mankato."

"Ed, I have to agree with some of what you say. Some things haven't turned out the way we expected, but most of what we were told has been right." He raised his voice so everyone could hear. "There were a lot of us to move and lots of belongings. For the most part the food's been good, we were treated real well in Seattle, and here we are only a couple days out of Seward." He looked out over the crowd. "We've been given free train fare, free passage by boat, free food. And it's been comfortable enough." Several were nodding. "And about being overloaded—well, we were given weight limits. If we went over, it was our own fault. We should be thanking the government for not forcing us to leave some of our belongings behind." He waited a few moments, allowing his words to sink in.

"He's right. We ought to be ashamed of ourselves," Patricia Lundeen said.

"Yeah, like Will said, we should be thanking the government instead of complaining," Robert added.

"A little thankfulness would take us a lot farther," Will said. "Even on this ship, we've been kept warm and well fed."

"Yeah, but how many of us can keep any of the food down?" Felix interjected. "I've been sick since we left Seattle."

"That's no one's fault," Norma Prosser said. "You've got to remember we've been kept safe and there's land waitin' for us in Alaska."

Drew Prosser joined the discussion. Readjusting a felt-brimmed hat and stroking a graying beard, he rested an arm around his solidly built, no-nonsense wife. "You folks need to stop your yammering and thank God you've been given a second chance."

"But what about this boat? It's got a crack in it," Alex pressed. "We can't even trust the government to keep us safe."

"You heard what the captain said. It's not going to sink, and it's going to be repaired."

Will smiled and nodded at the man, then looked at the people. "We're nearly to Seward; then we head for Palmer. There's plenty of land with good soil for farming, a new home for us."

A murmur of agreement moved through the people.

"Yeah, well, none of it will be ours if we're not there to draw for the parcels," Felix challenged. "We were told May 23."

"They know we're coming. They'll wait."

"You don't know that. If they go ahead, they'll leave us the scrub ground."

Will looked over the crowd. Everyone was standing now, even the sick. Luke pushed forward. His smaller brothers beside him, he stood next to his father. Will laid an arm across his son's shoulders. "We need to trust God. He's the one who oversees our lives. He's the one in control."

Will caught Adam Dunnavant's eyes. He seemed focused on the exchange, but he wasn't taking photographs or scribbling notes. Will even thought he'd caught a nod of agreement. They exchanged a smile, and he continued, "When most of us decided to settle in Alaska, we expected hardships; we knew it would be a struggle. And we've barely begun. We're going to have troubles. But does that mean we give up?" His eyes rested on Luke, then others who'd been sick. "I know some of you have suffered, and I'm sorry for that, but a new life waits for us. Our government has given us the gift of a new beginning, and we just have to accept that troubles and hard work come with it." He found Ed in the crowd. "And sacrifice." Wind snatched at his hat and he trapped it under one hand. "Have you forgotten what we left in the States?" He shook his head. "My farm was dried up, dead."

People nodded. Drew Prosser stepped forward. "Will's right. We have everything to hope for."

Robert added, "And we've got a lot to be thankful for." Again there were nods of agreement and more than a few "Amens."

Scowling, Felix conceded, "You may be right, but I won't believe it until I see it." He stomped away.

Drew joined Will. "Thanks for speaking up. We sure needed someone to keep a lid on these folks." He patted Will on the back. "You did a fine job of settling them. I was beginning to think they were going to mutiny." He smiled, and the creases in the corners of his eyes deepened. "You're good with people."

"They just needed to be reminded of their blessings. For the most part, these are good, solid folks."

Drew shoved his hands into his jeans pockets. "I agree. Seems people are the same everywhere. Up in Minnesota we had good neighbors. Hated to leave 'em." Norma joined her husband, and Drew laid an arm over her shoulders. "Like most of the others, our farm was in bad shape. With the children nearly grown, Alaska fit the bill for a new start."

"Just the word *Matanuska* sounds sturdy," Norma added. "It gives me hope."

Will nodded. "I haven't had a chance to thank you, Norma, for all the help you've been to my wife."

She smiled, her brown eyes warm. "Glad to do it. You have such a sweet baby, and I'm thankful for the chance to get to know Jean—she's a good woman."

"She is that all right," Will said with a grin. Leaning against the railing, he looked out over the ocean. "I have to admit I hate the holdup. I'll be thankful when I set my feet on solid ground again."

"Me too," Laurel said. She gave her father a hug. "I'm going to check on Mama." She hesitated. "I was really proud of the way you stood up to those men."

"Thanks, but I didn't do much. People want to hear reasonable talk."

"I was afraid you were going to have a fight," Justin said.

Brian grabbed hold of his father's hand and leaned back. "You should have hit him."

"Fights don't fix things," Adam said, placing a hand on Brian's head. The boy grinned up at him.

"Brian, Justin, why don't you come with me? I know Mama would love to see you." Laurel looked at her father. "Is there any water in our room?"

"No. It's farther up in the bow, and they're pumping it out. Your cabin's high and dry."

Laurel steered the boys toward the stairway.

Will gazed at deep swells. Instead of water, he envisioned dark earth plowed under, ready for planting. He could almost smell the heavy odor of rich loam and yearned for the day he'd turn his land with the plow.

Adam walked up to him. "I admire your faith, but you better be prepared for a letdown. I hate to agree with anything those guys say, but there's some truth to their words. The government may mean well, but this is an experiment. You're bound to have problems, and some you might not be able to overcome."

Chapter Ten

THE *ST. MIHIEL* MOVED INTO THE PROTECTED WATERS OF RESURRECTION BAY, and Laurel strained to get her first glimpse of Alaska. Justin stood in front of her, and Laurel rested her hands on his shoulders. She could feel his excitement. Will stood beside her, his arm protectively wrapped around Jean. Unaware of the significance of the moment, Susie slept with her cheek resting against her mother's shoulder. Brian had climbed onto the second rung of the railing and leaned outward. Luke kept a tight hold on his brother's belt. Rain splattered the calm waters of the bay, the ship's deck, and the eager colonists, but no one seemed to care.

Laurel peered at the bow of the ship, hoping to catch sight of Seward. All she could see was mist. *How much farther?*

Robert stood a few feet away with his mother and sisters. He glanced at Laurel and offered a smile. Laurel returned the gesture. For a moment her mind wandered to the possibilities—Robert, tall and powerful, working the farm and Laurel keeping a nice home. *You're being silly. You barely know him. Besides, he wants to farm in Alaska, and you're not staying.*

"Is this Alaska?" Brian asked, pushing himself up on tiptoe. "I can't see."

"I can fix that." Will lifted Brian onto his shoulders. "Is that better?"

"There's too much fog."

"Be patient. We'll see Seward soon."

A gull swooped over the deck, hovered as if looking for a morsel, then with a flip of his wings soared away and disappeared.

A small troop of birds, black with white faces and bright orange bills appeared out of the fog. They floated happily in the ship's wake. "What are those?" Laurel asked.

"Puffins," Adam said from directly behind her.

She swung around. "How do you know that?"

"I studied up on Alaska before leaving Chicago." With a smirk he added, "I figured a person ought to know something about a place before he visits it."

Laurel's ire rose. *Why does everything he says make me feel foolish?* "Oh," she said and returned to peering at the fog.

The rain slowed. Occasionally the haze thinned, and a patch of green or a rocky protrusion would appear for a moment before being swallowed once again in the damp soup. Wet and shivering, Laurel waited, unwilling to go below for fear of missing Seward's appearance. She felt the weight of a blanket being laid over her shoulders and looked up to see Robert.

"You're cold. I thought this might help."

Laurel pulled it close. "Thank you."

"Seems everyone's willing to get soaked just to be the first to catch a glimpse of Alaska."

Laurel nodded. "I can hardly believe we're here."

Pilings appeared, then the gray mantle fell away, revealing a sizable town. Someone shouted, "Hello Alaska." Another voice repeated the greeting and then another. Soon, "Hello Alaska" echoed all over the ship.

Clouds draped themselves over steep mountains that rose up from forested foothills. The range cut inland and stood like rugged scaffolding behind the Alaskan community. Rocks lay like dark rivulets between melting snows. This place was imposing and harsh, yet beautiful. Laurel leaned on the railing, barely breathing. The mist settled over the ship again, concealing the view. The gray wall occasionally swirled away, revealing a harbor crowded with small fishing boats, giant evergreens crowding the shoreline, and dark valleys between craggy peaks. One mountain stood above the others; larger and more imposing, it looked standoffish, almost hostile. Laurel had the distinct sense of being unwelcome.

The fog lifted, and sunshine bathed the town of Seward. Laurel's ominous first impression diminished. Homes and businesses huddled on the flat ground between sea and mountains. Crowds waited on the wharf. Laurel could hear a band playing.

Will and Jean embraced, cradling Susie between them. "We're here—finally," Will said.

Jean's eyes welled with tears.

Laurel wished she had someone to hug, so she folded her arms around Justin and pulled him close.

Robert laid a hand on Laurel's arm. "We're finally here," he shouted over the racket. Laurel nodded and would have hugged him, except that Mrs. Lundeen folded her son in plump arms and held him while she patted his back.

Laurel glanced at Adam, whose camera was recording their arrival. She turned back to staring at the fast-approaching dock. They were sliding through the dark waters fast—too fast. It looked as if they were going to ram the dock! Laurel braced her legs, grabbed hold of the rail.

"We're going to hit!" Justin cried.

"Get back!" Will shouted as he pushed his family away from the railing.

The ship plowed into the pier. The sound of grating and splintering wood pierced the air. The ship jolted to a stop, knocking some off their feet.

For a moment everything was quiet. Once the ship was sound and no one was hurt, Will laughed. "The perfect end to a perfect trip."

Everyone cheered.

"Do we get to go to our farm now?" Justin asked.

"Not right away, son. The men are going on ahead to draw for land plots. You, Brian, and Susie will stay with Laurel and Mama. I'll see you in a few days." Will looked at Luke. "I'd say being sixteen makes you more man than boy. You ready, Son?"

Still pale from days of illness, Luke managed a smile. "I'm ready. I'll be glad if I never see this ship again." He picked up his bedding and bag.

Adam stepped up to the railing, positioning himself between Robert and Laurel. "So, Mr. Hasper, the way I understand it the men are taking the train to Palmer immediately, and the women will join you in a couple days?" He had his pen poised to write in his tablet.

"That's what we were told. The drawing is tomorrow morning. We've got to be there."

"I'm going with you," Laurel said firmly.

"Sugar, I understand you want to go, but your mother's gonna need you."

Jean lay Susie against her shoulder. "Let her go, Will. I'll be fine. Justin's big enough to help."

Will looked out over the ship. Some men were already disembarking. Women were crying and embracing their husbands. He hefted his bag onto his shoulder. "You're sure?"

Jean smiled. "I can wait with the rest of the women." She glanced at a young woman sobbing into a handkerchief. "Some will need a calming voice."

Will nudged back his hat. "I'm not sure she'll be allowed. They said just the men."

"I can push my hair up under a hat and wear an oversized coat. No one will know the difference," Laurel said in a hurry. "Please, Daddy, let me go."

"All right, but if we get caught it's—"

"We won't." Laurel kissed her father. "Thank you. I'll get my things." She ran to the stairs.

"Just necessities," Will called after her.

~

The train blasted steam as if impatient for the last travelers to board. Wearing Luke's hat and her father's coat, Laurel walked up the boarding steps head down and straight into Robert's back, nearly tumbling off the steps. Her father caught her from behind.

Adam chuckled. *So much for remaining inconspicuous.* He boarded last and hoped he could find a place beside Laurel. *She'll probably sit with her father and brother, and that Robert is everywhere she is,* he thought irritably.

He wasn't even sure why he cared. She was just a plain-speaking Wisconsin farm girl—certainly not his type. He'd always been attracted to the more stylish, fashionable woman—educated and well-traveled, the kind who elevated the prestige of any escort. This was the first time Laurel had ever left Wisconsin. She certainly had no knowledge of fashion. Her long hair needed taming, and he'd never seen her wear anything but homemade cotton dresses and wool coats. Still, he couldn't free his mind of her. The dresses hung appealingly on her tall slender frame, and her auburn hair, although unruly, had a special allure. More than once he'd wanted to reach out and touch the soft curls.

I need to keep clear of her. I'll be leaving in a few weeks. This story ought to land me a juicy assignment overseas.

Luke had grabbed a seat beside Robert and was already involved in a discussion about hunting in the Alaskan wilderness. Will and Laurel sat facing them, Laurel next to the window. Adam had his sights on a seat toward the back when Will stopped him. "Adam, why don't you sit here by me?"

Adam sat across the aisle. The bench felt hard and cold. This might be an opportunity to gather more information for his story. He leaned his arms on his thighs. "So, I suppose you're eager to get to Palmer."

"Sure am. How about you?"

"Me? I suppose. It'll be good to finally see this great valley I've been hearing about. I've been to Alaska but never the Matanuska Valley."

"What do you have planned next?"

"I'll get my story written and head back to Chicago. Hopefully I'll be sent to Europe."

The train nudged ahead, then jerked. After a couple more bumps and shudders, they rolled forward. For a short while they followed Resurrection Bay, then began their ascent into the mountains.

"Wow, look how high up we are already," Luke said, peering out the window and down a sheer drop falling away several hundred feet.

Laurel glanced down at the rock face and sat back in her seat. "I'll be glad when we're out of these mountains."

"It's spectacular," Adam said.

Will glanced at the view, then turned to Adam. "I've never known a reporter before. Do you like the work?"

"Yeah. I travel and get to meet interesting people. Once I interviewed President Roosevelt."

"Really? What is he like?"

"Not a bad sort—pleasant, down-to-earth. They throw first-class parties at the White House."

"You've been, huh?"

Adam could feel his cheeks flush, and an embarrassed grin creased his face. "Well, that's what I hear," he admitted.

"Oh. You had me going there for a minute," Will said with a chuckle.

"I plan on going some day. My career is beginning to take off."

"And what do you want to do with your career?"

"I figure I'll be a reporter, but I'd like to get work overseas, preferably Europe."

"Things are in an uproar over there, aren't they?"

Adam threw an arm over the back of his seat. "Yeah, there's a lot going on. That's why they need good reporters—people who'll dig until they get the whole story. I'd like to get an interview with Adolf Hitler. He's the one who's really shaking things up right now."

Laurel leaned toward the aisle. "I heard he's an awful man. Why would you want to spend a minute with him?"

"Awful, maybe, but interesting for sure."

Laurel said nothing more and sat back, bundling into her coat. She returned to gazing out the window.

Will yawned. He leaned his head back against the seat and closed his eyes. "Think I'll get a little shut-eye while I can."

"Sounds good to me," Adam said, sliding to the seat next to the window. Frustrated, he folded his arms over his chest and stared out at a wall of snow alongside the tracks. He not only hadn't gotten anything new or remarkable for his story, but he'd sounded like a guy with a pipe dream in front of Laurel.

Light snow fell as they moved inland. The train rumbled over trestles traversing deep gorges, some with waterfalls streaming down mountainsides. They steamed across open meadows buried in white, made their way around large looping trestles, and traveled through several tunnels. Patches of huge spruce and hemlock, some draped in green moss, dotted the landscape. Mountains tall and rugged appeared like frozen giants, one range upon another.

Adam saw a bear lumber up a rocky bank and disappear into undergrowth. Adam went to work taking photographs and writing down everything he saw. Nothing was unimportant. It was all magnificent.

More than once, he caught Laurel watching him. What was she thinking? Why did he care? He kept his camera clicking—hiding in the work he loved and annoyed for allowing himself to care about anything else.

Chapter Eleven

THE TRAIN MOVED OUT OF THE MOUNTAINS, LEAVING STEEP RAVINES AND cliffs behind. It wound along an inlet where sleet-gray mud flats lay, left by a retreating tide. Rivulets of water trickled over the ooze, and small birds flitted across the mire, picking up tidbits left by the sea.

Laurel thought it ugly and turned her eyes to the heavy forest crowding the tracks on the other side of the train. Her empty stomach grumbled, and she hoped the rumors of a meal in Anchorage were true. She glanced at Luke and Robert who were dozing and wondered how they could sleep through such an important time in their lives. She studied Adam. He looked animated, taking in the scenery and occasionally holding his camera up to the window to click a photograph. He also jotted down notes.

He caught Laurel's eye and winked. "Remarkable, isn't it?"

"Uh-huh," she said, embarrassed at having been caught staring at him. "Do you know how far it is to Anchorage?"

"I was told Potter would be next. After that, it's Anchorage. We're nearly there."

She returned to watching the scenery slide by. Marshes brimming with rigid stalks topped with clusters of delicate white flowers, tall cotton grass, and broad-leafed water lilies gradually replaced the forest. The train wheeled past a small town, and Laurel's heart quickened. Anchorage would be next, then Palmer.

A mix of emotions tumbled through her. What would Palmer be like? Since leaving Seward, they'd seen little sign of human habitation. Would Palmer be so uncivilized? And what would the people be like?

Will dropped his lean frame into the seat beside Laurel. "That Drew will be a good neighbor. He's a fine man." Gray-blue eyes warm with concern gazed at Laurel, and he patted her hand. "You all right, sugar?"

Laurel nodded.

"Well, we're almost there."

Luke stretched and yawned. "Did you say we're almost there?" He straightened and peered out the window. "Hey, is that the ocean?"

"It's a bay," Laurel said dryly. "If you'd stayed awake, you'd know what's going on."

"Sorry. I was tired." He gazed out the window. "That looks like an island." He pointed at a strip of land rising out of the haze in the inlet.

"That's Fire Island," a passing porter said, stopping to gaze out the window. "My family and I've spent a few weekends there. It's beautiful. We like to explore the beaches, climb the cliffs, and in the evenings cook hotdogs and marshmallows over a bonfire on the beach."

"Sounds like fun," Luke said. Looking at his father he added, "Maybe we can do that."

"Maybe."

Adam changed seats. Sitting in front of the Haspers, he stared at the water. "This is Cook Inlet, isn't it?"

"Yes—the doorway to the rest of the world," the small porter said proudly, displaying large white teeth when he smiled. "It's free of ice year-round." He straightened. "You've got to watch the mud flats though. Sometimes they can be like quicksand. People get stuck and drown when the tide comes in."

Laurel's stomach turned, and she made a mental note never to step out on any mud flats.

"We'll be arriving in Anchorage in a few minutes," the porter said and hurried down the aisle.

The train followed the bay for several miles, slowing as it passed a few small houses. It approached a dock with long, low buildings with metal rooftops and a fishing boat moored alongside. Continuing to decrease its speed, the train wound around a bend and chugged to a stop in front of a small wooden building with a broad platform in front. Baggage carts were lined against the front wall. *This can't be Anchorage,* Laurel thought, trepidation growing. *It's too small.* "Where is the town?" she asked.

"There are houses up on that hill," Luke said, pointing at a rise not far from the depot. "I'll bet this is Anchorage."

"No. It can't be." A wave of disappointment swept through Laurel. She'd expected Palmer to be small but had hoped Anchorage would be a sizable city, a place she could visit and be reminded of the real world.

The porter stopped. "The young man's right. This is Anchorage, but the actual town sits up on the flat. You can't see it from here."

Laurel felt a rush of relief. "So there is a city?"

"Not exactly. It's small, only about twenty-five hundred people. But it's growing." With a smile, he trotted toward the front of the car.

Standing, Adam looked over the seat at Laurel. "Not what you expected, is it?"

"No," Laurel stated flatly.

Anxiety spiking, Will stood and waited while Laurel sidestepped to the aisle. He hoped this tiny depot was not a predictor of what they could expect in Anchorage. If the farms of Palmer were to be a success, Anchorage needed to be a thriving community. Laurel stepped forward toward the front of the car, and he followed. Luke, Robert, and Adam walked close behind. Disembarking, they joined other colonists gathered in front of the station.

A man wearing a pinstripe suit and a broad-brimmed hat stood on a platform. He smiled at the crowd, and his neatly trimmed mustache curved into an upside down half-moon. "Welcome. Welcome to Alaska." A smattering of applause rose from several onlookers. "I know you're anxious to get on to Palmer, but we wanted to give you a real Alaskan welcome, so we've had a feast of local dishes prepared for you. Cars are waiting to take you to the community hall. This way, folks," he said, stepping down and showing the crowd to the fleet of cars.

Laurel walked between Luke and Robert. Will and Adam led the way to a nearby car. Cameras flashed, and reporters pressed in.

"I'd better go to work," Adam said, lifting his camera and taking a photograph of Will. With a smile, he disappeared into the crowd. A man wearing an inexpensive suit stood beside a shiny Ford sedan. He held open the back door. "Welcome to Anchorage."

"I'll be glad when I can see it," Luke said casually, sliding onto the seat.

Will and Robert sat in the back beside Luke. Laurel took the front seat. The driver seemed taken aback at Laurel's appearance, but he said nothing and closed the door, then hurried around to the driver's side. His hands on the wheel, he glanced over his shoulder and said, "I'm Harold Iverson. We're happy to have you here. We sure hope you like it."

"I'm Will Hasper, this is my son Luke," Will nodded at Luke. "And this is Robert Lundeen, a friend. And sitting beside you is my daughter, Laurel."

Harold smiled nervously and nodded at Laurel. "We heard it was men only, but I thought you might be a girl."

"I just couldn't wait on the ship," Laurel explained.

"Will we make it to the drawing on time?" Robert asked.

"Absolutely. You'll be sleeping in the valley tonight. But we wanted to make sure you were well fed before sending you up to Palmer."

The train pulled out of the station, crossed a trestle over Ship Creek, rumbled through the railroad yards and past coalbunkers, then headed up a small valley. A massive range of mountains rose up from the flat just beyond the town of Anchorage.

Will's stomach knotted. He studied a handful of homes built into the hillside. The stopover in Anchorage had been enlightening. The city was smaller than he'd expected, but he'd been told there were other towns that would need fresh produce. With careful handling, there might be enough demand to support the colony, but it wouldn't be easy.

Remembering the promises made by the government agent in Wisconsin, Will's ire rose. *He lied. The market's not nearly as good as he said. It's possible we won't make it. Then what?* Slowly and deliberately he let the air out of his lungs, trying to calm himself.

Adam sat beside Laurel, across from Will. His eyes met Will's. "So, how's it look to you?"

Will hesitated. He didn't want to inflame an already volatile situation. He'd heard others worrying aloud about where they would sell their goods. "I'd hoped Anchorage would be bigger, but with the support of folks in Palmer and the other towns, we ought to make out all right."

"Hope you're right."

Seated nearby, Luke and Jason, Drew Prosser's son, began to talk about the hunting trip the two planned to take in the fall.

"Do men ever talk about anything else?" Laurel asked.

"What else is there?" Robert tucked a pillow behind his head.

"Baseball," Adam said.

"I once saw the Yankees in St. Paul." Robert fluffed the pillow and repositioned it.

"Yankees are out this year. It'll be the Detroit Tigers all the way. Not that it matters. Won't get a chance to see many games, if any."

"Aren't you going back to Chicago?" Laurel asked.

"Yeah, but probably not until late summer."

Will shut out the chatter and gazed at the passing countryside. *How am I going to support my family? If even one thing goes wrong, we're sunk.* Groves of birch with stark white bark stood like soldiers among tangled thickets of alder. Beyond, mountains blanketed with snow gazed down on hazy purple valleys and rolling foothills. They moved on toward the valley, the tracks clicking rhythmically beneath the train's wheels.

The miles passed, but Will's pondering brought no solutions. The train rattled over a trestle, and he gazed down at a river coursing through a canyon. The water ran clear and swift.

"We're almost there," Robert said. "Won't be long now."

"I'm sad to see it end. I like travel and adventure," Adam said.

Will wished he could recapture his enthusiasm, but all he could think of was Jean and the children. How would he provide for them? He'd signed a contract promising not to work at anything but the farm, but farming might not be enough. At least the government would provide supplies and tools for now. He wouldn't have to start making payments for another five years.

Once more, the tracks followed the inlet. The tide had come in, and waves washed the beach. Luke moved across the aisle and stared at the ocean. "Do you think we'll see any seals or whales?"

"You never know," said Drew Prosser, leaning over the back of Luke's seat. "I've heard tell there are adventures waiting at every turn for Alaskans."

Will's eyes roamed over the landscape to the north and rested upon a monstrous mountain. Buried in snow, it appeared to be floating upon the clouds. Nearby peaks were dwarfed by its mass. He couldn't tear his eyes away; it was compelling, stirring. In all his life he'd never seen anything like it. Strength flowed from it as if it were alive. Will's fears ebbed. God had created that mountain and everything else on the earth. Was the plight of a few colonists beyond his authority and power? Peace settled over him.

"Are you all right, Daddy?" Laurel asked. Will didn't answer. "Daddy?"

He looked at Laurel. "What, sugar? Did you say something?"

"Is something wrong? You've been awfully quiet."

"No. Everything's fine." He smiled. "Everything's good. I'm looking forward to some real adventures."

"All I want is a soft bed and a warm bath. Adventure can wait," Laurel said, resting her head against the seat. She closed her eyes and folded her arms over her chest. "It will feel good to get off this train. I think every inch of my body aches."

Will smiled and nodded. He studied a broad swamp where clumps of tall grasses protruded from murky water and ducks and geese paddled between thickets. Clouds of insects hovered over the waters. "Not long now, sugar. Not long."

Chapter Twelve

LAUREL TRIED TO SLEEP, BUT THE SUN'S RAYS SLANTED THROUGH THE window and onto her face. She turned away from the window, but the sunlight was still too bright. Finally, giving up, she stared at a sprawling grassy marsh. It looked dreary. Gradually, fields with bright pink star-shaped blossoms, wild iris, and a collection of other brightly colored flowers replaced the bleak landscape.

"It won't be dark before we get there, will it?" Luke asked.

Will grinned. "That shouldn't be a problem. Remember, this is the land of the midnight sun. I expect it'll be light at least until ten. And by this time next month, the days will be even longer."

"Really? Wow." Luke scanned the inlet, then turned and looked at the flats and distant mountains. "When you told us we were moving to Alaska, I didn't think I'd like it much. But I do. It's wild-looking and real pretty." He straightened and pointed out the window. "Hey! A moose!"

Everyone gazed at a huge brown animal with a bulbous nose. She stood beside a pond in a willow thicket, a calf at her side. Soggy vegetation hung from her mouth, and water dribbled from her lips while she methodically chewed, undisturbed by the passing train.

Luke pretended to point a rifle at the giant beast. "Pow!" He grinned and rubbed an emerging beard. "That would hold a man and his family for a good long while."

"What would you know about being a man?" Laurel asked, knowing she should hold her tongue but feeling miserable enough to share her unhappiness.

"And you're so grown up?"

"All right, you two," Will said. "Hold on to your tempers a while longer. We're almost there."

There? Where is there? Laurel thought. *A piece of ground in the backwoods of nowhere?* For miles there had been nothing but wilds—no homes, no towns. The forests, marshes, and mountains seemed endless. Feeling small and insignificant, she had the sense of being set adrift in a wilderness ocean. Closing her eyes, she wished she could sleep away her feelings of isolation.

The next thing Laurel knew, someone was shaking her shoulder. "Wake up. We're here. We're in Palmer."

Adrenaline shot through her, and she opened her eyes. All she saw at first were Adam's deep blue eyes and charming face. "Where's my father?"

"Down there." Adam nodded toward the front of the car.

Laurel looked around, then pushed herself upright and gazed out the window. The train had stopped beside a small depot with a broad wooden platform where people were milling about. The edge of the sun touched the top of a nearby mountain range. Laurel took a deep breath. She didn't want to leave the safe haven of the train.

"Laurel?" Adam urged. "We need to go."

She stood, grabbed her coat and bag, and stepped into the aisle. Will stood at the front of the car and flashed a smile at her. She hurried to catch up to him. Adam followed.

Her father disembarked and waited at the bottom of the steps. Laurel stood on the landing, then slowly took the steps. "You look like you're half asleep," Will said, taking her hand.

Laurel wasn't paying attention. Instead her eyes moved beyond the station to rows and rows of tents with metal smokestacks protruding from canvas roofs. They'd been pitched in an open, muddy field. *This was home, a tent city in a sea of mud?* she thought. Dejected, she walked beside her father and brother.

The camp had been erected in a broad valley. Rugged, snow-capped mountains bordered the basin like giant guardians. Forests bordered lush meadows and cleared ground. Beyond the tent city, Laurel could see farmhouses, barns, and fenced pastures with grazing cattle. She felt slightly better. At least there was some sense of order and domestication in this wild place. And she couldn't deny that although it was remote, the Matanuska Valley was beautiful.

She felt a sting on her cheek, then one on her hand. Mosquitoes had descended. She swatted at them, but they persisted, their whine setting Laurel on edge. A man shouted instructions, but she didn't hear, distracted by her battle with the determined insects. Finally, fumbling to hang on to her bag and hold her coat over her head as a shield from the biting pests, she followed her father and brother to a waiting pickup. She could feel the itch of rising welts.

Adam ran ahead. He snapped a picture of the driver, then climbed into the back of the truck and focused his camera on the approaching colonists.

A young man wearing a netted hat glanced at Adam. Deciding to ignore him, he turned to the newcomers. "Welcome to the Matanuska. Sorry about the mosquitoes. They're always bad this time of year." He hefted their bags along with several others onto the back of the pickup. "Climb in," he said and scrambled into the cab.

When everyone was settled, the engine fired and the truck jumped forward. Laurel toppled into Adam, who caught her and gently set her back in place. "Thanks," she mumbled, wishing it had been anyone else.

Mud churned under the tires and splattered into the back of the truck and onto the passengers. Gritting her teeth, Laurel wiped a clump of black muck off her arm.

They bumped over a rutted, muddy road and pulled into another camp of tents. The truck stopped midway, tents on both sides. If it were possible, the mire was worse here.

Still swatting at mosquitoes and keeping her lips pressed tightly together to make sure none found their way into her mouth, Laurel climbed out of the truck. She slipped in the mud, but Robert grabbed hold and kept her from falling. She smiled her thanks and lifted her feet, sludge sucking at her shoes.

Holding a list of names, the driver stood in front of the small collection of newcomers. "Sorry for the mess, but we just got these tents up. We'll have duckboards set down in a day or two."

"What's a duckboard?" Laurel whispered.

"Wooden slats," Will explained.

"That should make walking easier," the driver continued. "We've had a warm, wet spring, but it ought to dry up soon. We've had a couple of dry days, and we're hoping it lasts." He glanced at his list.

Before he could continue, Laurel asked, "Are the mosquitoes always this bad?" She knew she sounded whiny but was aggravated enough not to care.

The young man offered an apologetic smile. "They're pretty awful most of the summer, but you'll find hats with netting and Citronella in your tents. Here in Alaska, you take the bad with the good." He glanced at his list, then looked at the colonists. "Also . . ." He cleared his throat. "There aren't enough tents for all you folks plus the families that'll be joining you. So, until we can get more set up, some families will have to share."

Laurel nearly groaned out loud. With mosquitoes buzzing around her face and her feet sinking deeper into the mud, she waited beside her father and brother while tent assignments were read. The handle on her suitcase cut into her hand.

Since the Haspers were a large family, they weren't asked to share a tent. Kicking up mud, Luke ran to their designated home and disappeared through a canvas door. A few moments later he stuck out his head. "Come on. Hurry up. It's not bad." Again he disappeared inside, and the door fell back into place.

Will draped an arm around Laurel's shoulders and gave her a quick hug. "It can't be that bad."

They walked to the tent, and Will held the door for Laurel. She stepped inside, thankful to get away from the mosquitoes. Their temporary house was one large room with wood planking for a floor. A coal and wood-burning cook stove stood against the wall to her right, and a large cabinet stocked with food took up the space beside it. The other three walls were lined with beds, five in all. Small meshed windows let in fresh air and light. Though the room was bare, it was clean and tidy, except for Luke's fresh mud prints.

He plopped down on a bed. "This is pretty nice."

Will walked through the tent, surveying the space. "They've been real nice to give us beds with springs and mattresses." He smiled at Laurel. "When your mother gets our things in here, it'll look real homey."

"Where will we put everything?" Laurel asked.

"We'll manage." Will set his bag on the floor beside one of the beds. "I'd sure like to get a look at the land tracts."

"Knock, knock," someone called from outside.

Will pulled aside the flap. "Robert. Come on in."

Wearing a friendly smile, Robert removed a netted hat and bent over so he could fit his six-foot-three-inch frame through the door. He nodded at Luke, then turned warm, serious eyes on Laurel.

"Is your tent this big?" Luke asked.

Robert glanced around the room. "I'd say it's exactly the same." He turned to Will. "I found a local who said he'd take us out to look at some of the plots. Would you like to go?"

"You betcha. I was just sayin' I'd like to get a look." Will glanced at Laurel and Luke. "You two want to go along?"

"You couldn't keep me away," Luke said, striding out of the tent.

Laurel set down her bag. "What about the mosquitoes?" She scratched a welt on her wrist.

"Some of these were in my tent," Robert said as he held up his netted hat.

Will scanned the room. "Here's some," he said and walked to the cabinet, picking up three. He placed one on his head. "This should help."

"Thank goodness," Laurel said, taking one and pulling it down over her hair and carefully arranging the netting around her face and neck. She followed Robert and her father outside.

A wagon with two large plow horses in harness waited in front of the tent. A tall, slender man sitting in front looked down at them. He smiled and removed his hat, revealing dark brown curls. "I'm Tom Jenkins. Welcome to the valley."

Will shook the man's hand. "Will Hasper. This is my son, Luke, and my daughter, Laurel." He chuckled. "She's been trying to pass as a man, but I guess it doesn't matter now."

"You're too pretty to overlook, ma'am, even in that getup. I expect the officials chose to let you pass."

Laurel blushed. "Thank you, Mr. Jenkins."

"And I guess you've already met Robert," Will continued.

Tom nodded. "Climb in and I'll take you on out."

"Is it all right if I sit up front?" Luke asked.

"Fine by me," Tom said.

Luke scrambled onto the wooden seat beside Tom.

Tom looked back over his broad shoulder. "Any place in particular you want to see?"

"Do you know where there are some good parcels?" Will asked.

"There's lots of good land. I've got a farm myself." He clicked his tongue and flicked the reins. The horses plodded forward. "I'll take you out toward my place—the soil's good there, and some of the government parcels border my property."

Laurel pressed her back against wooden slats and tried to get comfortable. She was tempted to pout but had grown weary of her sour mood and resolved to put it behind her. Still, she hoped it wasn't far to the land.

"Hey there! Wait!" Adam Dunnavant called, running after them.

Oh, no. Not Adam, Laurel thought.

The driver pulled on the reins, and the horses stopped.

"Mind if I come along?"

Wearing a smile, Tom looked down at Adam. "The more the merrier." He gripped the reins, steadying the horses. "Name's Tom Jenkins."

"Adam Dunnavant," Adam said and climbed in, settling his six-foot-one frame against wooden sideboards directly across from Laurel. He nodded at Robert and Will.

"You still looking for a story?" Will asked.

"There's a lot to write about, but today I'd rather be a sightseer and just enjoy the scenery." He gave Laurel a charming smile.

Laurel couldn't help but notice his warm, expressive eyes. And although he had a ruggedly handsome face, there was something boyishly appealing about the set of his mouth and the way his hair always seemed to find its way onto his forehead. Still, she gave him what she hoped looked like a disinterested nod.

He grinned. "Feeling a little cantankerous today, are you?"

Laurel folded her arms over her chest. "I'm not."

"So, how do you like Palmer so far?"

The wagon jolted forward. "It's interesting—pretty, but I could do without the mosquitoes," Laurel added with a small smile.

"They're always especially hungry this time of year," Tom said.

"How's the writing coming along?" Robert rested his arms on bent knees.

"Good. The *Trib* likes what I've sent so far."

"You writing about the colonists' failure or success?"

"I'll write what I see. It'll be the truth." Adam kept his eyes on the countryside.

In spite of the sun, the air had a cold bite to it. Laurel pulled her coat close, careful to keep her hands tucked inside the sleeves to protect them from biting mosquitoes. "What time is it?"

Will pulled out a pocket watch. "Nearly nine," he said, surprise in his voice. "It seems earlier."

"Yep," Tom said. "The daylight this time of year can fool ya'. The days are long, the nights short. We work long hours—sometimes as many as twenty in a day. It's a busy season."

"Don't you get worn out?" Luke asked.

"Sure. We thank the good Lord that summer lasts only a few months." Tom chuckled. "Then we sleep during the winter to make up for the lost hours."

"Have you lived here long?" Adam asked.

"Me and the missus came up in twenty-five. It was just the two of us then. We have two boys now. I guess we might consider ourselves *sourdoughs* after ten years here." He smiled and shook his head. "Boy were we *cheechakos* when we got here—as green as they come." He chuckled. "But we learned."

"What's a sourdough and what's a cheechako?" Luke asked.

"A sourdough's someone who's been living up north a good long while. And a cheechako is a newcomer, a greenhorn." He settled mischief-filled eyes on Luke. "That would be you."

Luke straightened and threw back his shoulders. "I don't know that I'd call myself a greenhorn. I've lived in the country all my life, and I know a good deal about farming."

"That may be, son, but until you've spent a few seasons in Alaska, you're a cheechako." He grinned. "You'll see." He focused on the horses and flicked the reins. "Get up there." Glancing over his shoulder, he said, "It takes a while for some folks to accept outsiders. Some of 'em aren't happy to see the colonists come to the valley."

"I'd heard rumors," Will said solemnly. "I was hoping there wouldn't be any trouble between us and them."

Tom shook his head. "I doubt you'll avoid it. A few are as cross as a grizzly in the spring."

"Why?" Laurel asked.

"Well, when they came up here, they didn't have any help. They did it on their own and figure the colonists are freeloaders taking a government handout."

Luke looked outraged. "That's not true."

"No, but that doesn't change how they feel." Tom leaned his forearms on his thighs. "I figure we'd do a lot better to work together. It's not easy making a go of it up here." He gazed at the mountains. "I s'pect it's in God's hands though."

The wagon dropped into a deep rut, and Tom flicked the reins. "Come on there, boys," he said affectionately. The wagon bounced out of the hole, mud clinging to the wheels. "The pieces I was thinkin' about are just around this bend." He pointed toward a cabin with a wisp of smoke rising from its chimney. "That's my place." A large barn sat west of the house, and black and white cows grazed in a fenced pasture.

Laurel studied the house. It was small but had two stories and a porch that ran across the entire front. Rows of orange nasturtiums mixed with pink and lavender pansies and pink hyacinths grew in well-tended beds bordering the home, and the grass growing around the house was deep green and clipped short. Except that the house was made of logs, the place reminded Laurel of the farms in Wisconsin before the drought. Hope bloomed.

The horses clomped across a wooden bridge. A small stream washed beneath it, then gushed out the other side, swirling over rocks and tufts of grass. Willows, berry bushes, and horsetail clung to the banks.

Tom Jenkins guided the horses to the side of the road. "Whoa." He pulled on the reins, and the horses stopped. After pushing in the brake, he tied off the reins and climbed down. "This is it. There are four parcels along this stretch."

Laurel stood. Hands pressed against the small of her back, she stared at the land. A meadow of lush grasses and long-stemmed white and yellow flowers stretched out before her. Beyond stood a forest of spruce, alder, and birch, where ferns, berry bushes, and other greenery sheltered. Rising behind the forest were mountains, rugged and strong. Like a fortress they hemmed in the valley. Laurel felt uneasy. She was used to wide open prairies.

Will jumped from the wagon and walked through the field, leaving a trail in the grass. Luke followed. Slowing his steps, Will stopped occasionally to pull up clumps of grass and dig in the soil. He lifted dark, damp loam in his hands, and breaking it up, sifted it through his fingers. He turned around and around, gazing at the fields and mountains. "This is it! This is what God had waiting for us. Your mother will love it."

Laurel climbed out of the wagon and walked through the lush grass, the stalks slapping her legs. Fine particles of dust and pollen filled the air. She stopped beside her father, and he sifted the dark, musky-smelling earth into her hands. Crumbling the soil between her fingers, she let it filter to the ground, then looked at her father. "Grandpa would like it here. He'd plant an orchard."

"This is it then," Will said with a smile. "This is where we belong."

"But what if we don't get this piece?" Luke asked.

"We will. I know it," Will said.

Chapter Thirteen

MOMENTARILY CONFUSED, LAUREL ROLLED TO HER SIDE. *WHERE AM I?* SHE wondered. Staring at the dreary canvas wall, she remembered—the docking in Seward, a hurried trip by train to Palmer, and a visit to a plot of land. *Today is the day!*

Yawning, she stretched her arms over her head. It had been a long night. Her busy mind kept her tossing and turning, and sunlight had intruded long before it should have. Adjusting to the lengthy daylight hours would take some time.

Laurel fluffed her pillow, resettled her cheek against the cool cotton, and closed her eyes. Still, her mind would not rest. In frustration, she opened her eyes and studied the nearly bare room. Her father and Luke were both still sleeping. She smiled. *What is it about men? They can sleep anywhere, anytime.*

She closed her eyes again, but her mind immediately turned to thoughts about the day. *We'll be drawing for land. I wonder if we'll get the piece across from Mr. Jenkins?* Remembering the fertile acreage, she thought about the farm they would have one day; then college and a career swept the image away. A sense of emptiness settled over Laurel. Her family would be here and she'd be in Wisconsin.

"Well, I guess there's no sleep for me," she finally said and sat up. Will and Luke didn't stir. She peered out the tent window. Although the sun was up, there was no activity outdoors. *Of course not,* she told herself. *Reasonable people are still sleeping.* She dropped back onto the mattress and pulled the blankets over her face, hoping she might fall asleep if she closed out the light. Instead, the air became stale and warm.

With a sigh, she threw back the covers and dropped her feet over the side of the bed. The coolness of the room raised goose bumps on her arms and legs. Certain the fire needed tending, she stood on the chilled wood floor, and cold pierced her bare feet. Walking quickly and promising herself she'd wear socks after this, she crossed to the stove, poked in two pieces of wood, then returned to bed, hoping the rest of the world would wake up soon.

Today would be the beginning of their new life. They already had experienced milestones—the day they'd decided to leave, the morning they left the farm, their departure from Seattle, the landing in Seward, and their ultimate arrival in Palmer, but today was the true beginning—the day they claimed their land. Today they would know what piece belonged to them—their new home.

Laurel's mind drifted back to Wisconsin and the home she'd known there. Dust would be piled on the windowsills, the floors, and the porch. Wind would sweep over the dried-up prairie, lifting dirt and carrying it into the empty house. It would moan under the eaves and lift dried paint from the shingles.

She felt the desperation that had driven them from that place and shivered and also wondered how David and his family were. She missed him and their casual, comfortable relationship. Unshed tears burned her eyes. *That's enough of that,* she told herself and sat up. There was no use staying in bed. She pushed back the blankets and sat on the edge of the mattress. Although the fire crackled, the room was cold, so she dressed quickly.

Luke rolled over and mumbled something. His eyes were still closed, so Laurel guessed he was dreaming. She pushed her feet into her shoes.

"What you doing?" he asked.

"Getting dressed."

Luke stretched and yawned. "What time is it?"

"I don't know. Early. No one's up and about yet."

"Boy, I slept like a log," Luke said, stretching again. He climbed out from under his blankets. He was still wearing his clothing from the day before. Looking at the floor, he asked, "Hey, where are my shoes?"

"Look under the bed," Laurel said, retrieving her brush from her bag and pulling it through her long hair.

Getting down on hands and knees, Luke peered under the bed. He dropped to his stomach, reached under, and came up with the shoes. Sitting right where he was, he pulled them on, then tied them and stood.

Laurel stared at her brother. "You know, your clothes *look* slept in."

"That's because I slept in them," he said with a grin.

"You should have hung them up. Everyone's going to think you're a tramp." She tugged on the brush as it caught on a tangle. "I don't suppose you really care though."

"I'm not trying to impress anyone." He smirked. "I don't think Adam Dunnavant or Robert Lundeen care how *I* look." He picked up his belt off the floor and passed it through the loops on his pants.

"What's that supposed to mean?"

Luke cinched the belt and smiled. "Nothin'."

"I don't care a thing about either one of them." Laurel pulled her hair back and braided it, then let the thick plait hang straight down her back.

"Well, they sure seem to care about you. Everywhere you are, they are. It's sickening—reminds me of the moths we used to have flitting around the front porch light during the summer." He grinned. "And it don't look like you mind. I think you like the attention. You're probably sweet on both of them."

"I'm not! Absolutely not! They're just friends." She threw her brush back in the bag, then pulled up the bed sheets and blankets.

"What are you two squabbling about?" Will asked sleepily, pushing up on one elbow.

"Nothing, Daddy. I'm sorry we woke you." Laurel smoothed the blankets and tucked them in. She buttoned her coat. "We need more wood. I wonder where we can get some?"

"I'm sure we'll find out soon enough." Will sat up, rested his feet on the cold floor, and leaned his arms on his thighs. For a few moments he stared at the wood slats running beneath his feet, then ran his hands over his face and brushed back unruly blond hair. He smiled at his children. "Good morning. It's a great morning, isn't it?"

"Morning, Daddy." Laurel kissed her father's cheek. "There's coffee on the shelf, but there's nothing to cook it in."

"Don't worry about that. I'm sure there'll be some at breakfast. Last night they told us we'd all eat together in the mess tent—wherever that is." Turning his back to his children, he grabbed blue jeans lying across the foot of the bed and pulled them over long johns. He lifted his shirt off his bag where he'd draped it the night before, sniffed it, then pushed his arms into the sleeves. "I'll be glad to get the washing machine hooked up and running. I'm beginning to have trouble tolerating myself." He grinned and buttoned the shirt.

"Me too. I look awful. I might as well be a hobo." Laurel smoothed her skirt.

Laurel opened the doorway flap and peeked outside. A man and three children walked past. The youngest, a girl, skipped ahead. They didn't notice Laurel. Smoke rose from round metal chimneys, and a woman in the tent straight across from them was hanging diapers on a makeshift clothesline. She smiled at Laurel, then returned to her work.

Ducking back inside, Laurel said, "I don't see any mosquitoes, and people are up. Plus, I can smell coffee. I suppose if we follow the aroma, we'll find breakfast. I'm hungry."

"I'm starved." Will finished lacing his boots, then walked to the doorway and stepped outside. Luke and Laurel followed. Taking a deep breath, he scanned the compound, then the clear sky. "Another nice day. Just as it should be." He gazed at the nearby mountains. "This is a real beautiful place." For a moment he seemed lost in thought, and then he looked at Luke and Laurel. "So, you two ready for some breakfast?"

"Long past ready," Luke said.

"All right then," Will said. "Let's get to it."

After a breakfast of flapjacks, bacon, and coffee, families gathered in a clearing where a temporary platform had been erected. A map with numbered lots had been nailed to a wooden pole, and several colonists were gathered around it, hoping to get a clearer picture of the valley's layout and the plots available. Laurel tried to get close, but it was no use. From a distance she could see numbers and lines but couldn't make out what any of it meant. Finally, in frustration, she stepped away.

"I wonder which one we'll get?" Luke asked.

Will rested a hand on his son's shoulder. "The one God means us to have." A breeze caught at his blond hair. He smiled, and creases laid down by years of sun and wind deepened. Yet his blue eyes looked young and were alight with anticipation. "I expect we've already looked at it."

First, a lottery was held to determine in what order the men would draw for their lot numbers. Will was number twenty and took his place in line. Laurel and Luke stood beside him. "I'd say we're pretty lucky to have drawn number twenty," Will said. "We won't have to wait long to find out which piece is ours."

"Hey, Robert," Luke called to their new friend who stood just five people behind them.

"Hi, Luke," Robert said with a smile and nodded at Laurel. His eyes settled on Will. "Maybe after the drawing we can go out and look over our places together?"

"Sounds good to me."

Laurel swatted at a mosquito and hoped the hordes weren't about to descend. She'd left her netted hat at the tent. The pest buzzed her again, and she swiped at it but missed. Finally it moved on to someone else.

Laurel glanced down the row of men. "I'd hate to be number 204." Another mosquito winged its way around her. She watched it land on her arm, then slapped it. Lifting her hand, she grimaced. All that remained was a splotch of red and an insect skeleton. "I hate mosquitoes," she mumbled and flicked it away. She heard the click of a camera and looked up to find Adam with his Kodak trained on her.

He lowered it and smiled. "Just recording the story." He moved away, seeking out other interesting shots.

"What's taking so long?" Luke asked, shifting his feet. "I wish they'd hurry."

"Be patient. We'll know soon." Will grinned. "The only time I can remember feeling this eager was the morning I married your mama, and she was worth the wait. When she walked down that aisle, I knew I'd never seen a more beautiful woman." He winked. "And I still feel that way."

Ed Ketchum and Felix Pettersson stood together at the end of the line. They'd been such trouble on the ship that Laurel was pleased to see they'd be the last to draw. *Serves them right,* she thought.

Felix lit a cigarette with the butt of another, then threw the butt to the ground. He didn't bother stomping it out. He caught Laurel's eye but acted as if he hadn't seen her and said something to Ed.

The thin young man with straggly hair grinned at Laurel. Unwilling to be rude, she smiled at him and hoped he wouldn't decide to be friendly and join her. Ed Ketchum was repulsive, dirty, and unkempt. She turned her back to the two men and watched a heavyset man climb the steps to the platform.

Facing the colonists, he yelled, "Quiet!" He raised his arms over his head. "Quiet everyone, and we'll get started!" He looked at the crowd, and a hush settled over the group. All eyes were on him. "Good morning." People pressed in. The man removed his hat, wiped sweat from his brow, and replaced it. "It's pretty warm out here for May. Should make for a good growing season."

The people cheered. "Come on, get on with it!" someone shouted.

Laurel noticed a group of men standing off to one side. They looked angry, and Laurel wondered who they were. A tall, broad-shouldered man with a full beard and brown hair that hung in wild curls around his head seemed to be the leader of the group. Gray eyes lit with hatred swept over the crowd. Laurel had never seen him before. He couldn't be a colonist, or she would recognize him. Their eyes met and locked for a moment. Laurel could feel herself shrivel beneath his gaze. Then, as if he hadn't even seen her, his eyes moved on. With a shiver, and hoping she would never have to deal with him, she turned back to the man on the podium.

"I want to welcome you all to our beautiful valley," he said. "As I'm sure you all know by now, there's no place like it on earth."

"I'll say," Alex Pettersson said derisively. "Nothing like living in a mosquito swamp."

"Put a lid on it," another man said. "Go on. We're waiting," he encouraged the speaker.

The man cleared his throat. "I know you're here with high expectations, and you should be. The United States Government has put a grand plan into place, and I'm proud to be a part of it. This day will go down in the history books." He studied a sheet of paper Laurel guessed was his written speech.

She glanced at the man who'd been angrily watching the proceedings. He had his arms folded over his chest and glared at the speaker. "Daddy, do you know who he is?" she asked, nodding at him.

Will followed her gaze. "Ray Townsend. Tom Jenkins told me he's the leader of a group of homesteaders who want us to leave. Those are settlers with him."

"What is he going to do? Can they make us leave?"

"No." He gently took hold of Laurel's forearms and turned her to look at him. Smoothing back a strand of her hair, he said, "There's something more important going on here than those men. Don't let them spoil the moment."

Laurel nodded and returned to watching the speaker, hoping her father was right.

"You all know there's a lot of hard work ahead of you," the spokesman said. "There's no other way when it comes to farming. But I've been told you have what it takes, and I believe if you and the government work together, we'll make this one great farming community!" His voice boomed. People clapped and cheered.

"Now, then," he continued. "I won't make you wait any longer. I have 204 slips of paper in this box." He held up a cardboard shoebox. "Let's begin."

The first man in line needed no prompting. He ran up the steps leading to the platform, took long strides across the wooden stage, reached into the box, and pulled out a piece of white paper. He peered at it, then held up the slip and shouted, "Number 168!" He jumped off the platform and ran to the map. The next man drew his number and hurried away, then the next and the next. Each man headed out to inspect his land.

Laurel chewed her nails. Her stomach churned. Any minute they'd know which lot belonged to them. She prayed for God's favor. When the man in front of Will went up, Laurel clutched her father's hand.

Then it was Will's turn. He gave the back of Laurel's fingers a quick kiss and hurried up the steps. Reaching into the box, he took out a slip of paper, looked at it, then smiled and jumped down from the platform. "Number ninety-one," he told Luke and Laurel without stopping, but striding toward the map. "Ninety-one, ninety-one," he repeated, searching the map. "Here it is." He poked his finger at a lot with the number ninety-one printed in black.

"How do we know which one it is?" Luke asked.

"Hold your horses." Will studied the map. "Looks like it's over where we were last night." He looked around. "We need a ride out there." He spotted Tom Jenkins who was sitting in his wagon and watching the activity.

Robert ran up to Will. "What number did you get?"

"Ninety-one. You?"

"Ninety." Robert grinned broadly. "We're neighbors!"

Tom jumped down from the wagon and joined them. "So, what pieces did you draw?"

"Ninety and ninety-one," Will said. "Looks like they're out by your place."

Tom scanned the map. "I'll be hanged! Those are the pieces you looked at yesterday!" Grinning, he said, "Welcome, neighbors." He shook Will and Robert's hands. "I'll take you out." He led the way to his wagon.

Will, Robert, Laurel, and Luke piled in. Luke took the seat beside Tom. Laurel stood just behind them, hanging onto the back of the seat. The sun felt warm and energizing. In spite of her resistance to the move, she felt a flush of excitement. They owned a piece of land!

When they arrived at the parcels, they realized that Robert had drawn the piece along the creek and the Haspers had the one next to it. Laurel was only slightly disappointed. She'd liked the idea of having land bordered by a stream.

Laurel and Luke walked beside their father. There was plenty of open ground to begin farming right away, but there were also several acres of forest. They'd been promised that if they cut and skidded the trees, the government would pay them sixty dollars per cleared acre. The money would be needed.

Will pointed at a grove of birch. "I think we ought to put the house there, by those trees. They'll give us shade in the summer and will be a windbreak during the winter." He surveyed the acreage. "We can put in root vegetables over there." He pointed to a portion of land not far from where the house would sit. "And we'll plant oats there," he said, nodding toward the north end.

Striding across the adjoining piece of property, Robert joined them. "Nice acreage—all of it." He let his eyes roam over the land. "But I drew the piece you wanted."

Will patted Robert's back. "I'm glad you got it. I couldn't have a better neighbor."

Robert looked at Laurel. "I know you wanted to live by a creek."

"I did, but this piece will be just fine."

He reached into his pocket and pulled out the slip of paper with number ninety written on it. Holding it out to Will, he said, "Me and my family will be just fine on parcel ninety-one."

"No, son. That's the piece you drew. It's where you belong."

"I want to make the trade. I want you to have it."

Will stared at the paper, then looked at Robert. "You sure? With the creek bordering it, it's more valuable."

"Makes no difference to me."

Will shook his head. "I can't believe you're doing this." He pulled out his paper with number ninety-one written on it. "All right then." They exchanged slips. "You're quite a man." Will's voice broke. "Anything you need, you let me know. And you can have all the water you want from that creek." He shook Robert's hand. "Consider yourself family."

Robert nodded. "Thank you, sir. I count that a privilege." His eyes settled on Laurel.

She felt a wave of gratitude and admiration for Robert. He was a fine man.

"Well, we need to get our names and pieces of property registered," Robert said. "We can always come back later and make plans."

Will threw an arm over Robert's shoulders and headed toward the road. "We've got our places." He glanced back at Laurel. "Our new home."

Laurel's eyes took in the open fields, heavy forests, and imposing mountains. She couldn't deny it was extraordinary, and she did feel a sense of hope. Still, it didn't feel like home, and she doubted it ever would.

Chapter Fourteen

HER FATHER ON ONE SIDE AND LUKE ON THE OTHER, LAUREL WALKED DOWN the bustling tent-lined street. A man chopped wood while his wife hung laundry on a makeshift line. They passed a young man hauling water. Another pushed a wheelbarrow filled with coal.

The mud was beginning to dry, and wooden walkways had been laid down, making foot travel easier. Swatting at mosquitoes, Laurel chided herself for forgetting her netted hat. Her mother, Brian, Justin, and Susie were supposed to arrive by train later that day, and she felt her anticipation mounting. "How much longer until the train gets here?"

"We've got a few hours yet," Will said. "It's supposed to roll in late this afternoon, around four. Your mother will like it here." With a wry smile, he looked all around at the mud and temporary housing. "Well, not exactly here, but our new place."

"I'm hungry," Luke said. "What are we s'posed to do for lunch? Is the camp gonna feed us?"

"Nope. Not today. But we can pick up supplies at the store. Until we get our first crop in and sold, we're supposed to charge at the market. The government's given us five years to start paying back the debt on the land, house, and our other expenses. I don't intend on spending one dime more than we have to."

"We can do some hunting to keep meat on the table," Luke said enthusiastically.

"I meant to talk to you about that." Will cleared his throat. "It'll cost us fifty dollars apiece to hunt."

"What? Why?"

"They say we're nonresidents and have to buy a special hunting license."

Luke grimaced. "But we live here."

"They say we've got to be here a year or pay up."

"That's not fair."

"I know, but it's the law."

"Those government agents lied to us! They said we could hunt and fish all we wanted. Now what are we gonna do?"

Will raised an eyebrow. "We can fish, but the hunting will have to wait."

"We don't have the fifty dollars?" Luke asked.

"Nope."

"What if I earn it? Would you let me hunt?"

"Sure."

"All right then. I'll find a job."

"Some of the land can be tilled and planted right away," Will said. "Your mother is one of the best gardeners I know. The vegetables will help."

"We don't have to wait for the house to be finished before we put in a garden?" Laurel asked.

"Nope. As soon as I can get my hands on a plow, we'll turn the soil and get seed in the ground—that is, if the equipment and seeds are here. Seems things aren't exactly what we expected." Will stopped in front of the administration office. "I'll know soon enough what's in and what's not."

"While you're doing that, I'll go to the store and get supplies," Laurel said. "We'll need something for supper. Where is the store?"

"Not far. Just down that way." Will nodded in the direction of the mercantile. "You'll find it easy enough. Just stay on this road."

Laurel was in no hurry and strolled down the rutted road, navigating around puddles and soft mud. The sun felt good. Not exactly hot, but warm.

It was easy to find the market. It had a sign posted over the door that read Palmer Post Office and General Store. It wasn't large, and was deeper than it was wide. A few people stood out front waiting their turn to enter. Most had wagons or wheelbarrows. Realizing she had no way of carrying supplies home, Laurel wondered if she ought to get her father and Luke. Not wanting to lose her place in line, she decided to get just necessities. She could return for more tomorrow.

"I can't believe the piece of property we got," Laurel heard a woman complain. "It's no more than a swamp. And there's no timber on it. We could have starved just as well back in Michigan."

The woman was small and thin with dark brown hair pulled back severely and twisted into a bun. Her face looked pinched and dried-up. A little girl in a faded dress stood off to one side, and a small boy with dirt on his face and hands clung to the woman's skirt. Tears had left pale streaks on his grimy cheeks.

"So, what're you gonna do?" a plump woman wearing a plaid dress asked.

"We're filin' a complaint, that's what. They'd better give us a better piece of land, or we're packin' up and headin' home."

The boy pulled at his mother's dress. "I'm hungry."

Without hesitation, the tiny woman cuffed the boy up the side of the head. "Stop whinin'."

Sticking a dirty thumb in his mouth, he leaned against his mother.

"I heard there's lots of unhappy folks," the small woman continued. "And I s'pect there'll be a whole bunch who'll pack it in."

"Can't say that I blame them. There's been a lot of lyin' goin' on. That bunch up in Washington D.C. don't know what they're talkin' about, and the government agents have been lyin' to us from the beginning."

The waspish-looking woman nodded. "I s'pose you got a bad piece too."

"No." Her eyes flickered away. "We got good land, but we sure do sympathize with you." She closed her coat over a heavy bosom. "Are you really thinkin' of leavin'?"

"You're darn tootin'. What do we have to stay for? If they don't give us a decent piece of ground, we'll be outta here faster than a hound can chase down a possum." She folded her arms over her chest and tipped up her chin a notch.

Laurel thought she might be pretty if her face weren't so puckered and angry. This woman hadn't given Palmer a chance yet.

"Do you think you can get another parcel?"

"Hmm," she sniffed. "They'd better give us one. I'll let someone spit in my eye before I pay one red cent for a worthless piece of ground. After all they put me and my family through, they ought to give me a new parcel plus let me keep the one I have."

The line moved, and the two women disappeared through the doorway.

"Hey there, Laurel. How you doin'?" a familiar voice called.

Laurel turned to find Robert striding toward her. He carried his tall frame with ease. "Hi, Robert. I'm well. How about you?"

"Can't complain. I'm itching to get a plow in the ground. It's good soil out there." His deep brown eyes radiated excitement. "One day I'll have a fine farm."

"You plan on staying then?"

"Of course. Where'd you get the idea I'd leave?"

"I heard some people are heading back to the states because things aren't what they expected. I guess I just . . . I don't know. Of course, you wouldn't leave. I know that," she ended lamely, embarrassed at her suggestion.

"The only way I'm ever leaving this valley is if God pries me out. I belong here." Sucking in a lungful of air, he scanned the meadows and mountains. "There's good hunting and fishing, and I've never seen better soil."

He looked at Laurel. "You're still set on leaving?"

"Yes. I want to go to school. I want more than this. I'll stay until next summer's harvest is in though."

"Sometimes more is less," Robert said, nudging a stone with the toe of his boot. He looked at Laurel, his eyes serious. "Sometimes in the battle to get what we want, we lose sight of what's really important."

Laurel felt uncomfortable under Robert's gaze. Trying to make light of his words, she said, "You sound like a philosopher. You sure you never went to college?"

He chuckled. "I swear. I barely made it through high school. Never liked school much. I like working outdoors where you can smell the earth and plants. And it's a wonder the way things grow. I even like the feel of sweat rolling down my back."

Laurel knew the mindset. Her father had it. "I understand; I just don't feel the same way."

The women who'd been complaining earlier walked out with boxes of food in their arms. Their children followed, carrying smaller packages. The line moved forward, and Laurel stepped up to the door.

"Are you next?" a woman asked.

Laurel peered into the nearly dark store. A young woman about her age smiled from behind a counter. She was pretty with blonde, wavy, shoulder-length hair and sky-blue eyes. She reminded Laurel of a forget-me-not.

"Can I help you?" the girl asked, smiling at Laurel, then looking at Robert. She tossed her hair off one shoulder.

Laurel stepped up to the counter. "We need supplies."

The girl turned a ledger around so it faced Laurel. "Sign your name and your husband's and any children's names." She held out a pencil.

"We're not married," Laurel said, taking the pencil. She could feel heat rush to her cheeks. "I'm Laurel Hasper, and this is Robert Lundeen. We're just friends."

The clerk smiled. "I'm sorry. I just assumed." She cast a flirtatious glance at Robert. "I'm Celeste Townsend. It's good to meet you both. I hope you'll like living here." She looked at Laurel. "Are you here with your family?"

"Yes," Laurel said, wondering about Celeste's last name. Wasn't it the same as that awful man at the drawing?

"Well, you'll have to sign for you and your family."

Laurel wrote the names of everyone in her family, then handed the pencil back to Celeste. "Did you say your last name is Townsend?"

"Yes."

"I think I saw your father at the drawing yesterday."

"He was there." Celeste wrote in the ledger, then turned the page so quickly she tore it. "I hope he behaved himself." She offered a smile.

"As far as I know," Laurel said, confused by Celeste's intonation.

"He's mad as a bull locked in a barn. He thinks this valley belongs to the homesteaders and no one else."

Laurel stared at her, uncertain what to say.

"I'm glad the colonists are here. The valley could use more young people." She pushed the ledger toward Robert. "And there certainly aren't any local boys I'd want to marry." She let the sentence hang like an invitation.

Laurel suppressed a smile.

Looking at Robert, Celeste asked, "Are you the head of a family?"

"Yes."

The light dimmed in her eyes.

"My father died before he could make the trip, so I'm taking care of my mother and two sisters."

Celeste's smile returned. "You'll need to sign the list."

"Sure." He leaned over the counter and began writing.

Turning her attention to Laurel, Celeste said, "You have a big family. Are you the oldest?"

"Yes. Nineteen."

Celeste lifted two boxes from a stack and set them on the counter. Walking to a row of shelves along a back wall lined with canned goods, she grabbed several cans. She set them in the smaller of the two boxes. "I was told to start you off with basic goods, then when you need more, you can come back in." She hefted a bag of flour off the floor and set it on the counter.

"I didn't bring anything to haul this home," Laurel said.

Celeste set a bag of sugar in the bigger box. "I can help you. I'll be off work in a few minutes."

"I wouldn't want to put you out."

"It's no bother. I haven't got anything else to do."

"All right then."

"I suppose you have to look after your younger brothers and sister," Celeste said.

"Sometimes, but I don't mind."

"I wish I had brothers and sisters. My mom died trying to have my baby brother. I was fourteen. Since then, it's just been me and my dad."

"I'm sorry," Laurel said.

"It's all right, I guess. Dad and I are buddies." Celeste reached into a candy jar and took out five pieces of peppermint. She wrapped them in wax paper and placed them beside the sugar. "These are for your brothers and sister."

"Thanks."

While Celeste filled Robert's order, Laurel wandered through the store, which stocked a little bit of everything—sewing supplies, kitchen utensils and dishes, fishing gear, rifles and shells, and a myriad of other items. Celeste seemed to be taking a long time with Robert. Clearly she was interested in him. He seemed oblivious.

When Robert headed for the door, he had only one large box in his arms. He stopped and smiled at Laurel. "I'll probably see you later."

"Probably," Laurel said.

He pushed against the door and stepped outside.

Celeste waited on two more customers, then an older woman walked in. She nodded and smiled at Laurel. Tying on an apron, she took her place behind the counter.

Celeste joined Laurel. "I'm free. You ready?"

"Uh-huh."

"There's a wagon out back. I'll get it, and we can load your groceries." She disappeared through a door in the back of the building and reappeared a few moments later pulling a rusted wagon.

After loading the food, the two young women headed out the door with Celeste hauling the supplies. Laurel walked beside her. "Thanks for helping. I guess I'm just empty-headed these days. I didn't even think about how I was going to get this stuff home."

"I could use a walk after working inside all day." She glanced at Laurel. "And I'd like to get to know you."

"You're very direct," Laurel said.

"I am, but I figure you ought to say what you mean and mean what you say. Anyway, I'm glad you came into the store. There aren't very many people my age around this place, well, that is, before you colonists got here." The wagon bounced over a rut, and Celeste glanced back to make sure none of the groceries had spilled out. "Course, as you noticed, my father feels differently."

"He did look angry."

"He doesn't hide his feelings. He and I are alike that way." Celeste was quiet a moment, then asked, "So, you and Robert aren't a couple?"

"No. He's just a friend I met on the train. His property borders ours."

"He's awfully cute."

"He is. Do you live on a farm?" Laurel asked, changing the subject.

"No. My father's more of the mountain-man type. He hunts, fishes, and traps mostly. He's a hunting guide, so he knows his way around these mountains."

"Isn't it dangerous work?"

"Yeah. But he's been doing it so long I don't worry about him. He's good." Celeste stepped around a puddle. "We've got a small garden and some chickens and a cow. That's about it."

"Why is your father so angry about the colonists?"

"He and my mom homesteaded our place long before I was born. They built our cabin, put in a garden, and made their way without any help. He figures the colonists are taking a handout from the government and will be a bad influence on the community." She jumped over a puddle. "Don't take it personal."

Laurel stepped over a sizable rock. How could she not take it personally?

"He and some of the others think it's unfair that the government's helping you. Most of the families here are real poor. They could use some help too."

"Hard times are everywhere. Where we came from there's a drought, and farms are literally blowing away. Our farm is dead. When the government said they'd move us, we didn't have a choice. Coming here was the only way we could survive."

As she explained, Laurel's hurt grew. She stopped and looked directly at Celeste. "We haven't done anything wrong. We did what we had to."

"I believe you." Celeste gazed at the mountains. "But you need to know that even though this valley looks beautiful, it's not an easy place to live. It takes courage and sacrifice, and a person's got to stick with it."

"We know that. And we know how to stick with it." Laurel could feel herself growing angry.

"I tried to tell my father that, but he and some of the other homesteaders are so sure you're—" Celeste stopped mid-sentence.

"They're sure of what?" Laurel asked. "What are they saying?"

Celeste glanced at the ground. "It doesn't matter."

"Yes it does." Laurel stared at Celeste.

The pretty blonde pursed her lips, then met Laurel's gaze. "They're saying you're welfare moochers, too lazy or too weak to homestead on your own."

The injustice felt like a slap. "People are saying that?"

"Yes."

Anger rising, Laurel stared at the ground directly in front of her. "Do they know we have to pay back everything—our house, the land, the food we eat, everything? It's not free."

"I don't think you've done anything wrong, Laurel. And I wish my dad and his friends felt differently, but it's going to take time." She smiled. "I'm glad you're here."

Chapter Fifteen

THE AROMA OF COFFEE AND BACON PENETRATED LAUREL'S SLEEP. SHE DIDN'T want to wake up; she'd been having a lovely dream. In the setting of a hazy sunset, a man for whom she cared deeply was sitting beside her. She couldn't see his face. Laurel tried to hold on to the delight, but it faded. Then it was gone.

She opened her eyes. White canvas walls stared back at her. Reality hit. She wasn't at home but in a tent in Alaska. Laurel scanned the room, which was crowded with boxes and furniture. *Where are we going to put everything?* she thought gloomily, wishing she could return to her dream. It had been much nicer.

Melancholy replaced contentment, and Laurel sat up. She tried to shake the gloomy thoughts. *This is only temporary,* she told herself.

A steady drumming sound resonated from all around. Jean stood at the stove, seemingly unaffected by the droning. She was humming. Jean glanced at Laurel. "Good morning."

"Morning." Laurel looked around the tent, trying to distinguish where the noise was coming from. Her mind still felt fogged. She could hear bacon frying, but that wasn't making the drumming. "What's that sound?" she finally asked.

"Sound?" Jean listened. "Oh, you mean the rain. It's been pouring all morning." She glanced at the tent ceiling. "It's loud on the canvas, but after so many months without rain, I think it's wonderful."

Just means more mud, Laurel thought dismally.

Her mother smiled. "You hungry?"

"Yes. Breakfast smells good." Throwing back her blankets, she dropped her legs over the side of the bed. "Where is everyone?"

"They went down to the toilet and bathhouse."

"I can't believe I slept through my brothers' racket." Laurel slipped her dress on and pushed her feet into shoes. "What are we going to do today?"

"First thing, your father and I are going to the architect's office and pick out our house. Then you and I can get this place in order. Your father and Luke are going out to the property to begin clearing." She speared a slice of bacon, turned it, and set it back in sizzling fat. "Your dad's anxious to get his hands into that soil. He says the sooner we get started, the sooner we'll be able to move." She peeked out the tent window. "This is a beautiful valley. I'll be glad to get out onto our own place with a proper view."

"It's a valley of mud and mosquitoes," Laurel said, her tone surly.

Jean looked at her daughter. "You're not usually such a grumbler, Laurel. It's not attractive." She turned back to her cooking. "I know you didn't want to move, but there's nothing to be done now. Growling about it won't make things better."

"I know. I'm sorry." Laurel pushed back wild hair. "I don't know why I'm so out of sorts."

"You've forgotten to be grateful." Jean gave Laurel a challenging smile. "There are mosquitoes and mud, but they won't go away because we complain. We have to take the bad with the good."

Using a fork, Jean lifted strips of crisp bacon out of the pan and set them on a plate, then cracked eggs into the hot grease. Sighing, she said, "I could use a rest. It's been a long trip."

Laurel studied her mother. Although she wore a smile, shadows smudged the skin under her eyes, and she looked thin. The move had been hard on her. A flush of guilt spread through Laurel. "Maybe you should rest today. I'll set up the house. You can tell me where you want everything."

Jean walked to Laurel and hugged her. "That's sweet of you, but I'm fine. We'll do it together."

"All right," Laurel said, thinking over all the sacrifices she'd seen her mother make through the years. She couldn't remember a day when Jean Hasper hadn't been there to care for her family. It seemed a thankless job, and Laurel wasn't sure she wanted the same kind of life.

～

That afternoon, Will, Luke, Justin, and Brian set out for their land. They'd begin clearing. Laurel and Jean set about getting their temporary home in order. Jean laid a teary-eyed Susie in her crib, then turned and faced the chaotic room. Hands on hips, her eyes roamed over their belongings. "I'm not sure where to start."

"I'm sorry I didn't get more done. Susie was so fussy when you and dad were meeting with the architect."

"I think she's teething." Jean picked up a box. "Why don't we stack the boxes we don't plan on emptying along the wall there. That'll give us a little more room."

The two went to work, and a couple hours later Laurel sat in her grandmother's rocker with Susie in her lap. She studied the room. It was crowded but orderly.

Jean sat at the table. "That's better." She took a deep breath. "We'll do just fine."

A knock sounded at the door, and a woman called, "Hellooo. Anyone home?"

Jean walked to the door and opened it. Norma Prosser stood on the step. A stocky, cheerful woman, she seemed meant for farm life. "I hope I'm not bothering you."

"No, of course not. Please come in."

Norma stepped inside and glanced about the room. "This is real nice. It's a sight better than my mess. I think I brought too much from home." She folded her arms over her chest. "Drew is always saying I have pack rat in my blood." She chuckled. "I was just thinking that since our men are all out on our places working it might be a good time for the ladies to get acquainted. I was hoping we could gather at my place for a cup of tea and a visit?"

"I'll stay with Susie, Mama," Laurel said.

"Oh, don't worry about the baby. Bring her along. I'd guess most of us have children, and we'd be in a mess if we couldn't take them with us when we left home."

"Well, I'd like to meet my new neighbors," Jean said. "Laurel?"

Tired, Laurel would rather have stayed home, but she *was* curious.

Susie stood, flashing a nearly toothless smile at Mrs. Prosser. "I guess Susie's decided. I'll go."

"Wonderful," Norma said. "I'm just three tents down toward the main road. I'll see you in about fifteen minutes?"

"All right." Norma disappeared, and immediately Jean walked to the mirror above one of the dressers and unpinned her hair.

"What are you doing?" Laurel asked. "We're in the wilderness. I don't think anyone cares about your hair."

"That's no excuse to be uncivilized." Jean brushed out her shoulder-length, auburn hair, then pinned it up again.

Laurel watched. Her mother was still beautiful. Her hair shimmered, her face was nearly free of lines, and the hazel eyes that looked so much like her own still radiated with spirit. "Mama, why don't you leave it down? It's so pretty."

Jean looked at her daughter. "Why, thank you. I know that's the style nowadays, but I don't know that it's proper for a woman my age."

"You're not that old."

"I'll think about it. Why don't you clean up while I get Susie ready."

"Is that your way of telling me I'm a mess and I'd embarrass you?" Laurel teased.

"Well . . . you have been working hard. And we're about to meet some of our neighbors for the first time. First impressions matter."

"All right." Laurel handed the baby to her mother and crossed to the washbasin where she rinsed her face and combed out her long hair. Tucking in her blouse, she turned to her mother. "Is that better?"

"You look fine." Jean brushed out a wrinkle in Laurel's skirt.

When Laurel and Jean arrived at Norma's, a sheep dog tied along the side of the tent barked and lunged on its rope. Jean eyed him cautiously.

"Don't mind him," Norma said, opening the door. "He's harmless as a fly. Poor thing had to stay in the hold the entire trip. I think it'll probably take him a month to work out all his stored energy."

A dozen women had crowded into Norma Prosser's tent. Laurel had seen most of them during the trip, but the only ones she actually knew were Miram Dexter and her mother. As usual, Mrs. Dexter's expression was haughty and unfriendly. Laurel wondered why she bothered coming.

A woman who looked to be about Laurel's age sat straight across from Laurel. She was wearing slacks, and Laurel knew her attire would raise a stir. No one would say anything to her face, but later there would be gossip.

After serving tea and cookies, Norma stepped into the center of the room. "I'm so happy you've all come," she said warmly. "I know you're probably tired, what with getting your houses set up and after such a long trip, but I thought it would be good for us to get acquainted. How about if we introduce ourselves first. We can go around the room clockwise. I'll start. I'm Norma Prosser, and I'm real thankful to be here. I grew up on a farm in Minnesota, but in recent years Drew and I have been running a small general store. We're real happy to get back to farming."

The next woman nodded shyly. "I'm Jane McDougal. My husband and I have three children. We're from Michigan."

They moved around the room until each woman had introduced herself and told a little about her background. As they shared, the tension eased. The discomfort of meeting new people quickly faded, and the women began the process of building friendships.

All seemed well until Miram asked the woman wearing pants, "Delores, can you tell me where you got your slacks? I'd love to have a pair."

Before Delores could answer, Mrs. Dexter said, "You'll do no such thing. A proper young woman does not wear pants."

Laurel could barely suppress a gasp. She couldn't believe Mrs. Dexter could be so rude.

Norma stepped in. "I know it's been the accepted thing for women to wear dresses, but I think we can make allowances, bein' as we're living in the wilderness."

"Well, wilderness or not, my daughter will live up to a higher standard," Mrs. Dexter said.

Delores shifted uneasily in her chair. "I don't usually wear slacks." She combed back short, black curls with her fingers. "But with the mosquitoes and all the rain and dirty work, it just seemed to make sense." She looked at Miram and smiled. "And to answer your question, these belong to my husband. He doesn't mind at all that I borrowed them."

Laurel admired Delores. She'd certainly handled Mrs. Dexter well and seemed mostly unruffled at the disapproval. Wearing pants did make sense, and Laurel decided that as soon as she could get her hands on a pair, she'd adopt the more reasonable dress.

Mrs. Dexter held her cup in one hand and crossed one stubby leg over the other. "I'll be glad when we get moved into our houses. But I must say I was appalled at the lack of . . . facilities. We might be living in the wilderness, but I don't see any reason to be primitive."

Norma set her cup on the table. "Living here is going to take some getting used to, but I like it. And we need to be thankful for what we have. Where would we be without the help from our government? They've given us so much."

"Given?" Mrs. Dexter asked, her voice sharp. "They haven't *given* us anything. We have to pay for every last thing we get."

"Well, and we should," Jean said. "But we didn't have to pay for our passage or our stay in Seattle. And the houses are real reasonable, and since we don't have to start making payments for five years, we have plenty of time to get on our feet. I think the government has been very generous." She set her cup in its saucer. "And considering our circumstances, who else would have loaned us anything? The banks back home were foreclosing on folks. I'm grateful to the people who set up this colony."

"Just because we're poor doesn't mean we owe our government." Mrs. Dexter sniffed and took a sip of her tea.

"I don't care so much about the outhouses," Delores said, "but I'm afraid of meeting up with a bear or a wolf on my way to the toilet." She leaned forward, rested her elbows on her thighs, and said almost in a whisper, "Last night, in the middle of the night, I had to go so bad, but I was afraid to go outside alone."

The room broke out in laughter, relieving tension.

"And what about the winters here?" another woman asked. "We don't have electricity or lights. I was told it's dark most of the time, and it's cold. The snow piles up all the way to the roof."

"I grew up in Minnesota," Norma said. "We didn't have electricity, and we got along just fine. And it's plenty cold in Minnesota. Last year our vegetables froze in the ground in August." She sipped her tea. "I don't expect it can get much worse than that."

The women's griping reminded Laurel of how sour she'd been since arriving. She didn't like their grumbling and knew her own had made her look ugly. She vowed to change. She had a lot to be grateful for.

Norma refilled the women's cups with tea. "I must say I'm looking forward to my first summer and winter here. I expect there'll be adventures, joys, and sorrows. Those things come with any home." She smiled. "What's important is that we learn to lean on God and to share each other's burdens. Sharing will make the going easier."

As if she hadn't heard Norma, Mrs. Dexter said, "I ran into that Mr. Townsend yesterday at the store. He was downright rude. I was talking to that Celeste girl, and he cut in and said she wasn't to talk to me. What right does he have telling people who they can talk to?"

"Celeste is Mr. Townsend's daughter," Laurel said softly.

Mrs. Dexter sniffed. "Oh. Well, I told him he wasn't going to run this town and you know what he did? He sneered at me and said he'd do whatever he wanted."

Norma set the kettle on the stove. "We can't be worrying about Mr. Townsend. We need to be thinking about our new lives here in Alaska. We need to be thanking God for his many blessings."

There were murmurs of agreement, but Laurel remembered Ray Townsend's eyes. He wasn't going to stand by while they settled the valley. He would try to stop them.

Chapter Sixteen

The church building was simple and practical. Laurel followed her family inside. Sunlight spilled into the sanctuary through narrow windows along the outside walls, and hardwood floors glistened in the warm glow. A wide aisle in the middle of the room divided pews, and a raised platform reached from wall-to-wall across the front. A lectern stood in the middle of the stage, and a large wooden cross was suspended on the wall behind it.

A woman with a gray bun peeping out from beneath a small hat sat at a piano in front. She softly played "At the Cross." Adults sat straight-backed and still. Some were praying silently. Celeste Townsend sat beside her father. His shoulders almost filled a quarter of the pew. Laurel could only see his profile, but he looked cross. She wondered why he attended church. So far she hadn't heard anything positive about him, except from Celeste.

Celeste spotted her and waved. Her father turned and scowled at Laurel, then his hateful eyes roamed over her family.

Laurel stifled a shudder. She nodded and smiled, ignoring Mr. Townsend's disrespect. Celeste offered an apologetic smile.

Laurel realized that Robert was sitting beside her new friend. She wondered if Celeste had invited him or if Robert had made the choice. He caught her eye and winked. *He's certainly good looking,* Laurel thought. *Celeste could do worse.*

Adam Dunnavant walked into the sanctuary and sat across the aisle from her. Glancing her way, he nodded and removed his hat. Laurel smiled, thinking he looked stiff and awkward, his usual confident air absent.

As the notes of "Onward Christian Soldiers" resonated throughout the room, a choir filed onto the stage. A plump woman stood in front of the group, facing the congregation. "Please stand and turn to page 221 in your hymnals."

Adam knew the song. He'd heard it often enough. Every morning the boys at the orphanage had met in the main hall for prayer, worship, and a sermon. "Onward Christian Soldiers" had been one of the director's favorites.

At one time he'd embraced Christianity and even liked morning devotions, but Eli Hirsch had stripped away the pleasures in Adam's life. He could still feel the boyhood terror and sorrow.

Eli Hirsch oversaw the boys, their chores, studies, free time, and morning services. He wasn't a big man, but he was brutal. He had a mustache that looked like a rubber band stretched across his upper lip. When he smiled, which was infrequently, his lips would draw tightly over his straight, crowded teeth. The overseer's eyes were blue and cold, always detached. Under his gaze Adam had felt as important as an insect.

His stomach turned queasy at the memory. Eli had a love for the strap and used it often. He often misquoted the Scriptures, using Christianity to justify his brutality. Not only did he employ beatings, but he would starve or lock up boys for the smallest infraction. Adam had decided that either God didn't exist or didn't care about little boys without parents. Either way, it made no difference because Adam had washed his hands of the Christian faith.

The director, Mr. Owens, had turned a deaf ear to the outcries of abuse. He seemed to fear Eli Hirsch as much, or more, than the boys.

Adam's eyes roamed over the choir. Some voiced the words with vacant eyes and deadpan expressions; but others sang with reverence, eyes closed and faces uplifted. He had a vague memory of what reverence felt like. When he first heard the Bible stories about Christ, he thought he knew what it meant to be loved and to love—for a moment anyway.

Glancing at Laurel and her family, Adam's cynical outlook wavered. They were real. Their faith seemed genuine. The Haspers were good people, and although they held no special fondness for him, he knew that if he needed anything they'd be there to help. They cared about others. More than once he'd seen Will, Jean, or even Laurel come alongside someone to encourage and help.

They made no apologies for their faith and lived what they believed. Adam considered Will's religious convictions. Clearly he was intelligent, and yet he embraced a belief in an unseen God. The concept made little sense to Adam, but he still respected the man.

And Laurel, well, he'd never met anyone like her. She was beautiful and spirited like many women he'd known, but she was different in other ways. She didn't pretend to be anyone other than who she was—strong but vulnerable, complex and uncomplicated, angry yet repentant, stern but forgiving. She was real. And, like her father, she also professed a trust in God. Although Adam had always shied away from religious types, he found himself thinking about Laurel and wanting to be with her. However, he knew better. She'd only distract him from his work and his dreams.

Laurel glanced his way and smiled. Against his will, he felt himself soften and returned a smile. He looked down at his hymnal. A moment later he glanced back. The Haspers possessed something he'd never had. He was drawn to them. He wanted what they had. He wanted them to like him and hated himself for caring.

A tall, good-looking man with sandy brown hair stepped onto the platform. He crossed to the lectern, set a Bible on the stand and opened it. Resting his forearms on the podium, he scanned the congregation. "Good morning. It's good to see so many of you here."

The preacher straightened. "I especially want to welcome the colonists. We're happy you've joined our community. It is my hope and prayer that your transition to this valley will not be too difficult."

Adam had to admit the man looked and sounded like a decent person, but then, didn't all ministers?

He stepped around to the front of the podium. "It won't be easy. Change rarely is. We," he extended his arms, "this family, want to help. If you have any questions or needs, please tell us."

Ray Townsend coughed and leaned forward. Several eyes turned to him. He settled his back against the pew, then shifted forward again. Adam couldn't contain a wry grin. He understood Ray Townsend. He'd known others like him, men who needed to control, who resented newcomers because they threatened their domination. Someone like him could be trouble, real trouble.

"We pray you will come to love this valley as much as we do," the minister continued. He returned to his place behind the podium and rested his hand on the Bible. "Please turn to Philippians 3."

Adam folded his arms over his chest. He knew what was coming. The minister would read Jesus' *sacred* words, then demand that the flock obey them. He'd heard it before. His thoughts wandered to the colonists and the story about them that he still had to finish.

"Don't wait another minute," the preacher nearly yelled, pulling Adam from his reverie. Let Christ change your life." The minister nodded to three men standing in the back, and they came forward. Two of them carried baskets of bread. "This morning, as we take communion, let us remember Christ's love, a love that is so powerful he allowed himself to be nailed to a cross and willingly gave up his life for us."

The woman returned to the piano, and prayer books were opened. *That's it,* Adam thought. *No more.* While everyone's heads were bowed he slipped out of his seat and left.

When he was out of sight of the building, he stopped and leaned against a birch. Taking a pack of cigarettes out of his shirt pocket, he lit one and inhaled deeply, then slowly exhaled. He took another drag, then tapped the cigarette, spilling ashes at his feet. One day, when he was working as a journalist in Paris or Rome, he'd have himself to thank for his success, no one else. *Life is what you make of it. It's got nothing to do with an invisible God who supposedly loves you.*

~

When Laurel stepped out of church and onto the porch, she looked for Adam, but he was gone. She wished he'd stayed.

Robert, with Celeste on his arm, joined her. "Hello."

"Hi, Laurel," Celeste said with a friendly smile. "How are you adjusting?"

"I'm getting used to it."

"Maybe we can go to a movie some time."

"Sounds like fun."

Celeste looked at Robert. "Would you like to go?"

"Sure."

Patricia Lundeen walked out of the church. "Oh, Robert, there you are. We need to get home. We have a lot to do this afternoon." Joanna and Veronica skipped down the steps and headed toward the tent compound. Patricia smiled at Laurel. "It's good to see you, dear. How've you been?"

"Very well."

"And your family?"

"They're fine. Daddy and Luke are clearing the land, but Daddy's beginning to worry that the house won't be finished before winter."

"Oh, I know. It's a worry for all of us." She brushed a stray hair off her face and gazed at the nearby mountains. Unexpectedly, her eyes shimmered with tears. "I just wish my Charlie had lived to see it."

Robert placed an arm around his mother's shoulders. "He has."

Patricia patted her son's hand and offered him a brave smile.

"We need to get home," Robert said. Looking at Laurel, he added, "I'll see you later." He offered Celeste a smile, then escorted his mother down the steps.

Celeste watched him go. "Too bad."

"Too bad, what?"

"Too bad he's crazy about you."

"He is not. We're just friends."

Celeste walked down the steps, and Laurel followed. "There aren't enough good men in this valley, and it's just my luck that when one comes along he's interested in someone else." She took Laurel's arm. "That's all right." She smiled brightly. "I won't hold it against you. I like you too much."

Laurel stopped. "Why do you think he's interested in me?"

"It's plain as the nose on your face." She shrugged. "What is—is."

"What's as plain as the nose on my face?"

"Well, for one thing, he's always looking at you. And his tone changes when he talks to you—more considerate, you know."

"I'm not interested in Robert. If you like him—"

"Oh, no. I'm not falling into that trap. This is how it works. You reject him, he needs a friend and I'm it; then when he gets over you, he doesn't need me anymore."

"You're much prettier than me. You must have lots of boyfriends."

"There've been some, just not any I'm interested in." Celeste picked a buttercup. "I might have to leave the valley to find someone."

"Would you really?"

Celeste frowned. "No, I couldn't do that. I'm the only one my father has. I couldn't leave him." They strolled toward the road. "Besides, I like it here. I don't guess there's any place like it in the world." Celeste plucked the petals off the buttercup while reciting, "He loves me. He loves me not. He loves me. He loves me not." She continued until the last petal. "He loves me not." She tossed the stem aside. "See, I told you."

"It's just a flower, not a prophecy."

"Time we got home," Ray Townsend said, striding up to his daughter and casting a hateful glance at Laurel before leading Celeste away.

Will sat in the rocker, reading the latest edition of the Anchorage newspaper. All of a sudden he slapped it onto his lap. "I can't believe what they're saying."

Laurel stopped peeling a potato and said, "Who's saying what?"

"Nothing. Never mind. It's nothing."

"Daddy."

"Won't do any good to read it. It'll only get everyone all hepped up."

"Daddy," Laurel said again.

"All right. It says that some of the colonists are unhappy and grumbling about conditions. Several want to return to the states. They have quotes I can't believe. If they're true, I'm ashamed." He scanned the story. "Some are saying conditions are bad, that we're mistreated because we live in tents. One man's complaining because we don't have radios or free movies for the kids." His voice grew louder. "Another fella's griping because his house is the wrong color."

He looked at Jean. "I haven't heard any of that kind of talk. There's some griping about the mud and mosquitoes and the government's foul-ups, but this is foolishness."

"What else does it say?" Jean asked, settling Susie in her crib.

"Some congressmen want to send all of us back to the states. They say the plan was a bad idea."

"Well, I'm not going back," Jean said.

Will shook his head. "This kind of talk is just going to get people stirred up. We don't need more trouble; we're already at odds with the homesteaders." He folded the newspaper and pushed himself out of the rocker. Walking to a screened window, he gazed out. "We need to have a meeting between the homesteaders and colonists."

Luke stepped in from outside. "I've got some friends I want you to meet." He held the door open, and an Indian boy about Luke's age and a girl a little younger walked in. The boy was stocky and handsome with a broad, friendly face, and the girl was tiny with long black hair and large brown eyes. "This is Alex and Mattie Larson. They live on the river."

Brian and Justin's eyes were riveted on the newcomers.

"It's good to meet you," Will said.

"This is my dad, and that's my mom." Luke nodded at his parents. "And that's my sister, Laurel."

Laurel smiled. "Hi."

Alex returned a smile, exposing a row of perfect teeth. Mattie nodded shyly.

Luke placed a hand on Brian's head. "This is Brian and that's Justin."

"Happy to meet you," Alex told the boys.

"Do you live near here?" Jean asked, wiping her hands on her apron.

"Not far, about a mile."

"Are you Indians?" Brian asked.

"Brian, shush," Jean scolded.

Alex smiled. "It's all right." He looked at Brian. "Yes. Our mother is native, but our father was Scottish."

"Wow, I never met an Indian before." Brian's eyes were wide.

Mattie broke into a smile. "We're not that different from you. Although some think we are."

"Alex is going to teach me how to hunt and fish the native way," Luke said. "Then I can teach you, Dad."

"Would you like to stay for supper?" Jean asked. "We have plenty."

"Thank you, but we can't. Our mother is waiting for us," Alex said. "We welcome you to the valley. Some people don't like that you're here, but not everyone feels that way."

Mattie nodded.

"So, do you expect we're in for trouble?" Will asked.

Alex shrugged. "Maybe yes. Maybe no."

"It's not easy to be different," Mattie said solemnly. "Some of the people in this valley are good and kind, but some are not."

Chapter Seventeen

JEAN REFILLED WILL'S CUP WITH COFFEE, THEN SAT ACROSS THE TABLE FROM him, glancing at Justin and Brian. "Those two boys were completely tuckered out. I think Brian was asleep before his head hit the pillow."

Will sipped his coffee. "There's always a new adventure waiting for them. We need to keep a closer watch. Some of the kids have been wandering off into the woods."

"All they can think about is fun. I worry about bears." Jean stirred sugar into her coffee. "And the river." She glanced out the tent window, then looked at the clock. "I still can't get used to the long days. It's nearly ten o'clock and still light. From the look of things, you'd think it was the middle of the day."

"That's June in Alaska," Will grinned. "From what I hear, we better enjoy it because once winter sets in, we won't see much daylight. The days are short."

"I don't think I'm going to like that much." She leaned her elbows on the table. "Do you know how much longer it'll be before we can start work on the house?"

"Soon, I hope. Some places are going up, but there's a shortage of lumber, hammers, nails—the list goes on and on." He gave her a lopsided grin. "Seems the government's having trouble remembering in what order a house is built. The window frames are here, and the kitchen sinks arrived—there's a whole pile of them down by the depot. But they'll stay there until we get some of the other materials we need."

He stared at the dark brew in his cup. "They're still not letting us work on our houses. They expect us to stand by and watch transients build them. It makes no sense. And from what I've been hearing, a lot of those men don't know the first thing about building. Things would go faster if we could help."

"Why won't they let you men build your own homes?"

"Something about government regulations." He shook his head. "I'm grateful for the new start they're giving us, but I think whoever's making up the rules has rocks in his head."

Quiet settled over the couple, then Jean said, "I visited Norma Prosser today."

"How are they faring?"

"Good. But she said the Johnsons are leaving."

Will sat back in his chair and exhaled heavily. "I heard they were thinking about it. I was hoping they'd change their minds."

"From what Norma said, Ruth's still got a bad cough. She can't get her breath. It's worse since the weather warmed up and with all the rain. Things never dry out. It can't be good for her. People are saying she has TB."

"That's nothin' but gossip," Will said with disgust. "I talked to Tim a few days ago. She doesn't have TB. It's just a cough is all. I wish people would spend more time working and taking care of their own families and less time trying to get an earful."

"People are scared, Will. They're talking about a possible quarantine. There's a lot of sickness. Some children are down with measles. I guess one of the Ericson boys is real sick. And there's no doctor." She glanced at her sleeping youngsters. "I pray we all stay healthy."

"We'll have a doctor soon." Will emptied his cup and swirled the small pool of brown in the bottom. "Maybe we should talk to the Johnsons. I hate to see them go. There's been a steady trail of families leaving. At this rate, there won't be more than a handful left by winter." He set his cup on the table. "Let's go over and talk to them."

"Right now?"

"Sure. Why not?"

"It's late."

"Folks don't get to bed so early these days, what with daylight hanging on so long. Tim told me they've been up close to midnight every night. Laurel and Luke can keep an eye on the kids." He stood. "Besides, I could use a walk."

"All right." Jean grabbed a sweater off the back of her chair and pulled it on.

Will walked to the door and held it for her, then took her hand. "Tim thinks we ought to have a town meeting with the government supervisors."

"Would that help?"

"Maybe."

~

Will surveyed the crowded hall. The benches were filled, and people lined the walls. He wasn't surprised; he'd expected a big turnout. There were a lot of angry, frustrated citizens in the valley. Some residents were quietly tense, some griped among themselves, others argued. Adam Dunnavant stood just inside the door, camera around his neck and a writing tablet in his hand. He looked eager, keyed up. Ray Townsend and a few of his friends stood against the back wall. They talked among themselves, occasionally throwing disdainful looks at someone in the room. More than once Will noticed that Ray was casting hateful glances at Robert and wondered why. When he and Ray made eye contact, Will could feel the man's venom. *How did I let Tim talk me into this,* he thought. He felt a soft hand take his and looked down at Jean who sat beside Laurel.

Her eyes were heartening. "Trust the Lord. He'll sort this all out."

Will squeezed her hand, then walked to the front of the room. "Could I have your attention, please?" No one heard. He raised his voice. "Could I have your attention, please?" He waited, but only a few stopped talking and looked at him. Finally he shouted, "Sit down. Please. We have a lot to talk about." The room quieted.

"Thank you. I'm glad to see you all here tonight. I know a lot of you have questions and complaints for the camp supervisor, Mr. Sweet." Will nodded at a pudgy man wearing an overly tight suit sitting at a table in the front. He looked uneasy. Will couldn't blame him. "Mr. Sweet will do his best to answer your questions. It will go more smoothly if only one person speaks at a time." He smiled, hoping to set a pleasant tone. "I understand emotions are running high, but fighting among ourselves won't solve anything. So, please remember to respect your neighbor."

Ray sneered and leaned against the wall, folding his arms over his chest. Will acted as if he hadn't noticed.

Alex Pettersson stood. "When are our houses going to be finished? And why can't we work on them?"

The administrator stood, removed his glasses, and peered at the stout, longhaired troublemaker. "I'm sorry about the holdup, but several houses are well on their way to being finished. The government decided it would be better if we hired men to build your houses. They know construction."

"That's a laugh," someone shouted.

Mr. Sweet glanced in the direction of the voice, then unable to determine who had spoken, looked at the crowd. "You folks are farmers and can't be expected to know how to build houses."

A large man wearing blue overalls stood, and in a booming voice, asked, "Who do you think we are—know-nothings?"

"We know a lot more than you think we do," another man called.

"Yeah, you're treating us like children," Ed Ketchum added.

Drew Prosser stood. He had his hands in his overall pockets and appeared calm. Keeping his voice low and steady, he said, "Mr. Sweet, the resentment you hear comes from frustration. These men know how to take care of their families, but they're feeling hog-tied." Murmurs of agreement moved through the crowd. "A lot of us know carpentry. We've been farming all our lives, which means we have to know how to do most everything on our places, including building. And just like the rest of these men, I want to help build my home."

Mr. Sweet wiped his glasses with a handkerchief and resettled them on his nose. "I'm sorry, Drew, but it's been decided. The answer is no."

His face red and taut, Tim Johnson stood and stepped into the aisle separating the rows of benches. "See, Will, like I told you—domination. They loan us thirty-two hundred dollars and feel they've got the right to run everything. We've lost control over our own lives. It's dangerous. We might as well be living in a Communist country." He glared at Mr. Sweet.

Beads of sweat had popped out on the administrator's forehead. He mopped them with a handkerchief. "We're not power hungry. We're not Communists. We have a plan if you'll just let us implement it. Try to be patient. I agree it's not a good idea to keep you from building your houses, but I don't make the decisions."

Knowing it was time to take a stand, Will faced Mr. Sweet. "Sir, I don't mean any disrespect, but this colony is running out of time. We only have two or three months before winter sets in. We're going to work on our houses whether you or anybody else says we can. We have a right, and we're starting tomorrow. I'll be out at my place first thing in the morning."

Cheers and words of agreement echoed around the room. It was clear the government wouldn't have its way in this.

Ray Townsend stepped away from the wall. "What I want to know is why these freeloaders got a house at all? Us homesteaders came up here and proved up our places on our own. We got no help from the government." His curls shook as he bobbed his head in anger. "Nothin' was handed to us. We're still scratching to make a living and you're giving away houses, food, animals, and farm equipment. Anything these people want, they get," he bellowed. "There are families in this valley who can barely feed themselves." He folded his arms over his chest and turned a condemning gaze on Mr. Sweet, then Will.

"Mr. Townsend, isn't it?" the administrator asked.

"That's right."

"We're not giving them anything. They're merely borrowing from the government. They have loans that will have to be paid back."

Alex Pettersson jumped to his feet. "Yeah, so if we've got to pay it back, why has the government put us on a budget? We can't work anywhere but on our farms, and we need more money."

Resentful murmuring snaked through the room.

Mr. Sweet glanced at Will as if looking to him for the answer.

Will turned to Alex. Just as he'd feared, people were getting riled. If something wasn't done, they'd soon be out of control. *Father, give me wisdom,* he prayed silently. "Alex, is anyone in your family going hungry?" he asked, making sure his voice remained steady and calm.

"Not exactly. But we can't get a lot of things we need."

"I'd like to answer your question," Mr. Sweet said. He looked at Alex. "Sir, the fact is that every penny you borrow you'll have to repay. We wanted to be certain that families don't find themselves in such deep debt they can't pay it back. We decided a budget would help. After much consideration, we came up with an amount we considered reasonable." He sipped water from a glass that sat on the table in front of him. "If you have a special need, you can always file a request for additional money."

Robert Lundeen was the next to stand. "There's something else we need to talk about. It may not seem important to some of you, but my sister had a run-in with a pack of dogs the other night. If I hadn't come along when I did, she might have been hurt or even killed. Some folks aren't keeping their dogs under control."

"I tell you what, if any dogs come grousing around my tent at night, I'm gonna shoot 'em," Alex said.

"Why not tie up the dogs?" a man in the back row asked.

"That sounds fair to me," Will said. "Is that all right with the rest of you?"

Several nodded agreement.

"All right then, from now on the dogs are to be tied up at night," Will said. "If not, they'll be confined and . . . if we have to . . . destroyed."

A man Will had never seen before stood. "I think it's high time we gave this town a new name. Some of us have been talking and we like the sound of—"

"No!" Ray Townsend hollered. Like a rumbling storm cloud, he strode to the front. He stopped only inches from Will, his gray eyes narrowed, and said, "The name stays." He turned and glared at the crowd. "We've made room for you interlopers, we've tried to be patient, but this is where it ends." Spittle dropped onto his heavy beard. "Palmer it is, and Palmer it will stay."

Will forced himself to remain composed and said calmly, "I see no reason to change the name." He looked at the room of colonists. "As newcomers we've no right." Some people nodded, while others folded their arms over their chests and glared at Ray Townsend.

Drew Prosser stood. "I have to agree with Will. There are people who've been living here for years. This is their town. We've no right to come in and start changin' things." He removed his broad-brimmed hat and looked over the crowd. "We need a man to speak for us. Someone we can trust. Someone who's level-headed." He turned to Will. "Would you be our spokesman—a go-between who'll speak to the government officials for us?"

"He's right," Robert Lundeen said. "We need someone. Will you do it?"

"Say yes," someone else shouted.

Will looked out over the crowd. He glanced at Ray, and if it were possible, the man looked angrier. Will hadn't wanted to get involved in the conflicts. All he'd wanted when he left Wisconsin was a new beginning. Still, he had to admit that a go-between was a good idea. "Is everyone all right with that?"

Heads nodded, and several said, "Yes."

"All right then," Will said, running his hand over a day's stubble. "I'll do what I can."

"Shouldn't we have a town mayor?" Miram Dexter asked.

"And what about a police department?" Alex Pettersson added.

"I think both of those are good ideas." Will looked at the camp supervisor.

"Good ideas, yes, but not good timing," Mr. Sweet said. "Until you're in your homes and your farms are up and running, the U.S. government will remain the overseer of this community."

"That's not a democracy," Tim Johnson said.

"The government has a big investment in this colony, and it isn't ready to let go just yet. When the time is right, you'll have local government."

"The government doesn't know what it's doing," Felix pressed. "We've all seen the piles of sinks for houses that don't exist, desks for a school we don't have, and timber that needs to be sawed. And there are not enough hammers or nails. Why should we trust you?"

Mr. Sweet grabbed his handkerchief again and wiped perspiration from his face. "I'll admit, there've been mix-ups. We're working on them. This is the first time anything like this has been tried."

Alex shoved his hands down into his pockets and glared at the administrator.

"What about a school?" Miram asked in her usual whiny voice. "We were promised a school."

"And you'll have one. But it will take time. I promise we'll have something for the children before winter sets in."

The meeting went on and on. Frustrations were vented, fears voiced. By ten o'clock, Will was ready to adjourn the meeting when Alex Pettersson stood. *Oh, no,* he thought. *What now?*

"We've been lied to from the beginning," Alex said. "The agents back home told us we'd be able to hunt. Now we find out we can't unless we pay for a special license."

"You're still hunting," someone snickered.

Alex ignored the comment. "They started working on my house, and again I find out I've been lied to. I was promised a concrete foundation, but they laid the timbers right on top of the mud."

"No one was promised concrete foundations," Mr. Sweet said. He looked pale and cross. "And if you were, it's the agent's fault—not ours."

Ray Townsend grabbed an empty chair and threw it. It nearly hit several people, then bounced across the floor, stopping against the wall. "I've heard enough. You're nothing but a bunch of government moochers. You've been handed everything you could possibly need, and all you can do is bellyache. Go home! All you! And if you don't, we'll force you out."

Will understood Ray's disgust. People were expecting too much and complaining too much. He was ashamed of their behavior.

He walked up to the big man. "I can see what you're saying, Mr. Townsend, but I was hoping our two groups could work together—overlook each other's weaknesses. We've got to live in the same community, and things would work out a whole lot better if we could get along. Maybe we can help each other." He held out his hand.

Ray looked at Will's hand. Without a word he turned and walked out.

Chapter Eighteen

RAIN DRUMMED AGAINST THE CANVAS CEILING. IT HADN'T LET UP FOR TWO days. There was talk of flooding. Only a few months before, Laurel and everyone she knew had been praying for rain, and now they were praying for it to stop.

Brian and Justin were sprawled on the floor, a checkerboard between them. Justin jumped two of Brian's checkers. "Gotcha now." He laughed.

Brian pouted. "You always win."

"No, I don't."

"Yes, you do, except when you *let* me win."

The tent door opened. Cool air and moisture swept into the room. Will strode in, closing the door behind him. Water dripped from his hat and coat, creating a puddle at his feet. "The river's still rising," he said, sloshing across the room and sitting at the table. "Can you get me some socks?" he asked, unlacing his boots.

Jean crossed to his bureau, opened a drawer, and took out two pairs of wool socks.

"It's not looking good. We've got to evacuate families along the river."

"It's that bad?" Jean set the socks on the table beside him. "I can hardly believe weather like this in July."

"Yep." He pulled off his boots. Shucking his socks, he wiggled pink, wrinkled toes. "My feet are so cold, I can barely feel them. These are soaked." He handed the socks to Jean, then pulled on dry ones—two per foot.

"Do you need anything?" Jean asked, dropping the wet socks in a clothes basket. "I can fill the vacuum bottle with coffee."

He shoved his feet back into his boots. "Sounds good, but there's not time."

"Where's Luke?"

"He's waiting in the truck."

"Daddy, can I come?" Laurel asked.

"I don't know, sugar. It might be dangerous. The river's looking mean."

"I'm not afraid, and I want to help."

"All right then. You better get into a slicker and boots."

"Can I borrow a pair of your overalls?"

"Sure. There's an extra pair in the bottom drawer."

Will kissed Jean and gave her a hug. "Keep the coffee hot. We'll need it when we get back."

"It'll be here. I'll be praying. Please be careful."

"We will," Laurel said, planting a kiss on her mother's cheek. She followed her father out the door and into the downpour. The mud was deep and sucked at her boots. It was impossible for the trucks to travel into the compound, so she and her father headed for the main road where several pickups and cars were parked and waiting.

Will walked up to Drew Prosser's truck and opened the door. Drew's son, Jason, and Luke were sitting in front. "Can we ride with you?" Will asked.

"Sure." Drew started the engine, pushed in the clutch, and shifted into gear.

Luke and Jason scrambled into the back, ducking beneath a tarp while Will and Laurel slid onto the front seat. Drew pulled onto the road and headed for the river.

Rain pelted the fogged window. Drew leaned over the steering wheel, peering through a small clear spot on the windshield. "I've never seen it rain hard like this for so long." He wiped the window. "Tom Jenkins is going to follow us. He's got a couple of men with him."

They approached the river, and Laurel couldn't repress a gasp. Although it was a good-sized river, the muddy Matanuska had never seemed frightening. Now it had become a swirling brown torrent of branches and logs that grabbed at the floor of a wooden bridge they would have to cross.

"We don't have much time," Drew said. "If we don't get those folks out, they'll have to hightail it into the hills." They bumped across the wooden span, the river washing dizzily beneath them. "One of the old-timers was sayin' this is the highest the river's been in fifty years." Drew peered through the side window. "I don't think the bridge is gonna hold."

Following a road that ran alongside the river, Drew stopped between two houses. "You and Laurel take that one," he said, nodding at a log cabin. "And me and the boys will see about the folks in the next one."

Tom Jenkins's truck moved past. Adam and a man Laurel didn't know sat in the back. Adam peered out from beneath a broad-brimmed rain hat and waved.

Laurel waved back. A gust of wind swept up river, swirling through the trees and bending them toward the ground. A loud crack came from above Laurel. She ducked just as a limb fell from a cottonwood and crashed to the ground beside her.

"You all right?" Will called.

"Yeah. I'm ok."

"Come on. We've got to hurry."

Laurel followed her father to the cabin, the wind whipping at her slicker. Smoke rose from a rock chimney, giving an odd sense of warmth and welcome in the midst of the storm. Will stood on a stone porch and knocked.

Almost immediately an elderly woman with shoulder-length gray hair and smiling oval eyes opened the door. "Hello. What can I do for you?"

"Hello, ma'am. I'm Will Hasper, and this is my daughter Laurel. The river's rising fast. You're gonna have to leave. We're here to help."

The woman glanced at the river. "It's that serious?"

"It looks bad, ma'am. We don't have much time."

"Come in." She closed the door, shutting out the howl of wind and rain. "My name's Jessie Harrison. It's kind of you to help." She smiled, not appearing to be the least bit distressed.

Laurel looked about the room. It was small and cluttered, filled with bookcases that reached to a low ceiling. They were overcrowded with books, boxes, and piles of papers. Lovely paintings of wild flowers decorated free space on the walls. At the back of the room was a door. Laurel guessed it led to a bedroom.

Jessie hobbled into an adjoining kitchen. She picked up a wooden spoon and swirled the contents of a cast iron pot sitting on a stove. "I was just about to have a bowl of soup. Would you like to join me?"

"No, thank you. We've got to go. You can't stay."

"I've been here a lot of years, and this stretch of river has never flooded. Do you really think we're in danger?"

"Yes, ma'am, I do."

"Oh, dear." She scanned the bookshelves. "My husband's notes. I can't leave years of work behind." She looked at Will. "I must take Steward's notes. I won't leave without them."

"All right, but we'll have to hurry. Show us what to take."

Jessie walked to the closest bookshelf. "Some of them are on the top here. Can you reach them?"

He hurried to the bookshelf, grabbed down a box full of papers, and handed it to Laurel. "Put it in the truck and lay the tarp over it. I'll get the rest down."

"The stacks of papers have to go too," Jessie said. "And there are more boxes over there." She nodded at a bookcase on the opposite wall.

Will handed Jessie a box. "Do you have something we can put the papers in?"

She thought a moment. "Well, I think I've got a couple of apple crates out back. I'll be right back." She hurried outside.

He lifted down boxes and set them on the floor. Laurel reappeared. "Can you take two at a time?"

"Sure." Laurel picked up one box, and Will set another on top of it. Staggering a bit under the weight, Laurel hurried out the door.

Jessie returned, carrying two apple boxes. Her hair was wet, plastered to her head and forehead. "Will this do?"

"Perfect." Will picked up a box filled with folders. "I'll take these while you fill the others with the loose papers." He placed a second box on top of the one he already carried and headed out the door.

Laurel passed him. "I think the storm's getting worse."

"Just hurry," he said and kept moving.

Laurel ran into the house, feeling her panic grow. "Are there many more? Daddy says we have to hurry."

"Only a few, dear," Jessie said, grabbing another stack of papers and setting them in the box.

Laurel stooped and picked up another container of notes.

"Do be careful, please. These are important."

"I will," Laurel promised, wondering what possessions could be of such consequence this woman would risk her life to save them.

"How many more?" Will asked, walking back into the house.

"Just those," Jessie said, nodding at four small crates.

Picking up one, Will set it on top of the box Laurel held. "I'll take care of the rest. You get her to the truck."

Laurel followed Jessie, trying to hurry the old woman.

"Oh, dear, some of these are going to get wet," Jessie said. "I hope the ink doesn't run. I might not be able to decipher my husband's writing. I've been planning on getting these in order for years. Now I wish I had."

Laurel set the boxes in the back of the truck, covered them with the tarp, and hustled Jessie into the cab. Will returned with two more, then ran back inside for the last one.

A very pregnant woman and two small children ran toward the truck from the other house. She looked as if she'd been crying. A man, whom Laurel guessed to be her husband, followed with a toddler in his arms. Drew carried what looked like a stack of photograph albums. Luke had a box of dishes, and Jason followed, toting a box with a lid.

"All right, everybody climb in," Drew said, setting the albums in the truck bed.

The woman climbed in beside Jessie, and the man handed the toddler to her. Then he lifted the other children into the back and climbed in beside them, holding them close. Luke set the box of dishes next to Jessie's boxes and clambered in. Handing up his carton, Jason sat on a hub opposite Luke.

"We better get moving!" Drew called over pounding rain and gusting wind. "The river's rising fast! Where's your father?" he asked Laurel.

Before she could answer, Will walked out of the house carrying the last of the boxes. "That's it," he called, nearly running. "Let's get out of here!"

"Oh, dear, I forgot about Albert," Jessie said, climbing out the driver's side of the truck. "I can't leave him here." She walked toward the house, calling in a high voice, "Albert. Come on, Albert." A longhaired, multicolored cat ran out of the bushes and rubbed against Jessie's ankles. "Oh, there you are." She picked him up and cuddled him against her.

Will ran to the woman. "Come on! We've got to hurry!" He circled his arm around her small shoulders and hustled her toward the truck. "Get in!"

The other woman scooted in, and Jessie settled on the seat next to her. Resting her free hand on Will's arm, she said, "Thank you. Thank you so much."

"You're welcome." Will smiled. Drew slid in behind the wheel, and Will slammed the door. He helped Laurel into the back, then climbed in behind her. "Let's go!" he called, pounding on the roof.

Laurel sat in the corner next to the cab, opposite the man and his children.

He smiled. "Name's Bruce Miller. These are my girls, Sally and Lucy. Thanks for your help."

Laurel nodded. "Laurel Hasper. Nice to meet you." She was soaked through and shivering hard. She stared at the river. Water flowed over the bank!

The going was painfully slow as they wallowed through mud and runoff from the wild Matanuska. Another truck loaded with people and possessions fell in behind them.

Adam stood in the back, peering over the cab. Laurel barely recognized him in his drenched state. He smiled at her. She didn't know why, but somehow his presence made her feel less afraid.

With each passing minute more water washed over the muddy road. *Lord, protect us. Please help us get home,* Laurel prayed. What would they do if the bridge had washed away? She peered around the side of the cab, trying to get a view of the crossing. It stood amid a violent, muddy deluge.

Drew stopped the truck before crossing. A shudder went through Laurel. The river swept across the bridge, swirling around the railings and over the roadway.

Will jumped out of the back, joining Drew, Adam, and another man. The four studied the bridge for several moments, talked, then returned to the trucks. Adam stopped beside Laurel. "Everything's going to be all right," he assured her. "Don't be afraid."

"I'm not," Laurel lied.

He patted her arm and ran back to his truck.

Will climbed in and returned to his place behind the cab. "There's no more than a foot of water on the bridge, maybe less. We can still drive across."

Laurel's stomach somersaulted. "It looks bad. Are you sure we can make it?"

"Yep. God will see us through." He looked at her. "We don't have a choice, sugar."

The engine sputtered to life, and the truck moved forward. "Find something to hang on to," Will called. "It could get rough." He braced his legs and pressed his hands on the roof of the cab.

Bruce wedged himself more tightly into the corner, pulling his children in closer. Both boys moved from the hubs to the truck bed and hung onto the frame. Pulling her legs close to her chest, Laurel pressed her back into the corner. Working hard to keep her breathing slow and even, she tried to quiet her shaking. *God, please carry us across safely.*

The truck ground through mud, sliding as it dipped down an incline leading to the bridge. The rising waters had created a small ditch, and the back tires became wedged. Drew gunned the engine. The tires spun. He stopped, and Laurel could see he was praying. He put the truck in reverse, backed up, rocked forward, backed up again, then rocked forward with enough momentum so the tires bumped free. They started across.

Water swirled under the truck nearly reaching the hubs. For a moment the pickup lifted and floated, slamming them against the bridge wall. Laurel's stomach pitched, and her shaking increased. She choked back a scream. Somehow the tires found the wood slats of the bridge, and they inched forward. Laurel wiped wet hair from her eyes and craned her neck so she could see where they were heading. They were nearly halfway across.

The swirling brown torrent carried an enormous log toward the bridge. It barreled straight at them. "Daddy!" one of the children screamed, burying her face against her father's chest and clinging to his neck.

"It's all right, honey. It's all right," he said, but his voice shook, belying his words.

Laurel stared at the log. It rammed the sidebeam, and the bridge shuddered. She waited for the collapse, but the structure held. They kept moving.

"Hurry!" Luke yelled. "It's going to come apart!"

Still hugging her knees, Laurel buried her face in her arms. She didn't want to see.

The truck turned and climbed slightly. They bumped over another small channel where water had eaten away the soil. Finally the tires found solid ground. They stopped.

Laurel stood, hugged her father and Luke, and then turned to watch the truck that followed. She pressed her hand against her mouth. "They aren't going to make it! They won't make it!"

The truck had stopped in the center of the bridge. Surging water lifted it and turned it sideways. The bridge quaked; its girders fell away. Like ocean surf, muddy water washed over the structure, pushing it sideways. "No!" Laurel screamed as it buckled. She looked at her father. "Daddy!" she yelled, the little girl within wanting to believe he could do something.

Will grabbed two lengths of rope and jumped out of the truck. He tossed them to Luke and Jason. "Tie these off! Make sure they're good and tight." While the boys secured the ropes to the truck's bumper, Will looped one around his waist, knotted it, and ran toward the river. Drew grabbed the other line, tied it to his belt, and followed.

The bridge tipped onto its side in the wash, and two little ones fell into the surge. The driver and a man from inside the cab climbed free and swam for shore. Another man and a woman leaped out of the truck, swimming after the children. The woman flailed. Unable to fight the current, she was carried away. The man grabbed one child and fought for shore. Will swam for the second youngster. Before the swirling flood could carry him away, he grabbed hold of the back of the child's shirt. Luke and Laurel hauled on the rope.

"Hang on. We'll pull you in!" Luke yelled.

Bruce joined Jason on the other line.

Drew headed for the man with the boy.

With the child clinging to his back, the stranger grabbed a downed tree stretching out over the river. The surging waters nearly stripped them away, but the man hung on.

Drew fought his way to them, then shouted something. The roar of the river and blustering storm carried away his voice. Arms around his father's neck, the boy hung on. The man grabbed the rope just above

Drew. As soon as Bruce and Jason were sure he had a good hold, they pulled on the line. Jessie handed her cat to the pregnant woman and joined them.

Laurel and Luke continued to drag Will and the child toward shore. The car tumbled into the water and bobbed down river. Laurel watched, horrified, as another child was pitched out of the back. Adam dived in after him.

"God! No! Please help them!"

"Pull, Laurel!" Luke called. "Harder!"

Laurel did as she was told, still watching the raging waters carry away the truck. Adam and the child disappeared in the turbulent tide. Laurel's tears flowed. The rope burned her hands, and she dug her feet into the mud. There was nothing she could do except work to save her father and the child with him.

"Can you drive?" Bruce yelled at Jason.

"Yeah."

"All right then. I'll hang on here, and you drive them out," he shouted over the roar of river and wind.

Jason let go of the rope and ran for the truck. Bruce dug his feet into the mud and groaned as he struggled to hang on to the two men and one child. "Hurry! They won't last long in this cold water!"

Jason revved the engine, grinding the gears as he searched for first. He finally found it, and the car edged forward, then slid backward in the slime. Jessie and the other woman pressed their backs against the tailgate. Jason tried again, finally climbing away from the river.

Will and the child, Drew, the man, and boy were dragged from the river. Like muddied carcasses they lay in the rain and mud, not moving.

Laurel ran to her father and knelt beside him. "Daddy?" There was no reply. "Daddy!"

Will opened his eyes. Looking at the youngster in his arms, he loosened his hold. It was a little girl. Her clothes were nearly ripped off her body. She whimpered softly.

Jessie picked her up. "Now. Now. Everything is all right." She sat down and rocked the child, holding her close.

"Are you all right, Daddy?" Luke asked.

Will nodded and sat up, panting for breath.

Luke hugged his father. "I thought you were going to die."

The man Drew had hauled in sat up and pulled his drenched boy close, then claimed the little girl. Sitting in the mud, he held his children and stared at the river, his face grim.

"We've got to get all of you to the clinic," Jessie said. "Right now."

Drew looked at the grieving man. "I wish we could have saved them all." They limped to the truck and managed to climb onto the open tailgate where they sat shivering.

Laurel stared at the last place she'd seen Adam. He'd given his life trying to save a child. Choking back sobs, her tears mingled with rain on her cheeks.

Jessie stood beside her, an arm around Laurel's dripping wet shoulders.

"Do you think they might still be alive?"

"They're in the Lord's hands," Jessie said. "He'll see to them."

Chapter Nineteen

BUNDLED IN A WOOL BLANKET, LAUREL SAT ON THE CLINIC BENCH HOLDING a cup of coffee between her hands. Her shivering had stopped, but inside she felt empty and cold. She kept seeing Adam and the others disappear into the muddy water.

"Sugar, you all right?" Will asked, sitting beside his daughter and placing an arm around her.

Shaking her head no, Laurel leaned against her father. Burying her face against his chest, she allowed tears to flow, but the ache inside didn't subside.

Suddenly, the roar of a truck and hollering came from outside. A moment later a soaking-wet Ray Townsend pushed open the door and stepped in. A woman hung limply in his arms. "I need a doctor. Where's the doctor?"

Another man carrying a child wrapped in a blanket followed Ray. It looked like a little girl.

Laurel's heart caught in her throat. Were these the people who'd fallen into the river? What about Adam? Was he alive? She let her blanket fall to the floor and ran to the door. Two men stepped inside with Adam draped between them. "Is he alive?" Laurel asked.

"Yeah, but just barely," one man answered.

A nurse appeared. "Bring him back here." Taking short, quick steps, she led them to an examining room. Laurel followed. "Get him on the table," the nurse said.

The men laid Adam down, then stepped back. The one who'd spoken earlier said, "We found the lot of them tumbling down the river. We barely got them. If it weren't for Ray, this one would have been done in

for sure. But Ray wouldn't give up—not 'til he dragged him to shore."
He stared at Adam. "Sure hope he appreciates what Ray did for him."
With that he walked out of the room, the other man close behind.

Laurel leaned over the table. "Adam? Adam, can you hear me?" He
looked awful; his skin had a pale blue tinge, and his breaths were shallow.

The nurse stripped off his wet clothes and bundled him in warm
blankets. "He's real cold. We need to warm him." She looked at Laurel.
"You his wife?"

"No, a friend. Can't the doctor see him?" Laurel asked.

"He's with the little girl. She's badly hurt."

Adam moaned. His eyes blinked.

"Well, why don't you get your friend some coffee?" the nurse said.

Laurel sat on the front step of the tent, reflecting on the past few
days. The rain had stopped, and sunshine filtered through puffy clouds,
making mirrors out of puddles. She smiled. God truly was in control.
The day the bridge had collapsed, she'd believed Adam and the others
had perished. Who would have thought someone down river, especially
Ray Townsend, would have been there to help them. "Thank you,
Father," she whispered.

If not for Mr. Townsend, Adam would have died. Two other men
had pulled out the woman and child, but Ray was the one who'd gone
after Adam. The incident had shown her the man had another side. The
day after the accident, Laurel went to Mr. Townsend to thank him. He
didn't want her thanks and acted as if what he'd done was nothing out
of the ordinary.

Laurel's mind wandered to Adam. She could see his handsome, boyish face, his easy manner, the way he stood, the way he moved. His
appealing, confusing blend of toughness and sensitivity puzzled her. She
didn't understand the man or the way she felt whenever he was near. She
didn't want to care about him. It was foolish. He was nothing like her,
and soon he'd be leaving the valley. Though she fought it, Laurel wanted
to be with Adam, to talk to him, to share her dreams and aspirations.

"Let's go," Brian said, walking out of the tent waving a fishing pole.
"Justin, you said you'd go fishing." Brian looked at Laurel. "He promised. Make him go."

With a sigh, Laurel stood and walked into the tent. "Justin?"

"I don't wanna go. I don't feel good." Justin crawled onto his bed and lay down.

"You look all right to me," Brian said.

"Well, I'm not." Justin pulled a coverlet over himself and closed his eyes.

Laurel crossed the room and looked down at her brother. "What's wrong?"

"I think I'm sick. I have a headache and my throat hurts."

Laurel rested her hand on his forehead. It felt hot. She studied his face. His cheeks were flushed, and his eyes looked too bright. "I'll get Mama." She walked outside where Jean was hanging clothes. "I think Justin's sick."

Jean clipped a pair of blue jeans onto the line, then lifted overalls out of the basket.

"He said he's got a sore throat and a headache. He feels hot."

"I'll be right there." After hanging up the overalls, Jean hurried inside. "Well, let's take a look at you." She leaned over Justin. "Open your mouth."

Justin did as he was told. Laurel could see her mother tense.

Jean lifted his shirt, exposing a bright red rash. "Laurel, get your father," she said, her voice tight. Gently she pulled Justin's shirt down, then tucked the blanket under his chin. "Do you hurt anywhere?" Laurel hadn't moved. Jean looked at her. "Laurel, get your father," she said sternly.

Laurel hurried outside. She knew something was wrong. "Daddy," Laurel called. In mid-swing, Will didn't look up. "Daddy, Justin's sick. Mama wants you."

The blade cut through a chunk of birch, splitting the wood in two. "He's sick?" Will rested the axe against a wood slab. "What's wrong?" he asked, striding toward the tent door.

"I think he has a fever. And he's got a rash."

Will stepped inside. "Justin's sick?"

Jean intercepted him in the middle of the room. Her hands on his arms, she whispered, "I think he's got scarlet fever! We've got to get him to the doctor!"

"Why do you think that?" Will asked, his voice tight.

"He has a rash, a red sore throat, and a high fever." Jean returned to Justin's bedside. "Honey, show Daddy your tummy." Justin pulled up his shirt.

Will nodded. "Looks like scarlet fever, all right."

"Is that bad?" Brian asked, leaning on the bed.

"No. We'll take him to the doctor, and he'll fix him right up." He looked at Jean. "Good thing we've got a doctor now."

"Laurel, I'll need you to stay with Susie and Brian," Jean said.

Laurel nodded. "Where's Luke?"

"He's off with Alex again," Brian said petulantly. "He's always with Alex. He never plays with me anymore." He looked up at his mother. "Can I go to the doctor's with you?"

Jean kneeled in front of her son. "We need you to stay and help with Susie."

Brian stuck out his lower lip. "Can I find Luke?"

"No," Will said, bundling Justin in a blanket and lifting him. "You stay here. We won't be gone long." He walked to the door. "Drew was home a few minutes ago. I'm sure he'll drive us."

Jean kissed Brian and Susie. "We won't be long," she promised, then followed Will outside.

❧

Laurel refilled the basin with cool water and walked back to Justin's bedside. Dipping a washcloth into the water, she wrung it out and gently sponged the boy's face. Justin was getting worse. *Why?* she asked herself. The doctor had said most children rebound from scarlet fever. He had prescribed aspirin and keeping Justin quiet, but that hadn't helped.

Two days before, his elbows, ankles, and wrists had begun to swell, his fever raged, and the rash had changed, now looking more like bruises. Sometimes delirious, Justin thrashed about calling for his mother or others.

The doctor sadly explained that he'd developed rheumatic fever, a severe complication of scarlet fever. He'd been to see Justin nearly every day, but nothing seemed to help. This morning Dr. Donovan left shaking his head. There was nothing he could do.

The rocking chair creaked as Jean rose slowly so not to waken Susie.

She lay the little girl in her crib, then crossed to Justin's bedside. "Is he any better?"

Laurel shook her head no, cringing inwardly at the anguish in her mother's eyes.

"I'll sit with him," Jean said.

Brian placed his hands on his brother's mattress, then rested his chin on his hands. "Mama, how long until Justin's better?"

"We don't know, soon maybe." Jean sounded weary. She smiled gently at her young son. "God knows. We must trust him."

Brian nodded, her answer seeming to satisfy him. "I hope it's soon so we can go fishing. Justin likes to fish." He sighed. "I miss Daddy and Luke. When are they coming home?"

"Just as soon as we're all healthy and the doctor lifts the quarantine."

"I don't like it when everyone's sick." Brian ambled to the toy box. He took out a wooden truck and half-heartedly pushed it across the floor.

"Mama, he's not going to die, is he?" Laurel whispered.

Jean didn't answer. She gazed at Justin, her eyes filling with tears. Finally she said softly, "It's God's choice. Justin belongs to him, not us."

Laurel walked into the kitchen, picked up the kettle, and poured a cup of tea. "Do you want some?"

"No. I think I've had enough to last me a lifetime." She rewet the cloth and tenderly laid it across Justin's forehead.

All that night Jean didn't leave his side. Laurel sat in the rocking chair, falling in and out of sleep. Her brother's breaths became shallower and more labored. At one point Jean looked at Laurel and said, "He's fading. He's going to leave us." She covered her face with a handkerchief and cried softly.

Laurel looked on, not knowing what to do. She gazed at her brother. *Please, Justin, live. Please.*

"Laurel, get your father," Jean said, her voice trembling. "Quarantine or not, he needs to be here."

Norma cradled Jean against her shoulder. "Sometimes God takes our babies home to him. It's not for us to understand why."

"Justin was such a sweet, gentle boy," Jean sobbed.

Brian clung to his mother's skirt. "Mama, is Justin in heaven?"

Jean bent and scooped up her youngest son. She held him tight, then kissed his cheek. "Yes. Justin is in heaven. He's not hurting anymore."

"But if he's in heaven, how come we buried him?"

"We buried his body," Will said sorrowfully "His spirit, the part of him that made him Justin, is in heaven."

"I didn't want him to leave. I want to go fishing." Tears spilled onto Brian's cheeks.

"I know, sweetheart." Jean softly kissed his cheek. "One day, when you get to heaven, you can go fishing together again."

"We can? You think there's good fishing in heaven?"

"I'm sure of it."

Brian wiggled out of his mother's arms and ran outside.

Jean stepped into her husband's embrace and sobbed against his wool shirt. "We should never have come to this valley."

Will smoothed her hair. "It's not this place that killed Justin. Sickness is part of the world." He rested his cheek against her hair. "Justin loved it here."

Laurel couldn't listen anymore. Blindly she pushed through the door. The sun was warm and bright, people came and went, a butterfly danced through wild flowers, a car passed. The world seemed normal. How could that be?

She started to run, but her skirt caught at her legs. Hitching it up above her knees, she ran. She didn't know where she was going; she just ran. After a time her legs ached and her lungs burned, but it felt good. She kept running. The thought, *We should never have come—We should never have come—We should never have come,* tumbled through her mind in rhythm to her pounding heart.

Laurel finally stopped in front of their property. The house stood like a skeleton. Framed and roofed, it had no walls. It would be finished soon. But Justin would never live there. He'd loved this place. Every day he had come here with his father and brothers, helping carry lumber and tools. He'd even pounded a few nails.

Laurel walked up the driveway and wandered through the garden. The cabbage already had large tight heads. They were nearly ready to cut. Carrottops stood tall and leafy. Laurel bent and pulled one. A slender orange root pulled free of the dirt. She dusted it clean, smiling as she remembered how Justin always loved to eat carrots right out of the ground, still warm and fresh.

Laurel took a bite. It was sweet and tender.

She ambled on to the house. Stepping through the doorway, she entered the open structure. *This will be nice,* she thought, walking through the framed-in rooms. The air smelled of fresh-cut lumber, and her steps echoed as she walked across the kitchen floor. Looking at the plumbing already set in the wall, it seemed amazing that indoor plumbing existed in this wilderness.

Stepping out the back door, she stood on the porch. Her eyes roamed over open meadows and forests, then traveled to mountains that looked as if they'd literally been thrust up from the valley floor. Taking a deep breath, she felt the peace, its stillness. Quiet spread through her. God must certainly be in this place.

Her eyes went to the creek that bordered their land. Brian and Justin had fished there, played tag in the open fields, and sat among the grasses talking about their dreams—little boy dreams, but important nonetheless. Tears blurred her vision. *Justin loved living here.*

Suddenly, Laurel couldn't imagine living anywhere else. The mountains, open fields, and forests felt like home. The mountains no longer made her feel closed in but instead gave her a sense of protection. And she realized she didn't want to leave. She belonged here.

She strode to the side of the house where her apple seedling still sat in a pot. Since arriving she'd lovingly tended it but hadn't wanted to put it in the ground. Now it was time. And she knew just where it belonged.

Grabbing a shovel, she lifted the seedling and headed toward the creek. She could feel Justin's presence as if he were walking beside her. At the creek she could see him skipping along the bank. She stopped just above the pool where the boys had fished and swam.

Setting down the tiny tree, she dug into the fertile soil. When the hole was large enough, she removed the tree from its pot, loosened the root ball, and set it gently in the hollowed-out earth. She scooped dirt around the seedling and pressed it down firmly.

When she was finished, she sat back on her heels and looked at the little tree. "One day when you're all grown up, you'll bear fruit." Tears filled her eyes. "And I'll remember how Justin loved it here."

Finally she stood, brushed dirt from her legs and skirt, and looked out over the farm. Closing her eyes, she soaked in the sensations all around—the warmth of the sun, the smell of fresh dug earth, the aroma of wildflowers, and the breeze that tickled her bare arms. This was home.

With a shuddering breath, she said, "I'm sorry you weren't able to stay, Justin. I'll miss you."

Chapter Twenty

LAUREL KICKED A ROCK, SENDING IT INTO THE DITCH, THEN SHUFFLED THE lunch basket into her left hand. Looking at her mother and baby sister, she said, "Susie's getting so big. She looks more like a little girl and less like a baby."

"I know. She's nearly a year." Jean kissed Susie's cheek. She scanned berry bushes growing alongside the road. "The berries are nearly ready. Looks like there'll be plenty for picking."

Laurel looked at the smooth, round blackberries. "They don't look anything like the blackberries back home."

"They're supposed to be good for pies and jellies. Come January, they'll be a wonderful reminder of summer." Jean's expression turned sad. "Justin loved berry pie." Her voice broke.

Laurel rested an arm around her mother's waist and gave her a sideways hug. "I miss him too. Sometimes I can almost see him running through the field, or I think I hear his voice. It's hard to believe he's gone." She scanned the meadows on both sides of the road. Brilliant pink paintbrush, tufts of squirrel tail, navy-blue monkshood, and clusters of white aster grew among deep grasses. Her eyes followed the driveway, coming to rest on their home. "I wish Justin could see the house now." She bent and picked a daisy growing alongside the ditch. "After lunch let's pick a bouquet and take it to his grave."

Jean nodded, brushing away tears. "Sounds like a good idea."

Turning off the road, they walked up the drive. Pounding and sawing noises came from inside the house. "It's nearly finished." Holding the basket in front of her, Laurel gazed at the cabin. "It's nice. I like it."

"Your father's already fretting about getting the barn up. Winter's not far off." She glanced at the mountains. "We'll need a barn soon. But he's got to get a paddock built right away. I'm sure we'll get a cow or two in the drawing this weekend."

"A paddock won't do much to protect cows from wolves or bears," Laurel said. Shrugging, she added, "Maybe we won't see any. So far I haven't."

"From what I've been told, if you stay here long enough, you'll see both."

"Do you really think the farmers need to carry rifles with them while they're working?"

"I don't know. Maybe. It's wild here, not like Wisconsin." Jean shuddered slightly. "One night when your father and I were working here late, we saw a big sow lumbering across the field. She had two cubs with her. They headed down to the creek."

"You did? Why didn't you say something?"

"We didn't want to frighten anyone. And to tell you the truth, I forgot all about it until just this moment."

"Do you think they'd really attack someone?"

Jean thought a moment. "Yes—if the stories are true. I guess it doesn't take much to get their dander up, but lots of folks have been living here for years and have never had trouble with bears."

Will stepped out of the front door. "Hello," he called. "Boy, I'm glad to see you. I'm starved." He stuck his head back inside the house. "Hey, lunch is here," he hollered.

"Oh, boy! I'm hungry!" Brian shouted, dashing out the door. He raced to his mother, threw his arms around her legs, then leaned his head back and looked up at her. "We've been workin' hard. I'm real hungry."

Will unbuckled his work belt, set it just outside the door, and stepped off the makeshift porch. Taking long strides, he met Jean and gave her a sound kiss. "You look real pretty." He brushed back a strand of her hair. "Just as pretty as the day I met you."

"You're fibbing," Jean said with a smile. "But thank you anyway." She glanced around. "Where do you want to eat?"

"I'd say right here is fine. No place on this property is more beautiful than any other."

"All right, then," Jean handed Susie to Will.

"Hello, sweetie pie," he said, hefting the little girl above his head. She giggled her delight.

Jean spread out a blanket on the ground and sat. "How's the work been coming along?"

Will sat beside her. "Good. I figured it might go slowly, what with the extra carpenters working over at Robert's place, but we've made real progress." He nudged his hat off his forehead and turned his eyes to the spot a little east of the house. "As soon as I get the paddock done, I'll get to work on the barn. Hopefully winter will hold off a while yet. Don't know though. It's only August, and already the nights are cold."

Laurel sat across from her parents and opened the basket. She handed her father a cheese sandwich. A shadow fell across the blanket. Expecting to see Luke, she looked up and said, "We were wondering . . ." Her sentence died in her throat when she saw Adam standing over her.

He grinned. "Good to see you, Mrs. Hasper, Laurel."

"Hello, Adam," Jean said.

Adam looked at Laurel. "How've you been?"

"I'm fine." Laurel knew Adam had helped her father before but hadn't expected to see him today.

"Adam showed up this morning with his hammer and a hankering for work," Will said with a smile. "For a reporter, he's a darn good carpenter." He looked up at Adam. "How about something to eat?"

"You sure there's enough?"

"I made plenty," Jean said.

"All right then." Adam sat, folding his legs Indian style.

Brian took a sandwich from the basket and leaned against his father. "Daddy pounds nails real fast," he told his mother. "I tried, but it takes too long. I'm no good at it."

"You do fine," Will said. "You'll learn. You've still got some growing to do."

Laurel handed Adam a sandwich. "How have you been? Haven't seen you since . . . well, since the funeral."

"I'm good." Sadness touched Adam's face. "I'm sorry about Justin. He was a nice kid."

Somehow, hearing Adam's regret renewed Laurel's pain. Tears burned her eyes.

"Hey, you guys left me some, didn't you?" Luke asked, bounding off the porch. He stared down at his family.

"Course. You know your Mama always packs enough for an army." Will grinned and gave Jean's cheek a peck.

Luke rummaged through the basket and took out two sandwiches. Stripping wax paper off one of them, he said, "I think I'm going to stretch my legs. Alex said he might be down at the creek."

"And his sister, Mattie?" Adam asked, his eyes alight with mischief.

"Uh, maybe. She might be there." He strode off across the field.

"What was that about Mattie?" Jean asked.

"Nothing really," Adam said.

Laurel smiled. "Seems Mattie's always part of the group, especially when Luke's there. I think they like each other."

"Can't say I blame him. She's real pretty and sweet too." Will handed Susie a piece of his bread and the little girl shoved it in her mouth.

For a few moments everyone ate in silence, accompanied by the whistles of chickadees and raucous calls of whiskey jacks.

Jean leaned back on her hands. "It's lovely out here. I can hardly wait to move in."

"Me too," Laurel said.

"You're looking forward to it?" Adam asked, sounding doubtful. "I thought—"

"Yes," Laurel interjected. She hadn't told Adam she'd decided to stay. The last time they'd talked she'd still planned on leaving for school. Not wanting to inflict any unnecessary pain on her parents, she quickly added, "I'm looking forward to moving. I like it here. It feels like home."

Adam raised an eyebrow but said nothing more. Plucking a long stem of grass, he leaned back on one elbow and chewed the drying shoot. His gaze rested on Laurel for a few moments.

Adam's eyes were warm and approving, and Laurel wished he'd look elsewhere. She grabbed an apple out of the basket and bit into it, acting as if she hadn't noticed he'd been staring.

"So, Adam, how much longer will you be staying?" Will asked.

"Probably another month. I'm already due back at the paper, but I convinced them to give me a little more time to wrap things up."

At the mention of Adam's leaving, Laurel's mood wilted. For reasons she still didn't understand, she wanted him to stay.

"I'm hoping to return next fall for the colony's first harvest." He scanned the fields and mountains, then his deep blue eyes settled on Laurel again. He cocked his square jaw slightly to one side, and his mouth nearly curved into a smile. "Have to admit to having mixed feelings about leaving. I'm going to miss this place and the people."

Laurel felt heat rush to her cheeks. She looked away, hoping Adam hadn't noticed.

Will stood, picked up Susie, then held out his hand to Jean. "How about a walk before I go back to work?" Taking his hand, Jean allowed him to pull her to her feet.

Brian skipped ahead down the drive toward the road. "Can we go see Mr. Jenkins?" he called over his shoulder.

"Not today." Will rested an arm around Jean's waist.

Adam and Laurel watched the two stroll away. An uncomfortable silence settled between them. Adam finally asked, "What happened to your plans for school?"

"I decided to stay." Laurel took a bite of her apple. Juice squirted, and she wiped a droplet from her lower lip.

"You could get your schooling, then come back."

"I suppose, but I don't want to leave. This feels like home now, and I just left my home in Wisconsin. I'm not ready to go through that again—not yet anyway." She took another bite. "I might go to school some day, maybe if a university opens in Anchorage. I'm sure it sounds foolish to someone like you, but I don't think I ever want to leave."

Adam bent one leg, leaned on his knee, and settled a disquieting gaze on Laurel. "You want to be a farmer's wife?"

"Maybe."

"If you stay, that's what will happen. I thought that's the last thing you wanted."

"There's nothing wrong with being a farmer's wife," Laurel said defensively. Taking another bite of the apple, she hurled what was left of it into the bushes.

"I didn't say there was. You're the one who said it would be boring and thankless. I think you'd make a great farm wife." His gaze didn't falter.

Laurel watched her parents. "I don't know what I'm going to do, but I do know I'm not getting married anytime soon."

"What about Robert? Do you think he's going to wait long?"

Laurel met Adam's eyes. "Robert? Why would you think I'd marry Robert?"

"Why not? He's crazy about you." He gave her a slow smile. "Laurel, I can't see you settling for a mundane life. You won't be happy if there's not something new and exciting on the horizon all the time."

Angry, Laurel stood. "How do you know what kind of life I want?" She glared at him. "Life here is exciting enough for me."

Adam shrugged. "If you say so."

"Well, what about you? You're going back to the same place you've always lived, and you'll be doing the same thing you've always done. That isn't exactly exciting or adventurous."

Adam pushed himself to his feet. "I'm not staying in Chicago. I'll be heading for Europe, probably before the year is out. The paper's been real happy with my work, and I was told by someone I trust that soon I'll be sent to Europe to work as an overseas correspondent."

Laurel felt a catch in her throat. She didn't like the idea of Adam being so far away. "Well, good then," she said. "At least your life won't be *mundane.*" She tugged at the quilt. "Would you please get off the blanket? I'd like to fold it."

Glancing at his feet, Adam quickly stepped onto the grass. With a glint of mischief in his eye, he said, "Well, time to get back to work. Thanks for the lunch." He tipped his hat. "Nice seeing you." He turned and headed back to the house, carrying his tall, lean frame with his usual infuriating confidence.

～

The chiming of bells hanging from the door accompanied Laurel into the store. She hoped Celeste would be working. Since her conversation with Adam, she'd felt miserable. He'd been right. Farming life could be ordinary and monotonous. What would happen if she married a farmer, then found out she hated being a farmer's wife?

She considered the single men she knew in camp—none seemed interesting. She liked Robert well enough, but he felt more like a brother than a husband. Adam was the only one who intrigued her, but he was interested in world travel, excitement, and the high life.

"Hi, Laurel," Celeste called from behind the counter. "How are you?"

"Angry and mixed up." She glanced around the store to make sure no one was around to hear their conversation.

"What's wrong?"

Laurel sighed. "I don't know. I like living here, but sometimes I wonder if I ought to be doing something else with my life. I'd planned on staying just until my family got settled. I wanted to go to school—become a teacher." She shrugged. "Somehow it doesn't seem so important anymore."

"So? What's wrong with that?"

Laurel picked up a pen lying on the counter. "I don't know. When I look at my mama's life it seems . . . ordinary. She cooks and cleans, changes diapers, kisses scraped knees. I admire her, but I don't know that I want to be like her."

"You don't have to be like her. You can be a wife and mother and still have lots of other things in your life." Celeste placed an elbow on the counter and rested her chin in her hand. "I know I want to get married and have kids." She smiled dreamily. "Robert would make a good father." She straightened and shrugged. "Sorry. I can't help liking him."

"Why apologize? Maybe you ought to let him know how you feel."

"All he sees is you."

Laurel took a peppermint out of a jar sitting on the counter and popped it into her mouth. "Robert's just a friend."

"That's not how he feels."

Laurel glanced at a newspaper lying on the countertop. Adam Dunnavant's name leaped out at her from an article. Remembering he'd be leaving soon, sadness swept over her. "Adam's going to Europe."

Celeste brushed bouncy curls off her shoulder. She gave Laurel a smug smile. "Why don't you tell Adam how you feel about him?"

"What?" Laurel asked, staring at her friend. Finally finding her voice, she said, "I don't care about him like that. It's just that life will be less interesting without a reporter here."

"That's all, huh?" Celeste grinned. "I don't believe you."

Laurel leaned close to her friend and said softly, "All right. I admit I do think he's interesting, but we don't get along. In fact, he's the most infuriating man I've ever met. Every time we see each other, we end up in a fight."

"You know, they say opposites attract."

Laurel turned her back to the counter and leaned against it, folding her arms over her chest. "It doesn't matter anyway. He's leaving."

"Maybe you should go too."

"No. Palmer's my home now. My parents need me. I wouldn't like living like Adam. He wants to wander the world."

Celeste nodded. "Good. I don't want you to go."

The bells on the door jangled, and Jessie Harrison walked in. "Hello there," she said, brightly. "It's a wonder to see you again, Laurel. I've been thinking about you." She grasped Laurel's hand, her intelligent eyes animated. "I've never properly thanked you for helping me during the flood. Oh, what a fright we had," she added with a chuckle.

"I hope it's the last one I see. Did you get any water in the house?"

"Only a few inches. It was a mess, but there was no real damage."

Laurel glanced at Celeste, then looked at Jessie. "Do you know Celeste Townsend?"

"Oh, sure. I'm in here all the time." Jessie leaned a hip against the counter. "How are you, Celeste?"

"Good, Mrs. Harrison."

"And how about that cantankerous father of yours?"

"He's fine. But he says he misses your discussions."

"Debates you mean," Jessie said with a chuckle. "Well, I miss him too. Will you tell him for me?"

"Sure. I haven't seen you around much lately. You been feeling all right?"

"Yes, I'm fine. It's just that I nearly lost all my husband's work in the flood. And I've been slaving over those papers ever since, trying to get the information typed up and protected in notebooks." She rubbed swollen knuckles. "My arthritis makes for slow progress. I wish I could find someone who'd take on the job. I'd pay the person."

"I'd like to, but I'm already working here," Celeste said. "My father would have a fit."

"It's a blessing to be working in these hard times." Jessie turned a smile on Laurel. "You wouldn't be interested, would you?"

Laurel's normal heart rhythm picked up. Her family could use the extra money. "I might be. What would I have to do?"

"Oh, it's not hard, just takes some time. The university in San Francisco commissioned my husband to compile a compendium of Alaskan history, plants, animals, native customs, and so on. He had such a passion for it. There are piles of notes; some of them in boxes, some just stacked. You remember when you helped me during the flood?"

Laurel nodded.

"Well, all those papers are Steward's research." Her eyes shone with enthusiasm. "We came up from California in 1915 and traveled the territory, gathering information. The more we saw of Alaska and its people, the more we fell in love with it." She smiled. "We never wanted to finish the work because we enjoyed it so much. And we didn't finish. My husband died before he could complete it."

Laurel felt excitement build. "I love history. It's something I've always been interested in. I've even thought about becoming a history teacher."

"Are you interested then? It could take months, maybe even a year or more."

"I am interested, but I'll need to talk to my parents first." Laurel smiled. "I'm sure they'll say it's all right."

"Wonderful! Come by my house tomorrow, and I'll show you what I need. I even have an old typewriter you can use."

"I don't know how to type."

"Well, you can learn."

"All right. I'll see you tomorrow."

Jessie smiled, the lines in her face crinkling like parchment paper. "You've saved the day."

"I'll go right now and tell my folks. See you later, Celeste." Laurel walked out into sunshine.

Chapter Twenty-One

LAUREL PLUCKED A FIRM ROUND BERRY. STARING AT THE HALF-FILLED container, she said, "It takes a lot of berries to fill a bucket. I wish they were bigger."

"Nothing good comes easy," Jean said.

Laurel selected another cranberry, examined the small maroon fruit, then set it on her tongue. When she chewed, its taut skin popped and tart juice filled her mouth. Laurel puckered. "Oh, these are sour."

Jean chuckled. "They're supposed to go in your bucket, not your mouth. They'll make good pies and jelly. I'll make a pie for tomorrow." She looked across the road at their home. "I can hardly believe we're moving in."

"How many do you want?" Laurel asked, knowing it would take most of the morning to get a substantial quantity.

"Well, we didn't pick many raspberries, and I'd still like to get some of the high-bush cranberries. Norma made jelly out of some. It's the best I've ever tasted." She eyed the large milking bucket she'd brought. "I'd really like to fill the bucket today. We can come back for more after we get settled."

Laurel frowned. She'd rather finish packing. They could move some of their things into the house. The berries would still be here in a couple of days.

"Come mid-winter, we'll be glad for these," Jean continued.

"I know, but we have lots more days to pick. Shouldn't we be packing?"

"We'll have time this afternoon, and a lot of it is already done." Her fingers deftly searching, Jean added, "Plus, we can't know when the weather will change. It's been so nice. I'd rather be out here in the sunshine than the rain. And there are currants and mossberries still to be picked." She moved to another bush. "It's September. We've already had frosty nights, and I thought I saw a skiff of fresh snow on the mountains this morning."

Laurel dropped more berries into her bucket, then studied Mr. Jenkins's cows just beyond the fence. They grazed contentedly. She'd been told that as long as the cows were at ease there were no bears nearby. The colonists had taken to watching cows and carrying rifles. They'd never had to deal with grizzlies before, and after several sightings and some horrible stories, they'd grown leery. "Have you or Daddy seen any more bears?"

"We did see one pretty close to the camp yesterday, but he wasn't interested in us. He was busy eating berries. The bears are fat and happy these days. There's plenty for them to eat. From what I've been told, they become real gluttons this time of year, getting ready for their winter sleep."

Laurel glanced around. "They eat a lot of berries."

Jean straightened, kneading the small of her back. She smiled at her daughter. "Laurel, I think this would go more quickly if you thought more about picking and less about bears."

"There's no harm in being cautious." Laurel added another handful to her pail. "I heard a couple of Mr. Jenkins's calves were killed."

"Those two were up in his far pasture," Jean said as if distance made a difference.

"Was it a bear?"

"That's enough bear talk. I don't know what killed them. Let's just finish here."

Laurel nodded, but before bending to her task, she glanced about once more just to make certain they were alone.

The following morning Mr. Jenkins and Mr. Prosser arrived at the Haspers' tent to help load and move the family. Drew Prosser had his pickup and Tom Jenkins his wagon. Adam and Robert were also there ready to lend a hand.

While the men loaded furniture, Laurel and her mother boxed up the last of the food, dishes, pots, pans, and other small items. After everything was loaded, Jean climbed into Drew's truck, holding Susie on her lap.

"Climb on in here," Drew called to Laurel.

Laurel glanced around. It was a beautiful day; the sun felt warm. "I think I'll walk."

"All right then. We'll see you there." Jean closed the door, and the truck pulled away leaving a cloud of dust.

"Hey, do you mind if I join you?" Robert asked, falling into step beside Laurel.

"No, I don't mind," Laurel lied. She'd hoped to be alone to enjoy the beauty and serenity of the valley.

"I bet you're excited. My mother and sisters can hardly wait. Next week it's our turn. Mom said she'd stop by tomorrow or the next day."

"That'll be nice," Laurel said, paying more attention to her surroundings than to Robert.

Drew's truck steered around Tom Jenkins's wagon. Adam stood in the back of the wagon. He glowered at Robert. "Hey, we could use some help," he called.

"I s'pose I ought to go with them." Robert tipped his hat to Laurel. "I'll see you at the house." He loped after the wagon, climbing inside while it was still moving. Bumping over dried ruts, it nearly tossed him out before he found a seat on a wheel well. He waved to Laurel.

Laurel slowed her steps, wanting to enjoy the solitude of the valley. Red and yellow leaves still clinging to their hosts shimmered beneath fall sunshine. The pungent smell of moss and ripening berries hung in the air, and clusters of tall slender stalks of vivid pink fireweed bent in the breeze.

When Laurel arrived at the cabin, Susie already sat in her high chair, a half-eaten cracker in hand. Boxes waiting to be unpacked sat on the kitchen table, and Jean was bent over a flour bin, a large sack of flour in hand. She straightened and looked at Laurel. Blowing a strand of hair out of her eyes, she said, "Oh, good. You're here. Could you help me?"

Laurel crossed to her mother and held the bin open while Jean finished emptying the sack. "I'm sorry. I should have ridden with you."

"No. That's fine. But I'm glad you're here now."

"What do you want me to do?"

Jean scanned the kitchen. "How about putting away the dishes. They're in the boxes on the table." Nodding at an upper cabinet to the right of the sink, she said. "Put them in that cupboard."

Will and Drew Prosser walked through the door, a bed frame balanced on their shoulders. "Jean, you said Laurel's things went in the upstairs east bedroom, right?" Will asked.

"Uh-huh."

The excitement of being in their home caught hold of Laurel. She wanted to see her room. "Can I go up and take a quick look?"

Wearing an understanding smile, Jean nodded.

Laurel followed the men up the stairs and into her room. Her box spring and mattress were resting on their sides against a wall.

"Let's set up this bed before we get her bureau," Will said. He looked at Laurel. "Where do you want it?"

"How about next to the chimney? That way I'll be closer to the heat during the winter."

"Good thinking," Drew said.

After putting the bed together, the men left, and Laurel was alone. She could hear Brian's chatter from his room directly across from hers. Sitting on the bed, she was happy to discover she could still see outside.

After awhile she joined her mother in the kitchen and went to work unpacking dishes and placing them in the cupboard. The men kept moving past them, carrying chairs, tables, dressers, rockers, lamps, and other odds and ends. When they were finished, they filed out.

Will stood in the kitchen, watching Jean and Laurel. "It's coming together."

"It is," Jean said with a weary but satisfied smile.

"We've got to get the icebox and washing machine. Won't be gone long. When we get back, we'll be hungry," he added with a grin.

"I'll get supper on. It'll be ready by the time you return." Jean gave Will a peck on the cheek. "Is the crib up?"

"Yep. It's in our room."

"Good. Susie's cranky and tired of being trapped in her highchair. I'll put her down for a nap." She laid a hand on her husband's arm. "Thank you."

Giving Jean a quick hug, Will headed outside.

Jean lay Susie in her crib and returned to the kitchen. Susie's crying could be heard coming from the bedroom. Dropping into a chair at the table, Jean rested her face in her hand. "She'll fall asleep soon."

"I made coffee," Laurel said. "Would you like some?"

"Sounds wonderful."

Laurel filled a cup and handed it to her mother, then filled another. Sitting across from her, Laurel gazed around the room. "The kitchen's nearly done. I like it. It already feels homey."

Jean sipped. "I like it, too, especially the light. I've never had a kitchen with two windows in it." Setting her cup on the table in front of her, she asked, "Did Brian and Luke go with your father?"

"Yes. In fact, the last time I saw Brian he was on Adam's shoulders. He likes Adam."

"He's a nice young man. I'm sorry to say I misjudged him at first."

"Why do you say that?"

"Well, at first he didn't seem to have much practicality or resourcefulness. He seemed shallow. But after the flood and going after that little girl the way he did—well, not everyone would have done that."

"Yeah, I suppose."

"And the way he's helped around here. He's a hard worker, and he acts like he really cares for Brian and the rest of us. He just seems to be a real nice young man."

"Yeah, I guess," Laurel said, not at all certain she agreed.

"I better get to that supper," Jean said, pushing herself to her feet. "Could you finish unpacking that last box while I see to the food?"

Laurel took another drink of coffee, stood, and opened the box. She lifted out a mixing bowl and unwrapped it. Running a hand along the outside of the well-used glazed earthenware, she said, "It's good to see these dishes again. Seems like years since we packed them." Laurel smiled softly. "I remember thinking life would never be right again." She dipped the bowl into water, rinsed it, then dried it. "Things have a way of changing."

By the time the men returned, the kitchen was in order and chicken simmered on the stove. While Drew and Robert moved the gas washing machine onto the back porch, Will and Adam lugged in the icebox, settling it against an outside kitchen wall.

"Mmm, something sure smells good," Will said. "What's for supper?"

Standing on tiptoe, Brian tried to peer into the pot on the stove. "What's cooking?"

Jean swirled the hot stew, then dipped out a little so Brian could see. "Chicken and dumplings. I just have to add the dumplings." After dropping in balls of dough, she replaced the lid. Looking at the men, she asked, "You're staying for supper, aren't you?"

"I'd like to, but Norma's expectin' me," Drew said. "Thanks much."

"I don't think Adele would appreciate it much if I couldn't make it home for supper." Tom smiled. "But thanks." He headed for the back door. "We'll probably drop by tomorrow."

"All right," Will said. "Thanks for all your help."

"Glad to do it." Tom and Drew disappeared out the door.

"You sure there's enough?" Robert asked.

"Absolutely."

"All right then. My mother isn't expecting me."

"Adam?" Jean asked.

"Sounds good. Thanks. Could I get a drink?"

"Sure," Laurel said, filling a glass and handing it to him. "Robert?"

"Yeah. My throat's dry. I could use a drink." Laurel filled another, and Robert took it. He gulped down half the glass. "That's good water," he said, handing back what was left. "I still haven't gotten used to having water anytime I want. It's like a miracle." He looked at Laurel. "Our well came in good."

"I heard," Laurel said.

"There'll be plenty of water. Even if I put another house on the place, there'll be enough."

Laurel hoped he wasn't counting on her being the one to share it with him.

Adam handed her his glass. "Can I get a refill?"

Laurel filled the glass and handed it to Adam. This time he drank slowly.

Lifting the lid on the pot, Will peered inside and sniffed the rising steam. "Smells good."

Jean grabbed the lid and set it back on the kettle. "You'll ruin the dumplings."

He smiled down at his wife, circled an arm around her waist, and pulled her close. "The dumplings will be just fine. No one makes them as good as you." He kissed her, then unexpectedly danced her around the room. She laughed and followed his lead.

Laurel studied Adam as he watched her parents play. His blue eyes were alight with admiration; his mouth curved in an appreciative smile.

He turned warm eyes on her. For a moment she met his gaze, then embarrassed, Laurel busied herself by turning away and dipping flour out of the bin. "Does the stew need thickening?" she asked.

"Whew," Jean said with a laugh, stepping out of Will's arms. "Let me check." She moved to the stove. Lifting the lid, she poked the dumplings, then carefully swirled the meal. "It could probably use a little. I'll take out the dumplings and you can finish."

"Laurel's already a fine cook," Will bragged to Robert.

"Will, did you remember the pies?" Jean asked.

"I thought you knew me better than that," he said, a twinkle in his eyes. "I'd never forget one of *your* pies. They're on the seat of the pickup."

"I'll get them," Laurel volunteered, happy for an escape.

The air was chilly. The sun had dipped behind the mountains, and the valley lay in shadow. Laurel stood on the porch a moment, breathing in the air and enjoying the sensation of cold on her throat and lungs. Heading for the truck, she heard the back door creak open, then thump closed.

Adam leaped off the porch. "I'll give you a hand."

"It's just two pies."

"I wouldn't want you to drop one," he teased. When they reached the truck, he opened the door and stood aside while Laurel retrieved one pie and handed it to him. He allowed his hand to rest on hers for a moment. "Did you bake these?"

Adam's touch unsettled Laurel. She quickly withdrew her hand. "I helped Mama. We picked the berries yesterday."

"They look good. So your father was right when he said you're a good cook."

"I do all right." Laurel grabbed the other pie. When she turned around, he was standing close and staring at her. Holding the pie against her chest, Laurel met his eyes. "Adam, is there something you want?"

A look of discomfort flickered across his face. He didn't say anything for a long moment, then finally he lightheartedly said, "Just thought I'd give you a hand. I told you." He turned and headed toward the house.

Confused, Laurel followed.

Jean set the kettle on the stove. "Supper's ready. Everyone sit down."

Luke and Will carried in chairs from the front room, and everyone took their places around the wooden table. Jean set Susie in her high chair and handed her a spoon. The little girl babbled, beating the spoon against the wooden tray.

"Smells awfully good, Mrs. Hasper," Robert said.

"Thank you. I hope it doesn't disappoint you."

"I'm sure it won't."

Luke leaned forward on his elbows. "Adam, I read the latest article you wrote for the paper. It was good, but I'll betcha some people will get in a snoot over it."

"I suppose. But I don't write to please people. I write news."

"I didn't read it. What's it about?" Will asked.

"It was great," Luke answered for Adam. "He talked about all the work we've done, the progress we're making, and how the farms are starting to take shape. He even talked about the lies some folks have been tellin'."

"I'm glad to hear the truth's getting out," Will said. "Sometimes it seems the world only wants to listen to lies."

"Well, I'm not so sure it's what the paper wanted or what people like to read, but it's the truth, and everyone ought to know. I'm hoping the paper likes the story enough to consider me for overseas work." Adam's eyes momentarily found Laurel's, then he looked at Will and flashed a grin. "*The Trib* may be looking for a way to get rid of me."

Jean set a pitcher of milk on the table. "You're going overseas?"

"Well, I don't know exactly when, but I want to go. I'd like to be a correspondent in Europe. It's an exciting time—lots of changes, something rousing to write about every day."

"It's dangerous though, isn't it?" Jean asked.

"I guess so, but a reporter has to go where the news is. And I've always wanted to travel."

Will leaned back in his chair. "What about that Hitler fella? According to what I've read, he's stirring up trouble."

"The American government won't let him go too far," Robert said. "They'll step in."

Adam leaned on the table. "I'm not so sure of that. But whatever happens, I want to be there to write about it."

"Well then, Adam, I hope you get your wish," Robert said, his tone caustic.

"This is a big day," Will cut in. He smiled and looked around the table. "Our first meal in our new house here in the Matanuska Valley. We've had our joys and our sorrows. One of us is gone." His eyes met Jean's. An exchange of grief and support passed between the two. He took her hand. "I'd like to pray before we begin."

Will bowed his head. Everyone did the same. Even Susie stopped banging her spoon and tried to copy the adults by pressing the palms of her hands together.

Will began, "Father, this is a remarkable day, and we thank you for it. It is truly a miracle that we are sitting here at this table in this house in this magnificent place. Not so long ago, it was just a dream. We praise you for making it real."

He paused. "This house is made of wood and stone, but you're here. You'll make it a place of love. You'll make it a home, a place where we can live and grow in the grace you've given. May it be a safe shelter for our children and for every person who walks through our door."

He stopped and glanced at those sitting around the table. "Father, as I said a moment ago, one of us is missing—Justin. We wish he were here to share this time with us." His voice broke. "But we're thankful he's in your presence."

Laurel fought tears. She could hear her mother sniffle.

"And Lord," Will continued, "our friend Adam said he'll be going off to Europe soon. We ask you to keep him in your care. Remind him of your constant presence. Keep your hand upon him."

Laurel glanced up and caught Adam's surprised and grateful expression. Quickly she closed her eyes.

"And, Father," Will continued, "bless my beautiful wife who's always stood beside me, helping to keep me strong. She's been a steady helpmate. I couldn't make it through life without her." He glanced at Jean, then said, "Amen."

Adam leaned his arms on the table and said, "Thank you for the prayer. I'll remember it."

"You're welcome." Will smiled. "Seems to me you've been around enough to be considered part of the family—and we always hold family in high regard."

Adam stared at Will. "I never had a family. Thank you."

Chapter Twenty-Two

THANKFUL TO LEAVE THE COLD, LAUREL AND HER FAMILY WALKED INTO THE community building. The room smelled of baked goods, roasted meat, cigar smoke, and women's perfume. Some people stood in clusters, chatting. A few couples stood alone, talking quietly. A handful of children hovered near a row of tables laden with food, while their mothers made an effort to keep their youngsters' hands away from the fare. Dodging people as well as tables and chairs, a group of boys kicked a ball back and forth.

"I guess these belong over there," Jean said, carrying a pan of biscuits to the food table. Laurel followed with a pot of beans, setting them on the table beside her mother's biscuits.

Norma Prosser joined them. "Hello, Jean. Laurel." She smiled and nodded at each of them. "How does it feel to be in your new house?"

"Wonderful! For a while it seemed we'd always live in a tent." Jean chuckled. "I would have made it around for a visit, but we've been canning. Will and Luke's fishing's kept us busy putting up salmon. And with all the rest of the canning we've had to do, we haven't had time for socializing."

"It's the same at our place. I've been meaning to come by, but . . ." Norma shrugged. "That's how it is this time of year."

"The root cellar's stocked with carrots, potatoes, and turnips, and the shelves are crowded with canned fruits and berries plus the canned salmon and other meats." Jean smiled. "It's real comforting to see all that God's provided for our first winter."

Scanning the table of food, Norma said, "Looks like a lot of us have been blessed." She lifted her eyebrows in an exaggerated way. "But, oh, the work—although I must say, my Polly's been a real help even though she's just fourteen."

Jean hugged Laurel around the waist. "Laurel too. I don't know what I'd do without her."

Laurel forced a smile, hoping it didn't look phony. Normally she wouldn't have minded spending time at home, but she'd been longing to return to Jessie's so she could continue working on Steward's notes. It was much more interesting than gardening and canning, and the extra money was welcomed. Now, with most of winter's preparations completed, she hoped to return to reading and transcribing.

While Jean and Norma talked about their latest sewing projects, children, and recipes, Laurel searched for Celeste. Her friend always knew the latest talk of the valley or world news or the latest gossip about the movies and their stars. She spotted blonde curls. "Mama, Celeste is here." She smiled at Norma. "It was good to see you again."

"Wonderful to see you," Norma said. "You go along and join your friend."

"Thank you." Laurel crossed the room.

Celeste saw her and turned on a bright smile. "Hi. I was hoping you'd be here." She hooked her arm through Laurel's. "In fact, I was counting on it. My father didn't want me to come. He's really mad. But I wanted to celebrate with my colonist friends. So here I am." She tipped her chin up to emphasize her defiance.

"Is your dad really mad?"

Celeste nodded.

"Why? Why does he hate us?"

"I don't think he actually hates you."

"He has a funny way of not hating," Laurel said sarcastically, then immediately felt badly for degrading Celeste's father. "I'm sorry. I don't mean to be cruel."

"I know. Dad's changed. He didn't always act like this. It's just been since my mother died."

"When he pulled Adam out of the river, I saw another side to your father. I'd hoped maybe we could be friends."

"My mother was everything to him." Celeste's eyes turned sad. "She was wonderful." She looked straight at Laurel. "You're lucky to have your mother."

"I know," Laurel said, wishing there were some way to take back the harsh words she'd said about Mr. Townsend.

Miram Dexter walked toward them. She wore white gloves, a twill skirt, and a blue velveteen blouse with a matching hat.

"I wonder why she's so dolled up," Celeste whispered.

Miram joined them and smiled demurely. "Why, hello. How are you?" she asked, her tight nervous voice nullifying her classy dress. She sniffled into a handkerchief.

"Good," Laurel said. "Your allergies still acting up?"

Dabbing at her nose, Miram nodded.

Laurel hoped she wouldn't have to spend too much time with the nervous woman but immediately felt guilty at her selfishness. Miram had few friends. She wasn't really a bad sort, just different.

"How have you been?" Celeste asked Miram.

"Fine, except for my allergies." She smoothed back dull brown hair. "Poor Mama's been in bed with an awful headache all day. I almost didn't get to come. She thought it improper for a young woman to go out unescorted. She's so old-fashioned." Miram giggled. "I finally convinced her it would be fine." She searched the crowd. "Have you seen Ed?"

"Ed who?" Celeste asked.

"Ed Ketchum. You know, he's tall and blond."

Laurel remembered the young man. He was a horrible person. Why would Miram ask about him? She might not be a beauty, but even Miram could find someone better than Ed Ketchum. She was too nice for a man like him.

As if reading Laurel's mind, Miram said, "Ed's really not such a bad guy. He can be very sweet."

Laurel couldn't imagine that the man who'd challenged her father on the ship and who'd partnered up with Felix Pettersson could be sweet. "Oh," she said. Hoping to change the subject, she asked Celeste, "So, how long do you think until the first snowfall?"

"Anytime. It's awfully cold." She rubbed her bare arms. "I wish they'd turn up the heat. I'm thinking about putting my coat back on."

Will Hasper climbed the steps to a small stage at the front of the room. He'd been asked to be the speaker for the night's social. Standing with his hands in his pockets, he looked out over the crowd, waiting for people to stop talking. When they didn't, he raised his arms and called, "Good evening. Welcome." Gradually the room quieted. Will repeated, "Welcome. It's good to see so many of you here.

"The months have passed quickly. Back in May when we left our homes and headed north, most of us didn't know one another. Now we're neighbors and friends. Together we've accomplished a great deal, and we have much to be thankful for." People clapped and cheered. Will smiled. "We have a long winter ahead of us, but from what I'm hearing tonight, it sounds like we're ready for it. However, in the months ahead we need to remember the kinship we have and be ready to help one another. Together we'll make this colony a success." Cheers rose from the crowd.

When the people calmed, a man called out, "Don't forget there's still a lot of work to be done. The school and post office aren't finished. And we can use all the volunteers we can get."

"Did you hear that?" Will asked. "Our kids need a place for learning. And if you talk to our postmistress, Mrs. Wilkerson, she'll tell you how badly we need a post office. Guess there's not enough room for all the mail coming and going."

He stopped and gazed at the crowd. "But tonight's not about what we've still got to do. It's about celebrating all we've done. Please enjoy the good food. And I've been told there'll be music and dancing after we eat. First let's thank God for the food." Will bowed his head and said a short blessing, then looked out at those gathered and said, "Enjoy."

Laurel joined the food line along with Miram and Celeste. They moved around the table, filling their plates with a variety of family favorites—fried chicken, hot potato salad, biscuits, rolls, carrot salad, relishes, and wild meats. An assortment of cakes, pies, and cookies was at the end of the table.

The three young ladies found a table and sat. Miram barely found time to eat. She talked incessantly about trivial things, endlessly sniffled into her handkerchief, and in her strange way rearranged her glasses by crinkling up her right cheek to lift them. Laurel found her tiresome but tried to focus on what the woman was saying.

"So, my mother and I thought it would be best to use the tulip pattern. What do you think?" Miram asked.

"Tulips would be perfect," Celeste answered, then quickly focused on Laurel and asked, "So, Laurel, how does it feel to be settled on your farm?"

"Everyone keeps asking me that." She took a bite of carrot salad. "It's wonderful not to be crowded into that tent. I have my own room upstairs." She lowered her voice. "But I have to admit, I don't like living with an outhouse. I can't imagine what it'll be like in the middle of winter."

"I thought you had a chemical toilet," Miram said. "We do."

"There are seven . . . I mean six of us." A pang of grief hit Laurel. "Anyway, it comes in handy for middle-of-the-night trips, but for all day, every day?"

"You'll get used to an outhouse," Celeste said. "Well, maybe not." With a tilt of her head, she flipped curls off her shoulder. "It's all I've ever known, but I still don't like it." She grinned. "Just don't forget to watch out for moose when you're making a morning trip to the facility."

"Really? Why?" Miram asked, her voice shriller than usual.

"They're not usually a problem, but you've still got to give them a wide berth. You never know when one might be in a sour mood. And during the rut, they're real nasty."

"Hello, ladies," Robert said, planting himself beside Laurel and setting a cup of coffee and a plate piled with food in front of him.

"Hi, Robert," Celeste said, turning on her brightest smile.

He nodded at her, then turned to Laurel. "Haven't seen you since the day you moved in. How do you like it?" He took a bite of a biscuit.

Laurel looked at Celeste and Miram. "See, I told you that's all anyone asks." The girls chuckled, and Laurel turned to Robert. "I love it. But there's still a lot of work to do before the snow falls. The barn isn't finished yet, and we've got livestock that'll need shelter before long. One of our milk cows is nearly ready to calve, and we don't want it to become food for the wolves or bears."

"I heard Mr. Jenkins lost a couple calves to bears," Robert said, finishing his biscuit.

"How awful." Miram snuffled into her handkerchief. "I really don't like this wilderness living."

"Where did you live before?" Celeste asked.

"We had a dairy farm in Minnesota, but we lived close to town. We never had problems with wild animals, except maybe a fox or opossum getting at the chickens. But here . . ." She raised her eyebrows dramatically. "Why just the other day we had to stop for a big moose that was standing in the middle of the road. He wouldn't budge." Sounding indignant, Miram continued, "We had to wait for him. Imagine that."

Robert laughed. "I'm out scouring the woods for a moose, can't find one, and you nearly run one over." Shaking his head, he stabbed a piece of meat and put it in his mouth. "Life just isn't fair." He smiled. "I love the taste of moose." He took another bite, then stood. "In fact, I think I'll get me a little more before it's gone." Plate in hand, he walked away from the table.

Almost immediately, Adam took Robert's place. He had a cup of coffee in his hands. "Evening, ladies. I hope you're having a good time."

Miram blushed and nodded.

Celeste smiled. "Hi, Adam. We're having a great time. But I'm itchin' for some music. I love to dance. We don't get much opportunity around here."

Adam smiled. "Save me a dance."

"I will."

Laurel leaned away from Adam. He was sitting too close.

"What do you do for fun around here?" he asked. "Mostly all I've seen is work."

"Sometimes we go to the movies. They show films in Palmer. We don't get the new movies though. It takes a while for them to make their way up here." Pushing her plate aside, Celeste leaned on the table. "Did you see *Cleopatra?*"

Robert rejoined the group. "I saw *Cleopatra.* It was good," he said.

"I thought it was so exciting. And Claudette Colbert was wonderful!"

"Sounds like I missed a good movie," Adam said, taking a sip of coffee. "What else do you do for fun here?"

"Sometimes we go swimming, and of course, fishing. During the winter people skate, sled, and ski. And we have dog sled races. They're fun, but just for the men. Women aren't allowed." Celeste scowled. "I always thought that was unfair, but the men say dog sledding is too dangerous for women; plus it's too hard for us to handle the dogs. I think it's hogwash. I've done some mushing. It's not so hard. Someday I'll race."

The lilt of a fiddle carried across the room. A man with a heavy beard and knit cap stood in front. His fingers flew up and down the instrument's neck, while his bow whisked across the strings. "How wonderful!" Miram said. "I love the fiddle!"

Plates were quickly cleared away and stacked. People gathered around the musician. His bow hummed one tune after another. Onlookers clapped, and those who knew the words, sang. Wearing a smile, the man kept playing—songs such as "Ain't She Sweet," "Happy Days Are Here Again," and "I'm Looking Over a Four-Leaf Clover." The clapping and singing grew more exuberant. Some people danced.

The fiddler took a short break, guzzled a glass of cider, then returned to playing. This time the bow hummed a slow, soft melody. Two men joined the fiddler. One had a bass and the other a saxophone. People quieted, some swayed to the music "With a Song in My Heart."

Several couples moved to the middle of the room where they could dance. "I guess we ought to get out of the way," Celeste said, walking to the wall. Laurel and Miram followed. The three stood and watched the dancers. Celeste glanced at Robert, who now stood off a way. "I wish he would ask me to dance," she whispered to Laurel.

Ed Ketchum stepped up to Miram. Laurel barely recognized him. His unruly hair had been slicked down, and instead of ragged clothing, he wore a suit. He was clean and smelled of aftershave. Beads of sweat glistened on his upper lip. "Would you like to dance?"

Miram's face lit up, and she held out a gloved hand. "Why, I'd love to." She cast a coy smile at Celeste and Laurel, then walked with Ed to the dance floor.

"Isn't that something?" Celeste said. "I'd never guess—those two."

Adam joined Celeste and Laurel. "Looks like Ed cleaned up for the festivities," he said with a grin.

Laurel nodded. "He looks better than I thought he could, almost like a gentleman."

"Laurel," Robert said from behind her. She turned and faced him. "Would you like to dance?"

Laurel couldn't refuse without embarrassing him. Besides, she liked dancing. "Of course. I'd love to."

He smiled, took her elbow, and guided her onto the dance floor. The music stirred something inside Laurel, and she found herself enjoying the feeling of being escorted by Robert. Tall and handsome, he was a better-than-average partner. She could do worse. He held her close, but not too close, and Laurel was surprised at his confidence and skill.

They didn't speak, and Laurel wondered if they ought to be chatting. Other couples were. Oddly, she couldn't think of anything to say. She caught sight of Celeste and Adam dancing on the other side of the room. Celeste was smiling and talking. Adam laughed. Laurel felt a pang of jealousy.

The song ended, and Robert escorted her back to where she'd been standing. "Thank you," he said politely.

"Thank you. You're a very good dancer."

"Would you like something to drink?"

"Yes. That sounds good."

"There's punch on the table. I'll get us some." Robert walked away.

"I'm in the Mood for Love" resonated from the musical trio. Laurel leaned against the wall, swaying slightly.

Adam joined her. "That's a nice piece of music."

Laurel nodded.

"Would you like to dance?"

She didn't know how to answer. For some reason the idea of being in Adam's arms frightened her. He held out his hand. Without a word, Laurel placed hers in his. He led her to the dance floor, placed his arm around her waist, and pulled her close.

"You're tense," he said. "Relax."

"No, I'm not. Not really." Laurel forced a smile. *How stupid. Of course you're tense. He can feel it.* She loosened her hold on his hand and let her arm go slightly limp.

Adam smiled and his eyes warmed. Laurel liked his eyes—deep blue and passionate. He seldom let anyone see his tender side, but Laurel had seen it.

"I'll be leaving in the morning."

She stiffened again. "Leaving? So soon?"

"I have to get back to work. I've been stalling."

"Oh." Laurel felt her mood whither. "I hope you have a good trip back—no more rough seas."

"I'll be flying," he chuckled, "We had quite a trip up, didn't we?"

"Yes. It's hard to believe the months have gone so quickly." Laurel didn't want him to leave, but she couldn't tell him. "So, what will you do in Chicago?"

"Oh, just the usual—write local news. Hopefully they'll send me to Europe soon."

"Europe. It's so far away."

"You sound sad."

"I do? I guess I'm just tired." Laurel wasn't lying. She did feel tired. She wanted to go home to her room where she could close the door, turn out the light, and forget she'd ever met Adam Dunnavant.

"I'll probably be back next fall to finish the story. I talked with my editor, and he thinks it would be a good idea to finish it off with the colony's first big harvest." He scanned the room. "I'll miss this place, the people." His eyes settled on Laurel.

She thought they held a tinge of sadness. "I hope I'll see you then."

"You will."

The music ended, but Adam didn't release Laurel immediately. Slowly, he relaxed his arms but held onto her hand. "I'm going to miss you. Will you write?"

"If you give me your address."

"I left it at the post office."

"OK. Then I'll write. Will you?"

"Yes."

She could feel the pressure of his hand on hers and didn't want to let go.

Adam bent and rested his cheek against her hair. "I wish I could stay," he whispered, then brushed Laurel's forehead with his lips. "Good-bye." He turned and walked away.

Chapter Twenty-Three

LAUREL STUDIED THE NOTES IN FRONT OF HER. THEY WERE HARDER TO decipher than she'd expected. Transcribing would come later. For now Laurel had the task of sorting Steward's observations, which was difficult enough. "Are those the notes on the Athabascans?"

"Yes."

Laurel placed the folder with the others and returned to sorting. There were notes on native Alaskans, wildlife, plants, animals, topography, history, and more. When she'd accepted the position from Jessie, she had no idea the mountain of work that awaited her. There were hundreds of papers to be organized and cataloged. Every wall, including two bedroom walls, was crowded with books and notes. The notes in the bedroom had been forgotten when they'd evacuated Jessie. *Thank goodness the water didn't reach them,* Laurel thought.

She scanned the room. The papers had lain untouched for years. Disturbing the mounds of records had raised a dust cloud; a musty smell still hung in the air from the water that had creeped inside during the flood. Laurel wished it wasn't so cold so the windows could be opened to allow in fresh air. She watched her new friend lower herself onto the wooden chair in front of the oak desk. "Jessie, how did your husband get all this information?"

Her plain but serene face brightened with a smile. She hadn't bothered to put up her hair. Parted in the middle, it hung straight down on both sides, gray strands hanging in disarray. On Jessie, the wrinkles and silvery hair looked appealing and appropriate.

"Steward spent the better part of his life discovering Alaska. He loved research—not the kind you get in books, but the kind that requires leg work. He was devoted to it. When the college asked him to do this, he jumped at the chance."

She rifled through a stack in front of her and shook her head. "It's just a pity he didn't also relish organizing it." Gazing at the papers in front of her, she continued, "He expected me to do the sorting out, but I traveled with him most of the time; plus I had my painting to do. I just never seemed to have the time."

Her eyes took on a faraway look. "We traveled all through the state, even out on the Aleutians and way up north to Barrow. Steward talked to folks, researched history records in church archives, libraries, and even searched through people's attics. On occasion he visited grave-yards. Sometimes it wasn't easy to convince the natives to share their traditions and family stories, but Steward had a way about him. He'd wait patiently, make friends, and gradually build a person's trust." She smiled. "He made a lot of friends."

"It sounds interesting and exciting. I'd love to do something like that."

"It had its moments. We experienced discovery and danger. Some of our ocean excursions were challenging. It wasn't good enough for Steward to study a *baidarka;* he had to travel in one."

"What's a baidarka?"

"It's a long, narrow boat with two round seats cut in midway, and it's propelled by a paddle. The traveler has to lower himself through the holes and sit with his legs straight out in front of him. It's not very comfortable."

"Oh."

Jessie grinned. "Steward studied the bears too. We had more than one close encounter while he was trying to establish *true* bear behavior. He always believed they'd been unfairly judged, so we spent a lot of time with them. For the most part, they didn't want trouble, but we did meet up with a few bad tempers." She chuckled. "I discovered I could climb a tree faster than I ever imagined."

Jessie stood. Balancing a stack of papers, she carried them to a shelf and set them beside another pile. "When we started this work, we had no idea how big the project was. It was like an endless treasure hunt. One thing led to another."

Her eyes rested on an oil painting of a field of wildflowers. "We tried to photograph the flowers and plants, but we couldn't record the colors.

That's when I started painting." Her expression softened. "Those were truly glorious days. I remember sitting among God's creation on sunlit mornings, trying to duplicate on canvas what he'd crafted with his own hands. I could never do them justice. Each flower is exceptional and distinctive. God's paintbrush is far superior to mine."

"Your paintings are beautiful," Laurel said.

Jessie returned to the desk. "Thank you, dear. I still go out and paint occasionally, but my bones are getting old. I have to stick closer to home." She started to drink from her cup, but it was empty. "I need more tea. Would you like some?"

"Yes. Thank you," Laurel said, realizing her throat was parched. Jessie hobbled across the room. Laurel propelled herself out of her chair. "Why don't you let me do that?" She took the cup from Jessie and walked into the kitchen.

"I'm fine, really," Jessie said, following. Laurel refilled the cup and handed it to her elderly friend. "Thank you, dear."

Laurel poured golden liquid into her own cup, added sugar, and returned to her place at the desk.

Jessie lowered herself into the overstuffed chair and sipped her tea. "I miss my Steward. He was such a dear. His mind was always so much sharper than mine. But his drive to discover new things was so strong it sometimes blotted out reason. He got into a few scrapes." Her eyes sparkled. "I never had his depth of commitment or his knowledge. Even so, he never left me out. He always asked for my opinion." She settled back, getting comfortable in the chair. "The long dark winters didn't seem so long then."

"Do you have children?" Laurel asked.

"No, God never blessed us in that way."

"I'm sorry," Laurel said, not knowing exactly how to respond and wishing she hadn't asked.

"No. Don't be. Steward and I had a wonderful life. I don't know if we could have done all that we did if we'd had children. I believe God knows what's best for each of us. Not having children was his decision. I can accept that." She offered Laurel a sad smile. "Although, I must admit it was difficult in the beginning. We were young and had planned on a family. But I wouldn't trade a moment of my life."

Laurel wondered what it would be like to love someone deeply the way Jessie loved Steward and her mother loved her father. Her mind wandered to Adam. She missed him terribly.

After their last evening together, she'd been confused about her feelings. Adam seemed superficial, driven to prove himself, and bent on success at any cost. He was a flirt and obviously considered relationships between men and women to be some kind of game. He wasn't a man to be taken seriously.

However, when he'd started spending time with her family, Laurel had glimpsed another side of him. He was hardworking, willing to help whenever needed, funloving, and seemed to genuinely care about her and her family. Her feelings about him had changed. There was something very appealing about Adam, something she loved about him.

"So, how are the hunting and fishing going for your father and brother?" Jessie asked, cutting in to Laurel's thoughts. "It's such a shame they had to pay for their licenses." She shook her head. "Seems unfair to me."

"Luke worked hard to earn the money, but it was a good experience for him. The hunting's going well. They've brought home a Dall sheep and two moose, and they go fishing almost every day. We have a lot of canned salmon, and we smoked some of it. Alex, Luke's friend, showed us how. He's been teaching Luke and my father some of the native ways of hunting and fishing."

"Is that Alex Lawson?"

"Uh-huh."

"He's a fine boy. I like his family too. They're good people. It's so sad though. They haven't had an easy go of it—with no father in the house the last three years and the grandmother needing extra care."

"What happened to their father?"

"Douglas Lawson died in a fishing accident." Jessie set her tea on a small table beside the chair. "He was caught in an outgoing tide."

"Really?"

"Cook Inlet can have huge tide changes. They sometimes rise or fall as much as thirty-eight feet. Douglas got tangled in a net and was dragged overboard. The tide swept him away before anyone could do anything. He was never found."

"How awful," Laurel said, her sympathy for her two native friends expanding. "Alex told us his father was Scottish."

"That's right. He came to Alaska looking for adventure and fell in love with a native woman, Alex and Mattie's mother. It happens a lot."

Laurel glanced out the window. "It's snowing!" Setting her papers aside, she walked to the door and opened it. Snow and cold swirled into the room. After holding out her hand to catch a few flakes, she shut the door.

"It's about time. We've usually had our first snowfall long before this." Jessie rose from her chair and crossed to the window. Standing with arms folded across her waist and a contented expression, she gazed at the world, which was quickly turning white. "It's really coming down. You ought to head for home. Around here you can never tell how bad it's going to get."

Laurel scanned the room. "I still have so much work to do."

"It will be here when you get back," Jessie said with a grin. "I'd feel better if you left."

"All right." Laurel tidied up the pages she'd been working on, then pulled on her coat, drawing the hood tightly around her face and pushing her hands into gloves. "I love the snow." She opened the door. Stepping onto the porch, she said, "I'll see you tomorrow."

"All right, dear. But I don't want you walking over here if the weather's still bad. Now keep bundled; frostbite can get you before you know it."

"I'll be careful," Laurel promised and closed the door. In spite of her heavy coat, cold blew down her neck. She pulled her hood closer around her face. Fresh snow squeaked beneath her boots and swirled around her face, making her blink. Keeping her head down, she walked as fast as the slick snow allowed.

Cold and tired, she was grateful to see her driveway. Smoke rose from the chimney, and Laurel imagined the warmth waiting for her inside. She headed toward the house, then spotted the apple seedling bending beneath the weight of new snow. "Oh, no." She'd meant to protect it but hadn't made the time. If she didn't do something, it would die.

Laurel headed for the barn. Pulling the door open, she stepped into quiet and near darkness. She waited a few moments for her eyes to adjust to the gloom, then searched the cluttered interior for something to shelter the seedling. An empty wooden keg stood against one wall.

She loaded the container into a wheelbarrow, then steered it to a pile of wood chips her father had saved when he'd planed timber for the house. Grabbing a shovel, she filled the barrel with shavings, then, straining to lift the cart, she wheeled it toward the open barn door. As she stepped into the storm, wind and cold hit her. Shoving the rusty metal wheel through deepening snow, she headed for the stream bank. Cold air burned her lungs.

Be careful of frostbite, Jessie's words echoed. Laurel stopped, cupped gloved hands over her face, and blew warmth into the air pocket. Then, gripping the metal handles, she pushed through the snow. The wheel thumped into a deep rut and tipped the cart, spilling out its contents.

"Oh, no." Laurel grabbed the keg, set it upright, and dropped to her knees, scooping woodchips back into the barrel. When she'd refilled it, she righted the wheelbarrow, then tried to lift the container. It was too heavy. Immediately realizing her mistake, Laurel berated herself for the foolish error. She should have put the keg in first, then filled it.

"Laurel, let me help you!" Jean called over the howling wind. "Why didn't you come and get someone?" She grabbed one side of the barrel.

Gratitude and relief flooded Laurel. She took hold of the other side, and together they lifted the container into the cart. This time Jean held it steady while Laurel pushed.

When they got to the tree, Laurel and her mother carefully removed the snow that weighed down the seedling. It still drooped, but Laurel held it upright while her mother piled shavings around the base and around its fragile limbs. Together mother and daughter set the barrel over the seedling, fixing it in place.

"That should do it," Laurel said.

Her mother nodded. "We need to get you warmed up. I'll take this back to the barn. You go inside. I'll be right there."

Laurel was too cold to argue. "All right," she said, heading for the house and huddling against the snow and wind. She knocked her boots free of snow, pulled open the back door, and stepped inside. Warmth and the smell of fresh baked bread greeted her. Pulling off her coat and gloves, she hung them just inside the door.

A moment later the door opened, and cold swept inside along with her mother. Jean examined Laurel's face, ears, and hands for frostbite.

"Why didn't you get someone to help you?" she asked again, stripping off her coat and gloves. She hung them beside Laurel's.

"I don't know. I saw the tree and thought I could do it."

"It was foolish. You have to think, Laurel, if you want to stay alive here." Her voice was sharp.

"I know. I'm sorry, Mama."

"Well, as long as you're all right I suppose it's a good lesson. You're lucky you have no frostbite." She stepped into the kitchen and stared out the window. "The storm blew in all of a sudden. I hope your father and brother are all right."

"I'm sure they're fine. Winter storms aren't new to them."

"Yes, but we don't know what to expect here."

Laurel warmed herself at the stove. "It smells good. How long until supper?"

"Not long. There's a letter for you." Jean nodded toward the table.

"A letter? From whom?"

"Adam."

Laurel's heart leaped, and she nearly skipped to the table, snatching up the envelope. She started to open it, then decided she'd rather read it in private. "I'll read it in my room," she said, hurrying up the stairs.

Closing her bedroom door, she sat on the bed, took a deep breath, and tore open the envelope. Two newspaper articles written by Adam fell out. She set them aside and started reading.

"Dear Laurel," it began, "I'm sorry I didn't write sooner, but I've been very busy. Just as I'd hoped, the paper sent me overseas. I'm sitting here at my desk looking out over a London street. I can hardly believe my good fortune."

Laurel's heart sank. *London? That's so far away.* She continued reading.

"This is a fascinating place. In so many ways it's like America; but at the same time, it's different. There's a lot of history here. One of the articles I sent tells you about it. The people are friendly but different from Americans; I would say more standoffish. Several other U. S. correspondents are here, so I have American companionship—sometimes more than I'd like.

"I plan on visiting some neighboring countries. They're close, usually less than a day's travel. It's not so difficult getting around here. Trains take you most anywhere you want to go."

Laurel had never thought much about traveling overseas, but now she wondered what it would be like to see the world. For a moment she imagined herself alongside Adam, touring Paris, Marseilles, and Amsterdam.

"I've been reading Adolf Hitler's book, *Mein Kampf.* I shudder as I read. He's a madman. He considers people of any race other than blue-eyed and fair-skinned to be inferior, especially Jews. He intends to take over the world. He's already set up censorship over radio, films, and books in Germany. Jews have lost all rights as citizens, and any churches that preach against Nazi ideals are persecuted and their ministers imprisoned.

"There's talk of war. With Hitler as Fuhrer and Germany's buildup of arms, it seems only a matter of time. I don't believe the countries of Europe can stand against his forces. The United States will have to step in.

"Alaska and your magnificent valley look so good from here. I miss it—the peace and beauty. I look forward to visiting next summer. I wish it weren't so far from here to there, but this has been a good move for my career. Nothing holds me back now. I'm on my way."

Laurel let the letter rest in her lap. She wished he hadn't written. She didn't want to know about a possible war or that Adam's life was taking place on the other side of the world or that he planned to stay. Clearly, Adam's plans didn't include her.

She let the letter drop to the bed and crossed to the mirror. Picking up a brush, she pulled it through her thick auburn hair. "I'm acting like a schoolgirl," she told herself. "Adam never told me he cared for me."

A knock sounded at the door. "Would you like some soup and hot bread?" Jean called from the other side.

"Come in, Mama."

Jean opened the door and walked in.

"I'm not very hungry," Laurel said, setting the brush on the bureau.

"Is everything all right? Has something happened to Adam?"

"He's fine. He's in Europe." Laurel felt tears threatening and sat on the bed.

Jean sat beside her. "I know you miss him. I can understand. He's a good man."

Laurel rested her cheek against her mother's shoulder. "He's so far away," she whispered, sorrow spreading through her.

Chapter Twenty-Four

WILL OPENED THE BACK DOOR. A PIE IN ONE HAND, HE HELD THE DOOR FOR Jessie with the other as she stepped onto the back porch. Snow and cold blew inside.

"Brrr," Jessie said, brushing snow from her coat.

Will followed her. "If this keeps up, we'll be weathered in. It's a cold one."

"Jessie," Laurel said, meeting her friend and giving her a hug. "I'm so glad you're here."

Jessie unbuttoned her coat. "I was beginning to think we'd never make it." She took off the heavy coat. "Is this where you want it?" she asked, holding up the coat toward the hooks on the wall.

"Yep."

Resting an arm around Laurel's waist, Jessie walked into the kitchen. "My, it smells good in here."

Brian kneeled on a wooden chair and rested his elbows on the table. "That's cause Mama's been cookin' all day," he said proudly, "but there's no turkey. We got moose, rabbit, sweet potatoes, and—"

"All right, Brian, that's enough," Jean said, wiping her hands on her cotton apron. She took Jessie's hands and squeezed them gently. "I'm so glad you could come."

"It's an honor to be included in your family's celebration, especially on such a special day—your first Thanksgiving in Alaska."

Carrying the pie, Will followed the women into the kitchen. "It's blistering cold out there, and the temperature's still dropping. This could be a bad one." He handed the pie to Jean. "From Jessie," he said with a smile.

"It looks wonderful. What kind is it?"

"Lowbush cranberry. I got the recipe from one of the old-timers who came up long before Steward and me. I've been using it since my first summer. It's never failed me."

"I'll set it up here." Jean placed it in the stove's warming closet. "Can I get you anything? Coffee or tea?"

"A cup of tea does sound good. Might warm me up a bit." Jessie peeked into the front room, then sat at the kitchen table. "You've made this into a real nice home."

"Thank you," Jean said.

"We have three bedrooms—two upstairs and one down," Brian bragged.

"And we have a washing machine on our back porch."

Jessie smiled at the boy. "Your daddy must be a good carpenter."

"He is."

Steps sounded from the staircase, and a moment later Luke walked into the kitchen. "Hi, Jessie. Good to see you."

"Luke, how are you?"

"Good. Been doin' a lot of hunting."

"Yeah, he shot the rabbit we're eatin' today," Brian said.

"So, you're a pretty good shot?" Jessie asked.

"Not bad. Alex has been giving me some tips. He's got a lot more experience than me. He's gonna show me and Dad how to run a trapline."

"Good idea. There's always a market for furs."

Jean set a cup of tea on the table in front of Jessie. "Would you like sugar?"

"Yes. Thank you." Jessie scanned the room. "You've done really well for yourselves. You can be proud of your accomplishments. It's not easy to move to a new home and start over, especially one in the wilderness."

"I wish everyone felt like you," Laurel said, sitting at the end of the table. "Some of the homesteaders still don't think we can make it and want us to leave."

Jean set a bowl of sugar and a spoon on the table.

Jessie dipped out a half teaspoon of sugar and sifted it into her cup. Stirring, she said, "Not everyone feels like that, and more are coming around every day. Don't give up."

Laurel nodded. Ray Townsend, however, seemed to be getting worse. Celeste now had to make excuses to see her.

"Robert's here!" Brian shouted, running for the back door. He flung it open wide and jumped into his big friend's arms.

Robert picked up the little boy and threw him over his shoulder like a sack of potatoes. "Howdy, young man. Are you still full of goose feathers?"

Brian giggled and kicked his feet.

Joanna carried a pie. "Mama thought you might like this," she said, handing the pastry to Jean.

"Thank you." She smelled the warm pie. "Mincemeat?"

"Yep. I helped bake it," thirteen-year-old Veronica said, joining the group in the kitchen. "Hope you like it." She smiled, brown eyes sparkling and a deep dimple creasing her right cheek.

"I'm sure we will." Jean set the pie in the warmer alongside Jessie's.

Patricia Lundeen walked in, hung up her coat, then greeted every one of the Haspers with a friendly hug. She smiled, plump cheeks red from the cold. "I'm awfully glad we live close. I'd hate to think what it would be like to travel far in this weather."

"You girls go play and stay out of trouble," Patricia cautioned.

Sixteen-year-old Joanna flung a dark braid off her shoulder. "Mama, we're not babies."

"Oh, of course, I forgot for a moment," Patricia said with a wink at Jean.

The women settled at the table while the men headed for the barn. "What is it that men do in barns anyway?" Jessie asked.

Laurel opened a jar of string beans. "I've no idea, but they spend hours doing it."

"I think they talk about farming and politics. It's a place to get away from the women." Jean sprinkled brown sugar over a pan of sweet potatoes. With a wicked smile, she said, "I splurged and bought marshmallows. We'd decided to buy only necessities, but this is a special occasion."

"Oh, I know what you mean," Patricia said. "We're trying to be careful, too, but our debt is still growing faster than we planned."

"Daddy will love the marshmallows," Laurel said, hoping to reassure her mother.

Jean slid the sweet potatoes onto the oven rack beside the meat.

Heat and the aroma of roasting moose and rabbit drifted through the room.

"Oh, that smells heavenly," Jessie said. "My mouth is watering, and my stomach's growling."

A gust of wind shook the house, moaning as it blew beneath the eaves. "Sounds like it's getting worse," Patricia said a little nervously. "I heard we're supposed to have a hard winter. Makes me uneasy. I don't know what to expect." She finished peeling a carrot and set it in a pot.

"Winter can be rough," Jessie said. "Some years we had snow up to the rooftops. Sometimes we got very little snow, but then ended up with real cold temperatures. I'll take the snow any day."

Jean sifted flour into a bowl, added baking powder and salt, then mixed in lard, eggs, and milk. "I'm sure we'll be fine. These are good, solid houses. The pantry is full, and so is the root cellar."

"I'm sure you're right," Patricia said. "I'm probably worrying over nothing. That's my way."

After patting out the dough, Jean cut it into hefty biscuits. Setting them on two baking sheets, she opened the oven door and checked the roasting game. "The meat's done. All we have to do now is wait on the sweet potatoes, and cook the carrots and biscuits."

"Here are the carrots," said Jessie, handing Jean the pot.

Covering the vegetables with water, Jean placed a lid on the pan and set it on the stove to cook. "Laurel, could you set the table?" She added wood to the fire. "I'll check on those men."

"Sure, Mama."

An extra leaf was placed in the table, chairs were brought from the living room, and the food was set out. Will sat at the head of the table. "A real feast," he said as everyone found a place to sit. He looked at the expectant faces about the table. "We have much to be thankful for. I thought that on this special Thanksgiving we should each share our gratitude." He squeezed Jean's hand. "Would you like to begin, and I'll finish?"

Jean smiled and nodded. "There's so much." Her eyes filled with tears. She paused, trying to compose herself. "I thank God for my new home, and for my family. I'm grateful we're all able to be here, all except Justin." She glanced at Will. "But I praise God for taking such good care of our little boy. I'm sure this is a special Thanksgiving for him too."

Using a corner of her apron, she dabbed at her eyes. "There's no place sweeter than in the arms of Jesus. And I'm sure that's where he is."

Heads nodded; several shed tears.

Luke was next. "I'm thankful for this terrific place to live. I love it here. And I love to hunt and fish. I'm thankful for that."

Joanna smiled shyly, then said, "I'm glad we get to live on our new farm and that we're safe."

Veronica glanced at her mother. "I thank God for giving me a wonderful mother."

Eyes shimmering, Patricia squeezed her daughter's hand. "I praise God for all my children and for the wonderful comfort they've been to me since their father died and for everything they do for me. I couldn't have made it without all of you. And I thank God for giving Robert a heart so like his father's. He had a vision of what could be, and that's why we're here."

Jessie looked thin and small beside Patricia. She didn't speak right away but glanced at each person sitting around the table, her face serene as usual. "The Lord knows I've been on my own for many years, and sometimes it's lonely. But he always brings special people into our lives when we need them. Since I met Laurel, I've been given a whole new family, and I'm thankful for her and for all of you."

Robert was next. He glanced at his sisters and mother, then smiled at Laurel. "I'm grateful for special friends, too, and for a new beginning and the promise that God will see us through, no matter what hardship we face."

Brian grinned up at Robert, then at his mother. "I guess I'm most grateful for good food and for my daddy who hunts so we can have it and my mama who cooks." Jean and Will both smiled.

It was Laurel's turn next. She'd been trying to sort out what she should say. She had so much to be thankful for. She cleared her throat. "I thank God that I had a change of heart about Alaska. I'm grateful he gave me what I needed instead of what I wanted. I didn't know when I left Wisconsin that I'd love this place. I fought and kicked, but God kept his hand on me, and now this is home, and I thank him for his wisdom and his steadfastness."

Will bowed his head, and the others did the same. "I have so much to thank you for, Father—my family, this farm, good friends, a new beginning, and plenty to eat, but most of all, I want to thank you for your promise of a future. You always give us hope. The world says no, but you say yes; the world says quit, but you say carry on; the world says justice, but you say grace. You are our courage and strength. We cannot fail with you at our side."

He paused. "Lord, you know there are two special people who aren't with us today. Our Justin is with you." He was silent a moment. "And then there is Adam. He's across the sea in a place where frightening changes are taking place and maybe even war. We ask you to keep your hand on him and bring him back to this valley where he belongs."

Laurel looked up. *Where he belongs?* She glanced at her father. His head was bowed, eyes closed.

"And, Father, please continue to hold each of us in your hand; help us to value and respect one another. I think especially about the people in this valley who are filled with fear and hate. Show them a better way, Father. And help each of us to seek you in all we do. Amen." He looked up and smiled. "It's been a good year. We've worked hard. I'm hungry." Spearing a piece of meat, he held out his hand for a plate and asked, "Who's first?"

The meal was filled with compliments, good conversation, and laughter. After the feast, the pies were sliced and served. The children quickly devoured dessert. The storm had quieted, so they donned their coats and mittens and ran out into a white world to play.

Will, Robert, and Luke retired to the living room and the radio while the women cleared the table and washed the dishes. Laurel walked into the front room to see if anyone wanted a refill on coffee, but instead she stood in the doorway and listened to the radio. Jack Benny's familiar line, "Now cut that out," made everyone laugh. Robert looked up and winked at her. Laurel couldn't help but smile. "Anyone want more coffee?" she asked.

"None for me," Will said. "I couldn't fit in another drop." He patted his stomach.

"I'd like some." Robert stood and joined Laurel. "That was a fine meal. Thank you."

"My mother did most of it. I just helped."

"Well, thanks anyway." He held out his cup, and Laurel filled it. "Good coffee too," he said, taking a sip.

"I did make that. I learned from my father. He never thought Mama made the coffee strong enough, so he started making it when I was just a girl. One day he showed me how, and I've been doing it ever since. Some people think it's too strong."

"No, I like it. It's just right."

Replacing the pot on the stove, Laurel glanced at Robert. He was handsome—tall, with dark brown eyes and hair. He had an easy comfortable smile, and although reserved, his quietness never came across as arrogance. She liked him. *He'd make a good husband,* she told herself.

"Would you like to go for a walk?"

Laurel was wrapped up in her thoughts and didn't hear. "Did you say something?"

Robert smiled. "I thought you looked as if you were off somewhere else."

If he only knew.

"I asked if you'd like to take a walk."

"Sure," Laurel said, not exactly certain she wanted to be alone with Robert. He helped her with her coat, and Laurel wondered if she were being disloyal to Celeste, who was crazy about Robert. Laurel hooked the buttons, pulled the hood over her head, and pushed her hands into fur-lined leather gloves.

Robert opened the door and held it for Laurel. She stepped out onto the open porch. Cold air chilled her face and stung her lungs with each breath. The children were building a snowman and barely noticed them.

Snow crunched beneath their boots as Robert and Laurel walked toward the road. The world was white—snow blanketed fields, trees, the plow, and the wood shed, and the nearby mountains were buried. The landscape shimmered in winter's dusky sunlight. "I never thought about how bright snow could make the world look," Laurel said. "I always envisioned winter here as being dark. I love how it's all frozen and white. It's beautiful."

"I like it too." Robert linked arms with Laurel.

She felt a bit awkward. Was it wrong to allow Robert to think she might care for him? Maybe she did.

Robert pointed toward his farm. "My barn looks awfully small from here."

"That's because everything around it is so big—the mountains and the sky." She shook her head slightly. "I never understood how it would be to love a place so much. It's strange because I haven't lived here very long, but I don't ever want to leave."

"That's how I felt from the beginning, like I belong here. I'm never leaving," he stated flatly. Robert stopped walking and faced Laurel. "I know you're not interested in any kind of serious attachment, Laurel . . . but I was wondering . . . if you'd mind going to the dance with me tomorrow night at the community hall? It should be fun."

Laurel's first instinct was to say no. But what would be wrong with going to a dance with a friend? She let out her breath, and icy fog hovered between them. She remembered Adam's tender farewell and wondered if it held a promise? *No. He has his life, and it doesn't include me.*

She looked at Robert. "Yes. I'd like to go with you."

Chapter Twenty-Five

SOMETHING SIMPLE, LAUREL THOUGHT, SORTING THROUGH HER FEW DRESSES. She stopped at a light blue cotton. It had a scoop neckline, short sleeves, and a full skirt. Lifting it, she studied the dress. *This should work,* she decided, taking it off the hanger. *I don't want Robert to get the wrong idea.*

Pushing her arms into the sleeves, she pulled it over her head and smoothed the skirt over her hips. Standing in front of a full-length mirror, she studied her reflection. The pale blue softened her golden complexion and brightened her hazel eyes. Laurel pirouetted, and the skirt flared away from her legs. It would be perfect for dancing. She smiled, pleased with her choice—nice, but not too dressy.

Oddly, she was excited about going out. *It's only Robert,* she told herself, brushing her hair and clipping back a portion.

She smoothed a touch of rouge on her cheeks, then carefully applied a hint of lipstick. Standing back, she surveyed the effect and decided she liked it. Staring at her reflection, she reminded herself, *It's only Robert.* But Laurel knew things had changed. She'd decided to make room for him in her heart. It was the reasonable thing to do.

Adam's letter rested against the mirror on the bureau. Laurel picked it up and considered rereading it. She'd already read it several times and could recite much of it. She set it back on the dresser.

A soft rap sounded at the door. "Laurel? May I come in?" her mother asked.

"Yes." The door opened, and warm air from downstairs flowed in. Laurel had forgotten how cool the room was.

Jean stepped in, closing the door behind her. "You look beautiful. Since you took to wearing those overalls, it's easy to forget you've grown into a lovely woman." Jean smiled. "I just came up to tell you Robert's here, and I must say he looks awfully handsome. You know, he's such a fine young man. I'm happy you two decided to go out."

Laurel knew her parents considered Robert a perfect match for her. Holding her arms away from her sides, she turned around and asked, "This blue look all right?"

"Yes. It's perfect. Robert will love it." Jean glanced at Laurel's legs. "Are you sure you want to wear silk stockings? It's cold. Maybe your wool hose would be better?"

"No one else will be wearing them. It'll be warm enough indoors. I can put a blanket over my lap in the truck."

Jean nodded. "Well, I don't think you ought to keep Robert waiting."

Laurel grabbed her handbag from the dresser and followed her mother out the door and down the stairs.

Robert stood in the front room, hands in his pockets, his coat draped over one arm. He looked stylish, dressed in knit slacks and a sweater. His eyes followed Laurel down the stairs. "You look real pretty," he said when Laurel took the last step.

"Thank you."

Will set his newspaper on a table beside his wing chair. "You two be careful. The roads are icy." He looked at Robert. "What time can we expect you to have Laurel home?"

"The dance is over at ten o'clock, sir."

"All right then. You ought to be back here by ten-thirty." Will smiled, softening his decree.

"I'll have her home on time," Robert assured him, putting on his coat. "You ready?" he asked Laurel.

"Yes. I just have to get my coat and boots." Laurel headed for the back porch. Sitting on a bench by the door, she pulled a pair of galoshes over her pumps, then took down her coat from its hook. Robert held it while she slipped her arms into the sleeves. After putting on knit gloves, she gave her mother a kiss.

"Have a good time," Jean said, handing Laurel a lap blanket.

"We will," Laurel promised and stepped outside.

"Goodnight, Mrs. Hasper," Robert said.

"Night." Jean stood at the door and watched as the truck headed down the driveway.

The cold ran icy fingers up and down Laurel's bare legs. She shivered, and thinking she'd been foolish to wear silk stockings, laid the blanket over her lap.

Robert peered through a small section of cleared glass in the iced-up window. Weak headlights illuminated nearly imperceptible tire tracks in the snow. The pickup bumped over the rough, frozen roadway, snow and ice crunching beneath its tires.

"I wish we'd been able to bring our truck. Life would be simpler. Right now, just getting back and forth to town is a problem."

"God blessed me with this one. Mr. Sherstead and I made a trade. It was perfect timing, finding out he needed mending done and a part-time farmhand. Mama's patching his clothes, and I'm working for him when he needs me." They dropped into a rut. They ground their way free and Robert chuckled. "But I'm not convinced it's any faster than walking." He concentrated on driving, and the interior of the cab fell quiet.

Wiping her side window clear, Laurel gazed at the countryside. The moon, looking like a great round light, cast a glow across an ivory landscape. It illuminated white mountains and lay down shadows at the feet of naked trees. White hillsides stood like frozen sea swells.

The truck bounced over a mound of packed snow, jarring Laurel out of her reverie. The blanket had slipped off her knees and she replaced it.

Robert glanced at her bare legs. Embarrassed, he flashed her a smile before returning his attention to the road. "Your father told me your Guernsey's about ready to calve."

"Yep. He's spending more time in the barn than the house. She's been acting edgy, and he goes out to check on her every few hours. Good thing we got the barn finished. Otherwise, I'd be worried about the wolves." She glanced at the tree line. "Have you heard them?"

"Uh-huh. Some nights they sound close."

"They give me the willies."

Robert glanced at Laurel. "You don't have to worry about them. Howling is just their way of talking to each other. They're not threatening anyone."

"Yeah, but what if they're talking about where to find dinner?" They both laughed.

The lights of Palmer appeared out of the darkness. "Here we are," Robert said as they approached the small town.

A smattering of homes, buildings, cars, and people replaced empty frozen wilderness. Laurel's anticipation grew. She hoped Celeste was here, and she hoped her friend wouldn't mind that Robert was her escort.

Robert parked at the far end of the Grange Hall, then hurried around to Laurel's door. He opened it and offered his arm.

"Looks like a lot of people are here," Laurel said, taking Robert's arm and placing a foot carefully on icy ground.

As they entered the community building, warmth, music, and chatter greeted them. "I wonder if Celeste is here," Laurel said.

"She will be. You know how she loves parties."

Robert helped Laurel with her coat and hung it in an open closet just inside the doorway. Sitting on a bench, Laurel removed her boots. Quickly and as inconspicuously as possible, she ran her hand over her silk stockings, searching for snags. Thankfully there were none. Silk stockings were a luxury and too expensive to replace.

A band of four musicians—two saxophones, a clarinet, and a piano—were playing "Stardust." Robert and Laurel stood and listened. Robert leaned toward Laurel and asked, "Would you like something to eat or drink?"

"I am thirsty."

"I'll be right back." He headed for a nearby table.

"Laurel! Hi!" Celeste called, hurrying toward her friend and hauling along a pimply-faced boy. He was dressed in baggy pants, a sweater vest, bow tie, and saddle shoes. His hair was flattened against his head with hair grease. Celeste gave Laurel a quick hug. "I was afraid you wouldn't be here." She glanced at the young man. "This is Charles," she said flatly.

"Hi, Charles," Laurel said. "I haven't seen you around before. Are you new to the valley?"

"Nah. Just visiting. I came up from college to see my uncle. He's a friend of Mr. Townsend." Snapping his fingers and bobbing his head, he gazed around. "This place is jumping. You want to dance, Celeste?"

"No. I'm tired. Maybe later."

"All right." Charles seemed undaunted and headed for a group of girls standing along the wall.

"Isn't he something?" Celeste said with a giggle. "What a goon. I only went out with him because my father said I had to." She glanced around. "Did you come with someone?"

"Yes, I came with Robert."

Celeste's smile faded. "I thought you weren't interested in him."

"He asked me . . . just as friends . . ." Laurel hedged.

"I wish he would have asked me." She turned on a smile. "Well, can I be a bridesmaid at your wedding?"

"Don't be silly. It's not a date."

"He's smitten, and I'm telling you he won't settle for just being friends." She ran her hands through blonde curls. "Here he comes. It looks like he cleared the table of goodies."

"Hello," Robert said, balancing two drinks and a plate laden with cookies and cake.

Celeste flashed a smile.

Laurel took one of the drinks and a cookie. "Thank you."

Celeste turned to watch the musicians and the dancers. "The band's pretty good, don't you think?"

"Not bad," Robert said.

Charles jitterbugged back to Celeste. "Hey, babe, you ready for a dance now?"

Celeste shrugged and took his hand. "See you," she said with a resigned smile, allowing him to lead her to the dance floor.

"Who's that?" Robert asked.

"Charles. His father's a friend of Mr. Townsend. Celeste brought him as a favor."

Robert ate another cookie and finished his punch. "Would you like to dance?"

"OK."

He escorted Laurel to the dance floor. Taking her in his arms, Robert easily fell into the rhythm of a swing dance.

"You're good," Laurel called over the music.

"I used to do a lot of dancing back home."

Swing dancing was new and considered daring, but Laurel soon found herself caught up in the music. It was easy to follow Robert's lead. They danced nonstop through four songs.

Out of breath, Laurel asked, "Can we sit the next one out?"

"Sure," Robert said just as a short, redheaded man bumped into him.

"Watch it!" the man bellowed.

"Sorry."

A man with a bulbous nose collided with Robert from the other side. Another song began, and he swung his partner in close, peering at Robert through black curls. "Hey, look out where you're going."

Robert ignored the man, and taking Laurel's arm, headed off the dance floor.

The redhead stepped in front of him.

Robert stopped. "What do you want?"

"We want you to stop being so clumsy." He laughed, then his smile disappeared and his brown eyes narrowed. In a menacing tone, he said, "Don't much like outsiders. Sure feel a lot better if you all went back where you came from."

"Look, we're here to have a little fun. Why don't you guys leave us alone?" Robert tried to steer Laurel away from the men, but they walked alongside of them. A tall, skinny man with slicked-back blond hair joined the first two.

"We never wanted you colonists here," said the redhead. "And since you got here, we want you even less."

"Yeah," the tall one said, grabbing the back of Robert's collar. "We don't like you—never have."

"I don't know you." Robert shrugged free and glared at the assailant.

"Well, we know you." His eyes roved over Laurel.

"Leave us alone," Robert said.

"We'd feel a lot better if you left. Like my friend here said, we don't like you."

"Many other colonists are here. Why us?"

The redhead sneered. "Cause you're the one we were told to get rid of. We'll get to the others eventually."

Robert stared at the man. "We're not leaving."

Laurel laid a hand on his arm. "We can go. It's all right." Laurel's stomach tumbled. Ray Townsend had to be behind this. If Celeste knew, it would break her heart. "Please, Robert."

"We're staying."

Wearing a smirk, the tall blond grabbed Laurel, slid his arm around her waist, and pulled her close. "You can stay, sweetheart." He tried to kiss Laurel's neck. She wrenched free.

"Keep your hands off her!" Robert roared, taking Laurel's hand.

The man stepped in front of Robert. "You gonna make us?" He grinned, revealing small straight teeth.

"If I have to."

"Robert, let's just go," Laurel said. "Please."

At first he said nothing but continued staring at the man. Finally he said, "All right. We'll go." Keeping Laurel's hand in his, he led her to the coat closet, helped her on with her coat, then shrugged into his own while Laurel pushed her feet into her boots.

She stood, her heart racing. Glancing about, she asked, "Where did they go?"

"Probably looking for someone else to harass." He shook his head. "Those kind of guys make me mad. I'd like to . . . Never mind what I'd like to do. I hate to let them get away with this. It'll just make them worse." He steered Laurel out the door and down the steps. They rounded the building and headed for the truck.

When they were about twenty feet from the pickup, a familiar voice called, "Hey, leaving so soon?"

Robert and Laurel whirled around. The three hoodlums walked toward them. "Laurel, get in the truck," Robert said.

Laurel held on to his hand.

"Go," he whispered.

"No. I'm not leaving you."

Robert pushed her behind him. "We're going," he said. "We don't want any trouble."

The redhead sucked on a cigarette. The tip glowed cherry red. "Isn't that nice. You don't want any trouble." He looked at the other two. "Hey, Leonard, Billy, don't you think that's real nice?" He glanced at the blond. "What do you think? Should we just forgive and forget?"

Leonard gave a sick laugh.

Billy snickered.

"So, Teddy, what do you think we ought to do with them?" Leonard asked.

"My name's Ted," the redhead corrected sullenly. He walked toward Robert. "Seems to me he needs a lesson. Ain't that what we're supposed to do—teach him and all the rest of the freeloaders a lesson?" His grin crumpled into a grimace. He looked Robert up and down. "I s'pose you might buy your way out of this jam. You got any cash?"

"Some."

"We'll take it," Leonard said, standing beside Ted.

"No you won't," Robert said, sounding unruffled.

Ted smoothed back his hair. "So you say, but there are three of us and only one of you." He held out his hand. "Pay up."

Robert stared at the outstretched palm. "No." He squared his jaw and glared at Ted.

"That's fine by me," Billy said, striding up to Robert. "We'll get it either way, and I don't mind knocking your block off."

"Robert, give them the money," Laurel said, unable to quiet the tremble in her voice.

"Listen to the lady. She ain't stupid," Ted said.

"No." Robert backed toward the truck, keeping Laurel behind him.

"The money or else." Ted advanced. When Robert didn't respond, he threw himself at the bigger man, throwing a punch.

Robert deflected the blow but didn't see the one coming from Leonard, which hit him across the jaw. He stumbled. Ted hit him again. Robert fell to his hands and knees. Leonard kicked him hard in the side.

Laurel threw herself at the tall blond, but he easily tossed her away and continued to bash Robert. Pushing herself to her feet, Laurel screamed, "Stop it! Stop it!" She grabbed the brute's coat and pulled.

Ted got a hold of her from behind and lifted her off the ground. Laughing, he held her against him while she thrashed, trying to free herself. "I'll take care of her."

"Leave her alone!" Robert raged, pushing himself to his knees and staggering to his feet. This time it was Billy who swung at him, but Robert grabbed his hand and shoved him aside. "Leave her be, I said!" He came at Ted like an enraged bull.

"Someone's coming!" Leonard yelled. "Let's get out of here."

Ted kissed Laurel hard on the mouth, then let her loose. "I'll see you later," he pledged, then ran after his friends. They disappeared into the darkness.

Crying, Laurel ran to Robert who was leaning against the truck. She caressed his bloodied face. "Oh, Robert."

A man ran up to them. "You two all right?"

"I'm all right," Laurel said, wiping at her tears. "But my friend. They beat him up."

He looked at Robert. "They sure did."

Robert wiped blood from his mouth and nose.

"Looks like they really gave it to ya."

"They did that all right." Robert dabbed at his nose.

"Do you know who it was?" the stranger asked.

"No. They looked familiar. I've seen them around, but I can't say for sure." Robert focused on the man who'd helped him. "Who are you?"

"John Reynolds."

Laurel kept a hand on Robert's arm. "The one who seemed to be in charge was a redhead. His name is Ted. The blond was called Leonard, and the other guy's name was Billy."

The man nodded. "I know those three. They're always looking for trouble. Not much you can do about it. Their fathers don't take kindly to outside interference."

"It sounded like they'd been hired to attack us," Laurel said.

"By whom? Did they say?"

"No, but I can guess. I think it's Ray Townsend."

"You got any proof?"

"No," Laurel conceded.

"There's not much that can be done." Mr. Reynolds rubbed his stubbled chin.

"We must be able to do something," Laurel said.

"Oh, I can talk to their fathers and they'll catch it, but legally . . ." he shrugged. "You can try—"

"No need," Robert said.

"I'm going to talk to Mr. Townsend! He can't get away with this!"

"Leave it be." Robert dabbed his bloodied lip. "You don't know it was him. Let's get home."

Laurel's anger grew, and she pressed harder on the accelerator. Snow-covered roadway disappeared beneath the truck. It was all so unjust. In the morning, she'd give Ray Townsend a piece of her mind. They bounced through a hole, and Robert groaned. "I'm sorry." Laurel slowed. "You all right?"

"Yes," he said.

Laurel pulled into the drive. Her mother and father would help. "Let's get you inside," she said and started to open the door.

Robert grabbed her arm. "Wait. I don't want your parents to see me like this." He grimaced. "I want to talk for a minute."

"You need doctoring."

"I'll take care of it when I get home."

Laurel settled back. "You say *I'm* stubborn?"

Robert carefully turned until he faced Laurel. "I'm real sorry about tonight. I wanted you to have a good time."

"None of this was your fault."

"Yeah, I know, but I still feel bad." He stared at the dash. "I've been thinkin' . . . about you and me." He said nothing for several moments, then slammed his fist down on the dash. "I wanted this to be special. Instead I'm mad and all beat up."

His face and eyes were swelling and bruised. "Oh, Robert, your poor face." Laurel caressed his cheek. "I don't blame you for being angry."

He caught hold of her hand. "No. You don't understand. I . . . I wanted to talk to you." He paused. "I know you don't have special feelings for me, but I wish you'd give me a chance."

Her heart hammered. What could she say? She didn't want to hurt him. He was good and kind, everything she should want in a man. "Robert, I don't know how I feel about you just yet," she finally said.

"I'm crazy about you, have been ever since we first met. All I want to do is be with you—to look into your eyes, touch your hair . . ." He acted as if he might reach out to her, but he didn't. His eyes settled on her mouth. "Your smile makes the world come alive for me."

Robert's devotion stunned Laurel. She'd known he was interested but hadn't understood how deeply he cared. How could she hurt him?

He took her other hand in his. "I know you don't love me, but would you just think about giving us a chance?" He gazed at her, his brown eyes lit with love. "I'm not going to play games. I want to marry you, Laurel, but I know you're going to need some time. Would you just let me court you?"

Laurel's mind reeled. What was the right thing to do? Could she learn to love him? Her parents would be pleased if she married him. She searched his eyes. He was handsome, kind, honest.

"Laurel?"

"All right, Robert. We can see each other. And I'll think about the rest."

Chapter Twenty-Six

LAUREL STOPPED TYPING AND RESTED HER HANDS ON THE KEYS. AFTER working for several hours, she was exhausted. Stretching her arms over her head, then kneading the back of her neck, she gazed out the window. Snow had started falling again. She'd planned on stopping by Ray Townsend's on her way home. *Somebody has to stand up to him.* She stared at the snow. *Maybe tomorrow,* she thought with a sigh.

"You look tired, dear," Jessie said. "I'll pour us the last of the hot chocolate, then you can be on your way home."

"That sounds good." Laurel stood, stretching from side to side.

Jessie shuffled into the kitchen. "Looks like another storm is moving in. Hope it's not a bad one. We've already had our share this winter."

Laurel walked to the window and stared out at a white world. Snow had drifted against the house and would have buried the windows if she hadn't brushed them clear each visit. Icicles stretched from roof to white floor. Trees stood naked, their limbs encased in heavy frost.

Laurel squinted, trying to identify a pair of animal tracks, but the twilight made it difficult to see. She sighed. For weeks now, the days had seemed more dark than light. She missed the milder, brighter winters of Wisconsin. Mentally adjusting her mood, she walked into the kitchen. Wallowing in gloom wouldn't change a thing.

Jessie filled two mugs. "Here you go," she said, handing one to Laurel.

Laurel breathed in the rich aroma. "Mmm." She took a sip. "Good." Leaning against the counter, she gazed out a tiny window. "Don't the short days bother you?"

Jessie set the empty pot in the sink. "Sometimes." Using a hand pump, she filled the pan with water. "But I can't change things, so I try not to think about it." She turned and faced Laurel. "I get to feeling gloomy from time to time." She crossed the room, chucked two pieces of wood in the stove, then returned to her drink. "I think you've got cabin fever. A lot of Alaskans fight it. I expect it'll be rougher for you this year since it's your first winter." She smiled. "Don't despair. Spring will arrive before you know it, then summer. And you forget." She limped to the front room and eased herself into a chair.

Laurel sat across from her.

With a cup cradled in her hands, Jessie gazed out the window. "In spite of my winter gloomies, I wouldn't live anywhere else. Alaska is wonderful and awful, but it's real. Here, the cycles of life are fleeting but breathe vitality."

"Are you ever homesick for California?"

Jessie smiled whimsically. "Sometimes. Mostly what I miss is my youth." Her eyes sparkled. "I was quite lively and daring in my heyday, always searching for a new challenge."

She took a drink. "I was the only one in my family to go to college. In those days women became homemakers. My parents were proud of my achievements and encouraged me to go ahead with my education. I met Steward at the university. We were both majoring in history. The first time I met him he was studying for a final in the library. He looked up at me over his round, wire-rimmed glasses, his eyes so serious. I was smitten." She chuckled.

She looked at Laurel as if she'd forgotten anyone was there. "Oh, dear. I've gotten completely off track. Now, what was your question?"

"I just wondered if you missed your life in California."

"I guess I'd have to say no. My best years have been here in Alaska. The people welcomed us from the beginning."

"I wish I could say the same."

"Good things aren't always easy." Jessie set her cup on the table beside her chair. "Would you like to see my latest painting? I took a stab at a winter scene."

"I'd love to." Laurel drained the last of her chocolate and set the cup on a scratched end table.

Jessie pushed herself out of her chair, motioned for Laurel to follow, and hobbled to the back room. "These old bones don't like the cold." She opened the door and stepped into a chilly room. "I'd better leave that door open if I want to sleep tonight," Jessie said, shuffling to an easel beneath the window. "It's right here." She stood back and looked at the picture. "What do you think?"

Laurel's breath caught as she gazed at a scene of the snow-buried mountains that framed the valley. A frozen stream like shimmering glass meandered through foothills of frozen trees, bushes hugging its mounded banks. An abandoned barn stood at the base of a mountain, looking lonely amid the white expanse. A craggy peak scarred with dark fractures and rocky outcroppings rose up behind it. "Jessie, you're amazing! I feel as if I'm standing right there."

Jessie beamed. "Thank you. When it's dry, you can have it."

"Have it?" Laurel looked at the painting with new eyes. "Are you sure? It's so beautiful."

"Absolutely." She glanced out the window. "The snow's coming down harder. You better scoot on home."

Laurel bundled into her coat, pulled her hood tight around her face, and pushed her hands into her gloves. Standing at the door, she said, "I probably won't be back until after Christmas. Mama needs help with the baking, and I've got some projects I need to finish." She smiled, taking delight in the gift she was making for her mother. "I'm embroidering a handkerchief for Mama. It has a field of wildflowers on it. I got the idea from your paintings."

"I'm honored," Jessie said with a smile.

"Luke and Brian aren't hard to buy for, but I don't know what I'm going to do for Daddy. He loves woodworking. He used to make furniture and knickknacks. When we moved, he had to leave his lathe. I'd hoped Luke and Mama and I could put our money together and buy him one, but they're too expensive—fourteen dollars." She opened the door. "Maybe I can get it next year. Thank goodness for this job or I wouldn't have been able to buy any gifts."

Jessie smiled, "Steward used to enjoy working with wood. He was quite good."

"Are you going to the community Christmas party?"

"I thought it was just for the colonists."

"I guess, but you're like family. You ought to be there."

"Maybe. I'll see what the weather's like." She thought a moment. "I s'pose I could bring my famous fudge."

"That would be wonderful. Hope you'll be there. Bye."

Wind swirled underneath Laurel's hood and down her neck, making her shiver. She pulled out a wool scarf from her pocket and wrapped it around her face and neck.

Laurel stopped at the post office to check on a package for her mother. Heat radiated from a wood stove. "It's cold," she said to Millie Wilkerson, the postmistress, taking a moment to warm herself at the stove.

"That's what I've been hearing. I'm not looking forward to walking home."

Laurel stripped off her gloves and stepped up to the clerk's window. "It's nice and warm in here."

"I've been keeping that stove stoked," Mrs. Wilkerson said cheerfully.

The door opened, and Ray Townsend stepped in, his broad shoulders filling the doorway. He stripped back his hood, revealing flattened curls and a trimmed beard. His eyes rested on Laurel for a moment. He nodded and closed the door.

Laurel stiffened. Now was her chance.

"Ray," Mrs. Wilkerson said. "Good to see you."

He walked up to the counter. "You got anything for me today, Millie?"

Looking a little befuddled, Mrs. Wilkerson said hesitantly, "Laurel was here first, Ray." She glanced at Laurel. "Is there anything you needed to mail, dear?"

Laurel's mind whirled with all the things she wanted to say to Mr. Townsend. She focused on Mrs. Wilkerson. "No. I'm here to pick up a package for Mama. She's expecting something from Sears and Roebuck."

Millie smiled, and her pudgy cheeks rounded into apples. "Oh, that's right. Something came in just this morning." She waddled to the back of the room and picked up two boxes. "How exciting," she said, her eyes sparkling. She handed the packages to Laurel.

"Christmas gifts—a truck for Brian and a rod and reel for Luke." Laurel smiled.

Mr. Townsend leaned on the counter. He muttered, "Don't know why any colonist would bother to buy gifts—seems the government and the Sears store have already bought enough."

He'd said the words quietly and hadn't looked at Laurel, but she knew they were meant for her. She stared at him, outrage mounting.

"It's none of our doing that the government and the Sears people are sending gifts. I think it's kind of them since most of the families are too poor to buy much of anything."

Mr. Townsend stared straight ahead. "I don't begrudge the children their gifts. I just find it a little one-sided. Lots of homesteaders' children won't find anything under their trees Christmas morning."

Laurel hadn't considered how the gifts might look to the settlers. She'd simply been grateful. "I hadn't thought of that."

"I'm not surprised. Loafers rarely think of anyone but themselves."

"Loafers?" Laurel asked, her indignation growing. "Not a one of us is a loafer, Mr. Townsend! My father works harder than any man I know. Farmers don't know what it means to be idle. We're hardworking and just trying to make our way in this world. We have a right to a life just like you!"

Ray Townsend looked at her, and Laurel found herself staring into furious, gray eyes. "Young lady, you ought to talk to your father about manners. It doesn't seem you've been taught any."

"You're talking to me about manners? *You?* The mean, contemptible man who hired thugs to beat up an innocent man? Don't talk to me about manners! You don't know the meaning of the word! I don't think you have any scruples at all. Because of you, Robert Lundeen is spending the day in bed. His face is all beat up and he might have broken ribs!"

Mrs. Wilkerson watched, her mouth open and eyes wide.

"I don't know what you're talking about," Ray Townsend said evenly. "I don't even know anyone named Robert Lundeen."

"You're lying! You know him. He's a friend of Celeste's. You sent those men after him, and you can't convince me otherwise."

"Think what you like," he said, then looked at Mrs. Wilkerson. "My mail?"

At first Mrs. Wilkerson just gaped at him, then finally said, "Sorry, Ray, but nothing came in for you."

"Good day to you," he said casually as if nothing had taken place and walked out.

Laurel stared after him, still seething. She couldn't remember ever being so angry. Shaking, she pulled on her gloves. "I'm sorry, Mrs. Wilkerson. I . . . I didn't mean for that to happen."

"Oh, that's all right, dear. It isn't the first dispute I've witnessed in here."

Laurel picked up the packages and walked out. Pulling the door closed behind her, she stepped into the cold, swirling snow. She looked up and down the street, searching for Mr. Townsend. He was already gone. She headed for home, anger consuming her Christmas spirit.

That night over dinner, Laurel told her parents about her encounter. Will's face turned grim, but he calmly said, "You can't worry about him. His anger and bitterness have nothing to do with us, and we don't know for sure that he's the one behind the attack on Robert."

Laurel felt deflated. "I wish we could do something."

"I feel sorry for the man," Jean said.

"How can you feel sorry for him after what he did?" Laurel asked.

"From what I heard, he used to be a good man, but he's still grieving over his wife."

"I don't like him. He looks mean," Brian said, picking up a string bean with his fingers and putting it in his mouth.

"I do wish we could do something to help the children." Jean scooted her chair back and walked to the stove. Picking up a pot of coffee, she returned with it, filling Will's cup, then her own. "Laurel? Luke?" Both shook their heads no to the offer. Jean returned the pot to the stove. "Well, the colonists have lots of gifts. Why can't we contribute some to the homesteaders? Our children don't need so much." She smiled as an idea formulated. "We could invite them to the Christmas party."

"That's a wonderful idea!" Laurel said. "But how will we get the names and let them know about the party?"

"The one person who knows all the folks in the valley and will be certain to see them is Mrs. Wilkerson. Maybe she'll let us put up a notice in the post office, and I bet she'd be happy to spread the word."

"Slow down there, Jean," Will said. "You don't even know if the other colonists want to do this. Both sides have had hard feelings."

"Of course we'd have to ask them. Isn't there a meeting tomorrow night?"

"Yes," Will said. "I'll bring it up."

Although a handful of colonists didn't want to share their gifts, most agreed it was a good idea, so invitations were sent. Laurel returned to the post office a few days later to check on responses.

"I'm sorry, Laurel, but most of the homesteaders said they wouldn't be there," Mrs. Wilkerson said. She handed Laurel a piece of paper with a short list of names and ages on it.

"Why?"

"A lot of them said something to the effect that they didn't need a handout from outsiders."

"Oh. Why are they so stubborn?"

Mrs. Wilkerson sorted mail. "They have their pride. And I think that so much has been said about how the colonists are getting a free ride that they're afraid of being accused of the same thing."

Disheartened, Laurel left the post office and headed for the community building. The Christmas party was scheduled for the next evening, and several people were working on decorations. She walked up the steps to the hall and pulled open the door. Some women were decorating a tree; others were hanging decorations around the room. They stopped and looked at Laurel. She hated to tell them. They'd been hopeful it might mend some of the hard feelings. "I'm sorry, but only a handful of homesteaders will be here."

"Well, we tried," Norma Prosser said. "We'll have to do what we can for the ones who are coming. Not all our neighbors are angry. Some of them have been real nice and neighborly."

The night of the party, the Haspers piled into the back of the Lundeen pickup. Robert's injuries had healed. He'd pitched hay into the bed of the truck and laid out blankets. And now, Brian happily tossed hay into the air.

"Stop it, you little runt," Luke said. "You're getting hay all over everything."

Brian didn't take Luke's reprimand seriously. Bracing his hands against the cab, he jumped up and down.

"Brian, sit down," Will said. "If you're not careful, you'll get bounced out or you'll end up with a frostbitten nose."

Brian plopped down beside Luke. "Are we almost there?"

Will smiled. "Almost."

"Hey, Dad," Luke said. "You're going to be at the dogsled races, aren't you? Alex and I have been practicing. He's good, and King's a great dog—strong and smart. I think we can win."

"Of course I'll be there. You really think you can win?"

"Yep. We have another week to practice."

"Maybe I'll give it a try next year," Will said.

"I wish girls could race," Laurel said.

Giving Laurel a condescending look, Luke said, "Girls aren't strong enough."

"And you are? You're barely seventeen."

"That's enough," Will said, leveling a disappointed look at Luke. "I think girls ought to be allowed to race."

"Thanks, Daddy." Laurel hugged her knees against her chest, trying to hold in warmth. The air was so cold it hurt her lungs and burned her cheeks. She placed gloved hands over her face and breathed into them, warming her face. It helped a little. Then she stared up at the clear night sky. Stars winked out of a black blanket. "Daddy, do you think we'll see the northern lights soon?"

"Maybe. I hope so."

"Not me," Robert's sister, Veronica, said. "They sound spooky."

"I'm not afraid." Brian shoved his feet under a pile of hay.

"I think the lights would make Christmas perfect," Laurel said.

The pickup slowed and pulled into the parking area outside the community building. Several cars were already there. Laurel stood and was ready to jump out when she spotted the three men who'd assaulted Robert.

"What's wrong, sugar?" Will lifted her out of the truck.

"Those men," she said as she pointed. "They're the ones who attacked Robert."

"I'd say they need a talking to."

Robert stepped out of the cab.

"Are those the men who beat you up?" Will asked, nodding at the three hoodlums.

"Yeah, that's them."

"Come on," Will told Robert, taking a step toward them.

Robert grabbed Will's arm. "Let it go. I don't want any trouble. This is Christmas."

Will looked at Robert. "You know I'm not a violent man, but these fellas need someone to stand up to them. It'll make it easier on the rest of the colonists." He took another step. "I'm not going to say much," he promised, "just enough. Jean, you and the kids go inside. Me, Luke, and Robert got something we need to do." With Luke on one side and Robert on the other, Will strode toward the three.

The troublemakers straightened and stared at the approaching men.

Will stopped directly in front of them. Luke and Robert stood solidly beside him. Will's eyes moved from one to the other. Finally he said, "If you have a problem with one of us, you've got a problem with all of us."

"Ooh, I'm afraid," the redhead, Ted, taunted.

"If you had any wisdom, you would be."

"Yeah, well we ain't afraid of no outsiders." Ted spit tobacco juice at Will's feet.

Will glanced at the splatter, then settled his eyes on the young man's. "If I have to, I'll bring in the law."

Ted pushed his tobacco deeper into his cheek. "You think so?" He looked at his friends and chuckled. "Things ain't the same here as down home on the farm. No one's going to touch us."

"If that's the case, I'd be happy to deal with you personally."

"So would I," Drew Prosser said, joining Will.

"And me," said Tom Jenkins, stepping up beside Robert.

Ted no longer looked so self-assured. "We didn't do nothin'. This guy's a liar." He nodded at Robert.

"Sure," Tom said. He studied the man. "Your daddies would probably be real unhappy to discover you've been causing trouble again. I've been around a good long while, and I know just about everybody in this valley, including your daddies. You'd be smart to skedaddle on home."

"Yeah, we're goin'," Ted said and walked away, his friends at his side.

Wearing a smile, Robert watched them go. "Seems they've lost some of their bluster."

"Are those the boys who beat you?" Tom asked.

"Yeah."

"I don't think you'll have any more trouble with them. They know I'm not one to bluff, and they don't want their fathers knowing what they've been up to."

"Hope you're right," Will said. He headed toward the entrance. "Anyway, thanks for the help. How'd you know we were out here?"

"Your wife," Tom said.

Will clapped Tom on the back. "We've got a party to go to." He headed for the steps. Will met Laurel midway. Wrapping an arm around her shoulders, he asked, "You up for a party, sugar?"

"You bet."

People chatted and laughed. Streamers hung from the ceiling, a Christmas tree stood in one corner with mounds of gifts piled under it, a table crowded with Christmas goodies stood along one wall, and a real live Santa sat in the far corner. A line of children waited to visit him.

Looking around the hall, Laurel felt the warmth of friendship. Only a few months ago, these people met for the first time; yet a bond had already developed between them. Thinking over the last few weeks, Laurel realized she'd allowed the lack of daylight and the conflict between the colonists and homesteaders to steal her joy. *Enough is enough*, she decided. *From now on, I'm going to look at the bright side of things.*

She unbuttoned her coat. Robert quickly stepped up and helped her with it, then hung it on a hanger in the closet. "Thank you," Laurel said, wishing he wouldn't be quite so attentive.

Will scanned the room. "It's a shame so many families gave up and left. Good days are ahead for this colony."

"Yes, but we'll have some rough ones too," Drew Prosser said. "We've lost some calves. It'll make for a rough year. I'd counted on selling them to help make ends meet."

"The Lord will provide," Will said with confidence.

Drew nodded. "I know, but I'll be interested to see how he does it."

"How's that new calf of yours coming along?" Robert asked Will.

"Good. She's strong and hungry. In fact, if she doesn't slow down, we won't have enough milk for the family. I have to milk early to get our share," he added with a grin.

"When do you think Santa is going to hand out the gifts?" Brian asked.

"Soon," Jean said. "Brian, remember Christmas is more than just gifts."

Will rested a hand on Jean's arm. "For little boys, Christmas is about presents and good things to eat. I remember well." He kneeled in front of Brian. "Christmas is a time for gifts and goodies, but first it's a time to celebrate Jesus' birthday."

"I know. I didn't forget."

"Good." Will patted the youngster on the back.

People started singing, "God Rest Ye Merry Gentlemen," and Will hefted Brian onto his shoulders and joined in with the carolers.

His cheeks bright, Brian sang out, his falsetto voice carrying over the people.

Laurel's voice blended with those around her. A man standing beside her sang loudly, and she turned to see who it was. Adam smiled at her.

"Adam!" she yelled. Without thinking, she threw her arms around his neck and hugged him.

Adam held her tightly. "I missed you. I couldn't stay away."

Chapter Twenty-Seven

ROBERT'S TRUCK BUMPED THROUGH AN ICY POTHOLE. "THIS IS NEARLY AS rough as my plane trip here," Adam said with a laugh. "I think you might call it a white knuckle special."

"Was it scary on the plane?" Brian asked.

"Yeah, a little."

Brian looked up at Adam. "I'm glad you're here. You can sleep in my bed. I don't mind."

"No," Adam said, glancing at Laurel. "I didn't come here to force anyone out of his bed. I can sleep on the sofa or the floor. It wouldn't be the first time."

"Mama's already decided. Brian's sleeping with me," Luke said with disdain. He gave Brian a derisive look. "How long since you took a bath?"

"Saturday night like always."

"I don't want stinky feet in bed with me."

"My feet don't stink," Brian said defensively.

"Luke," Will cautioned.

Luke turned to Adam. "Say, would you like to go with me and Alex tomorrow? We're practicing for the dogsled races they're having after Christmas."

"Sounds like fun. I've never done any mushing."

"Great. We'll leave at first light."

"We were going to cut the tree tomorrow," Will said.

"I know, but I figured you and Brian could do it. This is important. Alex and I got to practice if we're going to win."

"All right." Will smiled at Brian. "It'll just be you and me then."

Brian climbed across the pickup bed to his father. He grinned up at him, clearly pleased.

Laurel searched for something to say. She'd figured that if she ever saw Adam again her mind would overflow with questions, but now that he sat across from her, she couldn't think of a single one.

"How are things shaping up in Europe?" Will asked.

"It's tense. There's a lot of speculation about Hitler and what he's going to do. He's building an army and recently announced the existence of a German air force, which is in direct violation of the Versailles Treaty. I think he's testing France and Britain. It doesn't look good. There's going to be war."

"Really?" Luke asked. He looked at his dad. "If there is, I want to fight."

"You're too young," Will said. "And if there is a war, it won't involve the United States."

"I wish I could agree with you," Adam said, "but I don't think Europe can stand alone against Hitler. If he goes on the offensive, European countries are going to need help from the United States."

"You mean American soldiers would have to fight?" Laurel asked, apprehension touching her.

"Yeah. I think so."

Laurel's trepidation grew. "And what about you? What would you do?"

"I'd serve my country." Adam plucked a piece of straw from the bale he rested against. "But right now we have peace. Anyway, I'd rather think about the English countryside. It's beautiful—green fields, heavy forests. And Paris. It's one of the most interesting cities I've ever visited. The Eiffel Tower is incredible. And when I was in Paris, I spent several hours in the Louvre."

"What's that?" Brian asked.

"It's an art museum that sits right along the Seine River. Art from all over the world is housed there. They actually have paintings by Leonardo Da Vinci and Rembrandt."

"I've always wondered what Paris was like," Laurel said. "I doubt I'll ever see it."

"I'll take you, as long as you're not afraid of flying," Adam said with a grin.

Laurel didn't know how to respond. "I don't think I'm afraid. I've never been on a plane."

"I've always wanted to fly," Luke said.

"I like it." Adam bundled deeper into his coat. "When you're high above everything, you get a whole new perspective. Farmland looks like a giant patchwork quilt, and rivers remind me of silver strands of ribbon."

"Wow! That sounds neat," Brian said. "Can I go to Paris with you?"

Adam gave the boy a quick squeeze. "Sure. Someday when you're grown up."

Laurel studied Adam. He seemed different, comfortable and happy. And if it were possible, he looked even more handsome than she'd remembered. He needed a shave, but the shadow only added to his appeal. When he smiled, his strong features softened, revealing the inner boy. The eyes were the same deep blue and intense. When she was with him, she often had the feeling he could see her very thoughts.

She glanced into the cab and caught Robert's eye in the rearview mirror. He wore a gloomy expression.

Laurel remembered how his face had dropped when she'd thrown herself into Adam's arms. He'd been unable to conceal his hurt, and guilt had washed over her for causing it.

Until Laurel had seen Adam, she'd convinced herself he didn't matter anymore. Now, each time she looked at him, her heartbeat picked up, her palms turned sweaty, and she fumbled for something to say. She fought the impulse to stare at him and felt like a schoolgirl with a crush.

The truck turned into the driveway and slid to a stop in front of Laurel's house. Robert climbed out and walked around to Laurel. "Let me help you." He caught her around the waist and lifted her down. Possessively, he kept his hands on her waist. "Will I see you tomorrow?"

"Uh, I don't know. Maybe. I don't know what I'll be doing. I guess it depends—"

"On what? Whatever Adam's doing?" Robert's voice was sharp. "Never mind. It doesn't matter." He turned and walked back to the driver's side of the truck. "Good night, Mr. and Mrs. Hasper." He ignored Adam, wrenched open the door, climbed in, and slammed it closed.

"What's wrong with Robert?" Brian asked. "Is he mad?"

"Shh. It's none of your business." Jean shuffled the baby from one arm to the other and took the little boy's hand. The truck's engine fired, and Robert bumped down the driveway. Jean headed for the back door. "Adam, I'll put fresh sheets on the bed for you."

Her arms folded under her head, Laurel stared at the ceiling. Moonlight illuminated the room. She welcomed its glow. It matched her mood.

She closed her eyes, but sleep wouldn't come. Finally she threw her legs over the side of the bed, pushed her feet into slippers, and walked to the window. The moon looked like a giant yellow ball resting in the night sky. Its brightness lit up the yard and pastures. The barn stood in the light, dominating the pasture. Beyond were the forests, the mountains rising up behind them like a white crown silhouetted against the night sky.

A wolf howled, his call sounding lonely, pitiful. The cold air penetrated Laurel's flannelette nightgown. She rubbed her arms as if doing so would scrub away the gooseflesh. *Why did Adam come? He could have spent Christmas with friends in Chicago.*

❧

Adam leaned his hands on the bureau and stared into the mirror. Brown hair fell onto his forehead; deep blue eyes filled with mischief stared back. He knew he was good-looking, but he'd always wanted to be seen as someone more reflective and serious, not just handsome. However, he wasn't averse to using his looks when he needed them.

Moving away from the mirror, he studied his build. He was tall and lean but well-muscled. Although most women found him attractive, Laurel didn't seem to care. Why wasn't she interested in him?

He pushed his arms into the sleeves of a flannel shirt, then did up the buttons. "Maybe she is," he said, remembering how she'd sometimes blush under his gaze. And last night her warm welcome seemed genuinely affectionate. *But afterwards, she withdrew and stayed away from me. Robert was at her side all night,* he thought, feeling a surge of jealousy. "I need to stop thinking about her and just enjoy my time here," he said, lacing a boot.

He was eager to spend Christmas with the Haspers. The idea of the holidays with a real family appealed to him. He felt at home here. He'd never had a home life, and this family drew him. He also hoped to find time alone with Laurel.

With a lull in Europe's tumult, it was easy to convince his editor to send him to Alaska to do additional research on the colony. The company had flown him north with a promise of better days to come if he found a good angle on the story. *I'd better come up with something exciting. Maybe this dogsled race will do the trick, especially the angle of Luke and Alex, colonist and native working together. I hope they win.* With one last look in the mirror, he headed for the kitchen. The smell of frying bacon and coffee greeted him at the top of the stairs. He hurried down.

"So, you ready for a practice run?" Luke asked him at the bottom of the stairs.

"You bet. Do you mind if I write about it?"

"That would be neat." Luke caught Adam's arm. "In fact, I've been keeping a scrapbook of all your articles."

Adam smiled. "Really?"

"Yeah. I've never known a real live reporter before. And you're good. I was thinking that maybe some day I'll give it a try."

Adam placed a hand on the boy's shoulder. "Give it your best try." He stepped into the kitchen. "Morning, Mrs. Hasper."

"Morning, Adam," Jean said, spooning batter onto a griddle.

"I could smell breakfast clear upstairs. My mouth's watering."

Laurel lifted a pot of coffee off the stove. "Would you like a cup?"

"Oh, yeah. I could use some. Thank you." Taking the coffee, he held it under his nose and took a whiff. "Smells good." He sipped then wandered to the kitchen window and looked outside. "When's it get light?"

"We've got nearly three hours yet," Luke said. "I know my way to Alex's. We won't have to wait till sunup."

The back door opened, and Will walked in. He pulled off his gloves, shoved them into his coat pockets, then took off the coat and hung it on a peg. "Cold this morning, and the wind's picking up. Looks like we might be in for another storm." He kissed Jean, accepted a cup of coffee from her, and sat at the table. "So, what do you think of Alaska in the wintertime, Adam?"

"What I've seen I like. I've missed Alaska."

Luke sat across from his father. "You missed it even when you were in Europe?" he asked incredulously.

"Europe's nice, but it's not home."

Will raised an eyebrow. "So where is home, Adam?"

"I never thought much about it. Being raised in an orphanage, I don't have a place to look back on. When I lived in Chicago, I rented an apartment, but it never felt like home." He raised his cup. "I guess this feels more like home than any place." His eyes met Laurel's, then returned to Will. "I know it sounds silly, but after spending last summer here, working on the house, fishing with you, Luke, and Brian, and just being with the family, I kind of feel like I belong." He shrugged. "Can't explain it."

Will smiled. "I understand. I've always had family, but I would think that growing up without one would feel like being set adrift on an ice flow." He placed a hand on Adam's arm. "I'm honored you chose us as your stand-in. You fit real well." He hesitated. "Have you ever considered staying? Ever wonder if this might be where you belong?"

Adam's cup stopped halfway to his mouth. Slowly he lowered it to the table. "I thought about it. Sure wish I could stay. But there's no future for me here. I've got my career to think about."

Jean set a plate of bacon and a platter of pancakes on the table. "Who's to say where a person's future lies? That's only something God can know. If we listen to him, he'll direct us." She looked at Adam. "Have you ever asked him where you belong?"

Adam speared two pancakes and set them on his plate. "Well, ma'am, not really. I know you folks put a lot of stock in God, but I can't give him much credit for the good or bad in my life. He's never done much for me." Adam's mind reeled with memories of the cruel and lonely institution where he'd grown up. He'd placed his trust in God once, but God hadn't rescued him. God had let him down, and Adam had no room for him. Trying to remain nonchalant, he drizzled syrup over pancakes. "I don't think God cares much about me."

"I'm sorry to hear you say that," Jean said. "He does care. God created you. He sent his son to die for you. You just need to believe."

Adam chewed and stared at his plate. "Ma'am, with all due respect, believing never did me any good."

Standing at the stove, Laurel listened, remembering what Adam had told her about his childhood. He'd been a lonely, frightened boy. She wanted to comfort him, knowing that child still lived inside. Gently she said, "It wasn't God who let you down. It was people."

Adam looked at Laurel. "Well, I guess you're welcome to your opinion." He took another bite of pancake.

After breakfast, Luke and Adam headed for Alex's. Adam struggled to adapt to snowshoes.

Although daylight touched the sky, the temperature dropped. "Looks like clouds are building up," Adam said. "Do you think it's a good idea to be out here?"

"Oh, sure. We'll be fine."

They approached a small log cabin nestled in deep snow amid a grove of spruce. A trail of smoke drifted from a chimney. Luke strode up to the door and knocked. A low, gruff bark answered from inside.

A few moments later, the door opened. A dark-haired girl with oval, brown eyes stood just inside. She smiled. "Hi, Luke." A huge dog with a heavy coat and gray and white markings on its face pushed its nose between the door and the girl. He growled.

"King, no. It's just Luke."

Adam studied the animal, wondering if he ought to step back. Its dark brown eyes were filled with suspicion, and they'd settled on him.

"Hi, Mattie," Luke said, reaching out and patting the dog. "Is Alex ready to go?"

"He's sick."

"What's wrong?"

"Sore throat and a fever." She glanced over her shoulder. "I don't think he's all that sick. He just likes to be babied."

"I am sick," came a croaky reply. A moment later Alex appeared at the door. He gave Mattie a disdainful glance. "Sorry, Luke, but I really am sick."

"I was hoping we could practice."

Alex nodded at Adam. "Hey, what are you doing back here? I thought you were off in England or somewhere."

"I was, but I had a little work to do here and thought it would be nice to spend Christmas in Alaska." He glanced at the dog. "Nice dog. What's his name?"

"King." Alex patted his head. "He's not mean. Just let him sniff the back of your hand."

Adam took a step forward. A growl rose from King's throat. Adam stopped, then hesitantly held out his hand, palm down. The big dog sniffed him, then pushed through the door, heading straight for him. Adrenaline shot through Adam, but he held his ground, allowing the large animal to sniff his legs and feet. "Good boy. I'm not a bad man. I'm a good man," he said.

Seeming satisfied, King wagged his tail and licked Adam's hand. Adam stroked his head.

"You can go without me. The sled's out back," Alex said.

"You think I'm ready?"

"Sure. You're good, a natural. And King is used to you. You can handle him."

Luke ruffled the dog's thick fur. "OK, King. I guess it's just you and me today." The dog leaned against Luke's leg, pushing his one hundred plus pounds against the young man. Suddenly he bounded past Luke and into the snow.

With King in the harness, Luke and Adam set off. At first the only sound was the swoosh of runners and jangle of the harness as they cut across the snow. "We've got a piece of open ground where we practice," Luke called to Adam, who struggled to keep up.

Adam's legs ached, and he fought for breath. The cold hurt his lungs. King seemed to be picking up the pace. "Hey, could you slow down?" he called.

Pulling the sled to a stop, Luke laughed. "Can't take it, huh?"

Adam caught up to him. Resting his hands on his legs, he bent at the waist and gulped in oxygen. "Keeping up with a sled in deep snow isn't running; it's torture. I'd like to see you do it."

"I told you to ride," Luke said with a grin.

"I should have listened to you."

"Why don't you take a turn?"

"I don't know how."

"Just stand on the runners. If you want him to go, say mush; gee means right and haw means left. King knows what to do."

"You sure?"

"Yeah."

"OK." Taking the traces, Adam stepped onto the sled. "All right, let's go," he said, jingling the harness. "Mush." King needed no coaxing. He lunged ahead, and Adam nearly toppled off backward. He grabbed hold of the sled and hung on. In spite of his hood, wind whistled past his ears. His cheeks burned with the cold, and he wished he'd remembered to pull his scarf over his face.

The snow slid past him, faster and faster. He headed down an embankment.

"Slow him down!" Luke shouted. "You're going too fast!"

Adam pulled on the lines and called, "Whoa." He didn't know what to say to stop the dog. King kept pulling hard, and the sled continued to pick up speed.

"Slow down!" Luke yelled.

"I'm trying!" Adam pulled hard. King didn't seem to notice. The sled whipped over a mound, nearly tipping over. King skirted a tree, and the sled pulled hard to the right and leaned into the snow. Adam felt a tearing, searing pain in his right knee. His foot wedged between the sled and the runners, dropping him onto his back. His body banged against the snow as it followed the sled down a hill. Suddenly his foot came free, and the sled sailed away without him, King still pulling strong.

Adam didn't move for several minutes. He gulped down air and held his throbbing knee between gloved hands.

Lunging toward him, Luke called, "Adam? Adam, you all right?" He kneeled beside his friend.

Speaking through gritted teeth, Adam said, "My knee, it's bad. I don't know what I did, but I can't move it." He sucked air between his teeth when he tried to move.

Luke carefully ran his hand down Adam's leg, then gently manipulated the knee.

"Ahh!" Adam yelled. "Stop! Don't touch it!"

"Can you stand?"

"I don't know. I'll try."

Luke bent down, and Adam threw his left arm over the young man's shoulder. Luke started to rise.

"No! No! Stop! Let me down!" Adam gripped his leg and settled back against the snow. "You'll have to get the sled or go for help. There's no way I can walk out of here."

Luke searched for King and the sled. They were gone. "It's a long way home without a sled." He turned and looked in the direction King had gone. "Alex will kill me if anything happens to his dog."

"Go get the dog. I'll wait. Maybe you can haul me back on the sled."

"It's real cold out here, Adam. I hate to leave you."

Adam gazed around. "What choice do we have? Get the dog."

"I'd feel better if I could make a fire. I didn't bring anything. Did you?"

"No. I hadn't counted on anything like this." Knowing it was hard for Luke to leave him, but realizing he had no other choice, Adam gentled his voice. "This is my fault, not yours. You need to get the dog before he goes too far."

"All right. I'll be back as soon as I can." Luke headed out, following the trail left by King and the sled.

~

Laurel hung a glistening red ball on the tree. "Mama, shouldn't Luke and Adam be back?" She walked to the window and stared out at the darkness. The wind had picked up and swirled snow against the glass.

Jean rested her hand on Laurel's back. "Your father has gone to get Robert. They'll look for them."

"But the weather's getting bad. If they go out—"

"Laurel, all this worrying won't help." She forced a smile. "I'm sure Luke just got caught up in some of Alex's stories and is heading home right now. They'll probably meet each other on the road."

"I hope you're right."

Hours passed and still there was no sign of Luke or Adam. Robert and Will returned after several hours of searching.

Will dropped into a chair at the table. "We went to Alex's. He hasn't seen them since this morning. He's sick, so Luke and Adam went without him."

"They could die out there!" Laurel said. "What are we going to do?"

"Robert and I came back to get warmed up. We'll keep looking. Tom Jenkins is going to help, and some of the old-timers said they'd look too." His face lined with worry, he cradled a cup of coffee between his hands.

"You'll find them," Jean said, pulling a shawl around her shoulders. "They'll be fine. Luke's a clever boy, and Adam's an intelligent man."

"Yeah, but Adam doesn't know anything about surviving under these conditions," Laurel said.

Will nodded. "I better get moving. Robert said he'd meet me in thirty minutes." He held Jean in a tight embrace, then kissed her before disappearing out the back door.

"Is Luke going to die like Justin?" Brian asked, his eyes brimming with tears.

"No, Luke isn't going to die. He'll be fine. We'll find him." Jean pulled the boy onto her lap.

Laurel paced, her mind creating frightening images of two frozen bodies. "God, help them. Please help them make it home." Unable to hold back her tears, she let them fall. She'd already lost one brother. Now Luke? And what about Adam? If something happened to him, she couldn't bear it. *I love him,* she admitted. *I love him.* She pressed her forehead against the cold window glass.

"Honey, they'll be all right." Jean eased Brian off her lap and walked to Laurel. Pulling her close with one arm, she said, "Try not to worry. They'll make it back."

"Oh, Mama, I feel so awful. I can't stand it if I lose Luke. I still miss Justin so much." She cried against her mother's shoulder.

Brian patted her back. "It'll be all right. Let's look at the tree. It'll make you feel better," he said and disappeared into the front room.

"Mama, I love Adam."

Jean pushed a strand of hair off Laurel's face. "I know."

"You do? How? I didn't until just now."

"I know you," Jean said with a maternal smile. "I see the way you light up when you get his letters and the way he unsettles you when he's around." She kissed Laurel's forehead. "I was young once. I haven't forgotten what it's like."

"You didn't say anything. Why?"

"What was I supposed to say? Adam was gone, and Robert was here."

"What should I do?"

"I can't tell you that; only remember that sometimes our hearts can lead us astray. Adam is a fine person, but his life is very different from yours. Robert is steady, he's ready to include you in a life you know, and he loves you."

Laurel kissed her mother. Walking back to the window, she stared out into the night. *If Adam makes it, I'm going to tell him how I feel,* she decided.

Chapter Twenty-Eight

OVER SHRIEKING WIND, LAUREL HEARD THE DISTINCT SOUND OF BOOTS BEING knocked free of snow. She ran for the door, flinging it open. Blowing snow swirled in. Will stood alone. He looked at her through anguished eyes. Laurel's legs went weak, and she grabbed the doorframe to steady herself. "Where's Robert?" she managed to ask.

"Home."

"You didn't . . . they aren't . . ."

"Will?" Jean asked.

"We didn't find them." Closing the door, he stepped inside, pushed off his hood, and unbuttoned his coat. "We looked and looked and didn't find them. We couldn't stay out longer." He hung up his coat.

Jean walked to her husband and slid her arms around his waist.

Will pulled her close. "I'm sorry. We'll go out again at first light." He looked at Laurel. "I'm sorry, sugar."

"There's coffee," Laurel said, "and Mama made apple cake."

Will managed a smile. "I can count on you baking when life gets hard. Coffee sounds good." He held his hands out to the stove. "Where's Brian?"

"He tried to wait up but fell asleep sitting at the table," Jean said, filling a cup with coffee and handing it to Will before she sank into a chair.

"I carried him up to bed," Laurel said. Her father looked weary, empty. Wind howled under the eaves.

Will shivered. "I'm cold to the bone."

"We need to get you into some warm clothes," Jean said, pushing herself to her feet and grabbing one of three shirts resting on the back of a chair beside the stove. She held it out to him. "Put it on. It'll warm you."

Will did as he was told. "Feels better. Thanks."

Wondering if it were possible for Luke and Adam to survive a night in this storm, Laurel filled a mug with coffee and sat at the table. "What do you think happened to them?"

"Don't know. We tried to follow the sled tracks, but they'd been buried in fresh snow."

"Do you think they're all right?"

Before Will could answer, Jean said, "Of course they are." She walked to the cupboard, opened it, and took down three plates, then set them beside the apple cake. "God hasn't forgotten those two. He's looking after them." She opened a drawer, took out a knife, and sliced the heavy, moist dessert. Lifting out a wedge, she gently placed it on a plate. "God knows just exactly where they are, and he'll make sure they get home." She handed the cake to Will. Meeting his eyes, she said evenly, "Tomorrow's Christmas. They'll be here." She turned and walked back to the counter, removing another piece of cake. She set it on a plate and gave it to Laurel. After cutting a piece for herself, she sat at the table.

Will stood beside the stove. After taking a drink of his coffee, he set the cup on the warming shelf above the stove, then with his hand shaking slightly, he cut off a bite of cake and ate it. He said nothing.

Laurel sat across from her mother. She speared her cake but didn't eat it. Her stomach ached. "Mama, how can you know they'll be all right?"

"I trust God," Jean said.

Laurel moved the confection around her plate, then pushed the dessert away.

She didn't want to hurt her mother, but unable to hold back the words, Laurel said, "God didn't save Justin."

"He won't take another son from me," Jean said softly. "I know it." Silence fell over the room. Jean set her fork on the side of her plate. Her eyes brimmed with tears.

Immediately Will set his dessert aside and crossed to her. Kneeling beside Jean, he wrapped his arms around her.

She cried softly. "I want them to be all right. They have to be all right."

Will held her tight. "They're in God's hands. All we can do is believe he'll do what's best." Staring at the window, he added, "Sometimes God's will isn't our will. We must trust him. He knows all things; he sees the beginning and the end. He'll do what's best," he repeated.

Jean looked into Will's eyes. "You're right." She kissed him. "What would I have done without you all these years?" She managed a small smile. "Let's get you warmed up and into bed. I'll bring in some hot bricks."

Will kissed her again. "Thank you for taking such good care of me." He released her, stood, and walked out of the room.

Using oven mittens, Jean grabbed three hot bricks and wrapped them in heavy towels. She kissed Laurel's cheek. "Try to get some sleep, honey."

Laurel rested a hand on her mother's arm. "I don't know if I can—not with Adam and Luke still out there."

"Maybe they'll be here in the morning." Jean gave Laurel a comforting smile and left the kitchen.

Laurel sat at the table. The cabin creaked and shuddered. The wind moaned, hurtling snow against the window. It sounded like hard pebbles hitting the glass. Laurel stared at her coffee mug. The sides of the cup were stained black, and the dark brew sat flat and lifeless like cold brine. She stood, crossed to the sink, and dumped it down the drain. Standing in front of the window, she stared out at white crystals swirling toward the window out of the dark. "Where are you? Please come home. Please."

She closed her eyes. "God, I beg you to keep them safe. I couldn't bear it if anything happened to them." Tears spilled onto her cheeks. Wiping at them, she walked stiffly to the stove, stoked the fire, put out the lantern, and wandered into the front room.

The Christmas tree that had looked merry earlier that day now only served to remind Laurel they had nothing to be cheerful about. Without Luke and Adam, there couldn't be any Christmas. Gifts were piled underneath it. Laurel kneeled and picked up one. It was for Brian. She knew what it was—a top. She smiled. Brian would like it.

She picked up another. The tag was made out to Adam. Laurel's breath caught. How had her mother found a gift for Adam so quickly? She smiled softly. "Mama. She must have gotten it for him today." She replaced the package.

The floor creaked in her parents' room, then footsteps followed. She stood and turned to find her father watching her.

He looked at the tree. "Doesn't seem much like Christmas."

"No, it doesn't."

Will shuffled into the kitchen and reappeared a moment later with his coat and boots on.

"You're not going out again?" Laurel asked, alarm ripping through her.

"No. I'm not that foolish." Will smiled, the creases deepening in his face. "I have work to do in the barn. I'd planned on getting it done this evening, but . . ." His words fell away. "I've been working on a sled for Luke—for the race. I figured he'd have a better chance with a new sled."

Fear, like a knife, twisted in Laurel's chest. What if Luke never used the sled? Softly, she said, "He'll like that."

With a slight nod, Will turned and walked out. Laurel heard the door open and close. With one last look at the tree, she shuffled up the stairs.

~

Laurel opened her eyes to a dark room. The sun wasn't up yet, but the world was quiet—no wind, no snow pebbles against the glass— just quiet. Shocked that she'd slept, Laurel sat up. *Maybe Luke and Adam are home,* she thought, throwing her legs over the side of the bed. She pushed her feet into slippers, pulled on a bathrobe, and headed downstairs. The house was empty. Hurrying for the back porch, she hoped to find Luke and Adam's coats hanging by the back door, but she didn't.

She walked to the stove and picked up the coffeepot. It was still half full, so she set it on a burner and started a fire. With that done, she sat at the table, her cheek resting in her hand. "Father, I thought you would save them," she whispered.

Laurel sat for a long while. Finally her mother joined her and quietly started cooking breakfast. "I figure I ought to have something for them to eat when they get home," she said.

"Do you really think they're coming home?" Laurel asked, desperate to believe.

"Yes, I do. In fact, I wouldn't be surprised if they were on their way right now." She glanced out the window. "It's getting light. They should be here soon." She turned a piece of sizzling bacon.

Laurel walked to the window. The world looked like it had been draped in white eiderdown. Fresh powder concealed tire tracks, footprints, and animal tracks. Tree limbs were encased in unspoiled crystals, and evergreen needles had turned into white fluff. No one had come or gone—the snow was unmarred. Even the tracks left by her father last night were buried. The snow no longer looked beautiful. Instead Laurel saw death. Resting her cheek against the cold glass, she wished she could believe.

The sound of a car engine fractured the quiet. Her heart quickening, Laurel peered up the driveway. A pickup truck bounced and slipped through the deep powder and stopped in front of the house. Laurel held her breath. Were Adam and Luke in the truck? Or had someone come to tell them they'd been found . . . dead?

The barn door opened. Pushing against snow, it created a mound. Will stepped out, his face creased with fatigue and worry. He stared at the truck. Then a smile smoothed away lines of anxiety. "Praise the Lord!" he hollered and ran for the truck.

Luke stepped out of the cab. He looked weary but healthy.

"Thank you, Lord!" Laurel whispered, hoping Adam would be next. He didn't appear. *Where is he?*

Then she saw Adam carefully lift his right leg and set his foot gingerly on the snow. His pant leg had been cut open, revealing a bandaged knee. He swung his other leg out and slowly stood, leaning against the truck. After saying something to the driver, he closed the door and watched the truck back away. He said something to Will, then looked at the house. His eyes stopped when they reached Laurel. Smiling, he swept off his hat and waved it at her.

Joy rolled through Laurel. She waved back and ran for the door, flinging it open. "Luke!" she yelled, throwing her arms around her brother. "I thought you were dead." Tears washed her face. She kissed his cheek.

Luke grinned. "Maybe I ought to disappear more often. I like this kind of welcome. If you treated me this way all the time, I'd be a much nicer brother," he teased and stepped inside.

Laurel came face-to-face with Adam, who had an arm draped around her father's shoulders. She didn't know what to say or do. She wanted to hug him, hold him close, and tell him she loved him, but knew she couldn't do that. It wasn't proper, and she had no idea how he would receive such a bold announcement. Besides, she'd already embarrassed him his first night in Palmer.

Adam let loose of Will and limped forward.

Laurel's eyes went to his knee. "Adam, you're hurt!"

He grinned and pulled Laurel to him in a bear hug. "It's nothing." He held her for a moment before releasing her. "For a while yesterday, I was afraid I'd never see you again."

"You were?" Laurel's heart beat fast.

Resting an arm around her shoulders, Adam limped into the house.

"What happened to your leg?" Brian asked.

"I twisted it when the sled crashed. It's sore and swollen, but it'll heal." Still leaning on Laurel, he hobbled inside.

Laurel liked the feel of his arm around her and the sensation of helping him. "What happened to you two?"

"It was like a miracle," Luke said. "We were out practicing for the race, and I let Adam have a hand at the reins. Everything was fine, and then King went wild. He wouldn't slow down. Anyway, Adam and the sled headed down a hill and tipped over. King kept going. We were stuck, and the weather turned bad."

"How about a cup of coffee?" Jean asked.

"Sounds good." Adam lowered himself onto a chair at the table, careful not to bend his knee.

"Anyway," Luke said, pulling out a chair and dropping into it, "I had to leave Adam to get help. The wind was picking up and it was snowing, plus it was getting dark. I'll tell ya', I was scared. I prayed as I walked." He smiled at his mother and father. "Thanks for teaching me right. Anyway, I stumbled onto this cabin. And would you believe it? King was standing right there on the porch, still in his harness, the sled behind him." He took the coffee offered and sipped it.

"A man named Mr. Applegate lives there. He was real nice and went with me to get Adam. That's where we stayed last night. We'd have come home, but the storm was too bad by then. I'm sorry if we worried you."

"All that matters is you're safe," Jean said.

"Mr. Applegate's kind of a recluse, but he's actually real friendly."

"Interesting man. I'd like to write a story about him some day—if he'll allow it."

Jean took a goose out of the icebox. "It's going to be a wonderful Christmas!"

"Yeah, can we open the presents?" Brian asked, running to the front room.

"I don't see why not," Will said with a chuckle.

Brian grabbed a package from under the tree. "This one's for me!"

Will joined Brian. With Susie on her lap, Jean sat on the sofa, and Laurel sat beside her. Adam lowered himself into the rocker, keeping his leg out straight in front of him, and Luke stood in the doorway.

"Can I open it?" Brian asked. Will nodded, and the boy tore through the paper and opened the box. "Wow!" he said, pulling out a metal dump truck. Immediately he set it on the floor, pushing it over the wood planking while making truck noises. "This is just like a real one!"

"I suppose we might as well open the rest," Will said, picking up a package. "Here's a gift for Susie." He handed a gift to the little girl. "This is for Luke."

Luke took the package and quickly unwrapped it. "A new fishing reel! I should be able to catch a string of fish with this." He assembled the pieces and held it out, giving it a flick of the wrist to get the feel of it. "This is nice. Thanks."

Will then handed a package to Laurel. She opened it and found a new pair of silk stockings.

Jean grinned. "I figured I might as well be impractical. I know how much you like dressing up."

Laurel hugged her mother. "Thank you, Mama."

"Hmm, there's one here for Adam."

"Me?" Adam asked incredulously. "You didn't even know I was going to be here."

"Santa knows everything," Jean said with a grin.

Adam quickly stripped away the wrapping paper. Inside lay a new notebook, a writing pen, and a scrapbook. He looked at the Haspers. "I don't know what to say. It's perfect. Thank you."

Laurel thought she saw tears in Adam's eyes and was touched that something so simple could trigger that kind of response in him. She felt more certain his surface bravado was simply a way of shielding himself.

"I never really had a family Christmas," he said. "Thank you."

Other presents were exchanged. Jessie had made a gift of her husband's wood lathe to Will. Plus there were handkerchiefs, pocketknives, cookware, and books. When the gifts were all opened, Will stood. "I think there's one more," he said mysteriously, "but I'll have to go and get it. I'll be right back."

He left the room and walked out of the house. A few minutes later a knock sounded at the back door. "Luke, I think that's for you," Jean said, a twinkle in her eye.

"Me?" He stood and walked to the door. The rest of the family followed. Opening it, he stared at his father and the fine mushing sled beside him. "Where did you get it?" he asked, walking down the step, his eyes never leaving the sled.

"I made it. Figured if you two boys were going to win that race tomorrow you needed a good one."

"Thanks, Dad!" Luke kneeled beside the sled, running his hands over the smooth wood and inspecting the metal runners. "This will be fast. We'll win for sure now."

Chapter Twenty-Nine

THE FOLLOWING MORNING, DAYLIGHT BROUGHT SUNSHINE AND SHIMMERING snow. Filled with anticipation, the Haspers piled into the back of Robert's truck and headed for town. The races would be starting in less than thirty minutes. Luke had already taken off. He and Alex had things to do to prepare.

When they pulled into town, the streets were crowded with contestants and spectators. The barking of dogs echoed from the end of the street where the races would begin. Already, two teams of mushers waited at the starting line. Several elimination races would be held, and in the end, only two teams would be left. The winners of that race would be the champions. Luke and Alex waited their turn. King was more than ready, pulling on his harness and barking at the other dogs. He was by far the biggest dog. Laurel hoped he was the fastest.

She felt Robert at her side. All morning he'd nearly hinged himself to her, often holding her arm. Laurel felt uncomfortable, especially after realizing her true feelings for Adam. She'd have to tell Robert.

Robert took Laurel's hand. "While we're waiting, can I talk to you?"

"Of course." Laurel tried to sound nonchalant, but she knew Robert well enough to know something was wrong. She suspected it had to do with Adam, and she wasn't eager to hear what he had to say.

Robert led her away from the crowd. With his hands on her upper arms, he looked down at her. "Laurel, you know how I feel about you, and I wouldn't ever do anything to hurt you, but . . ."

Laurel's throat tightened.

"So, do you think the boys will win?" Adam asked, stepping up to the couple.

Robert closed his eyes and let out an exasperated breath. "I don't know," he said without looking at Adam. "Laurel and I are talking. We need some time alone."

"Sure," Adam said and started to walk away.

"No, wait," Robert said. "You might as well stay. I'd like you to hear this too."

Laurel felt queasy. She didn't like the way Robert sounded. He seemed anxious and almost angry. "Do we have to talk about this now? Luke's race is just about to start."

"It won't take long." Robert sucked in a deep breath and looked at Laurel. "I know Adam leads an exciting life, and he's an interesting person, but I don't think it's a good idea for you to see him."

"What?" Laurel asked.

"He's not right for you."

"Robert, Adam and I are not *seeing* each other. He's just staying at our house. He's a guest."

Adam took a step closer to Laurel. "And if we were, I think it's up to Laurel to decide who she sees and who she doesn't see. You have no right to tell her what to do."

Robert's normal gentle demeanor faltered, and he glared at Adam. "In case you don't know, Laurel and I have an understanding. We're a . . . a couple."

Laurel gasped. "No, Robert. We're not. I told you we could go out together. That's all." She cringed at the pain that passed over his face. She didn't want to hurt him.

"Laurel, you know how I feel about you." Robert gripped her arms. "Adam's not good for you. He's a philanderer. You deserve better."

"Oh, you mean someone like you?" Adam challenged. "And where do you get the right to call me a philanderer? You know nothing about me."

"I know more than you think. The kind of man you are is common knowledge."

Robert looked at Laurel. "I can offer you stability, an honest living. He—"

"That's enough!" Laurel snapped. "You don't know Adam, and you have no right to say such things about him. And no one tells me who I will see and who I won't see." Laurel's anger goaded her on.

"You don't own me, Robert. I like you, or I did like you, but you've gone too far."

"I just want to protect you."

"Thank you very much, but I can take care of myself." Furious and embarrassed, Laurel spun around and headed back toward the racers. As she joined her parents, Jean raised a questioning eyebrow but said nothing.

A few moments later Adam joined Laurel. They glanced at one another but didn't speak. Robert stood with his mother and sisters. Each time Laurel looked that way, he was watching her, his face a mix of anger and hurt. Laurel wished she'd held her tongue.

Luke and Alex moved to the starting line. Streamers marked the course, which led through town, then around a willow thicket at the edge of town where riders and drivers were supposed to switch places before heading back down the street the way they'd come. The first to cross the finish line won.

King barked and snarled at the dog next to him. Alex called to him in his native tongue, and King settled down. Luke would ride first. He sat on the front of the sled, and Alex stood on the runners. When the gun sounded, both teams lunged forward. The crowd cheered. Alex and Luke quickly moved ahead of the other team. King was stronger and faster than his competitor, opening up more and more ground between him and his challenger as he ran the course. It was an easy win. Luke and Alex slid across the finish line several lengths ahead.

There were more heats, with Luke and Alex winning theirs. Laurel did her best to avoid Robert and concentrate on the races. Finally it came down to the last race. Luke and Alex were matched against a good team that clearly had experience. It wouldn't be an easy contest.

Laurel asked Adam, "Do you think they can win?"

"Absolutely. I'm betting on it. I've already got my story written in my head, and they win."

He smiled, setting off a fluttering sensation in Laurel's stomach. She'd decided to tell him how she felt, but now after what had happened with Robert, she wasn't sure. Life was complicated. *And what if he doesn't feel the same as I do?* she wondered.

The gun fired, and the two sleds took off, tearing through town, the other team in the lead. Their dog was big and pulled hard. King couldn't abide anyone being ahead of him, so he strained to catch them. Alex yelled commands, but the dog needed little coaxing. He closed the gap.

They rounded the thicket. While the sled was still moving, Luke jumped off and ran behind Alex, grabbing hold of the handles and the lead. Alex stepped off and ran alongside while Luke took control, then he jumped onto the sled and settled into the fur cushioning. The exchange took only seconds and was a maneuver they'd practiced many times. Soon they were on their way back toward town. The other team had an easy transition as well, and both teams were running side-by-side.

King snarled and snapped at his rival. The dog retaliated by sinking his teeth into the thick fur around King's neck. For a moment it looked like a dogfight would end the race. "Mush, King!" Luke yelled. Reminded of his task, the dog lunged forward and pulled ahead, gradually opening the distance between the sleds. Alex and Luke flew across the finish line first.

Cheers from onlookers erupted. The Haspers and Alex's family ran to congratulate their sons. Jean gave Luke a big hug while Will pounded him on the back. "Good job, son."

"It's a great sled," Luke said, wearing a broad smile.

"I knew you could do it." Adam hugged Luke hard, lifting him off the ground. "I knew it, and that's what I'm going to write. I think the Chicago readers will get a kick out of this. I got some good pictures too."

Laurel had never seen Adam so animated. It was as if he'd actually run the race himself.

"Maybe I'll do this one day. What do you think?" he asked.

"You'd have to stick around," Will said with a knowing smile.

Adam didn't answer, but his expression darkened, and he turned quiet.

Laurel waited, longing for Adam to say he would stay.

"I better get," he said and walked up the street, clearly wrestling with something and wanting to be alone.

Laurel hesitated. She needed to know what was going through his mind, and she needed to tell him how she felt. With a quick glance at Robert, she ran after Adam. "Wait," she called.

Adam stopped and watched her, his expression a mix of confusion and sadness. He caught Laurel's arm, clasped her gloved hand in his, and continued walking. "Where do you want to go?"

Laurel looked back. Robert stared at them, unable to conceal his hurt and anger. Laurel yanked her hand out of Adam's. "Anywhere's fine with me," she said. "It's awfully cold."

"They're building a bonfire. We could warm up there."

"No. Too many people. I want to talk to you about something." Laurel tried to think of a place. "There's a barn just at the edge of town. It's filled with hay. We could bury ourselves in it to stay warm." She glanced at his leg. "But what about your injury?"

"I'll be fine. Lead the way."

Laurel walked and Adam limped toward the barn. She didn't know what she was going to say. She'd never felt about anyone the way she did Adam. What if he thought she was silly?

The next thing she knew they stood in front of the barn. Adam opened one side of its double doors. "After you," he said gallantly.

Laurel stepped inside. It was dark and musty, smelling of hay. "It's not much warmer in here."

"That's all right," Adam said, catching Laurel in his arms. "We can make our own heat." He looked down at her, his passion obvious.

Laurel caught the mild scent of spicy aftershave. A mixture of alarm and desire coursed through her. What had she gotten herself into? "I . . . I . . ."

Adam quieted her protest with his lips. He pulled her close. His kiss was tender, not at all frightening. He smiled, planting a kiss on the tip of her nose. "I've been dreaming about doing that for months."

"You have?"

"Uh-huh," he said, his voice husky. He kissed her again, only this time with more urgency.

Her arms circling Adam's neck, Laurel answered his kiss.

He gently pressed his lips against her neck, then held her tightly. Pressing his cheek against her hair, he said, "I hate to go. I don't want to leave you."

"I don't want you to." Laurel stepped back. "Adam, when you and Luke were lost, I told myself I'd tell you how I feel about you if I had the chance." Her hands rested against his chest; she glanced at them, then back at his penetrating blue eyes. "Adam, I love you. I didn't want to, but I do."

Adam's eyes widened slightly, then a crooked smile touched his lips. "I love you." He kissed her again. "I've never loved anyone in my life.

Not really, not before you." He kissed her, first on the mouth, then her forehead, eyelids, and neck.

Laurel's emotions surged. She felt herself falling into a dizzying spiral. She opened her eyes and pushed away. "I . . . I've never been kissed like this."

"I'm sorry. I . . . I wasn't thinking. I got carried away."

"No, it's not that . . . It's just . . ." How could she explain her own passion? It was too embarrassing. "I just don't think we should. That's all." She walked to a pile of hay and sat down.

Keeping his injured leg straight, Adam sat beside Laurel, and took her hand. He kissed it, then pressed it against his cheek. "I've never felt like this. I do love you." He searched Laurel's face. "I love your family too. I've never had a family before. It feels good."

Afraid to ask, but knowing she must, Laurel gathered her courage. "Adam, please stay here with us."

Adam didn't answer.

"Can you stay in the valley?" she pressed. "Even Daddy thinks you belong here."

Anguish touched his face. He stood, walked to a window, and stared out. "I wish I could." He didn't say anything for a long moment. "I can't. I have my work. It's what I've always wanted. I *have* to leave." He turned and looked at her. "How can I give it up? I'm nothing without it."

"You're not nothing, Adam. You could never be nothing. The work you do isn't who you are. You could write here in Palmer. We need a newspaper."

"Here?" He couldn't hide a smirk. "*The Palmer Weekly?*" He shoved his hands into his pockets. "That's not a paper." He paced, then stopped. "Laurel, come with me—the two of us in Europe. It'll be fun."

Laurel had imagined traveling the world with Adam, and for a fleeting moment, she thought it might be possible. Then she remembered her family, sweet Justin, and the farm. She'd just found a new home. This is where she belonged, not somewhere on the other side of the world. "Adam, I can't leave. My family needs me. And . . . and this is my home."

Adam said nothing for a long while. "So, that's it then. I go back to England and you stay?"

"I guess so," Laurel said, her heart heavy. *Lord, there has to be a way,* she anguished. *Father, can I go?* No matter how much she wanted to be with Adam, she found no peace in the idea of leaving. God had another plan for her.

The sound of laughter and singing carried through the window. "They must have started the bonfire," Adam said morosely. Taking her hand, he said, "At least we can have one more evening together. My plane leaves tomorrow."

"Tomorrow," Laurel said, careful not to look at Adam. She didn't want him to see her tears. "I have to go, Adam. I'm sorry. Good-bye." She wrenched her hand out of his and ran from the barn, wishing she'd never met Adam Dunnavant.

Chapter Thirty

WILL SET HIS EMPTY COFFEE CUP ON THE COUNTER. "ARE YOU FEELING better?" he asked Laurel.

"I'm fine. I've just been a little tired." Laurel added the cup to the dishes already piled in the sink.

"Did something happen at the dog sled races? You've been kind of quiet ever since."

"No. Nothing," Laurel lied. She didn't want to talk about Robert's possessiveness, and she certainly couldn't tell her father about what had happened with Adam.

Putting on his coat, Will hollered, "Come on Luke, we've got to milk the cows. We've been lazing around here long enough." He pulled on his hat and gloves. "It's a cold one," he said, kissing Jean and heading out the door.

Jean lifted Susie out of her highchair, and carrying the little girl on her hip, headed for the bedroom. At the same time, Luke raced through the kitchen, grabbing his coat and hat off the back porch before disappearing out the door.

"Slow down," Jean called after him.

"He didn't hear you," Laurel said with a grin, clearing the last of the breakfast dishes off the table. She watched Luke run to the barn and sighed, wishing she could have his high spirits. She'd felt gloomy since Adam had gone. She shuffled across the room, lifted a pot of hot water off the stove, and carried it to the sink where she added it to the cold water. Bubbles danced and burst.

Laurel picked up a dish and ran a washcloth over the egg-encrusted plate. Her mind wandered back to the kiss she and Adam had shared.

For a moment it had seemed as if their life was as it should be, but to Adam, work was everything. *Eventually he'll find out it isn't enough,* she thought dismally, scrubbing the dish.

The back door flew open, and Luke ran inside. "Fire! There's a fire!" he yelled.

"Where?" Laurel asked, alarm pulsating through her.

"The Lundeen's place! Dad's already on his way!" Without bothering to close the door, Luke sprinted out.

"Mama!" Laurel shouted, dropping the plate back into the water. "The Lundeens' house is on fire! I'm going!" She didn't wait to see if her mother had heard. Stripping off her apron, she pulled on her boots and coat.

Susie in her arms, Jean ran into the room. "A fire?"

Laurel could hear Brian's steps on the stairway as he galloped down. "Where's a fire?"

"At the Lundeens'. I'm going." Laurel hurried out the back door.

"Me too," Brian said, following her.

"You wait for me," Jean told Brian, then called after Laurel, "I'll be there just as soon as I can."

Peering through the muted early morning light, Laurel headed for the gate, keeping her eyes on the smoke pouring out from beneath the Lundeen eaves. Her father and Luke, looking like hurdlers, had nearly made it across the pasture. She pushed on the gate, stopping just long enough to close it, then ran across the field. Pulling up her skirt, she plunged through deep snow, struggling to stay upright as her legs dropped through the crusted top and sank into white powder. Barely noticing the cold, she struggled to run faster. Smoke now billowed out a side window.

Will charged through the snow, Luke just behind him. When he reached the gate, he didn't stop to open it but catapulted over the top. Luke followed.

Cold seared Laurel's lungs, and her legs ached, but she kept going. *Please, Father, let them be all right,* she prayed, sorry that the last time she'd seen Robert she'd been angry. Too winded to climb over the gate, Laurel unlatched the bolt and pulled hard. Snow piled behind it, and she barely managed to open it enough to squeeze through. She sprinted the last few yards.

Patricia Lundeen stood in the driveway, her two girls clinging to her. Luke stood beside them. The girls were crying; Veronica hiccuped with each sob. No one else was in sight. Smoke rolled out the windows, and flames licked the rooftop.

Patricia glanced at Laurel; her eyes were tormented and sorrow-filled.

"Where're Daddy and Robert?" Laurel yelled, grabbing the woman's arm. "Where are they?"

Patricia looked at the house. "I told them to leave it, but they wouldn't listen." She pressed a trembling hand to her mouth. "He's inside. So is Robert. Your father went in to get him."

"No!" Laurel ran to the house, but radiating heat forced her to stop at the front steps. "Daddy!" she screamed. "Daddy!"

A few moments later Will and Robert stumbled from around the side of the house. Blackened from soot, they staggered, coughing. Robert dropped to the frozen ground, resting on hands and knees and gulping in air. Still panting, he sat up, rested his arms on bent knees, and stared at the burning house. Anguish etched his face.

Will stayed on his feet but bent at the waist and coughed again and again.

"Daddy, are you all right?" Laurel asked, wrapping an arm around his waist.

Will nodded. Straightening, he stared at the burning home. "It'll just take . . ." He coughed. "A few minutes for . . . me to . . . get my breath." He shook his head slowly. His eyes slid to Robert. "I'm sorry, son."

Patricia kneeled beside her oldest and wrapped her arms around him. The girls joined them, and the four sat in the cold, weeping and holding each other.

Finally Veronica stood. "What are we going to do?" she asked, chewing on the end of her braid.

Joanna pushed herself to her feet and draped an arm around her younger sister.

Still staring at the house, Veronica asked, "Where are we going to live?"

Patricia struggled to lift her bulky weight off the ground. "God will take care of us," She pulled her daughters close. The girls shivered. Both were in slippers and dressed only in their nightclothes.

"The first thing we're going to do is get you warm and dry," Jean said, approaching Patricia and the girls. She gave them all a hug, holding Patricia the longest.

"Where are Brian and Susie?" Will asked.

"Susie's in her bed, and Brian's keeping an eye on her."

"Brian?" Will raised an eyebrow.

"He'll be fine," Jean assured him. She turned to Patricia. "You can come home with us. We've plenty of room."

"I don't know what happened. The house was cold, so I built a fire. It was fine when I went upstairs to check on the girls." Patricia stopped, her mind searching for an explanation. A puzzled expression touched her face. "I heard a crash and breaking glass." She looked at her son. "What do you think that could be?"

No one answered, then Luke said, "I saw a pickup pulling out onto the road from your place this morning. I couldn't tell who it was."

Robert's expression turned pensive. He looked at Laurel. "I saw that redhead, Ted, stop out on the road a couple days ago. And then again yesterday."

Patricia put her hands to her mouth. "You don't think someone . . . ?"

"I don't know what I think, but I'm going to find out."

≈

After a quick cleanup, Will and Robert headed for Ray Townsend's. "It's Ray. I know it," Robert said, keeping his eyes on the road and gripping the steering wheel so hard his knuckles were white.

"I think we need to start with him," Will said cautiously. "We don't have any proof."

Robert turned into the Townsend driveway and slid on ice. He corrected, then skated toward a fence running alongside the drive. Finally, regaining control of the truck, he said, "No proof maybe, but he's the one."

Will had thought it might have been Ray who hired the young men to beat up Robert, but it was hard to believe he would stoop so low as to burn Robert and his family out. Robert stopped the car, threw it into gear, then turned off the key. Will rested a hand on the young man's arm. "Rein in your temper. We don't know what happened for sure. We're here to find out what we can."

Robert nodded and opened the door. Stepping out of the pickup, he waited for Will, and the two men approached the Townsend house together. It wasn't much to boast about. Like many homes in the valley, it was simple and made of logs, although it was slightly larger than most. They stepped onto a broad wooden porch.

Robert knocked on the door. Celeste opened it. Her face flushed slightly, and she smiled. "Why, Robert, how nice to see you." She glanced at Will. "Mr. Hasper. Good to see you. What brings you out our way?"

"We need to talk to your father," Robert said solemnly, swiping a lock of black hair off his forehead. He'd left in such a hurry, he'd forgotten a hat. "Is he here?"

"Yes. He's out back cutting wood." Celeste's smile faded. "Is something wrong?"

"I just need to talk to your father," Robert repeated, his voice tight and controlled.

"I'll take you to him. Let me get my coat."

"No." Will smiled kindly. "We can find him. Thanks." He nodded and stepped off the porch, then headed around the back of the house. Robert followed.

The crack of splintering wood told them where to go. Ray Townsend stood on the side of a shed, and he brought an ax down on a piece of pine just as Robert and Will stepped into his vision. The wood split and fell away. Ray looked at the visitors, his mouth set. He rested the head of the ax on the chopping block and leaned on the handle. "Something I can do for you?"

"We have something to say to you," Robert said.

"I've no time to shoot the breeze."

"You have time for this." Robert's words came out sharp and abrasive.

Will stepped forward. "There was a fire at the Lundeens' place this morning. Robert's house burned. Someone was seen leaving the property just as the fire broke out."

Mr. Townsend picked up another piece of pine and set it on the stump. "And what does that have to do with me?" He swung the ax up over his head and brought it down, ripping open the wood.

"More than once I saw you drive by my place lately," Robert said, "and one of those men you hired to beat me stopped on the road twice this week."

Mr. Townsend's mouth turned up in a sneer. "So the roads belong to you? I always thought this was a free country where a person could drive wherever he pleased." He threw the split wood aside and rested his ax on his shoulder. "None of this has anything to do with me."

"Someone set my house on fire! And it was one of your men!"

"My men? Now I have men?" Ray lifted the ax and let the end of the handle rest in his left hand. "I don't own anyone. If someone burned down your place, it was his choice. If I were you, I'd go and see . . . What did you say the man's name was? Ted?"

His hands rolled into fists, Robert stepped toward Ray. The big man held the ax in front of him. "Son, you might want to think twice before coming at me."

"Robert," Will said calmly, "this won't solve anything." He stepped between the two. "Ray, I've given you the benefit of the doubt more than once. No more. You've stirred up a lot of the trouble we've had since we came to this valley. It's true we have no proof you're behind this fire, but if we come across it we'll go to the law."

Ray let loose with a roaring laugh. "Go ahead, but you won't find any proof. I'd advise you to head back where you came from. I'd hate to see anything happen to you or your family."

Will struggled to control his temper. He wanted to pummel the man. He glanced at the ax. *He'd probably use it,* he thought. "Don't threaten my family. You're not running us off. We're here to stay. This is our home." He took a slow breath. "We can live as friendly neighbors or not. It's up to you."

"Get off my land. Now."

Disheartened and angry, Will turned to Robert. "Let's go. There's nothing we can do here."

"God knows the truth," Robert said. "And one day, you'll pay."

He and Will turned to walk away and nearly ran into Celeste. Anguish lined her face. "Robert, I know my father didn't do anything. He wouldn't do this."

"I hope you're right," Robert said and walked on.

Chapter Thirty-One

THE FIRE WAS REPORTED TO THE AUTHORITIES, BUT NOTHING TURNED UP THAT would implicate Ray Townsend. When Ted was confronted, his friends said he'd been with them. Nothing could be done.

Friends and neighbors donated food, clothing, and other odds and ends. The Lundeens moved in with the Haspers. Their house couldn't be rebuilt until spring, and they had no money for rent. Robert shared a room with Luke and Brian upstairs; Laurel gave her room to Patricia and the girls and took the sofa in the front room.

Two families sharing one house was a challenge, but the Haspers and Lundeens made it work. Everyone pitched in, and cooperation was the rule. All the women, including the Lundeen girls, shared housework and cooking. Robert looked after his place and also worked alongside Will and Luke.

Laurel was glad they'd been able to help but had to admit to feeling uncomfortable at having to share living space with Robert. He'd been unable to hide his feelings.

Although Adam had left the valley, he remained in Laurel's thoughts. He still wrote, and each time a letter arrived, her emotions were upended.

Early one afternoon, Joanna and Veronica burst through the back door. Their cheeks pink with cold and eyes bright, they ran to Laurel, who sat at the table visiting with her mother and Patricia Lundeen. "The boys have cleared away the snow on the creek," Veronica said, out of breath. "Celeste and Robert want to know if you can come skating."

"Celeste? She's here?" Laurel hadn't seen her in weeks. Celeste's father had made the Lundeens and the Haspers off limits to his daughter.

Veronica smiled and nodded.

"Do you need me for anything, Mama?"

"No, go. You work too hard for a young person. Have some fun."

"All right." She looked at the girls. "Tell them I'll be there in a few minutes." Laurel ran upstairs, opened the bottom drawer of the dresser she shared with Patricia, and dragged out a pair of long underwear, her overalls, and a sweater. Slipping out of her cotton skirt and blouse, she hung them on a hanger and quickly dressed in the warmer clothes. Taking the steps two at a time, she headed downstairs. Pulling on her coat and mittens, she fumbled to tie the straps on her hood, then grabbed her skates off the back porch shelf. With a hurried good-bye, she headed for the creek.

February cold and sunshine greeted her. She took a deep breath, relishing the sensation of cold air as it hurried down her throat and filled her lungs. Winter would be over soon. As much as she looked forward to the warm, long days of summer, she'd miss the special beauty and fun of the season.

A trail had already been laid down in the snow, which made the going easier. Shouts and sounds of laughter echoed from the creek. Laurel hurried her steps.

Standing on the top of the bank, she watched Luke and Alex race down the frozen stream. *Those two are always competing at something,* she thought with a smile. Joanna and Veronica were practicing spins and leaps. Veronica fell but with a shrug pushed to her feet and tried again, this time more successfully. Celeste had hold of Robert's hand and was leading him down the ice away from the others. Laurel felt a twinge of jealousy. *Don't be silly,* she told herself. *He doesn't belong to you.*

Veronica looked up at Laurel. "Hi. Hey, everyone, Laurel's here."

Celeste stopped and waved. Laurel waved back, then placing her feet sideways, she made her way down the slick slope. Alex skated up to her, snowball in hand. Wearing a grin, he hurled it at her.

Laurel ducked and scooped up a handful of snow and fired back. He easily skated out of range. "Where's Mattie?" Laurel asked.

"Grandmother's not feeling well. She's taking care of her."

"Oh," Laurel said. "Tell her we miss her."

"Yeah, Luke's the one who really misses her," Alex said with a smirk.

Luke charged him. Alex skated off, challenging his friend to a race. The two took off down the creek. Laurel smiled. They were still more boys than men. Sitting on a log, she pulled off her boots and slipped on skates.

Celeste glided to the edge of the ice. "Hi," she said, wearing her usual smile. Her blue eyes looked bright, her cheeks touched with pink. With golden curls peeking out from beneath a knitted cap, she looked prettier than usual.

"Hi. I've missed you."

"I know. Me too. But you know my father. I had to sneak over. He doesn't know I'm here."

"I wish he didn't hate us."

"Yeah. Me too."

Laurel finished lacing her skates and stepped onto the ice. She made a practice twirl. "It feels good to be outdoors!"

Robert skated up, shaving ice chips and sending them into the air. "You want to race?" He smiled at both girls.

Without answering, Laurel pushed hard against the edge of her blade and glided away. "Catch me!"

Immediately Robert raced after her, but Celeste didn't join in. She sat on the log and watched.

Laurel glanced over her shoulder. Robert was catching up. She hurried her strokes, loving the feel of the wind on her face and smooth, hard ice beneath her blades. She knew she was no match for Robert. He caught up easily, grabbed her around the waist, and swung her in a circle. They started to fall and Laurel squealed, then hit the ice.

She didn't get up right away. Instead, she lay on her back, cold penetrating her coat. Gazing at the vivid blue sky, she said, "I love winter. It's so beautiful."

Robert found his feet. Looking down on Laurel, he asked, "How long you plan to stay down there?" He held out a hand.

Laurel sat up. "It is cold." She took his hand, and he pulled her to her feet. "One of these days I'll beat you."

"Oh, you think so."

Celeste sat, face in her hands, watching them. Laurel felt a twinge of guilt. She was ignoring her friend. She skated back across the frozen pool and sat beside her. "So, what have you been up to lately?"

"Working at the store mostly." Celeste smiled. "But I believe that all work and no play will not keep the doctor away."

"Hey, we're going sledding," Luke called. "Alex knows a good hill."

"You want to go?" Robert asked Laurel.

"I just got here. I'd like to skate a little while. You can go."

"No, I'll stay here with you."

Celeste started to take off her skates. "I think I'll go with them."

"Please stay," Laurel said.

"No. I haven't done any sledding in a while. Sounds like fun." Her usual smile missing, she pulled on her boots and stood.

Laurel wanted to spend time with Celeste, but how could she change her mind now without hurting Robert? "All right. We'll skate a little while, then come up. Save some good runs for me."

"See you later," Celeste said quietly and headed after the others.

Laurel watched her friend climb the bank and disappear. "I think we ought to go with them. Celeste and I are best friends, and we haven't had a visit for a long while."

"I thought you wanted to skate."

"I do, but . . ." she shrugged, not knowing what else to say.

"Sure. We can go sledding."

Laurel sat and quickly untied her skates. "We'd better hurry. I don't want to lose them."

"I wouldn't worry about that," Robert grinned. "They'll leave a clear enough trail." He sat and started removing his skates. "I was wondering if you wanted to go to the movies next Saturday? They're showing *The Thin Man* with Myrna Loy and William Powell and Shirley Temple's *Littlest Rebel*." He smiled and shook his head. "What a combination. I guess they're trying to please everybody."

"Sounds like fun," Laurel stood. "What about your sisters and my brothers? Shouldn't we invite them?"

"Nope. I want it to be just us."

"All right," Laurel said a little hesitantly. They walked up the bank and followed a broad path of footprints through the snow.

Robert took her hand and helped her over a log. He flashed a charming smile, his dark eyes alight with admiration. Caught off guard by his open affection, Laurel suddenly felt drawn to him. She returned the smile. *I do care deeply for Robert. Maybe I could learn to love him.*

Walking side by side, they followed the path left by their friends. When Robert caught hold of her hand, she didn't resist.

~

A cab pulled to the curb, and the back door opened. "Come on, Adam, climb in," called Burke Sanderson. He shivered. "Brr. I hate London in February."

Adam slid onto the cushioned seat beside the veteran journalist and closed the door. "Hi, Burke. What you got?"

The cab left the curb and merged into traffic. The big man puffed on a cigar. He drew a mouthful of smoke in, then slowly exhaled. He studied the stogie.

"So, what's up?" Adam repeated.

"I got a wire from the *Trib* today. You have a new assignment."

"Yeah?" Adam asked, his adrenaline picking up. He'd been waiting for something big.

"You've heard the scuttlebutt about England's new king, Edward?"

"Yeah." Adam stiffened. He didn't like the direction this conversation was taking.

"Rumors are, he's still seeing that Mrs. Simpson, and the word is, he plans to marry her."

"The royal family won't stand for it." Adam leaned back against the seat. "He's got too much to lose. Do you think he'd actually marry her?"

"Maybe, but he could be thrown out on his ear for it."

"Can they, the royal family do that? He's king."

"Who's to say what they can or cannot do? It's the royal family."

Adam shook his head. "He'd be a fool to let go of his title for a woman."

"Either way, it's your job to find out what he's up to."

"What? You want me to cover this?" Fuming, Adam stared at the dreary, rain-soaked London street. "This is my new assignment?" he asked incredulously.

"Yep. It's hot stuff. There's a lot of interest back home. You know Americans—they always like a good love story."

"Stalin's jailing twelve-year-old kids, Hitler's flexing his muscles, there are riots and fighting in Ireland, and you want me to baby-sit a lovesick king?" Adam yelled. "I can't believe this!" He glared at pedestrians.

"Hey, this wasn't my idea. Don't yell at me." Burke took another drag of his cigar. He pulled one from his pocket and offered it to Adam. "It's a good story. Don't complain."

Adam stared at the cigar but didn't take it.

Burke slid it back into his pocket. "This is a good chance for you."

"I'm a newsman. This is soap opera stuff. Tell them I said no."

Burke shifted his bulk to face Adam. "Look, don't mess this up. If you do a good job, they'll give you more work, better stories."

Adam said nothing for a moment, then reached over and slid the cigar out of Burke's pocket. "He won't give up the crown for a woman," he said, meeting the reporter's eyes. "What man in his right mind would do a thing like that?"

"So, you'll do it?"

Adam nodded.

"I'll let them know you're on it." Burke patted Adam's shoulder. "Good choice. I think that man will surprise you. She's a real babe. A good woman can bring even a king to his knees." He grinned. "I've known a few like that." Signaling for the cab driver to stop, they pulled to the curb. Paying the cabby, he said, "Keep in touch," then left the car.

"Where to?" the driver asked. When Adam didn't answer, he repeated, "Where do you want me to take you?"

"I'll walk." Adam opened the door and stepped out. His foot splashed into a puddle. Slamming the door, he swore under his breath. Careful to avoid more puddles, he headed up the sidewalk, barely aware of congested foot traffic. He knew the story of King Edward and Mrs. Simpson. With the right slant it could be a good one. *So, why don't I want to write it? Maybe it hits too close to home,* he thought.

He'd been unable to put Laurel out of his mind. Everywhere he went, her spirited hazel eyes, playful mouth, and thick auburn hair went with him. He shoved his hands into coat pockets and walked faster, remembering the kisses they'd shared. Her lips had been soft and responsive. Her eyes had been filled with devotion and admiration.

He kept walking, no longer noticing the puddles, only seeing Laurel. He tried to imagine living in Alaska. He'd liked it there. And Will's words had haunted him. "Maybe you belong here? Maybe this is where

God intended you to be?" Adam smiled. He liked Will. He liked all the Haspers. They were like family.

"No!" he almost yelled, then looked around to see if anybody had noticed. *I like it here—the excitement, the status. I'm respected. And I have friends and women whenever I want.*

He started across a bridge. The rain had stopped. He watched the Thames flow beneath, then disappear. Slowing his steps, he ran his hand along the railing. "Where do I belong? Where?" He stopped and looked up at the arching trusses above. What if God did have a plan for him? And it wasn't here in London?

A large boat cruised toward the bridge. Adam wondered how many times it had traversed the river and how many more trips it would make. There were always more crossings, more opportunities. The ship passed beneath him. "I have time. I don't need to make a decision today or tomorrow if I don't want to."

He started walking again. "Maybe one day Alaska will be right. Now I have a career to build and a story to write about the king and Mrs. Simpson." He smiled. "And if God has a different plan for me, he can show me," he said offhandedly.

A memory of a boy who'd once believed and trusted flitted through his mind. He felt a twinge of regret, but shrugged it off. *I like the way things are. Life is good for me here. It's fast-moving, interesting. I'd be a fool to give it up.*

Chapter Thirty-Two

KNEELING IN THE SNOW, ROBERT SKINNED OUT A MINK, BUT HIS MIND WAS elsewhere. All morning he'd been searching for the right way to ask Will for Laurel's hand. Just how did a man go about asking a father if he could marry his daughter?

Will smoothed the snow, then positioned a trap. Opening the jaws, he reset the spring and baited it with a piece of rotted salmon, then carefully scattered snow over the trap and line. "That ought to do it." He stood.

Robert held up the mink. Running a hand over thick brown fur, he said, "Nice pelt."

"It's been a good season," Will said with a satisfied smile.

Robert added the skin to the others already hanging from his belt. "Thanks for letting me share the trapline with you. Having to build a new place puts a crimp on the money."

"I'm glad for the help, son. With you lending a hand, we've been able to set out more traps." Will pushed his feet back into his snowshoes. "I sure understand about debt. Seems the pile of bills just keeps growing. I'll be glad to get in our first harvest. Makes me uneasy watching my debt grow every time I go to the store." He gazed through the trees. "We've got a couple more traps to check. Better get moving." He started off.

Lying low over the valley like a dreary ceiling, slate-gray clouds hid mountain crests. Ice encased naked tree limbs. Deep snow lay in mounds around trunks and hung like giant white pillows on evergreen boughs.

Robert followed Will through the frozen forest, icy snow crunching beneath the slats of his snowshoes. He searched for the right words. He didn't know how Will would respond. The Haspers liked him well enough, but he also understood they knew Laurel wasn't in love with him. *That will come in time.*

At midday Will asked, "You hungry? Jean packed us a lunch."

"Yeah. Starved."

Will picked up his pack, plodded to a nearby log, wiped it clear of snow, then sat. Robert joined him. Digging into the pack, Will took out two sandwiches and handed one to Robert. He removed the wax paper and peeked between the pieces of bread. "Mmm, rabbit." He took a bite. "It's sure pretty out here."

"It is." Robert started on his sandwich. *I should ask him now.* He looked at the sky. "So, do you think we have long to wait for spring?"

"Some of the old-timers say it'll be an early one. Hope they're right. I'd like to start turning the soil as soon as I can. And to tell you the truth, the house is beginning to feel like a cave. I'll be glad for more daylight."

"Me too. Warmer, longer days will give me more time for the house." Robert took another bite of his sandwich. "I was thinking I'd make it bigger this time."

"Oh?"

"Yeah. I figure that one day I'll marry and will need more room."

Will chewed and nodded.

Robert struggled to swallow a bite. His mouth and throat were dry. "Uh . . ." His pulse picked up. *Now. Ask him now.* "Sir, I . . . I wanted to talk to you about something." He picked a crumb of crust off his coat and tossed it onto the snow. A small bird swooped down from a nearby tree and picked it up, then flitted back into the branches. "Wonder why he didn't fly south?"

"Don't know, some don't." Will looked at Robert. "You said there's something you wanted to talk about?"

"Yes, sir."

"If you're worried about living in our house, don't. Things are fine with us. We're a bit crowded, but we know you'll get your place built as soon as you can. There's no hurry."

"I figured as soon as the weather warms up, we can move back into a tent." Robert studied his sandwich. "But that's not what I wanted to talk about. I . . ." He looked at Will. "Well actually, sir, I wanted to ask you if I could have your permission to marry Laurel."

Silence fell between the two. The cushion of snow seemed to inten-sify the quiet.

Will met Robert's eyes. "What does Laurel say?"

"Well, I haven't . . . exactly asked her yet. I wanted to find out how you felt first."

Will watched the bird fly to another tree. "You know how me and Mrs. Hasper feel about you. You're like our own son. We couldn't choose better for Laurel. But . . ."

Robert steeled himself for the worst.

"There's Adam."

"I know Laurel had feelings for him, but she said he's gone—for good."

Will massaged his jaw. "That's right . . . probably. But even so, it doesn't change how Laurel feels about him. A person can't turn feelings on and off whenever he or she wants."

Robert brushed snow off the log. "I know Laurel's not in love with me, but she does care for me. She told me so. I'll make a good husband. I'll treat her right, and maybe in time she'll grow to love me."

"And what if she doesn't? Are you willing to settle for that?"

Robert took a deep breath. "Yes, sir. I figure I've got to have her on whatever terms she's willing to come to me. I can't imagine my life with-out her." He wiped away more snow, revealing brown bark. "I figure, if two people care about each other and treat each other right, love will follow."

Will took two bites out of his sandwich. Chewing, he stared straight ahead. He swallowed, then looked at Robert. "Well, I expect if you know what you're getting into, you have my blessing. Laurel certainly couldn't ask for a better man."

Robert smiled. "Thank you, sir." He shook Will's hand. "I figured I'd ask her tomorrow after the movies. She and I are going into Palmer. Just the two of us."

Will nodded. "I'll be praying for God's will."

∽

Laurel ran the brush through her hair, then pulled soft curls up into a barrette. She added a hint of rouge to her cheeks, then dabbed on lipstick. She stood back and studied her reflection. Wrinkling up her nose, she smiled.

Feeling a little on edge, she smoothed her skirt. *Honestly, why am I so nervous?* she wondered. Since her father and Robert had returned, a sense of expectation and disquiet hung in the air. Something was up. But what?

A soft knock sounded at the door, and Robert's mother stuck her head in. "Are you ready?"

"Yes. Almost."

Stepping in, Patricia stood just inside the door. Wearing a satisfied smile, she folded her arms over her bosom. "I'm s'posed to see if you're ready. My son is chomping at the bit. He's actually pacing."

"Really? He did seem kind of tense all morning. Do you know why?"

Patricia's eyes sparkled, and her pink cheeks rounded when she smiled. "No, I don't."

Laurel didn't believe her. "Is something wrong?"

"No. Nothing." She shrugged. "He's a man. Who can say why a man acts the way he does?" She chuckled. "Well, I told him I'd hurry you along, and I have." She started to leave, then stopped and added, "Have a wonderful evening." She shut the door quietly and left.

Laurel sat on the edge of the bed and slipped on her shoes. "What's gotten into everyone?" She tied the laces, and her mind flipped through her last encounters with Robert. He'd been especially considerate and kind. *He's always thoughtful, though,* she told herself. "Well, whatever's going on, I'll find out sooner or later."

Robert met her at the bottom of the stairs. "You look nice."

"So do you." Laurel had rarely seen Robert dressed up, except for church. However, tonight he wore a blue suit with a gray and blue patterned tie. The suit fit him perfectly, showing off his tall frame and making his wide shoulders look even broader. His shoes were polished to a sheen, and he'd used some kind of grooming cream on his dark hair. He looked tense.

Offering her his arm, he asked, "Shall we go?"

On the way in to town, they talked about inconsequential matters such as the weather and the latest gossip. People bet on when spring break-up would arrive, and Robert and Laurel made their own guesses. A moose grazed on willow limbs alongside the road, and they stopped to watch the animal.

When they arrived at the theater, Robert hurried around and opened the door for Laurel, then escorted her into the small theater. They sat near the back of the packed movie house. Robert's tension seemed to increase after they were seated. He fiddled with his tie, drummed his fingers on the edge of his seat, and bounced his legs up and down.

Finally Laurel asked, "Robert, is something wrong?"

"No. Why?"

"You're acting strangely—jumpy."

"Oh. I am? I'm sorry." He stilled his legs and stared at the curtain in the front. "I'm fine."

Laurel settled her back against the seat, folding her arms over her chest. "You're sure nothing's wrong?"

"I'm sure. Say, you want some popcorn or something?"

"No. I'm not hungry."

The theater turned dark, the curtains were pulled back, and lights flickered on the screen. Numbers flashed, counting down from ten to one. Music swelled, and the title *The Thin Man* blazed across the screen, then pictures of Myrna Loy and William Powell were shown. Intent on enjoying the movie and ignoring Robert's nervousness, Laurel relaxed her shoulders and settled back.

The movie was surprisingly good, leaving the audience spellbound one minute, frightened the next, and then laughing. She was sorry to see it end. "That was wonderful!" she told Robert. "Did you like it?"

"Yeah. It was good." He still seemed distracted. "Would you like to walk a ways before the next movie starts?"

"I could use a stretch," Laurel said, allowing him to take her arm and escort her outside. The air was cold, but it felt good after the small, stuffy theater. Both Laurel and Robert were quiet. Tension lay between them, and Laurel was glad when it was time to return to their seats.

The second movie was charming, but Laurel was thankful when it was over. She hoped Robert would tell her what was troubling him. "Shirley Temple's so cute," she said, searching for a conversation topic. Robert made no reply. "Don't you think?"

"What? What did you say?"

"Oh, never mind." Frustrated and annoyed, Laurel walked fast. She got to the truck ahead of Robert and didn't wait for him to open the door. She climbed in, and when he took his place behind the wheel, she stared ahead, silent.

It took him three tries to start the truck, but finally the engine sputtered to life and they headed home. Robert remained quiet. Laurel sulked. The truck lights glistened off ice layered on the road. "I'll be glad for spring," Robert finally said. Laurel nodded but didn't add anything. They pulled into the driveway and parked.

Laurel reached for the door handle, but instead of opening it, she asked, "Robert, have I done something to make you angry? You're not acting like yourself." She looked at him. "I wish you'd tell me what's wrong."

Robert turned to Laurel. "You haven't done anything. It's just . . ."

"What?"

"I've been thinking." He fell silent again.

"About what?"

He took Laurel's hands in his. "You know I'm crazy about you. I have been ever since I first met you on the train to Seattle."

"I know," Laurel said, unable to look at Robert, afraid of what he was going to say. Finding courage, she met his gaze. His eyes were tender, filled with affection. She wished she'd left well enough alone. *Why can't things stay the way they are?*

"Laurel, I love you. I want to marry you." Before she could answer, he continued, "I've already talked to your father, and he thinks it's a good idea. I know all about Adam and that you still have feelings for him, but . . . he's gone."

Laurel's heart constricted. Adam *was* gone, and Robert was here. What should she do? How did she really feel about Robert? *I'm not in love with him, but I do love him. He's a fine man. I'd be a fool to wait for Adam.*

"I know you're not in love with me," Robert continued. "Do you think you can learn to love me?"

Suddenly, compassion flowed through Laurel. She treasured Robert. Along with Celeste, he was her best friend. She smiled. "I do care for you, Robert." She caressed his hands, then turned them palm up. "Calluses. You work hard. I know you'd take good care of me. You're kind and decent." Laurel hesitated, then said, "I'd be proud to be your wife." As she said the words, Laurel was stunned. She'd meant them, and not until she'd spoken, did she understand how much Robert meant to her.

Wearing an astounded expression, Robert asked, "Really? You mean it?"

Laurel laughed. "Yes. Of course I do."

He caught her to him, holding her tight. "I was afraid to even dream you might say yes. Thank you, Laurel. Thank you." Gently caressing her hair, he touched his lips to hers, then quickly released her.

Looking into Robert's eyes filled with passion and devotion, doubts swept over Laurel. Could she love him enough?

"As soon as weather permits, I'll start on the house. It'll be a fine home." He kissed her hands. "It'll be wonderful! You'll be close to your family, and we'll have a farm and maybe even a passel of kids." He blushed, then chuckled. "Well, we can talk about all that later. Let's go in and tell your folks!"

Laurel waited while Robert went around to open her door. The kiss hadn't been anything like the one she'd shared with Adam. She knew she didn't feel the same about Robert as she did Adam, but was that wrong? Wasn't a relationship built on stability, respect, and commitment better than one based on passion and dreams?

Chapter Thirty-Three

ROBERT HELD ON TO LAUREL'S HAND WHILE HE WALKED OFF THE DIMENSIONS of their new home. "We'll have to make it bigger than the first house. I was thinking we ought to have our rooms upstairs. Mama and the girls can stay downstairs."

"Oh. I thought we would be downstairs and everyone else would be up."

"Well, it probably won't be long before Mama has trouble getting up and down the stairs."

"Of course," Laurel said. "I should have thought of that." She considered it a moment and at the same time tried to sort out her rising sense of insecurity. "What if we had our room downstairs and put the girls upstairs? That way I'll have better access to the kitchen." She looked at Robert. "I'll feel like a guest if I'm living upstairs."

Robert thought a moment, then scratched his head. "I don't know. I'll think about it." Pointing, he said, "We'll have the kitchen right along here. I figured we could have a big back porch so you'll have room for your washing machine."

"I don't have a washing machine."

"We'll get one," he said confidently. "And I thought we ought to have a large front room since there are so many of us, and when the children come along..." He squeezed her hand. "You do want children, don't you?"

"Of course. As many as God gives."

"I'd also like to put in a fireplace so the kitchen stove isn't our only heat. It'll help warm the upstairs too."

"That sounds like a good idea," Laurel said, beginning to feel a little left out of the process. Robert's ideas were good, but he hadn't asked her what she wanted. It seemed he cared more about what his mother wanted.

"Since our room is going to be upstairs, I thought we ought to put an extra bedroom up there for our kids. My sisters will be off raising their own families by the time we'll need their room."

"Maybe, by that time we can move into it. It's easier for stoking fires and such," Laurel said, feeling her resentment rise. He'd acted as if she'd said nothing about wanting a room on the main level.

Robert nodded. "Absolutely." He smiled. "See, we'll come up with the perfect house." Suddenly Robert caught Laurel up in his arms, lifting her off the ground. "Just think. Spring is nearly here, and we're almost ready to start building our home. The materials ought to be here any time, and I've already got most of the logs cut. Then, come December, we'll be Mr. and Mrs. Lundeen."

Laurel laughed. "Robert, put me down."

He set Laurel on her feet, then kissed her, gently as always, never demanding, never without respect. Sometimes Laurel almost wished he'd be a little less gentlemanly. *Of course he should be a gentleman,* she told herself, then said aloud, "I can hardly wait. Mama and I ordered material for the curtains. I hope your mother approves."

"I'm sure she'll love them. She thinks the world of you. In her eyes you can do no wrong."

Laurel smiled. She and Patricia had a good relationship, but their tastes were different. Laurel wondered how they would find common ground in decisions about decorating and other things.

Laurel didn't want to dampen Robert's mood, but she needed to express her feelings. She met his eyes, laid a hand on his arm, and said, "Robert, it sounds like a fine house, but . . . well, I was hoping we could have a place of our own."

An incredulous expression crossed his face. "We can't afford that."

"It wouldn't have to be a big house. Couldn't we have two small houses instead of one big one?"

"Why would you want two separate houses?"

Laurel's frustration grew. "Robert, I love your mother and your sisters, but if we live with them, I'll feel like we're living in your mother's house, not ours."

Confusion and hurt touched Robert's eyes. "I thought it was decided."

Laurel studied tufts of grass pushing through the snow. Without looking at Robert, she said, "It was, but *you* decided. You didn't ask me."

Robert took Laurel's hands in his. "I'm sorry. I didn't mean to overlook your feelings. I just figured it was the only way. Mama's kind and easy to get along with. She's happy to share a house with us."

"I understand that." Laurel's hopes sank, but she couldn't give up without trying. "She's older, more experienced. Your mother has ideas of her own. No matter what I do, it will feel like her house." Laurel gazed across the property. "I thought two small houses would work— one there by the barn and the other one on the northeast corner."

Robert was quiet for a long while. Finally, shaking his head, he said, "I wish I could do it, but it's not possible. Two houses means two roofs, and two kitchens with plumbing. It'll cost too much. Besides, I already have the go-ahead from the government agent on the one."

He gazed at the tent he'd brought out to the property. Smoke rose from the chimney. "I don't see why one house is a problem. Our families lived together for a long while, and it worked fine."

Unable to keep the sharpness out of her voice, Laurel said, "It wasn't your home; it was ours. And it did work well, but we all knew it was temporary and my mother and father were clearly the heads of the house. That's how it's supposed to be."

Instead of getting angry, Robert apologized again. "I'm sorry, Laurel. I wish you'd told me how you felt. I don't know what else to do."

Deflated, Laurel said, "It's all right. I know there's no other way. We'll make it work. We'll find a way."

He hugged Laurel. "Everything will be fine."

Laurel nodded, but she wasn't so sure.

～

Will set down his pencil and leaned on the table. "Our debt to the government is getting worse. By the time we bring in our first crop, we'll owe close to nine thousand dollars. I don't know how we're going to pay it back. I wish I could find a job." He took a drink of coffee. "Some of the other men are working. A few are up at the Copper River Mine."

Jean pressed a cauliflower seed into black soil, covered it, then moved on to the next space in the planter. She created a small hole with her finger and dropped in seed. Glancing at her husband, she said, "We signed a contract promising you wouldn't work anywhere but on this farm. And we've still got four years before we have to start paying on our loan."

"I know."

"Spring tilling and planting will begin soon. You won't have time for anything else."

"Luke can do some of that."

Jean gave her husband a skeptical look and planted another seed. "Maybe you can sell one or both of the calves. The cows give us more milk than we need, and we've been able to sell some of the extra cream and butter. We could cut back and sell more."

"That's just a drop in the bucket; it won't do much against this debt."

She turned and looked at Will. "Isn't that usually how you tackle life—one drop at a time—one penny at a time—one step at a time?" She dusted off her hands. "If they find out you're working somewhere else, we could lose the farm."

"They wouldn't do that."

"You don't know what the government officials will do." Jean held up the planter tray. "These will be up before you know it, and they'll need to be put in the ground. You'll also have to plant all the other crops, including the grain. And you're going to have to start tilling as soon as the snow melts and the ground dries out." She walked across the room, draped her arms around Will's shoulders, and hugged him. "Money's tight, but it always has been. We just have to be patient. We're so close."

Will brushed the remaining dirt from Jean's index finger and kissed it. "I know. You're right. I'm just not used to owing anyone."

Jean kissed his cheek, then straightened. Looking out the window, she watched Robert and Laurel walk across the field, their hands intertwined. "I'm more worried about those two."

"Why?"

Continuing to watch them, Jean said, "I can't say for sure, but I don't know how he's going to do everything—build a house and work a farm all at the same time."

Will stood. Standing behind Jean, he wrapped his arms around her. "I told him I'd help, and Drew and Tom said they'd be out at his place whenever they can. He'll do it. They'll be fine."

"Yes," Jean said, still hesitant.

Will turned her around so she faced him. "What else? What's troubling you?"

"You'll think I'm silly."

"Try me."

"Well, I don't see a light in Laurel's eyes when she looks at Robert."

Will chuckled. "A light?"

"Don't laugh."

"I'm sorry." Will pasted a serious expression on his face. "Tell me."

"Well, when a woman's in love, she has a light inside her that shows on the outside."

Will tightened his hold. "Oh, you mean like the way your face lights up every time you set eyes on me?"

"You're awfully full of yourself." Jean snuggled against him. "Yes, that light. And I'll have it until the day I die."

"She's a grown woman," Will said. "She ought to know her own mind. She loves Robert."

"Yes, she does, but Laurel's not *in* love with him. I'm not sure she's doing the right thing."

"Could you pick a better man?"

"A better man? No, but even so, he might not be the right one for her."

"You think she ought to marry Adam?"

"I didn't say that."

"Well, he's not here, and from what I've heard, he's not about to move here." He pulled Jean closer. "I think Adam's a nice young man, but he has a lot of growing up to do. He's so busy seeking self-fulfillment, he doesn't have time to even think about God or what God wants for him."

Jean continued to watch Robert and Laurel. "He won't find what he's looking for in Europe," she said sadly.

"I know, and I'm sorry. I like Adam. I even believe Laurel loves him." Will squeezed Jean more tightly. "I think he belongs here."

"Why do you think that?"

"I don't know—maybe because something about him settles down when he's here." Will straightened. "But while Adam finds himself, Laurel can't wait around. She's got her own life to live."

❧

Laurel gazed at the notes, trying to make sense of them. *Sometimes Steward's writing is illegible,* she thought in frustration and typed what she thought it said. She glanced at the two boxes she'd finished transcribing. *At least I'm making progress.* Another half dozen lay on the shelf, needing to be recorded.

The door opened, and Jessie walked in. She had a bouquet of bluebells and blue lupine. "Aren't these lovely? I couldn't resist. They're all over the forest floor." She walked into the kitchen, ran water into a canning jar, and arranged the flowers in it. Setting the bouquet in the middle of the kitchen table, she stood back and gazed at them. "I love flowers. Always have. From now until winter, I'll have real flowers in the house." She smoothed back gray hair and tucked a piece behind her ear. "How is the work coming?"

Unable to hide her frustration, Laurel said, "Slow, but my typing is getting better." She glanced at the boxes still waiting. "How did you and your husband find the time to dig up so much information about Alaska?"

Jessie added wood to the stove and moved the kettle to a front burner. "For many years, it's all we did. It was our life." She smiled and took a container of tea out of the cupboard. "Would you like some?"

"Yes. Thank you."

She spooned tea into cheesecloth, tied it off, then set it in the kettle. Hobbling into the living room, she sat in her overstuffed chair.

Laurel let her fingers rest on the typewriter keys. She suddenly felt deflated. Jessie had led an exciting life, one that had made a difference. She'd wanted to do something important with hers. How was being a farmer's wife going to contribute to the world? She looked at Jessie. "What do you think you would've done with your life if you and Steward hadn't come to Alaska?"

"Oh, I don't know. I suppose we'd have settled somewhere along the San Francisco Bay, probably taught history."

"Do you ever wish you'd done that?"

"Oh no. I've loved my life." She smiled and her eyes turned into slits. "When I was at the university, I never expected life to be an adventure.

Living here wasn't part of my plan. Had I known what waited for me, I'd probably have been too frightened to leave California." She studied Laurel. "Why do you ask, dear?"

Laurel shuffled and stacked papers. "No reason."

Jessie waited quietly.

"Well, I've been feeling a little uncertain about my future."

"In what way?"

Laurel stared at the typewriter. "Did you ever want to be something other than what you are?"

Jessie thought a moment. "For the most part I've been real happy with who I am, but I do wish I'd been a mother." She smiled softly. "Steward and I wanted children. I think I already told you that. What a gift it would be to bring a new life into the world. To be part of shaping a young person into a special, unique individual." Her eyes sparkled at the thought, then settled on Laurel. "Why?"

Laurel had never thought of parenting as a gift. It had simply been something a woman did, part of an ordinary life. "Sometimes I feel like I want to do more with my life than just be a wife and mother. I wanted to go to college, become a teacher."

"Do you think that's what God wants you to do?"

"I don't know. Do you think if someone wants something badly then it's what God wants for that person?"

"Sometimes, but not always. The world and its desires can cloud our thinking, keep us from listening to God. Sometimes the clatter drowns him out." She leaned forward. "What about Robert?"

"He's a wonderful man. I love him, but . . ." Laurel stood and walked to the window and stared at the rocked walkway, green shoots of spring grass, and blooming wildflowers. "Sometimes I feel like something else is pulling at me, and I'm not sure I should marry him."

"The wedding is in December?"

Laurel nodded.

"It seems you have a lot of time to think on it then."

Jessie pushed herself out of her chair. "No one can tell you whether or not it's right to marry or not to marry. Only you can know. Life comes to us just as it is." She crossed to Laurel. "Maybe you should think about what your life would be like if Robert wasn't in it. The answer lies in your heart. If it's meant to be, then no matter where you are or what life brings, you'll be content. Trust God to lead you. If you put him first, you'll find your way."

Laurel chuckled. "You sound like my father."

"Well, of course I do. He knows God, and so do I." Jessie grinned. "Now, I think it's time for that tea." She shuffled into the kitchen, took two cups from the cupboard, and filled them with the pale amber brew.

"I know I'm being silly worrying about all this. What you said about raising children, well, I'd never really thought about it that way. I guess it *is* a privilege."

Laurel walked into the kitchen. Taking both the cups, she crossed to the table and sat down, setting one in front of her and the other opposite her. "I love the work I'm doing for you. Maybe I can help you with the book when we're finished."

Jessie lowered herself onto a wooden chair. "I'm counting on it. A lot of work still needs to be done. I don't know how I'd do it without you."

When Laurel left Jessie's that afternoon, she felt better about her wedding plans and her future in Alaska. Still, she wanted to talk to Celeste. She could always count on her to speak the truth. Laurel trusted her. She stopped at the store, hoping her friend was working.

The bell hanging from the doorknob rang its usual cheerful chime when she opened the door and stepped inside. Heat radiated from a wood stove, and the store smelled of spices and coffee.

Leaning on the countertop, Celeste looked through a magazine. At the sound of the bell, she looked up. "Hi. I was just thinking about you." She held up the magazine. "There's a perfect wedding gown in here." Celeste laid the magazine on the counter, opening it to a page with a wedding dress.

Laurel studied an elegant white gown with a beaded bodice and princess neckline. It had long sleeves with beaded wrist insets and a long, full skirt.

"Isn't it just the thing for a December wedding?" Celeste asked. "I knew it was the perfect dress when I saw it. It will look wonderful on you."

"It's lovely, but we can't afford anything that fancy. My mother and I are going to make my dress. We've already ordered a pattern from Sears and Roebuck. I'll show it to you when it comes in."

Celeste walked out from behind the counter. "Oh, Laurel, you'll be the most beautiful bride. I can see you floating down the aisle with a long train sweeping behind you." She giggled. "And Robert will be waiting at the altar." She sighed.

"You're such a romantic."

"Maybe."

"Even if I wanted a wedding gown like that, we could never afford it. I don't know what we're going to do. Already there's talk that there won't be buyers for our vegetables."

Celeste's mouth turned hard. "And you think my father's behind it?"

"Well . . ." Laurel hedged. "I heard—"

"You and the others blame him for everything! You all talk about how unfair the homesteaders are toward you, but did you ever think about how they feel? I mean, you all came into town and just took over. Everything you've needed has been handed to you." Celeste slammed a can of green beans on the shelf. "Sometimes the world doesn't revolve around you and your farms, you know. Other people are also trying to make a living."

Laurel couldn't believe what she was hearing. Celeste had never even hinted that she was angry with the colonists.

"You complain and complain. It's never enough. You've all had so much help, but you want more." She swung around and glared at Laurel. "You know, you can't always blame someone else for your troubles. Sometimes it's just life. Sometimes it's your own fault!"

Doing her best to control her tears, Laurel looked straight at her friend. "I thought we were friends. I didn't know you hated me and the others."

Celeste's anger seemed to crumple. She leaned on the counter. "I don't hate you." Her face softened. "I'm sorry. I didn't mean to get mad. It's just that my dad gets blamed for everything." She glanced out the front window. "And I don't know what I believe anymore." Her eyes brimmed with tears. "Sometimes I'm afraid he really did those things to Robert and some of the others." Her chin quivered, and she pressed her hand against her mouth. "I know my dad's not evil. He was wonderful to my mother, and he's always been a good father. How could he do what they say he did?"

Chapter Thirty-Four

A DAY OF CELEBRATION WAS SCHEDULED TO COMMEMORATE THE one-year anniversary for the colonists. It was called *Colony Day*. It was also a day of no return. May sixteenth was the last day the government would send colonists back to their hometowns at no charge.

It hadn't been an easy year. Many had difficulties adjusting to Alaskan life—the difference in soil and climate, government errors, money worries, family tragedies, and on and on. And now, with a threatened boycott of goods by homesteaders, they were facing more trouble. As the May sixteenth date approached, some agonized over whether they should stay or go, but most decided to stay.

The celebration included speeches, games, music, and good food. Feeling very much like one family, the Haspers, Lundeens, Jessie, Celeste, Alex, Mattie, and Robert sat together, their blankets spread out on new spring grass. The sun felt almost warm. The fragrance of wildflowers, greenery, and moist earth filled the air. The mosquitoes had uncharacteristically taken a holiday and didn't bother picnickers.

"You want to be my partner in the three-legged race?" Luke asked, grabbing his friend Alex. "We'll beat the pants off everybody else."

"Sure," Alex said, jumping to his feet.

The two teens ran to the starting line, joining several other boys.

They were given a piece of rope and were tying it around two of their legs when a husky boy with dark wild hair walked up to them. "Hey, Luke, we don't want no siewashes in this race. You can run if you want, but not him." His eyes rested on Alex.

Adrenaline surged through Laurel, her anger rising. She'd seen this before. "Did you hear what he said?" she asked Robert.

"Yeah, I heard," he said glumly.

Laurel stood, glaring at the boy. Someone needed to put a stop to his bigotry.

Mattie stood beside Laurel, her eyes trained on the boy. "He doesn't want Alex to race," she said, her voice laced with hurt and resentment.

Luke straightened and stepped up to the bully. "This is a free country, and we'll race if we like, John." He said the boy's name with venom.

John glanced over his shoulder at his pals who, for the most part, were keeping their distance. "There ain't no stinkin' Indians allowed."

Luke's face turned red, and he shoved the young tyrant. "He races! You hear?"

"Will, stop this," Jean said.

Without taking his eyes off the boys, Will said evenly, "They're not children. They need to settle this on their own."

"Stinkin' Indian!" John taunted, wearing a smirk. "Siewash!"

Luke lunged at the boy, swinging his fist. It landed squarely on the bully's broad nose.

John fell on his backside, a stunned look on his face. He clapped a hand over his nose. "What did you do that for?" He looked at his bloodied hand.

Luke stood over him. "Don't never say nothin' like that again." He looked at the other boys. "Alex is my friend, and he's just as good or better than any one of you!"

John pushed himself to his feet and brushed dirt off his pants. Giving Luke a dirty look, he walked back to the starting line. Laurel didn't feel sorry for him. It wasn't the first time he'd taunted Alex and Mattie.

Luke walked back to his friend and proceeded to tie the string around their ankles. "Now we're really gonna beat their pants off," he told Alex with a grin.

Alex smiled and threw an arm over Luke's shoulders.

Laurel could see tears in Mattie's eyes.

Jessie patted the native girl's hand. "Don't let someone like him bother you. He's just one boy."

"It's not just one boy," Mattie said, her voice hard.

"Well, I think it's awful," Celeste said. "If Luke hadn't hit that John, I would have!"

Mattie smiled at Celeste. "Thanks."

A gun was fired, and the boys took off. Luke and Alex made a good team. They charged ahead of the others. Several got their legs out of sync, tangled their feet, and fell. John and his partner didn't make it more than ten yards. Laurel smiled with satisfaction. However, just at the finish line, another team lunged ahead of Luke and Alex. The two comrades ended up in second place. It didn't seem to bother them at all. They fell on the grass laughing and clearly happy to have run a good race.

"So, how are the wedding plans coming along?" Jessie asked Laurel and Robert.

"Good," Robert said.

"We still have plenty of time." Laurel tossed a braid back over her shoulder.

Robert took her hand in his. "We can hardly wait. It's too far away. I'm beginning to wish we'd picked June." He smiled at Laurel, and she returned the gesture.

"I get to be in the wedding," Brian said. "Laurel said I can carry the rings." He smiled broadly. "It's a very important job."

"That it is," Jessie agreed.

Ed Ketchum and Miram were across the clearing from the Hasper group. Ed was stretched out on the ground. Miram sat beside him, giving him sips of lemonade and bites of cookies.

"I don't think yours is the only wedding coming up," Jessie said. "Seems Miram and that young Ed Ketchum will be tying the knot soon."

Laurel chuckled. "I never would have thought those two would get together. Ed's looking pretty good these days. Seems love has helped him to turn over a new leaf."

"Love can bring about things you never thought possible," Celeste said dreamily.

Robert looked at Will. "Heard you have a new calf."

"We do." Will leaned back on his hands. "Can't decide whether to sell her or keep her though. I'd like to build a small herd of milk cows. We can't produce enough milk and butter for the folks around here. Trouble is, it'll be a long while before that calf comes fresh, and we could use the money now. It'll take a few more seasons to get the rest of my land cleared and producing."

"I'll buy from you," Jessie said. "I'm getting too old to keep up with a garden."

"Thanks." Will shook his head. "Sometimes I wonder why I ever decided to be a farmer."

"It's in the blood," Robert said matter-of-factly. "It's somethin' we have to do." He smiled. "I love working the soil—the smell of fresh-turned earth, the feel of the sun on my back, green sprouts shooting up. There's nothing like it, when I stand and look at rows and rows of crops, knowing they're growing because of my hard work and sweat." He leaned back on his hands. "I don't think I could do anything else."

"It's backbreaking," Luke said. "Makes you old before your time. You can never count on a crop. Weather and pests can wipe you out. I was thinking about hunting or tracking."

"Yeah. More and more folks are coming in from the outside to hunt. They need guides."

At that moment Ray Townsend approached them.

"What's he doing here?" Celeste asked, watching her father approach. "Daddy?"

Will stood.

"Now, Will, don't interfere," Jean cautioned.

"He's mad." Celeste wet her lips, pasted a smile on her face, and tossed blonde curls off her shoulder.

Ray Townsend, looking like a thunderstorm about to let loose, marched straight up to his daughter. "What are you doing here, young lady? I told you to stay away from these people."

"Laurel invited me. She's my best friend. I wanted to come."

Ray glared at Laurel. "Colonists are not your friends." He shifted his cold gaze to Will. "Keep your daughter away from mine."

"Laurel's a grown woman. She has her own mind," Will said evenly.

"What you really mean is, she's out of control. If she were my daughter, I'd do something about it."

"She's not your daughter, and she's not out of control. She's a fine woman, and I'm proud of her." He cast Laurel a quick smile. "Laurel makes up her own mind about things. She's not a child, and I won't treat her like one. Fact is, she's nearly a married woman. Soon she'll be running her own house."

"And I suppose producing more colonist brats," Ray spat.

"Daddy! Please! Don't!"

"I think you've said enough," Will stated, his tone sharp.

Ray studied the outsider. "You're the leader of this group, someone people look up to. Right?"

"This group has no leader. We all make our own decisions."

"But you might consider yourself a voice of reason?"

"Maybe. Me and others."

"Well, think about this. You and the rest of this lot aren't wanted in this valley. You're all nothin' but a bunch of government moochers. All you do is whine about what you don't have. I doubt any of you can wipe your own noses." He took a step closer to Will. "If I were you, I'd tell them all to pack up and move on. Life here ain't fit for the weak or timid."

"I told you, we're here and we're staying," Will said evenly. "We've got crops in the ground, and we'll be selling vegetables by the end of summer. This valley needs more than trappers and hunters. A whole territory needs produce, and we plan to be the ones to grow it for them."

"Try and sell your vegetables. None of us are buyin' them. We don't need nothin' you grow," Ray said through clenched teeth.

Will relaxed his stance. "We're having a little party here. Why don't you simmer down and join us?" He managed to smile. "We plan on staying in this valley. It would be best if we could be friends, work together." He extended a hand.

Ray stared at it.

Jessie joined Will, standing beside him. "Come on, Ray. These are good folks, and they'd much rather be a friend than an enemy. Most of the settlers have accepted them already. Why can't you? I've known you for a good many years, and you're better than this."

"Stay out of it, Jessie." Ray grabbed Celeste by the arm. "C'mon, we're going."

"Daddy!" Celeste yanked her arm free. "What's wrong with you? Why are you acting like this? If Mom could see you, she'd be ashamed." Eyes brimming with tears, Celeste stared at her father.

Without another word, Ray Townsend turned and walked away.

Celeste watched him go. Laurel joined her friend, placing an arm around her shoulders. When Mr. Townsend was out of sight, Celeste let the tears fall. "I don't know what's wrong with him. He never used to be like this. This is the worst it's been since Mom died. I'm afraid for him."

Chapter Thirty-Five

LAUREL PLUCKED ANOTHER WEED, THEN LEANING BACK ON HER HEELS, SHE closed her eyes, enjoying the sun's heat. Using the back of dirt-encrusted hands, she wiped sweat from her forehead and gazed at a row of cabbages.

Inhaling deeply the musky smell of loam and pungent aroma of damp vegetables, she smiled. *Robert's right. Farming gets inside you.* Laurel didn't understand the why of it; she simply knew it was true. No matter how much her muscles ached, no matter how badly her hands hurt, no matter how many crops were lost to insects or to frost, it was part of her.

Her eyes moved past the young cabbages to rows of peas. Small pods weighted the branches. The sweet vegetables were nearly ready for picking. A picture of warm afternoons spent on the porch shelling peas came to mind. Some of the best times had been spent on that porch. She would shell peas or snap beans and listen to her mother and grandmother tell family stories or share local gossip. Those had been gentle days.

"Laurel! Laurel!" Brian called. Holding a long stick with a sharp point above his head, he ran between rows, jumping over plants and kicking up dirt. "Mama needs you at the house," he said, running up to his sister.

Laurel stood. "Is everything all right?"

"Yep. She just wants to take lunch to Daddy. She says you need to keep an eye on me and Susie." He compressed his lips. "I'm not a baby anymore. I can stay by myself."

"Yes, but what about Susie?"

"I could watch her."

"I know, but you wouldn't be able to play then."

"Mama and Daddy are having a picnic at the creek. Mama said I couldn't go." He pouted, then lifted the stick over his head again. "Hey, watch this," he said, flinging the makeshift spear. It flew straight. The point plunged into the soil. It wobbled a moment, then stood like a skinny post. "Good, huh?" Brian said, running to retrieve it.

"Very good. One day you might throw a javelin in the Olympics."

"What's a javelin? And what's the Olympics?"

Laurel chuckled. "A javelin is a fancy spear. And the Olympics is a big contest where people from all over the world compete in sporting events. They run races, see who can jump the farthest, and throw the javelin to see who can throw it the farthest."

"Oh. Can I go and throw a jav . . . a . . . lin?"

Laurel smiled. "You're not old enough now, but maybe one day." Laurel pressed her hands against the small of her back and stretched from side to side. "The Olympic Games are going to happen soon. They're being held in Germany."

"How do you know that?"

"Adam told me about it in his letter."

"Can we go and watch?"

"Oh, no. It's too far away, but Adam might go."

"Is Adam going to be in a race?"

"No. He's going to write about them."

Laurel took Brian's hand and walked toward the house, her mind on Adam. She missed him and wondered what he was doing now. She hoped he did get to report on the Olympics. He'd said he thought he might be sent.

Brian jerked his hand out of Laurel's, lifted the stick over his head, and ran toward the house, stopping several times to throw his spear.

Laurel followed, enjoying his antics. *I hope Robert and I will still want to picnic together when we've been married as long as Mama and Daddy.*

She hadn't yet written to Adam about the wedding. He deserved to know. She decided to write him after lunch.

Jean met Laurel at the back door, a basket draped over her arm. "Thank you for watching the children."

"I don't mind. It was time for me to come in anyway. I'm hungry."

"Susie's eating a sandwich. When she's done, you can put her down for a nap. And I expect Brian will be running out of steam any time. He'll be ready to go down soon." She stepped out the door. "I'll be back in a bit."

When both children were napping, Laurel went to the cupboard, took out paper and pencil, and sat at the table. She stared out the window for a long while, trying to think of just how to tell Adam she was getting married.

She started with "Dear Adam. I received your letter. It sounds as if life is very exciting for you there. Here it is much quieter. Summer has finally arrived. The snows have melted, and the valley is literally overrun with blooming plants and flowers. It's beautiful. However, the mosquitoes are back, but they don't seem as bad this year."

She stopped writing and thought about what else he might be interested in. He'd seemed to like the idea of farming and clearly enjoyed her family. She continued, "The cabbages, potatoes, turnips, and carrots are up. The peas are nearly ready to pick. Everything grows amazingly fast. Daddy said it's all the sunlight. He's working hard, nearly from sunup to sundown, but it's wonderful to see everything growing so well. He's already cleared and tilled about four acres and planted them, two in vegetables, two in oats. He's working to clear more. It's a long, slow process, but he hopes to have two more acres finished by fall. The government will pay him sixty dollars for each acre. The money will help a lot. We may have trouble selling our vegetables. Ray Townsend is leading a movement to keep homesteaders from buying our produce."

She chewed on the end of her pencil, then returned to the letter and wrote, "December fifteenth, Robert and I are getting married." She stared at the sentence. It looked too bold. Erasing it, she wrote, "Robert and I have grown very close. We've decided to get married. December 15 is the day we've chosen." She stopped and read the sentence. It sounded better. "We both love winter, so we figured December would be a good time. We'd like you to come. I know it's a long way from London to Palmer, especially in December, but could you try?"

Unexpected sadness spread through her. Laurel set down her pencil. Part of her would always love Adam even if he didn't share her life.

She returned to the letter, telling him about Colony Day and the confrontation between her father and Ray Townsend and how Celeste was hurting and confused. She chatted about fishing and hunting and her work for Jessie and how much she enjoyed studying local history.

She signed the letter, "Sincerely, Laurel."

~

Adam read the letter, then sat staring at it. He'd known this was coming. Finally he folded it, keeping the creases just as they were, then carefully returned it to the envelope and walked to the table where he intended to set it. Instead he let loose a stream of profanities and hurled it.

He dropped onto a chair at the table. His insides felt raw. *You knew she'd marry him. You knew it.* The ache gnawed at him, and he groaned, covering his face with his hands. "I shouldn't have let her go."

He envisioned Laurel in Robert's arms, and then he saw her walking down an aisle with Robert waiting at the altar. Breaking away from the image, he stood and paced, fists clenched. How could he have been so stupid? He should have tried harder to get her to see things his way. His eyes fell on a vase with carnations. Without thinking, he grabbed it, hurling it against the wall. Splintering glass shattered the silence. Flower petals and crystal littered the floor. Water dribbled down the wall.

"I'm stupid! Stupid!" He crossed to the window and gazed down on the busy street three floors below. Thoughts of the farm and the valley pulled at him. He tried to imagine himself a farmer. Could he do it—give up his career? No. He couldn't give up all he'd worked so hard for—not even for Laurel.

He opened the window, and chilly afternoon air flowed in. It was cool for June. He leaned on the sill and studied a man hawking newspapers. Once, not so long ago, that had been him. He'd come far.

Again the memory of his conversation with Will nudged him. "Maybe God wants you here in Alaska," he'd said. "Maybe it's where you belong."

Adam respected Will. At the time the comment had stopped him. "It's not possible," he told himself, imagining what life would be like without writing, without the prestige, without the challenge. "Alaska's not for me." He leaned on the sill. "Even if it is God's plan, it's not mine. And if Laurel wanted me, she would have come to London."

Adam grabbed his coat, left the apartment, and headed for the stairs. When he reached the first floor, he pushed through the door and stepped onto a small porch leading to the street. He hurried down the steps, heading for the nearest pub.

He walked decisively, avoiding eye contact with passersby. When he reached the tavern, he pulled open the door and stepped into a dimly lit room. Small tables and chairs were scattered about. A long bar stood on one side of the room. The smell of stale cigarette and cigar smoke lingered from last night's visitors. A man and a woman sat at one of the tables. They talked quietly, sipping dark ale.

Adam walked to the bar and sat on a stool. Resting his forearms on the bar, he counted tumblers standing in straight rows on a shelf on the wall.

The bartender, a robust-looking man with a heavy mustache, greeted him, "Good day to you, Adam."

Adam nodded.

"You look a bit down in the mouth. What can I get for you?"

"Just a beer. Don't bother with a glass." Adam didn't look up. He heard a fizzle as the lid was pried loose. The bartender set the bottle in front of him, then wisely went about his business. Adam took a sip, then guzzled down half the bottle.

The door opened, and a rush of cool air and city street noise swept inside. Adam didn't look up.

"Hey, I thought that was you," a man said.

Adam recognized Joe's voice. He didn't bother to look at his friend.

"Hey, what's got you so down?" Joe said, sidling up next to Adam.

Adam glanced at his fellow reporter. As always, he wore a pinstripe suit and broad-brimmed hat, which he'd tucked under his arm. His hair was short and slicked back. Joe smiled, revealing a row of perfect white teeth—too perfect, Adam had always thought.

Ginger was with him. As usual, she was dressed in a stylish suit at least one size too small. She also wore a snug-fitting felt hat over short blonde curls. Her lips were painted red. "Adam, you look bad. What's wrong?" She slid onto the barstool next to him.

"I thought you were still out of the country, Ginger," Adam said unenthusiastically.

"I'm back." She smiled seductively. "Can I help?"

"No."

Joe took the seat beside Adam and signaled to the bartender. "Two more beers here." He looked at Adam. "So, what's up? You look like your best friend just died. And I know that can't be true because I'm here." He chuckled.

"Nothin's wrong. I'm fine."

"Oh, sure. I can see that." Ginger crossed one leg over the other, showing off shapely limbs. "Anything I can help with?"

Ignoring her question, Adam asked, "What kind of trouble you been up to?"

Ginger chuckled. "Trouble? Me?" She sipped her beer. "Is the paper sending you to the Olympics?"

"I doubt it," Adam said glumly. "I'd like to go though." He took a swig of beer. "It's predicted that Jesse Owens could bring home a fistful of gold medals."

"Who is he?" Ginger asked.

"Isn't he that Negro runner?" Joe said.

"Yes." Adam shook his head in disgust, wondering how a reporter, even if she were a woman, couldn't know about Jesse Owens. "Wish I were going to be there. Instead, I'm still dogging King Edward. The rumors about him and Mrs. Simpson are big news," he said sarcastically. He downed the last of his beer and signaled the bartender for another.

"I'd rather be following around a handsome king than some sweaty athlete." Ginger smiled; her lipstick glistened. She reached into her purse, took out a cigarette case, and opened the lid. After tapping out a cigarette, she snapped the case closed and tossed it on the bar.

"I thought you'd stopped smoking," Joe said.

"I did." She lit the cigarette, inhaled deeply, and blew smoke at Joe. "I enjoyed doing the write-up on the latest Paris fashions."

"That crowd? I heard they're nothing more than a bunch of sniveling prestige-seekers," Joe said.

"Maybe, but they dress nicely and smell good. I had a wonderful time." She sipped her beer. "Joe, you're the one who gets the best assignments," she said, flicking ashes on the floor.

The bartender pushed an ashtray toward Ginger. "My floor isn't an ashtray," he said dryly.

"Oh, sorry." She tapped the end of her cigarette against the tray as if to show him she was remorseful.

"I liked my last assignment." Joe grinned. "Writing a story on the latest Rolls Royces and Bentleys isn't work." He took another swig of beer. "One day I plan on having my own Rolls Royce, and I'll have a driver too."

"How do you plan on making that kind of money? You think you're gonna get rich in this business?" Adam asked derisively. He gulped down more beer.

"What's eating you?" Joe asked.

"Nothin'."

Ginger raised a well-defined eyebrow and snuggled up to Adam. "We were thinking about going out and having some fun. You want to come?"

Adam studied Ginger. He knew all he had to do was nod her way and she was his. He'd considered it. She was a real looker. The trouble was, since Laurel, he hadn't been interested in women. He chugged his drink. "Tell me, Joe, is any woman worth a man's job?"

Joe grinned. "I guess that would depend on the job and the woman."

"No, I mean it. I'm serious."

Joe leaned on the bar. "I wouldn't give up my job for any woman. It's me and the job, or nothing. She'd have to accept me just the way I am, and that includes my work." He stared at Adam. "Who's got your eye? Someone I know?"

"It's no one."

"I don't believe you," Ginger said. "Why don't you just spill it?" She smiled. "You'll feel better."

"I've seen that look before. You're in trouble, Adam." Joe placed his hat on his head, snatched Ginger's cigarette, stubbed it out, then took her hand. "Come on. A band's playing down the street. We can dance the night away. What about it, Adam?"

"Nah. I don't feel like it." He finished off his beer and ordered another.

"If you're not careful, someone will have to carry you home," Joe said.

"That's all right with me."

"Come with us." Joe eyed Ginger. "You think I can handle this broad all by myself?"

"You'll have to." Adam leaned on the bar and grinned. "You'll manage. Go on. Have a good time. I'm going back to my flat and hitting the sack."

"All right. We'll see you around." Joe tossed several coins onto the bar. "That ought to cover the drinks." He turned to Ginger. "Come on; my feet are already tapping."

Ginger leaned over and kissed Adam's cheek. It was a long, soft kiss. "Hmm. I like your aftershave." She smiled and straightened. "I'm pretty good at healing broken hearts."

Adam grinned and nodded. "I know. I may just give you a call."

Ginger's eyes lit up, then Joe dragged her out of the pub.

Adam downed two more beers.

Digging into his pocket, he pulled out money for the additional drinks and laid it on the bar. *I'll write to her. I'll tell her how happy I am for them both.* Stumbling, he walked to the door and stepped outside. Hands in his coat pockets, he walked toward his apartment, determined she'd never know how he felt. He'd opened up to her once. Never again.

Chapter Thirty-Six

LAUREL HEADED UP THE STAIRS TO CHANGE OUT OF HER SUNDAY DRESS. IT was too nice a day to spend indoors. She planned on working in the flower garden, and if time allowed, she'd throw in a line at the creek. She'd become a fairly good fisherman, and the stream running along their property had nice rainbow trout.

Robert told her he'd be working on the house but would try to find time to join her. She'd be glad to see it completed. At least then she and Robert would be able to spend more time together.

Laurel considered their wedding and the move to their new home. She was eager for it to happen, but the idea of sharing a house with Robert's family dampened her enthusiasm. In all her girlhood dreams, she'd never once envisioned living with her husband's family.

"Hey, Laurel," Brian called from the bottom of the stairs. "We're goin' to the lake! You want to come? Mama's packing a picnic lunch with fried chicken, and Daddy said we could go fishin'."

Laurel stopped at the top landing and looked down at her little brother. "Mmm. Fried chicken sounds good. Who's going?"

"Everybody. Even Alex and Mattie are meeting us there."

"All right. I'll go. When are we leaving?"

"Mama said I'd better get a move on, so I guess right away."

"I have to talk to Robert first." She was almost sure Robert would go. "Tell Mama and Daddy I'll meet you there."

"OK." Brian started to move away, then stopped and looked up at Laurel. "Daddy said I could use his fishing pole. I betcha I catch a big one." He grinned, then skipped off.

Laurel went on in to change her clothes.

"Laurel," Jean called from outside her door.

"Come in." Laurel finished buttoning her blouse.

Jean peeked in. "We're leaving. Brian said you'd be down later?"

"Yes. I was supposed to meet Robert at the creek, but I'll run over and see if he wants to go to the lake instead. I'm sure he will."

"All right. Don't be too long. We'll wait lunch for you."

Jean closed the door, and Laurel heard the squeak of the stairs as her mother headed down. She pushed her feet into casual shoes and tied them, then walked to the bureau and picked up her brush. The wind had made a mess of her hair.

Her eyes fell on Adam's most recent letter. He'd congratulated her and Robert on their upcoming wedding. She hadn't expected Adam to be as pleased as he'd sounded.

She pulled the brush through her hair and put it into a ponytail. Grabbing a towel from the closet, she laid it out and set her swimming suit in the middle of it. She rolled up the towel with the suit and headed for the door.

Her spirits high, she walked through the empty house, out the back door, and headed across the field to Robert's. The cows and their calves grazed. Chewing contentedly, they gazed at her as she passed. The two horses and three sheep they'd acquired paid no attention but nibbled grass.

Mountains, some still topped by snow, stood framed by a deep blue sky. The nearby forests shaded bushes heavy with green berries. They'd ripen soon. Laurel looked forward to fresh pies. They'd already used the berries they'd canned last fall.

When Laurel reached the gate separating the Hasper's land from the Lundeen's, she stopped and leaned on it. Robert was kneeling on the roof of their home, nailing down wood shingles. The sleeves of his cotton work shirt were rolled up, revealing muscular arms. His coffee brown hair was damp with sweat, and his dark eyes were serious as he concentrated on his work. He placed a nail on a shake, then swinging his hammer accurately and powerfully, he drove it through the shake. Still not aware of Laurel's scrutiny, he took another nail, set it, and pounded it in. *He's good,* Laurel thought, pride welling up.

The sun felt hot. Laurel could imagine how hot and thirsty Robert was. A swim at the lake would be just the thing. Stepping through the gate, she ran toward the house and called up to him.

He looked down at her, surprise on his face. "Hi, there. I didn't expect to see you so soon." He sat, bending his knees. "I thought I was coming to your place."

"The family went to the lake. We're invited. You want to go? Mama made a picnic lunch—fried chicken."

"How can I refuse?" He grinned. Leaving the nails, hammer, and shakes where they were, he walked to the edge of the roof and climbed down a ladder. "I'm glad to see you," he said, giving Laurel a kiss. He pulled a handkerchief from his back pocket and wiped perspiration off his forehead. Tucking it back in place, he said, "I'll change and tell Mama we're going."

A few minutes later, seated in the front of Robert's truck, the couple headed for the lake. "I've been thinking I needed a day of fun," Robert said with a smile. "Too much work can ruin a man."

"I have to agree."

"The minister gave a good sermon this morning," Robert said. "He almost always has something to say that inspires me. I have a lot to be thankful for."

"Me too. Sometimes I start thinking about what I'm missing in life, and I get to feeling restless. But I think God wants us to be thinking about our blessings and be thankful." Laurel shook her head. "I get so frustrated with myself—especially when I get caught up in the what-ifs." She chuckled. "I can make myself dizzy."

She studied the distant mountains. "I mean, look at that view. It's glorious. I remember when I stood up to my father and told him I wouldn't move here. I acted like a spoiled brat that day. It was killing Daddy to leave his home, and I could only think about me.

"When I think about the beatings Jesus took and how he hung on that cross and died for us, I'm ashamed at how selfish I am. He never took his eyes off God." Laurel gazed at a field ablaze with bright pink fireweed. "I want to be like him."

"Don't be so hard on yourself."

Laurel rested her head against the window frame. "I almost didn't move here with my family." She smiled at Robert. "I'm glad I did. Even though I have wonderful memories of growing up in Wisconsin—the farm, family, and friends, now I can't imagine living anywhere else."

Robert reached across the seat and clasped Laurel's hand. "I can't wait to have our own family."

"Me either." Although she'd said the words, Laurel felt a hesitation. Adam's face with his appealing smile and captivating blue eyes flashed through her mind. She closed her eyes and willed away the image.

"Did you?" Robert asked, then added, "Laurel?"

"What? I'm sorry. What did you say?"

"I was wondering if you brought a swimsuit?"

"Yes, of course." She tried to focus on the passing countryside, but her mind wandered back to Adam. *Maybe he's at the Olympics.* She glanced at Robert. "Have you ever thought of going to the Olympics?"

"The what?"

"The Olympics. You know, where people from all over the world get together and compete in different sports."

"Oh. No. I'm not much interested."

Laurel was unable to imagine someone not being interested in an international event like the Olympics.

Robert slowed and pulled in alongside several other cars parked at the lakeshore. "Looks like there's a crowd today. Everyone's trying to get in a last swim before summer ends." He climbed out, quickly came around the truck, and opened the door for Laurel. "I'm looking forward to your mama's fried chicken."

"It's the best," Laurel said, grabbing her towel. She stuffed it under one arm and held Robert's hand as they walked to the lake. Will and Jean were sitting on a blanket beneath a tree. "Hi, Mama. Daddy. It's warm out, isn't it?"

"It nearly is. Nothing like we used to get in Madison. But I s'pect for the valley, you might call it a scorcher." Will chuckled.

Jean kept an eye on Susie who toddled along the waterline, splashing in ankle-deep water. Falling on her bottom, she giggled. "That little girl has no fear."

"She loves the water," Robert said.

Brian raced up from the lake and jumped into the middle of the blanket. "I'm hungry. Laurel and Robert are here. Can we eat?"

"Yes," Jean said with a smile. "We can eat." She opened the picnic basket, then set out chicken, biscuits, a jar of pickles and pickled beets. She called to Luke. "It's time for lunch. Bring Susie with you, please."

Luke splashed water at Mattie, dunked her, and headed for the beach. Then he scooped up Susie and raced Alex and Mattie for the blanket. The three teens dropped onto the spread.

"Are those pickled beets?" Robert asked.

"Yes."

"I love pickled beets."

Will removed the lid and held out the jar to Robert. "Have as many as you like. Jean makes the best I've ever tasted."

Robert took several slices and ate them, then licked red juice off his fingers. "I ought to get the recipe for my mother. She'd like these."

"I'll write it down, and you can take it home to her," Jean said. "I thought it was my fried chicken you were really crazy about."

"I like that too." Robert took a chicken leg and bit into it.

Laurel's good mood had faded. Robert seemed to care more about food and recipes than he did about things like the Olympics. *What are we going to talk about for the next fifty years? Stop fretting. We have lots in common. He's just being nice to Mama.*

Robert took another piece of chicken.

"How's the house coming along?" Will asked.

"Good. I've got the interior walls set, and I'm working on the roof. We ought to have the whole house finished in another six or eight weeks." He winked at Laurel. "It should be ready in plenty of time for our wedding." He took her hand. "By the way, Mama found some material for curtains when she was in town. She wanted to show it to you."

"But I've already got material."

"I know, but Mama liked it so much that I told her it would be all right. I hope you don't mind."

Of course I mind! Laurel thought. Tension settled over the group. "I guess if she has her heart set on it," Laurel conceded, giving her mother a helpless look.

Jean offered a sympathetic smile.

"You want to go for a swim?" Robert asked Laurel.

"Right now? We just ate. I thought you were supposed to wait at least thirty minutes."

"We won't swim hard. And you barely ate." He stood and held out a hand to Laurel.

She took it, allowing him to help her to her feet. Laurel didn't feel much like swimming, although the lake sparkling beneath the sun did look tantalizing. "Let me get on my suit," Laurel said, heading up a path leading to a small dressing room. The short walk made her feel better, and so did Robert's admiring stare as she came out of the bathhouse.

Fed up with her changeable moods, Laurel was determined to have a good time. She raced Robert for the water and didn't slow down as she stepped into the lake. Its icy coldness sent spikes up her legs and into her body. Squealing in delight, she kept going.

Robert waded in beside her. As soon as the water reached his waist, he dove in. When he surfaced, he pushed his hair out of his face and smiled at Laurel. "Come on. Dive in."

"No. It's too cold." Shivering, she held her arms close to her.

"Either you do it, or I'll do it for you."

"Don't you dare." Pushing through the water, Laurel headed toward the beach. Robert grabbed her and twirled her around, dunking her. She came up sputtering and wiped wet hair out of her eyes. "You!" She laughed, then dove in and swam out a little way. Treading water, she waited for Robert, but Luke jumped at him and tried to dunk him. The two tussled.

Laurel's eyes roamed over the beach. Children played in the sand and in the shallows. Parents relaxed in the shade of trees. A young couple caught her attention. They were indiscreetly entwined in each other's arms. The woman reached up and ran her fingers through the man's blond hair. He gazed down at her, then kissed her ardently.

Laurel glanced around to see if anyone else had noticed the pair, but they could be seen only from the water. They'd set their blanket in a grove of birch. Laurel knew she was intruding, but she couldn't keep from watching.

The woman said something. They laughed, then held each other tightly. Then Laurel noticed the woman's bulging abdomen. She was pregnant. Laurel felt a pang of jealousy. *To be so in love would be wonderful,* she thought, aware she didn't feel that deep passion for Robert.

Chapter Thirty-Seven

LAUREL THRUST A PITCHFORK INTO THE EARTH, WEDGING IT BENEATH A potato plant. Pushing it deeper with her foot, she lifted the plant, which was heavy with potatoes, then dropped to her knees and began breaking up loam with her hands. When her fingers found the firm, round potatoes, she pulled them free of the root, brushed away the dirt, and dropped them into a wheelbarrow. Before moving on, she rested her arms on the edge of the cart.

Her mother bent over a plant in the row beside her. Glancing at Laurel, she said, "These are loaded!"

Laurel pushed the wheelbarrow a few feet down the row. She looked at the sky. Fingers of wispy clouds stretched across the pale blue ceiling. The sun was warm but not hot. Squawking echoed across the fields, and Laurel sought out the geese she knew were heading for their winter feeding grounds. Flying in perfect formation, they paddled the air. Laurel watched until they disappeared beyond the forest in their single-minded flight south.

Summer was coming to a close. Chilly mornings foretold of approaching fall. Soon the morning sun would reflect off sparkling, frosted earth. Already leaves were changing into their fall colors—red, yellow, and orange. Autumn, with its iridescence, would settle over the valley.

Leaning on the pitchfork, she stared at the home she and Robert would share. He'd done a good job. It was a nice house, but it just didn't feel like hers.

"You're not going to get many potatoes dug that way," a man called, cutting into Laurel's thoughts.

The voice sounded familiar. Laurel whirled around. "Adam?" She stared at him, thinking it might be her imagination. Sunlight shimmered off his light brown hair, which curled onto his forehead as it always did. He was wearing blue jeans and a pale blue work shirt. A charming smile lit his face. The closer he came, the faster he walked, his long legs carrying him toward her.

"Adam!" Laurel repeated, refusing to obey the compulsion to run to him.

Adam had no such reservations. He ran to her and swept her into his arms.

Automatically, Laurel's arms went around his neck. She didn't fight his embrace.

He held her against him and whispered against her hair. "I've missed you. Oh, I've missed you."

Laurel could smell his mild, spicy aftershave. It reminded her of the kiss they'd shared. *I'm engaged!* her mind yelled. *What am I doing?* She pushed against his chest. "Let me go!"

Adam grudgingly released her, but he stood close, his captivating blue eyes searching hers. She felt his passion and his love, and fought a rush of emotions that threatened to drive her back into his arms.

"I'm sorry for that. I didn't mean to. I know you're engaged. It's just that when I saw you . . ." Adam brushed the hair off his forehead. "I wasn't thinking. Sorry," he ended lamely.

Laurel took a steadying breath. "I . . . I didn't know you were in town."

"I flew in this morning." He gazed at the fields and rows of lush green crops. "You've done well." He looked at Jean, who was studying him with a puzzled expression. "Afternoon, Mrs. Hasper."

"Hello, Adam." Jean stepped over the row of potatoes and joined the two. "It's good to see you. What brings you to the valley?"

"My story. I still have the final piece to write—the first harvest. By the looks of things, you've made it."

"It's been a good year."

"You'll be taking part in the fair?"

"Of course," Jean said. "Nearly every farmer will have something entered."

Adam smiled. "That's why I'm here." He glanced at Laurel. "Then I'll be heading back to Europe. Things are heating up over there."

Reality hit Laurel. Adam wouldn't be staying. Sadness seeped through her.

"We're happy to have you," Jean said. "Can you stay for supper?"

"I've been dreaming about your cooking. Of course I'll stay." Adam's eyes swept over neat, mounded rows of vegetables and dark loam, then moved to the mountains. He breathed deeply. "In London I'd remember how beautiful it is here, but the memories aren't nearly as good as the real thing." He glanced at Laurel. "It'll be hard to leave."

The following morning Laurel headed for the forest to pick cranberries. Adam tagged along. She carried an empty lard bucket, hitting it with a stick periodically as they walked.

"Why are you making that racket?"

"The bears are filling their bellies before winter gets here. It's best to let them know we're coming. It's not a good idea to surprise one."

"Oh." Adam searched the ground and picked up a branch. He started beating his own pail. "So, this will send them off, huh?"

"Usually. I've never had a problem, but bears are unpredictable." Laurel wasn't sure she liked the idea of Adam joining her. It probably wasn't a good idea to spend time alone. She knew Robert wouldn't like it.

They entered the woods and immediately found bushes heavy with clusters of red berries. "They're loaded. These make great jellies and syrups."

Adam immediately plucked a firm, round fruit and held it to his nose. "Smells funny." He popped it in his mouth, then spat it out. "They're sour. How do you eat these?"

Laurel laughed. "I told you, Mama makes jelly and syrup out of them. She adds lots of sugar." Laurel untied a length of rope she'd cinched around her waist and ran it through the bucket handle, then looped the rope around her waist, pulling it snug and tying it. "This way your hands are free to pick."

"Good idea," Adam said, unbuckling his belt to secure his pail. He picked a handful of berries and set them carefully in the bottom of his pail. "So, you and Robert are still planning on getting married?"

"Yes. December fifteenth. I wrote you."

"Yeah, I remember." Adam's voice took on a hard edge.

"We'd like you to come."

"I think I'm going to be busy that day," Adam said dryly.

"Oh." Laurel had known he wouldn't be there. "Our house is nearly finished. Robert's done a fine job. Would you like to see it after lunch?"

"Actually, I've got work to do." Adam stepped further into the bush, stretching to reach a bunch hanging from an upper branch. "Remember, I'm here to finish my story." He looked at Laurel. "Do you know how many families have left?"

"No. You'd have to ask Daddy. I know there've been a lot. But other families have come and taken over some of the places."

"Really? Looks like your farm's doing well."

"It is, but that doesn't mean much money is coming in. Markets are lean."

"Sorry to hear that." Adam stared into his nearly empty bucket. "Are you going to the fair?"

"Yes. We're excited about it. My father entered some of our produce. The Matanuska Valley grows the biggest cabbages and turnips you've ever seen."

"I'll be there taking pictures, and I'll make sure to get one of you and your turnips." He grinned in that charming boyish way of his, and again Laurel wished he hadn't come.

Laurel sat in the rocker. She'd been dressed and ready to go for an hour, but Robert hadn't shown up. Her family had left for the fair early that morning, but she'd decided to wait for Robert.

"Where is he?" Laurel fumed, pushing herself out of the chair. She walked to the window and stared at the Lundeen tent. A trail of smoke rose from the stovepipe.

She marched to the back porch, grabbed her coat from its peg, pushed open the door, and stepped outside. Angry, she walked fast. Robert knew she'd wanted to leave early. It wasn't like him to be late. Laurel picked up her pace. Maybe something was wrong.

She stepped up to the door of the tent and called, "Hello." There was no answer. "Hello," she called again. Still no answer. She peeked inside. The tent was empty.

She searched the barn and scanned the fields but couldn't find Robert. *He wouldn't have gone without me.* Uncertain whether to be angry or worried, Laurel headed down the road toward the fairgrounds.

A pickup approached, stirring up dust. Laurel stepped to the side of the road and waited for it to pass.

It slowed and stopped. Adam rested his arm on the open window. "Hi. I was coming to get you."

"How'd you know I needed a ride?"

"Robert's sister remembered she was supposed to tell you that Robert went into Anchorage yesterday. He planned on being back in time, but he didn't make it." He grinned. "I figured you could use a chauffeur, so I volunteered. Hop in." He reached across the seat and opened the door.

Laurel climbed in. "Why did Robert go to Anchorage?"

"Something about selling vegetables."

"He said he'd be back this morning?"

"That's my understanding."

"I hope he's all right."

"You know how bad that road gets. He'll be along soon."

"You didn't have to pick me up. I could have walked."

"Yeah, but then I would have missed your company." Adam grinned, naughtiness touching his eyes. He turned the truck around, and they headed for the fairgrounds.

Sitting beside Adam was unnerving. He affected her in a way no one else could. Laurel hugged the door, keeping plenty of space between herself and Adam. "Have you already been to the fair?" she asked. *Of course he has. He just told me he talked to Robert's sister,* Laurel thought, feeling dimwitted.

"I just came from there."

"What do you think? Is it a good one?"

"Well, it's no Chicago Expo, but it's not bad. Reminds me of the ones I went to when I was a boy. Lots of simple down-home fun and good food. I was thinking I might take a shot at the greased pig race." He grinned, his eyes sparkling with mischief. "You think I can win?"

"You just might."

Adam pulled into a grassy area congested with cars, trucks, and wagons. He parked, then reached across Laurel and opened her door. "Do you mind if I tag along with you for a while?"

"No, I'm on my own," Laurel said, knowing she should have refused and spent the day with her family. *What's the harm? I'll never see him again,* she reasoned.

They walked through a bright display of flowers, then moved on to tables laden with vegetables. Adam was stunned at the size of the cabbages and turnips. They continued on to an exhibit of local crafts.

Jessie sat amidst a display of her paintings. She was working on one, but stopped when Adam and Laurel walked up to her. "Hello, there." She stood, gave Laurel a hug, and then shook Adam's hand. "It's good to see you, young man. I was hoping you'd return to us."

"I'm not staying. I've got to get back to London. I'm working as an overseas correspondent these days," he added, unable to keep the pride out of his voice.

"Yes, Laurel told me. So, what are you doing here?"

"Finishing the story about the colonists." He lifted the camera hanging from a strap around his neck. "You mind if I take your photograph?"

"Oh, no. Not at all."

"OK, just stand between these two paintings," he said, gently steering her into position.

Jessie placed a hand on a picture of wild sweet peas. "How's this?"

"Perfect." Adam took several photos. "I ought to be able to get a good one out of these," he said.

"I don't know. My face has never been very camera-friendly." She chuckled and sat. "So, have you been around to see much of the fair yet?"

"Some of it," Laurel said.

"Well, you've got to watch the rodeo. They had one this morning, and there's another competition this afternoon."

"Sounds fun." Laurel gave Jessie a hug. "I'll see you later this week?"

"I'm counting on it."

Laurel and Adam moved on. They made the rounds of several exhibits and games. Adam stopped at a booth where the challenge was to knock over a stack of weighted bottles with a baseball. Laurel eyed the prizes—an assortment of stuffed animals and dolls. One doll was especially beautiful. It had big blue eyes and a headdress of pink feathers. "That's what I want," she said, pointing at it. "Can you get it for me?"

"I'll try." Adam grabbed three balls, and in rapid succession, pitched them at the bottles. He knocked them down on his third try.

The barker took down the doll. With a wink, he handed it to Laurel. "I think this is what you wanted?" He looked at Adam. "You've got a good arm. Ever think about taking up baseball?"

"Oh, sure. The Yankees can't wait to sign me," Adam said with a laugh. He circled Laurel's waist with his arm and escorted her away from the booth.

The gesture felt natural, but Laurel stepped away. "Robert should be here by now."

"He's probably heading into town right now."

"I hope so." Laurel held the doll at arm's length. "She's kind of silly-looking, but I like her. Thanks."

"Glad to do it," he said with a small bow.

They looked at the livestock, then munching cotton candy, moved on to the rodeo. Young men climbed onto the backs of wild horses and bulls. A few stayed on until a bell rang, but most were dumped in the dirt. Laurel couldn't understand why men would do such a thing, but it was entertaining.

At one point, she saw Ray Townsend staring at her from across the arena. Instinctively she moved away from Adam. She knew Ray had been relieved at her engagement to Robert. It meant Celeste was safe from the arms of a colonist.

Ray made his way around the corrals and walked straight to her. With only a glance at Adam, he turned his eyes on Laurel. "Where's Robert? Don't suppose he'd be too happy to know you were here with someone else."

A mix of anger and guilt swept through Laurel. "Adam and I are friends. That's all. And Robert's in Anchorage trying to sell his produce. He'd be here if he could, if there were a market here. You've made sure that can't happen."

Ray's lips turned up in a satisfied sneer. "Going into Anchorage won't help him. It won't save his farm." He glanced at a calf kicking up dust as it bucked past, then his cool eyes settled back on Laurel. "He won't make it. None of you will." With that, he walked on.

"He makes me so angry," Laurel growled, watching his back.

"Don't let him get to you. He's nothing but a lot of hot air."

"I wish that were true."

"Forget about him. Let's enjoy the day."

By the time twilight fell over the valley, Laurel had forgotten about Ray Townsend and his threats, and she felt all too comfortable with Adam. It seemed as if they belonged together. Her mind was filled with questions and uncertainties about Robert and their wedding, and she felt guilty for enjoying herself when Robert was late returning. "I'm worried about Robert."

"I'll bet he got tied up with business and decided to stay over. Maybe it means he's selling a lot of vegetables."

"I hope so."

Darkness settled over the fairgrounds, but lights turned night into day. Luke ran up to Laurel. "I've been looking everywhere for you. Mama said it's time to head home."

Laurel wasn't ready to leave. She glanced at Adam.

"If Laurel doesn't mind, I'll take her home," he offered.

Trying to remain nonchalant, Laurel said, "I suppose that would work." She turned to Luke. "Tell Mama Adam's taking me."

Luke stared at her a moment, then said, "All right. I'll tell her." He headed toward the parking area, glanced back, then kept going.

"I'm glad we have a little more time together," Adam said.

Butterflies took flight in Laurel's stomach. If she loved Robert, how could she feel this way about Adam? *We're not doing anything wrong. We're just friends enjoying the fair,* she told herself. But she knew it was a lie. Laurel glanced at Adam. He'd had a good time. It was clear he loved the valley. Maybe he would stay. If he did, then what should she do?

Robert's sisters, Joanna and Veronica, walked past. Thankfully the girls didn't see them. Guilt enveloped Laurel. *I should leave now.*

"Do you want to walk a while?" Adam asked.

"Sure," she heard herself say. "The fair is beautiful at night."

Adam took her hand. She didn't attempt to withdraw it. He led her to a bench alongside a small pond on the edge of the fairgrounds. "Do you want to sit?"

"That sounds nice."

Adam sat and pulled Laurel down beside him. He rested an arm over her shoulders, and they stared at the pond where carnival lights shimmered. The night sounds of frogs and settling birds mingled with carnival music and the voices of hawkers.

For a long while they said nothing. Laurel's guilt grew. Although she listed all the reasons to go, she couldn't make herself leave. Instead, she gazed at the pond.

Finally Adam asked, "Are you serious about marrying Robert?"

"Yes," Laurel said, knowing she sounded ridiculous. If she were serious about Robert, why was she here with Adam? "I mean, I thought I was." She was afraid to look at him.

He turned toward her, gently placed his hand under her chin, and tipped her face to him. "After I got your letter, I vowed I'd never approach you again. But I can't help myself." He gazed into her eyes. "You don't love him. You love me."

The passion in Adam's eyes enveloped Laurel.

"You shouldn't marry a man you don't love. Marry me."

"You?" Laurel's voice came out a whisper. She wanted to flee. Loving Adam wouldn't work. They were too different. Laurel couldn't breathe. She had to get away. Standing, she stepped to the edge of the pond and turned her back to Adam.

He followed, resting his hands on her shoulders. "Think of it. We'll visit the Colosseum in Rome, travel the canals in Venice . . ."

Laurel stiffened. "You want me to go away with you? You won't stay?"

Adam turned her around so she faced him, keeping his hands on her arms. "No. I told you, I can't."

Misery wrenched at Laurel. If she wanted Adam, she'd have to leave the valley. "You want to wander the world?"

"Yes. It would be wonderful! Just the two of us! There's so much I want to show you!"

Laurel stepped back. She'd known better. Still, when she looked at his charming face and captivating eyes filled with love and longing, she asked, *Could I go? Lord, can I go?* She waited, hoping to hear a yes. Instead, the sense that it was wrong grew stronger. She sighed and looked at her hands. "I wish I could go with you. I want to, but I can't."

"Why?"

Feeling empty and ashamed, she gazed at him. "I want to be with you, but it's not what God wants. Whatever plan he has for me is here." She blinked back tears.

Adam swiped his hair back. "How can you know that? Don't you think God wants you to be happy?"

"Yes, he does. But *our* most excellent plans aren't always what they ought to be. His way is always best."

"And what about us?" Adam paced, then stopped directly in front of Laurel. "How can anyone know God's plans? Does he talk to you?"

Regret washed over her. She shouldn't have let this happen. She gazed out over the water and said softly, "Yes. Sort of. He speaks to me through his Word and I know him in my heart; he whispers to me in my mind."

She looked at Adam. His face had become a mix of anger and anguish. "Since I came here I've grown closer to God. I'm learning to listen to him. I don't get it right all the time, but I know that leaving with you is wrong."

"So, you want me to give up my life and stay here? To give up all I've worked for?"

She glanced at the ground, then back at Adam. "Success won't bring happiness. Anyway, not the kind of success you're talking about."

"I won't give it up. Not ever. I can't."

Laurel knew he spoke the truth. Tears spilled onto her cheeks. "I'm sorry, Adam. I shouldn't have come here with you. It was wrong, unfair to you, to me, and to Robert. I can't fit into your life. I'm just plain me, Laurel Hasper, farm girl."

Adam's eyes flashed anger. "I'm sorry too." He turned to walk away, then stopped when he spotted Robert standing only a few yards away, his face a mask of anguish. He strode toward Robert, brushing past him. "You win. She's yours," he said, then disappeared into the darkness.

Pain knifed through Laurel. "Oh, Robert." Tears spilled onto her cheeks. "Robert, I'm sorry." She'd done a terrible thing. She'd been disloyal to the man who'd been her best friend, a man who truly loved her, and she'd driven Adam further from God. *How could I have done this?* She crossed to Robert. "I'm sorry, Robert. I'm so sorry."

Robert's anguished expression turned tender. Laurel rested her forehead against his chest. "Adam's gone. Forever. Can you forgive me?"

Robert's arms tightened around her. "I forgive you."

Laurel snuggled against his chest, then remembered her earlier confrontation with Ray Townsend. "Robert, I did something else. I told Ray Townsend what you were doing in Anchorage."

"I'm not going to worry about Ray Townsend." He held Laurel at arm's length. "I did well today. Sold a lot."

"That's wonderful." She hugged Robert tighter. What would she do if he were forced to leave?

Chapter Thirty-Eight

HUNKERED DEEP IN HIS COAT, ADAM MARCHED DOWN THE SIDEWALK. KING Edward had an announcement. Much had been speculated over the king's decision. Some believed he'd abdicate; others said no. Adam hoped it was the latter, but contemplating why he felt this way was dangerous territory, so he'd avoided introspection. After all, his job was simply to report the news, not puzzle it out.

Adam hurried up steps, pulled open double doors, and walked inside the meeting hall. Others were hurrying toward the conference room. He followed the flow.

The room, already teeming with reporters, resonated with chatter from newsmen. Some took bets. For months Adam had listened to the rhetoric, watched the king, and waited for him to make a move. Adam hoped the king's statement would put an end to his vigil so he could move on to something of greater importance.

The romance between King Edward VIII and the American divorcee, Mrs. Wallis Simpson, had raised a stir, but it seemed of little significance to Adam. However, the British monarchy had taken a strong stand. No concessions would be made. A king could not marry a divorcee, no matter what the circumstances.

Adam took a seat at a long table crowded with journalists. *A man ought to be free to choose whom he would marry, no matter what his position,* Adam thought. Taking out writing tablet and pencil, he waited. Adam couldn't comprehend a man giving up a kingdom for a woman.

Against his will, his thoughts carried him back to Alaska. No matter how hard he'd tried to put Laurel and the Haspers behind him, he couldn't. Everywhere he went, she went with him. Her passion and strength shouted at him. Her beauty drew him.

In four days she would walk down an aisle and promise herself to someone else. Adam envisioned how she would look. Laurel would be stately, proud, and stunning. She'd wear her hair up off her neck, allowing a few soft auburn curls to caress her face. Hazel eyes would shimmer from behind a veil. A soft smile would touch her lips.

He wanted to be the one waiting at the altar.

Stop it! This is getting you nowhere, Adam told himself. *Concentrate.* He tried to focus on the activities in the room. He recognized many of the reporters but made no attempt to talk to anyone. He tapped his pencil on the pad. "Oh, no," he groaned as Joe and Ginger walked in. He didn't feel like explaining his sour mood or fending off Ginger's advances.

Joe immediately spotted him. He waved and grinned, exposing his perfect teeth. Taking Ginger by the elbow, he propelled her toward Adam. "Hey, so you got the call too," Joe said, sitting beside Adam.

"Yeah. What are you doing here? I thought this was my story."

"It's big. What can I tell you?" Joe smoothed his thin mustache.

"I think it's very romantic," Ginger said, settling herself in the chair on Adam's left. She smiled provocatively, dipped into her purse, and fished out a lipstick. Without using a mirror, she expertly ran the bright red tube over her full lips, smacked them, and replaced the makeup. "I think he's going to abdicate. After all, love is stronger than anything." She smiled at Adam. "What do you think?"

"I don't care. I just wish he'd get on with it."

"Touchy today, aren't we?" She ran a hand over Adam's shoulders. "Oh, your muscles are so tight. Would you like me to massage them?"

"I just want you to do your job," Adam said. "And I'm not it."

"All right, all right," Ginger said. "Just trying to be friendly. You look like a storm cloud."

"You do look pretty jumpy. What's eating you?" Joe asked.

"Nothing. Everything's fine. I just want to get on to something else." He stared straight ahead, hoping his friends would leave him alone.

The tumult in the room became a droning hum as his mind returned him to the last time he'd seen Laurel. She'd said God's plans aren't always our plans, and then she'd told him pointedly that success wouldn't make him happy. *How does she know? Why can't I have success and be happy too?*

Will Hasper's words played through his mind. "Ever wonder if this might be where you belong?" *Could he be right?* Adam wondered. *What would I do in Palmer? I'm a writer, not a farmer, not a hunter or a trapper.*

Remembering his mushing experience with Luke, he smiled. *No, I don't belong in Alaska,* he thought sadly.

The radio crackled, and a man standing in front turned up the volume. "Quiet," he called over the din.

Adam pushed through the turmoil of his mind and listened. The king was about to speak.

In a monotone voice, a man said, "This is the BBC. Tonight King Edward VIII has an announcement. The king . . ." the broadcaster said in a deep voice.

There was a long pause, then a solemn voice said, "Good evening. Tonight I come to you with a heavy heart. After long and anxious consideration I have determined I must renounce the throne."

"I knew it! I knew it!" Ginger said.

"Shh. Be quiet!" a man with pencil-thin eyebrows and a narrow face shouted over the uproar. Remembering there was more to come, the reporters closed their mouths and listened intently to the king's next words.

"I, King Edward the VIII of Great Britain, Ireland, and the British Dominions beyond the seas, King Emperor of India, do hereby declare my irrevocable determination to renounce the throne for myself and for my descendants and my desire that—"

"He's done it," Adam said. "He's actually given up his life, everything he is." Astonishment pressed down on him. While the king spoke, Adam scribbled down notes for his story. As he wrote, questions tumbled through his mind, and he couldn't shake a vision of Laurel walking down the aisle to another man.

His voice grave but decisive, Edward continued, "I find it impossible to carry the heavy burden as king without the help and support of the woman I love."

Adam stopped writing. He stared at the radio. He imagined what his life would be like without Laurel. He could see it—flat, lifeless, no flavor or meaning. King Edward had decided a kingdom without the support of the woman he loved was meaningless. Was that Adam's answer? Was God speaking to him?

Memories of times he'd shared with the Hasper family pummeled Adam. The months he'd spent with them had been the best he'd known. As a boy, he'd felt the presence of God. He struggled to remember, but after years of abuse and loneliness, he'd closed himself off to love—the love of God and the love of people. He'd refused to seek and to trust. And up until he'd met the Haspers, he'd believed he'd done well for himself. He'd thought life's successes would be enough to fill the emptiness.

Adam opened his eyes to the truth. He'd been wrong. The sickening sensation in his stomach twisted into a knot. He'd known he was wrong. Since returning to London, he'd sought happiness in work, but it had given only superficial satisfaction. And when he'd had successes, he had no one to share them with.

Adam remembered the little boy who'd climbed from his cot one night and kneeled before God and accepted the gift of salvation and love. God had promised never to leave him nor forsake him. He hadn't. Adam had walked away from God. All through the years God had been near, calling to him, pleading with him to listen and to follow. Adam had closed his ears. He'd abandoned the relationship. Now he understood. Possessions and status would never bring true joy.

Amidst the confusion of hungry reporters, Adam didn't hear the madness, he heard God. Tears burning his eyes, he prayed, *God forgive me. I've been so foolish. Show me what to do. Show me the way.*

Laurel's face filled his mind, and heartache returned. *How could I have been so stupid? She's all that matters. God, what should I do?*

Then he knew. "I've got to tell her," he said, standing.

Adam looked at Joe. "I have to go. You write the story."

"What? You nuts?"

"No. For the first time in years, I'm not." Adam pushed his hat down on his head. "I'm going to Alaska. I just hope I'm not too late."

Adam hurried out of the room. All that mattered to him was to tell Laurel he'd found his way. She needed to understand he loved her, wanted to marry her, and if Alaska was where they belonged, then that is where they would live.

He walked through the conference room, leaving the bedlam

behind. Pushing open the door, he ran down the hallway. He'd send a wire. *Lord, I pray I'm not too late.*

~

Laurel stood on a stool while Jean pinned the hem of her wedding dress. It was the last detail that needed tending to before the wedding. Laurel looked at her reflection in the wood-framed mirror. The gown was lovely, with a princess neckline, fitted bodice, long sleeves, and a floor-length skirt. She smoothed the material, enjoying the feel of soft crepe.

"Hold still."

"Sorry." Laurel held her arms out straight in front of her, admiring the pearl buttons on the cuffs. She also had matching buttons edging the neckline. It had been a splurge to buy them, but now it seemed worth it. The dress was much more elegant with the delicate adornments.

Jean pushed the last pin through the material, then straightened and stepped back. Studying Laurel, her eyes filled with tears. "You're so beautiful. It was certainly worth a dollar a yard." She took out the handkerchief she kept in her pocket and dabbed at her eyes. "My little girl is about to become a married woman."

Laurel stepped off the stool and hugged her mother. "Things won't change that much. I'll just be next door."

Jean nodded, her chin quivering. "No. Things will change greatly. I'm being silly. It's just that . . ." Her eyes refilled. "It seems like yesterday you were jumping rope and climbing trees."

Laurel smiled. "I remember." Tentatively, she asked, "Mama, were you scared when you and Daddy got married?"

"Oh, yes." She blew her nose. "Well, not scared exactly, but a bride always has some anxiety." She smiled. "You don't have to be afraid of Robert. He's a gentle man."

"I know. He's wonderful. It's just that . . ." Laurel didn't know how to explain what she was feeling. She looked at her reflection again. She didn't look blissful. "Shouldn't I be ecstatically happy that I'm getting married?"

"I can only tell you what I felt. I was overjoyed at the idea of becoming your father's wife. I could barely wait for the day."

"Mama, I don't feel overjoyed, exactly. I mean, I'm happy. Robert will be a wonderful husband, but—"

A knock sounded at the door, and Jean hurried to answer it. David Phillips, a young man who sometimes delivered mail, stood on the porch. "Good day, Mrs. Hasper."

"Hello, David. Please, come in out of the cold."

"Thank you, ma'am, but I have to get back." He held out an envelope. "I have a telegram for Laurel."

"A telegram?" Jean's voice sounded tight. "From where?"

"London, England, ma'am."

Jean took the envelope.

He held out a ledger and pencil. "Could you sign here, please?"

Jean signed.

"Good day to you." David walked away.

Closing the door, Jean turned and faced Laurel.

Fear surging through her, Laurel stared at her mother. It had to be from Adam! "Something must be wrong!"

Her face lined with worry, Jean held out the envelope to Laurel.

Her mouth dry, her heart thumping, Laurel stared at it. "Do you think something's happened?"

"I don't know. You have to open it to find out."

Her hands shaking, Laurel took the envelope from her mother and opened it, steeling herself for the worst. "My dearest Laurel." *STOP.* "I love you." *STOP.* "Please don't marry Robert." *STOP.* "I'm coming." *STOP.* "Adam."

"Laurel, what is it? You look like you've seen a ghost." Jean took the telegram and quickly scanned it. "Oh, dear."

Laurel sank into a chair. *What should I do?* she thought. Adam had told her before that he loved her, but he'd believed his career came before anything else, including her.

She looked at her mother, her eyes brimming with tears. "I can't hurt Robert that way. I just can't. How dare Adam do this!"

Adam folded the frayed newspaper he'd picked up at the Seattle airport. He'd read it, then folded it and refolded it so many times it was tattered. He'd left London four days ago, knowing he couldn't make it before the wedding. Now he was nearing Palmer. He stared at the white countryside passing by the train window. Aspen and cottonwood stood like ghost trees, their bare arms stretched out, skinny and knotted.

Even if she got my wire, she probably married Robert. He's a good man. I was foolish to believe she'd call off her wedding just because she got a wire from me.

The train rumbled over a trestle. Clouds hung like a low ceiling above a gray inlet. It looked desolate and lonely, matching Adam's mood. He'd rediscovered God, but what if he'd awakened too late? What would he do without Laurel?

He opened the paper. In large bold letters the headline announced, "King Gives Up Throne For The Woman He Loves." Below it quoted the king's words, "I found it impossible to carry the heavy burden without the help and support of the woman I love." Ever since Adam first heard those words, they'd echoed through his mind.

He closed the paper, letting it rest in his lap. *Why didn't I understand sooner?* Even as he asked the question, he knew the answer. He'd been too busy trying to be important. Now he was paying the consequences.

He rested his head against the seat. *I'll be a farmer. I'll be anything. Nothing matters without her.*

The train slowed and stopped in front of the Palmer depot. Adam grabbed his bag, walked down the aisle, and stepped off the train. He had the distinct sense that he was going to an execution—his. What would he do if Laurel told him she was Mrs. Robert Lundeen? How would he react? He tried to prepare himself for the worst.

He looked around and remembered when he'd first arrived in Palmer; he'd been full of himself, ready to show the world who he was. Now he was simply a man who'd made a terrible mistake.

The first time he'd set foot in Palmer, it had seemed to be nothing more than a tent city, up to its armpits in mud and mosquitoes. Now the tents and piles of sinks and hardware were gone. There were new buildings. This corner of civilization sitting in a white wilderness had a sense of order and peace.

He walked into the depot. A thin, balding man looked up from behind a counter. "Can I help you?"

"I was wondering if I could get a ride out to the Hasper farm. I'm willing to pay."

"Well, Jeff Hutchinson was here a while ago." The man rubbed his chin. "I don't know if he's gone yet though." Walking slowly and methodically, he crossed to the door and opened it. Stepping outside he called, "Hey, Jeff! Can you give this fella a ride out to the Haspers'? He says he'll pay." The clerk walked back inside. "He's coming."

A moment later a man wearing an overly large fur coat and peering out from beneath a puckered hood stepped inside. "Need a ride?"

"Yes. Do you know where the Hasper farm is?"

"Not sure. I'm kind of new around here. You know the way?"

"Yes. I'll show you."

"All right then. Let's go."

Adam followed Jeff to his car, dropped his bag on the back seat, then climbed into the front beside him.

They drove in silence for a long while. Finally Jeff said, "Looks like we're going to get more snow. We've had a gentle winter so far, but I heard January and February can get pretty bad."

"I don't mind snow."

Jeff glanced at Adam. "You aren't from around here, are you?"

"No." Adam didn't want to explain. He just wanted to see Laurel. He prayed she was still Laurel Hasper.

They bounced over the wooden bridge just before the Hasper driveway. Adam told him to slow down and showed him where to turn.

"Oh, yeah. I think I know them. Seems I heard they were having a wedding or something out here."

Adam's stomach tumbled. He made no reply. The car stopped, and Adam stepped out, wondering why he was bothering. Handing Jeff a dollar, he said, "Thanks."

"Thank you." Jeff stuffed the money into his coat pocket.

Adam grabbed his suitcase and closed the door. He stared at the house. No one came out. *She's not here,* he thought dismally. *If she were, she'd have come out to greet me.*

Jeff backed around and headed down the driveway. Adam walked toward the porch, snow crunching beneath his city shoes. He felt sick and wished he hadn't come. Gripping his suitcase handle, he headed for the door, unaware of anything but his pounding heart.

The door flew open. Luke jumped past the step and ran to Adam. "Hey there! Adam! I heard you were coming! It's good to see you!"

Adam clasped the young man in a tight hug, then stood and looked at him. "You've grown." He smiled, but all he could think of was Laurel. "That beard makes you look like a real mountain man."

Luke grinned. "Thanks."

Adam saw movement at the door. Laurel stepped onto the porch. She was more beautiful than he remembered. Long, soft curls cascaded over her shoulders, her cheeks were flushed, and her amber eyes looked like warm gems. She didn't speak.

"Laurel." Adam's voice caught in his throat. He felt like a schoolboy.

Unaware he was moving, Adam walked to the porch. Dread filled him, but he grabbed hold of his usual confident charade. It was a safe place for him. Stepping up to the porch, he asked casually, "Did you get my telegram?"

"Yes. You said you were coming. Why? Why are you here, Adam?"

All the way from London, he'd practiced the words; now they failed him. He looked at the ground, his stomach knotting, then lifted his eyes to Laurel's. "I told you in the wire."

"No, all you said is that you loved me and were coming here." Her tone was sharp.

Adam swallowed past the lump in his throat and glanced at her left hand to see if she was wearing a wedding ring. Her hand was hidden in the folds of her dress. "Are you Laurel Hasper, or Laurel Lundeen?"

Laurel stared at Adam. Her voice controlled and reserved, she asked, "Why?"

"Laurel, you're tormenting me." He stepped closer. "Why do you think I came all this way?"

"Why did you?"

"I love you. I want to marry you."

"You've told me that before. What's different now?"

Adam remembered the paper he'd been carrying. He'd stuffed it into his coat pocket before leaving the train. Now he grabbed it. Opening to the front page, he held it out so she could see the headline. Leaving his façade behind, his eyes filled with tears, and he choked out, "This earthly king helped me to understand what the heavenly King has been trying to tell me. The world's riches are like refuse when compared to the riches God wants to give us. Faith and love are what matter."

Laurel gazed at the headline, her eyes shimmering.

"Please tell me you haven't married Robert. I'll do anything, be anything. Just say you're not Mrs. Lundeen. I was stupid and stubborn, Laurel. But now I understand. And I'm trying to listen to God. I know he wanted more for me than I wanted for myself." He dropped the paper and grabbed her hands. "Are you Mrs. Lundeen?"

"You must be awfully special. God doesn't usually use royalty to speak to people." A slow smile emerged. "No, Adam, I didn't marry Robert. I couldn't. I'm in love with you." She glanced at the snow-covered ground. "It would have been unfair to him. He deserves someone who's crazy about him." Tears glistened.

Relief and joy flooded Adam. He pulled Laurel into his arms. "Thank God." He stepped back, cradling Laurel's face in his hands. "I love you, Laurel Hasper. Together we can seek God's will for us. I don't want to do it on my own anymore. I want to do things God's way. And nothing in this life matters without you."

"I love you," Laurel said.

Adam searched her eyes. "I'm sorry it took me so long to listen. I forgot God loved me and that he wanted the best for me. He knew you were the best and this place was the best. We belong together here." He kissed Laurel's hands, then pulled her into his arms. "We'll make a life in this valley. I don't know how. It doesn't matter—just as long as we're together. God will show us the way." He grinned. "You're a better listener than me."

"You're learning fast," Laurel said with a smile.

Adam took Laurel's hands, turned them over, and gently kissed her palms. "Can we discover God's way for us as husband and wife? Laurel, will you marry me?"

She smiled up at Adam. "Yes, I'll marry you."

Adam kissed her and pulled her close, knowing that God had blessed him in a way he hadn't deserved. "Being your husband will be my greatest achievement."

From the Author

DEAR READER,

In 1994, while doing research for "The Northern Lights Series," I discovered a little known piece of history—the development of the Matanuska Colony in Alaska. I tucked away the information in the back of my mind. Little did I know that my cousin was married to a descendent of these first colonists. When I came across this information I decided it was time to take a closer look at the government experiment of the 1930s.

Historical books and newspaper columns were mailed to me and I dove in, reading ravenously. Long before I was finished, I knew the story had to be told. I must confess in the beginning, I was most impressed by the adventures and hardships, but as the story unfolded it was the people who touched me.

They hadn't intended on making history—their main concern was simply to survive during one of America's most difficult eras. For the most part they were like you and me—real people, but living extraordinarily because of circumstances, a situation that revealed their strengths and weaknesses to the world.

The characters in this book are fictional, but I believe they are an accurate depiction of humankind. Will Hasper did what he had to do; his family trusted and followed. The people in this story moved forward, some fearful, others angry, many displaying courage and strength. And as is true in life, there were those who whined and complained and even exploited the circumstances. But as is often the case, God worked through even the weak.

After many months of living with the people in *Valley of Promises,* I know them well. I relate to each—for I have been afraid, angry, and tempted by the riches of the world. And because of God's strength and goodness I have even, on occasion, been courageous.

It is my prayer that the Haspers as well as Adam, Robert, Celeste, Miram, and even Ray Townsend have helped you to see yourselves more clearly. No one is above reproach, and yet gratefully none of us are out of God's reach. Allow him to come near, for it is his love that lifts and carries mankind. He draws us to himself, and it is only because of his love that we will one day know perfection.

May the Father bless you richly as you walk with him.

❧

You may reach Bonnie at:
Bonnie Leon
P.O. Box 774
Glide, OR 97443
leon@rosenet.net